THE LIFE
OF
ROSE BRAMBLES

Book 1

~

By

Lesley Tréville

ISBN-13: 9781674900605

CONTENTS

ACKNOWLEDGMENTS

My sincere thanks go to two very important places of huge interest. Firstly, Madame Tussauds in London and Paris, for advising me of what waxworks were actually in their museums at the time of writing.

Secondly, The Élysée Palace in Paris, for allowing me to describe, in detail, the rooms in the palace.

CHAPTER 1

———————~——————

"Brambles. Brambles." BANG. The noise of the wooden ruler hit Rose's desk and she jumped. Rose had been daydreaming. She hated school, most of the teachers, but most of all Mrs Billows, who took History and Geography. She was tall, willowy and very stern looking. "What question did I just ask Brambles?" she snapped.

Rose stood slowly, but kept her eyes down. The girl sat at the side of her, showed her a piece of paper, from underneath her desk. On it read "Battle of Hastings." Rose spoke quietly and said, "My apologies Mrs Billows. You were telling us about the Battle of Hastings, and I was thinking about the horrors of what that battle had on the men, women and children. It must have been dreadful." She held her breath waiting for Mrs Billows to tell her to hold her hand out. Rose usually got the ruler at least once a week. To her surprise she told her to sit down. After that lesson eventually finished, it was lunchtime. On purpose Rose had made no friends, and had only been at Watchford Boarding School for three months. She loved being out in the fresh air, running through the fields, watching the animals at play. This school was like a prison.

A voice interrupted her thoughts, "Hello, my name is Ruby.... Ruby Smith," said the girl who had sat at the side of her in lessons. "May I join you?"

Rose looked her up and down and said, "I'm Rose ... Rose Brambles. Thank you for what you did, and yes, please sit down." Ruby and Rose chatted through lunch, and Rose liked her. Maybe they could be friends? Every day after that Ruby always saved the seat next to hers, and they became good friends.

One day the headmistress called Rose to her office. *Now what have I been blamed for,* thought Rose. Some of the girls had it in for her since day one, and every time something happened, she got the blame. Rose knocked on the door.

"Enter," said a brusque voice. "Ah Brambles, sit down," said Mrs Pickett. "As you know another couple of weeks and it will be the Christmas and New Year holidays. I'm sorry to tell you that your uncle and aunt are going abroad and will not be able to take you with them, and so you will be staying here." Rose's heart sank and she could feel tears spring to her eyes, but was determined not to cry, and she didn't. "The school doors will be closed and locked, so along with some others, you will stay in your dormitory. That's all Brambles, now back to class."

Rose returned to class and straight away Ruby could see something was dreadfully wrong. Later on in their dormitory Rose told her what had happened. Ruby was horrified to think her friend would have to stay at the school and started to devise a plan. The day of the holidays arrived and most of the girls were excited and packing. Rose watched Ruby packing and felt downhearted, as it would be nearly two weeks before she would see her again.

The door of the dormitory opened and a voice bellowed, "Brambles, headmistress's office now."

Rose sighed and said, "Now what? Bye Ruby and have a lovely time." Rose sauntered down the corridors until she arrived at the office, knocked and entered. A couple were seated and smiled at Rose. Rose eyed them suspiciously.

"Now then Brambles, this is Mr and Mrs Smith, and you are going to spend the holidays with them." Rose was taken aback. She would rather stay in the school than go to strangers, but she knew she had to accept.

"Thank you Mr and Mrs Smith. I would be delighted to spend the holidays with you," said Rose politely.

Mrs Pickett replied, "I'm sure you will have a wonderful time Brambles, now go and pack." Back in the dormitory there was only Ruby left.

"What happened?" asked Ruby. "I'm going to some strangers' house for the holidays. Never thought I'd say this but I'd rather stay here."

Ruby smiled and said, "What's the name of these people?"

Rose replied, "Smith. I'd better pack as they're waiting downstairs."

A little while later Rose and Ruby arrived at the entrance hall.

"Mum, Dad," said Ruby running towards them. Rose looked stunned. Ruby turned and looking at Rose said, "You coming Rose, and as you've gathered, these are my parents." Rose's smile lit her whole face up.

Once settled in the back of the car, Rose said, "How did you ...?" Ruby told her she had written to her parents and asked them if she could join them and they said they would be delighted. "Thank you Ruby, you're the best friend ever." Soon they arrived at the town of Birn, and just on the outskirts, Mr Smith turned into a drive where a small detached house stood.

"Home at last," he said and pulled up outside the front door. He opened the boot and gave Ruby and Rose their suitcases. Mr and Mrs Smith and Ruby walked towards the door. Rose stood frozen to the spot, with her suitcase in her hand, as a distant memory resurfaced. The house slowly changed into a very large, dark, gloomy building, and Rose, at the tender age of five, stood looking at it, with her small suitcase in her hand. She looked up at the stranger who had hold of her hand and felt alone and very, very scared. That was six years ago.

"Rose, Rose, are you alright? You look like you've seen a ghost!" asked Mrs Smith, who had gone back to her.

Rose blinked and saw the house was back to normal and said, "Sorry. I just had a bad memory." Mrs Smith took Rose's hand and led her inside. In the hall, was a large Christmas tree with presents wrapped up and placed underneath.

"Ruby, why don't you show Rose her room and the house," said Ruby's dad. Ruby grabbed Rose's hand and they ran up the stairs.

"Here's your room Rose, and I'm next door." Rose peered in to see a lovely room decorated in blue. There were light blue walls, heavy dark blue curtains, a single bed with a blue satin cover, and a deep blue thick carpet. There was also a wardrobe and dressing table, a desk and chairs. For once, Rose was overwhelmed and didn't know what to say.

Ruby took her hand and led her into her room, which was in

peach. "Rose, are you sure you're alright?" asked Ruby with concern.

Rose smiled at her friend and said, "It's just so beautiful Ruby. I have never been so happy, and I don't know what to say or do, if that makes sense."

Ruby replied, "Bit different to the boarding school isn't it? You and I are going to have a wonderful Christmas and then we'll both see a New Year in together. Mum and Dad have a New Year's Eve party, but we can stay up here and make our own fun." Ruby showed Rose the bathroom, where her parents' bedroom was, the study, the dining room, the sitting room and the kitchen. The kitchen was large and Ruby's mum was boiling the kettle.

"Now you two, I expect you're thirsty and hungry so what would you like?"

Ruby replied, "A cup of your lovely tea please Mum, and a slice of cake."

Rose replied, "I'll have the same as Ruby please Mrs Smith."

"Now Rose, my name is Monica and my husband is George." Rose was startled at that remark.

"Please forgive me," she replied a little afraid of upsetting anyone, "but I was brought up to respect my elders, so I would rather call you Mr and Mrs Smith."

A male voice behind her said, "Quite right too Rose. Mr and Mrs Smith is fine. I hope you like the old place? Ruby will no doubt show you the surrounding gardens tomorrow." They all sat round the kitchen table, drinking and eating, and slowly all got acquainted.

"Tomorrow as you know is the day before Christmas Eve, and so we thought we'd take you girls into town. We can have lunch somewhere and then come back later on and enjoy a lovely dinner," said George. Monica noticed that Rose had paled slightly and was chewing her bottom lip.

"I can't wait to show you the shopping centre," said Ruby to Rose, "You'll love it." Rose smiled.

"How about doing a jigsaw?" asked Monica. Hours later, after they had finished a jigsaw of the world, Monica went to the kitchen and made some beef, cheese and tuna sandwiches. Also on the table was a Battenberg cake and a jam sponge cake. A large pot of tea was also made. Monica called to everyone, who then sat at the kitchen table and ate their meal.

Later on as they were relaxing in the sitting room, George said, "Where were you born Rose, if you don't mind me asking? I noticed you have a Lancashire accent."

Rose, without thinking, replied, "I was born in a village called Hayleigh."

George said, "Well, what a small world. My father use to live in the village of Blackthorn, about fifty miles south."

Rose paled and said quietly, "Did you say ... Black ... Blackthorn?" George nodded. Suddenly Rose felt hot and sick. The room started spinning and she fainted.

"Oh heavens, Rose, Rose, are you alright? George, get me the smelling salts." Rose came round slowly.

"My dear girl, did I say something to upset you? I'm so sorry if I did," said George.

Rose replied in a hushed voice, "My apologies, but I'd rather not talk about it." Monica and George looked at each other, both concerned. Soon it was time for bed and Monica told the girls she would be up soon to tuck them in. Ruby and Rose cleaned their teeth and had a quick wash, changed into their nightdresses, said goodnight to each other and went to their bedrooms. Rose heard Monica go into Ruby's room, and then knocked on her door and entered.

"Rose, are you feeling better now?" Rose replied she was fine. "I hope the bed is nice and comfy. If you need another pillow or blanket there are some spare ones in the wardrobe." Rose replied she was more than comfy, and thanked her again for letting her stay.

Monica took Rose's hand and said, "I hope you don't mind me asking, but I noticed when we talked about going shopping, you looked a bit concerned."

Rose felt embarrassed, and replied, "I don't have any money and I only have my school uniform and underwear. All my clothes are at my uncle and aunt's house." Monica felt for Rose and asked her where she lived. Rose replied in the large village of Rilford.

"Oh that's only a short drive from here. We could drive over there tomorrow and get some of your belongings."

Rose replied, "It would be of no use, as I don't have a key to the house."

Monica smiled and said, "Don't worry Rose, we'll sort something out. Now snuggle under the sheet and blanket, and I hope you sleep well." Bending over she kissed Rose's forehead. "Night Rose."

Rose replied, "Night Mrs Smith." After Monica left, Rose had a tear in her eyes, as another memory came to her. The last time she had been kissed goodnight was by her mam.

Once Monica and George were in bed, Monica said, "What do you think of Rose? I quite like her."

George replied, "So do I. I've never seen Ruby so happy, and I think they'll be friends all through school." Monica then started to read her book, whilst George read his newspaper.

"George, why do you think Rose fainted? She was fine until you mentioned Blackthorn."

George put his paper down and replied, "I'm not sure. I was never there, as you know. My father met my mother and moved here. I do remember him talking about a huge black building, on top of a hill, that overlooked the village. It was called Blackthorn Orphanage. If Rose was there, then she had a really bad start to life."

Monica sighed and cuddled into George's arms. "Rose told me she has no money and only her school uniform with her. I feel for her. What can we do?"

George kissed Monica's forehead and said, "I'm sure Ruby will let her have some of her clothes, and as to the money, you leave that to me. You finished reading?" Monica nodded and so George turned out the bedside lamp.

In the morning, after breakfast, Ruby let Rose have a look through her wardrobe and pick out some clothes, and then they all went to town. George parked the car and they all headed for the shopping centre. "Now you two go and enjoy yourselves and we will meet you at the cafe on the ground level at twelve o'clock." As they went to go, George took Rose's hand and put some money in it. "Just in case you need something Rose," and winked at her.

Rose nodded and smiled and said quietly, "Thank you. I'll pay you back." Ruby and Rose had a great time going in and out of the various shops. Ruby bought various things, and Rose bought a box of chocolates to give Mr and Mrs Smith on Christmas Day, and a book for Ruby. They had lunch and then returned to the house. Ruby gave Rose some wrapping paper for her presents. Christmas Day arrived and all four of them had a wonderful day. Monica cooked a large chicken and served it with vegetables, stuffing, sausages, Yorkshire puddings and gravy. Christmas pudding followed this, with sixpences in it, and custard/cream. Afterwards they sat in the sitting room, and opened their presents. Both Ruby and her parents loved her presents. Rose received a couple of books, and some toiletries. Later on, apart from Rose, they all fell asleep. Rose was happy and for once felt part of a family. The rest of the week flew past and Rose and Ruby had a wonderful time. Ruby took Rose down to the park and showed her how to roller skate in the bandstand. They went for long walks and chatted about everyone and everything.

Soon it was New Year's Eve, and both the girls helped Monica get ready for the party. It was a buffet and tables were put in the dining room, and all the various foods were laid out and covered until the evening. As a surprise Monica had made Ruby and Rose a new dress for the party. They were delighted. Soon the guests started arriving and Rose and Ruby stayed in one corner of the sitting room making their own entertainment, until it was time to get something to eat. Monica and George kept their eyes on them to make sure they weren't bored. Both of them fell asleep about 10pm, but woke about 11.30pm. Then the clock struck midnight and everyone saw in a New Year. Lots of hugging and kisses did the rounds and then they sang "Auld Lang Syne". Monica helped the girls to bed and kissed them goodnight.

Two days later they were on their way back to school. The teachers noticed a vast improvement in Rose. She knuckled down to her schoolwork and started socializing more with the other girls. The Easter holidays Rose went home, and had a boring time. When the summer holidays arrived, Rose spent half of the holidays at home and the other half at Ruby's. On a beautiful sunny day, Rose, Ruby and her parents, went to the seaside for the day. Rose had never been before and was scared of going in the sea, but with Ruby and her parents' help, she was soon running in and out of the sea enjoying herself. That evening, for some unknown reason, George asked Rose if she was happy.

Rose replied, "I have never been so happy and it's all thanks to both of you and Ruby."

Monica replied, "We love having you Rose, and if you need anything, you only have to ask."

Rose chewed her bottom lip and said, "Now I know you, and trust you, can I, maybe ... tell you my story?"

George took her hand and said, "Only if you want to Rose, as you don't have to."

Rose replied, "I want to."

CHAPTER 2

———————～———————

"I was born Rose Clark, and my parents were Robert and Doris Clark. My mam worked at the corn mill and the cotton mill. My pa worked down the pits. Sometimes he would have to go to other pits, why I never knew. I had two brothers Stephen and Frank, who were two and four years older than me, and we lived in the large village of Hayleigh, in Lancashire. At one end of the village was the corn mill, and on the outskirts at the other end, about five miles away, was the large coal pit face. The village was on the banks of a large river, where a dam had been built to channel the water to the wheel of the corn mill, so that wheat, barley etc could be ground up. In the middle of the village was a War Memorial to the First World War. Shops included a greengrocer, post office, chip shop, co-op, two pubs, and a garage. There was also a parish church, the remains of an abbey, a school and a viaduct. On the other side of the river was a large forest.

The first memory I had was my mam taking me to the infant school. Once there, I was taken to a small classroom, where there were ten other children. I held onto my mam's hand tightly. "Now come on lass, be a good girl and go play. Look there's a Wendy house, and lots of toys. Frank and Stephen will collect you at lunchtime and take you home to Aunt Jean's." I looked at my mam and said, "Don't leave me our mam, I'm scared." At that moment the teacher arrived and looking at my mam, knew the problem. "You must be Rose. I'm Miss Brown and your teacher. Do you want to come and play with the other children?" I shook my head. Another girl, who I had noticed had been watching us, walked up to me and said, "I'm Susan. Do you want to play in the Wendy house?" I looked at my mam, who smiled and said, "There's nowt to be scared of Rose." Within minutes I was playing happily, and didn't see my mam leave. Later on we had a break and were given milk and biscuits. Soon it was time to go home. Only Frank turned up and we walked back to Aunt Jean's.

"Well young Rose, did you have a good day?" asked Aunt Jean, who was my pa's sister. I told her all about it. "Well lass, that's good. Now I've made you a cheese sandwich, so eat that and then go out and play." I ate the sandwich and then went and sat on the doorstep playing with my doll and teddy bear, looking down the road for my mam to come home. I did this every day, unless it was raining. As soon as I saw her I would skip down the road and hug her, and she would hug me right back, and then walk home hand in hand. Over the next couple of months, I noticed my mam was getting very tired and putting on weight. Then one weekend my mam told all of us she was expecting another bairn. I hoped it would be a girl, so I would have a sister, but it never happened. Mam became ill, and died in childbirth, along with the child. Pa started spending a lot of time down the pub and coming home drunk, but he never hurt us.

One day after school, about two months later, I was surprised to see my pa waiting for me. I ran to him and hugged him, but he pushed me away. We walked home in silence. As we got to the house a car drove up and a lady got out. "Mr Clark, I am Mrs Bronlew from …" My pa replied, "I know who you are, so you'd better come in from prying eyes and twitching curtains." In the kitchen I noticed a small suitcase. My pa said, "Rose, I have to go away to another pit for a time, and your Aunt Jean can't look after you all day, so I have arranged for you to go on an adventure. I've packed a case for you, and I'm sure you'll have a wonderful time. I hope you understand it's what I need to do?" I replied, "Yes pa. I'll miss you, Frank and Stephen so much, but you'll be back soon and then I can come home." The next minute I was in the car being driven away. The motion of the car made me sleepy and I closed my eyes. Little did I know I would never see my pa or brothers again."

***

Some time after Rose had been driven away, Jean walked into the kitchen.

"Rob, where's Rose, as I haven't seen her today?"

Rob glared at his sister and replied nastily, "She's gone."

Jean paled and replied, "What do you mean she's gone? Gone where?"

"She's gone where you'll never find her. I know bloody well what happened Jean, and I'll be damned if I'll bring up a bastard, and the worst thing is you never told me," and with that slapped her hard across her cheek.

Jean staggered back and said quietly, "Who told you?"

Rob replied, "Angie Turnbull. She's always fancied me and thought I should know the truth. Now you going to tell me what happened you bloody bitch?"

Jean sat down at the table and said shakily, "It was the factory owners' son Tom's twenty-first birthday party, and we were all invited to the Black Bull. I stayed home and looked after the bairns. The following morning I found Doris in a bad way. She told me when she'd had enough she decided to come home. Yes, she was the worse for wear, so when Tom offered to walk her back, she thought nowt of it. Walking up the back ginnel, he tried to kiss her, but Doris pushed him away. Once in the house, Doris felt faint and went upstairs, after saying thank you and goodnight to Tom.

"She passed out on the bed, and then slowly became aware of someone undressing her. She thought it was you. Your hands were roaming over her body, your lips kissing her breasts and sucking her nipples. She remembered saying, 'Oh Rob, give me a good un tonight.' Your lips were on hers and you were spreading her legs apart, and then she felt you enter her. You brought her to climax a few times, and then she slept. It was only in the morning, that her world shattered as she realised she'd slept with Tom. Distraught wasn't the word. She tried to avoid him at the factory, but he would always get her on her own and he would try to fondle her. He even thanked her for his own personal twenty-first birthday present. In the end she told him to "bugger off" or she would tell you, and then god help him. Two months later she realised she was up the duff. She was petrified of losing you and so we kept quiet. I strung Tom up by his throat and said if he told anyone I'd kill him on the spot. A week later he left for London."

Rob was pacing up and down and replied, "So that little bugger raped her then. I'll have the cops on him."

Jean replied, "Rob it wouldn't be any good. Doris thought it was you and let him have her. Please tell me where Rose is. She can live with me, and, if necessary, I'll move away."

Rob turned on Jean and said, "You're no bloody sister of mine anymore, and so do what you want. You're not welcome in my house, or the one you rent from me. Now GET OUT, and be gone before the morn."

Jean was horrified and said, "But Rob where will I go and what about Frank and Stephen?"

Rob replied with venom in his voice, "I don't bloody care woman, just go. By the way, you'll never find that little bastard now." Before the sun rose Jean had packed her bags and left.

When the boys returned from school, Rob told them that school was finished. They needed wages coming in to pay the bills, and he had arranged for them both to go down the pit. Frank and Stephen were stunned, but knew they had to do what their pa told them, or have a beating inflicted on them.

"What about Rose?" asked Frank.

Rob replied, "Your Aunt Jean is looking after her for the time being. Now eat your dinner, then bed, as you'll be up at 5am."

The following morning at 5.30am, Rob and his sons walked down the back ginell, meeting other men and boys on the way from the terraced houses, to meet the work bus that would take them to the pit. When they arrived, they went to a large room filled with lockers. Rob went to his and they all changed into their work clothes. Rob had his safety helmet with headlamp in his hand. Then they made their way to the lift cage, which would take them underground. The cage was full of men and boys. Once down, a man covered from head to foot in dust and soot said,

"These your bairns then Clark?" Rob nodded. The man said, "Right, you two with me."

"You scared Frank?" asked Stephen. Frank nodded. Rob told them to stay in the locker room once they had finished, and wait until he arrived. They were led down a long tunnel, only lit by dim lanterns.

About halfway the man said, "This is where you work from. See all these pieces of loose coal, you pick 'em up and put 'em in wagons as they pass by. Work fast, no slacking, or stealing, or else. Understand?" Both boys nodded and started working. They were allowed a break, when they ate their sandwiches that their pa had made, and a drink of water. At the end of the day they were shattered. As told, they waited for their pa in the locker room. Eventually he turned up and told them to strip, like himself. Then he took them into the showers where they all soaped each other down until they were clean, then dried and put their other clothes on. "Put clothes in me bag, so I can wash em when we get home," said Rob.

Once home, Frank said, "Pa, can we go and see Rose?" Rob nodded and told them not to be long as dinner would soon be on the table. About a minute later they were back. "Pa, Pa, Aunt Jean and Rose aren't there. The house is all locked up, and when I looked through window, all her stuff's gone."

Rob looked at them and replied, "Don't talk daft lad. She's probably in front room. Let's go look." Rob grabbed the spare key and they entered the house by the front door. All was in darkness, so Rob put the lights on. He looked over the whole house and said furiously, "What the bloody hell ... she's gone and taken Rose with her. Stephen run to cop shop and tell em to get here NOW."

A short while later, Stephen returned with a copper. "Mr Clark, your lad ere says his sister's gone missing. That right?"

Rob replied, "Yes sir. My sister Jean was looking after her, as me and my bairns all work at pit now. With me Mrs dying, Jean always looked after Rose till I came home. I don't understand, it's not the sort of thing she would do." Later on the copper left with full descriptions of Jean and Rose and said a full search would start in the morning. Soon the whole village knew. The women felt sorry for Rob and the boys and would leave meals for them to be heated up. The men not down the pit would join in the searches, but nothing was found.

About a month later, the detective in charge knocked on Rob's door. "Detective, have you some good news for me?" he asked full of concern.

The detective replied, "There's no easy way to say this, but we found a woman's body on Treeburn Moor. We think it's your sister, and need you to identify her."

Tears fell down Rob's face and he said emotionally, "Oh please no. I've just lost me Mrs and now maybe me sister. What news of Rose?" The detective told him there was no trace of her, and did he know why his sister would be heading in that direction. Rob replied he didn't. After Rob had identified his sister and the body released, a funeral was held. That night after a farewell party to Jean, he reminisced about the last time he had been in the pub. He had about three beers and a game of dominoes with his mates and then left.

At the bottom of the ginell two men were waiting. "You wanted to see us Clark?" one of them asked.

"I'm calling in that favour you owe me," said Rob. Years ago he had been in the wrong place at the wrong time and saw a murder. They threatened to kill him unless he kept stum, and he did. Now he wanted that favour. "I want you to deal with me sister Jean. I've told her to leave tonight, and if I know her she'll do a moonlight flit. Take her far away, but go north, and then dispose of her."

One of the men replied, "It'll be done and then none of us need meet again. Agreed?"

"Agreed," said Rob and they all shook hands. "If you're interested, me sister has never bedded a man, so if you want to show her what's she's been missing, you have me blessings."

CHAPTER 3

As Jean slipped quietly out of the house, she was unaware of being watched. The car trailed behind her for a couple of minutes, and then before Jean knew what was happening, she was grabbed and something put over her nose and mouth. When she came round, she was in the back of a car with two men in the front. She had no idea where she was as it was pitch black. Then the car stopped, but the headlights were left on.

"Out you get slag," said one of the men.

Jean was scared and said, "Where are we, and why are you doing this?" She realised her hands were tied behind her back, and her coat was gone.

"Your brother asked us to show you a really good time, if you get my drift." Jean tried to run, but they caught her, and dragged her back to the car headlights and so she started to scream.

"Scream as much as you like, as there's no-one out here to hear you. Now let's see what you're hiding under that hideous dress. Hold her still while I cut this thing away." He produced a knife and grabbing the front of her dress, slashed it straight down the middle. He put his hand round her back and unfastened her bra, and then cut the straps. "Cor, nice titties," he said. He grabbed them and started kneading them, and brushing his thumbs over her nipples. Then he was kissing and sucking them. "Looks like she's enjoying this, feel how hard her nipples are." The other man, stood behind her, started fondling her breasts and agreed. Next her panties were cut away. "Need to lay her down. Look there's a flat rock slab over there where

15

we can put her, and have good access, and then we can have some real fun."

Jean was desperately trying to plead with them not to do it, as they laid her on the slab, with her legs hanging down, but they ignored her. The slab was cold and Jean shivered as it touched her back. The man stood in front of her dropped his trousers. "Now look at this, isn't it nice, long and big. Guess where it's going Jean?" He parted her legs and ran his hands over her thighs and up towards his prize. He parted the lips of her entrance and rubbed his finger up and down, and then slipped it into her, pumping it in and out. "You really are a virgin. Feels like you're getting wet Jean. Well can't wait any longer so here we go ready or not." He lifted her legs up towards her shoulders and then rammed himself into her repeatedly. Jean screamed like she'd never screamed before. Once he'd finished he offered her to his mate.

His mate said, "Roll her over, don't want to stick this where yours has been. I need me bottle of water." Jean was struggling and the other man slapped her hard as he rolled her onto her front, and then pushed her dress up out of the way. Suddenly she felt water being poured between her buttocks. Her legs were kicked far apart and she felt him massaging the water round her back passage and then rammed his thumb in and out, pouring the rest of the water over her. "Nice and slippy now," he said, and pushed himself up inside her. He took her with a violent force, but as he was pumping her a piece of protruding stone, which was smooth and round and wet with the water, was rubbing Jean's sensual nub and she felt her body responding and moaned. "Bloody hell, I can feel her coming." He rammed in harder and harder and as her climax hit her Jean blacked out. When he'd finished they rolled her over and the other one took her again. They both took her three times.

Once satisfied one said, "You fed up with her now?"

"Yes, let's beat the crap out of her as she's just a whore now." They beat and kicked her until she was black and blue, and was hardly conscious. They untied her hands and took the remains of her clothes off. Totally naked they wrapped her in a large blanket and dumped her in the back of the car. They drove another five miles and stopped by a fast flowing river. They got her out and took her to the river's edge.

"Well Jean, been a pleasure to have screwed you. Hope you enjoyed it as much as we did?"

Jean looked at them through half closed eyes and said nastily, "Laughs on you boys, as it was a stone that made me come, not you." That was the last thing Jean said. Making sure they only touched the blanket, they pushed her naked body into the river, but as they did one of them cut her throat.

"That should wash away any evidence. Fancy a pint?" The other nodded and threw the blanket in the back seat. "Pity we had to end her as she was a good screw. Nice and tight." They both laughed and drove off.

The detective told Rob when they found Jean she was naked, had been badly beaten and raped repeatedly, front and back, which led them to believe two, maybe three men had been involved. She also had her throat cut. Her suitcases were never found. Rob was distraught to think his beloved sister had to endure such a horrific assault.

Back home he opened a bottle of beer and laughing said, "Here's to you Jean. At least you died knowing what it was like to have a man between your legs." He'd got rid of both of them and nobody suspected a thing. It had however changed him, as now he would never trust a woman again. If he wanted sex, there were plenty of tasty prostitutes around.

***

Rose carried on with her story. "When I awoke, we were driving through rough countryside and up a long steep hill. There was nothing around at all. At the top of the hill, the road levelled out and I saw the biggest building I had ever seen. It had high walls round it, with another wall inside separating the building in two. There were two large gates with notices that said 'Males' and 'Females' on each. In big letters above the gates was a sign that said "Blackthorn Orphanage." We drove down a long drive and pulled into a space. "Out you get lass. This is your new home now. Here's your suitcase," said the woman. I took the case and turned and looked at the building in front of me. It was even bigger close up and was black, gloomy and high, and as I stood there I felt scared. "I want to go home," I said. The woman just grabbed my hand and took me inside.

"The inside was as gloomy as the outside. We went up some stairs and came to a door that had 'Governess' written on it. The woman knocked on the door and we were told to enter. Inside the room was dimly lit, and I saw a woman sitting behind a desk with lots of papers and files on it. "Who's this?" asked the woman, peering over her glasses. "This is Rose Clark from Hayleigh governess." "Ah, another bastard I believe." I didn't know what that word meant. The woman stood and was tall, quite big and had her black hair scraped back into a bun, and looked frightening. "I am the governess, and you will address me so at all times. Do you understand?" Quietly I replied, "Yes governess." She explained she ran the female side, and her husband, the governor, ran the male side. "Come here and let me look you over." I went and stood in front of her and she removed my hat and coat. She looked through my hair, made me open my mouth and stick my tongue out. She poked and prodded me, and wrote whatever she was doing on a piece of paper. When she sat back down at her desk, she opened a large book, and looking at the other woman said, "She needs to go to Infant 2 dormitory, and will be number 16. She needs to be washed from top to toe, and her hair cut. Take her away."

"I was taken to a room, where two other women were, and the one who had brought me said, "She's all yours," and left. They stripped me of my clothes, which one woman took away. The other woman grabbed my hair, which was quite long, and cut it from ear to ear. I started crying. "Stop that blubbering girl or else I'll lock you in the cupboard." A bucket of cold water was poured over me and I was scrubbed from head to toe. Something was rubbed into the remains of my hair, which stunk. After I had been dried, the woman said, "Put these on girl." I was handed a pair of briefs, green dress, socks and shoes, and a cardigan. Afterwards I was taken to another room. "Sit there and I will get you something to eat and drink." I was given a stale bread roll and a mug of water. As I finished eating yet another woman came in. "You must be 16. I am Miss Cook and I run Infant 2 dormitory, so you will be under my charge. Follow me." We went down a corridor, and then along another. "This room here is where you will wash yourself and clean your teeth. There are also some toilets. You cannot use the toilets after lights out. Do you need to go now?" I replied I did, and so I used the toilet. She then opened a door opposite, which was a large room with lots of beds in it. "This bed is yours, undress, and put your nightie on, no noise and no talking." I didn't realise darkness had fallen and so the only light was from the moon shining through the slats on the windows. I saw my suitcase was at the side and quietly opened it. Inside were some of my clothes and shoes, my colouring book and crayons, and my small beloved teddy bear. I took him out, changed and got into bed cuddling him and started crying. "Hush now, stop crying or we'll all get into trouble. Move over and let me get in with you," said a hushed voice. I moved over and she got in. "I'm Yvonne. Here, let me cuddle you like your mam would." She wrapped her arms round me, and slowly clutching my teddy, I drifted off to sleep.

"I was awoken by lights being switched on. Miss Cook stood there. "Time to get up and wash." There must have been over thirty girls who lined up. I noticed two slept to a bed. "17 you're in charge of 16 so show her what to do." "I will Miss," said Yvonne. We stood in the line, on the cold flagstones, and quietly Yvonne whispered in my ear, looking round to make sure Miss Cook didn't see her, "What's your name? We have to call each other by our numbers, but in the dormitory, when we're alone, we use our proper names, so we don't forget." I told her it was Rose. When we reached the bathroom, Miss Cook handed me a flannel, towel, small piece of soap, toothbrush and toothpaste, and a comb. All had the number 16 on them. Yvonne said, "You keep these 16. There is a locker by your bed with a drawer, so put everything in there. At the side is a bar where you hang your flannel and towel to dry." After we'd washed in cold water and been to the toilet, it was back to the dormitory, where Yvonne showed me how to make my bed properly, and then I dressed in the uniform given me. That was when I noticed all of it had 16 on it. Next, in a line, we walked to the end of the corridor and down the steps to the dining room. This room was large, with long tables set out in lines, with another long table raised up on a platform. We had to stand and wait for the governess to arrive.

"She went down the first line, checking hands, necks and behind the ears had all been washed properly. One girl hadn't and that was the first time I saw someone get the cane across her hands. Once she'd inspected the line we went and stood by the table that was for our dormitory, which had a bowl, spoon and mug. Again everything had numbers on it. This was done until every girl was checked. The governess and teachers then stood by their table. The governess then said," Prayers please." We had to say a prayer for the food we were receiving. One woman then filled the mugs with water, whilst the other slopped thick, hardly warm, porridge into the bowls. It tasted vile, but I ate it, and drank my water. Looking around I saw girls of all different ages. Nobody was allowed to talk. At the end of the meal, the governess again walked up and down, making sure every girl had eaten her food. If you didn't - punishment was given. The bowls, spoons and mugs were then quietly passed down to the end of each table, where two girls would then take them and place them onto a trolley, to go to the kitchen. We then returned to our dormitory, where Miss Cook checked all the beds had been made properly. If it wasn't done properly, everything was pulled off, and you had to remake it, followed by a punishment. After this was done, we were taken to another room, where we had lessons. The room was dimly lit, like the other rooms, with no windows. I was given chalk and a small slate to write on. There was a short break when we had bread and dripping, and a mug of water, then back to lessons. Once lessons had finished, Miss Cook asked me to stay behind, so she could talk to me. "Sit down 16. Do you know the reason why you are here?" I replied, "My pa told me I was going on an adventure. Can I go home soon?" Miss Cook sighed and said, "I'm sorry 16 you won't be going home again. Your pa doesn't want you anymore." Tears filled my eyes and I said, "What did I do wrong? Does my pa and brothers not love me anymore?" Miss Cook then explained to me what a bastard was. I was only five, but I understood, and it hurt badly."

CHAPTER 4

Miss Cook said, "I know this place isn't what you're used to 16, but if you do as you're told and not misbehave you will have a passable life. Misbehave and your life will be hell. Now back to the dormitory, as it will soon be time for supper. Can you remember the way?" I shook my head and so she showed me. Back in the dormitory all the girls were talking quietly. Yvonne told me all their names, but too many to remember. I just looked at them. "It's alright Rose, don't worry, you will soon get the hang of everything. Carol, over there, has a small notebook hidden away and puts a small line down for each day. When she has seven, she puts a line through them and we know it's a week, and …" At that moment the door opened and a voice shouted, "Dining Room." As with breakfast we went to the dining room. This time instead of porridge, something that looked disgusting was put in my bowl. The meat was fatty and hard to chew, the vegetables were hard, and again it was nearly cold. I started to gag, and Yvonne passed me my mug of water, of which I drank some. She mouthed, "Eat it, please." I did and felt so sick, but after drinking the rest of my water, I managed to keep the food in my stomach. After supper we had an hour to get ready for bed, and make sure we all went to the bathroom/toilet. It was then that I noticed my suitcase had gone. I looked round for it until Yvonne asked me what I was looking for. She told me that it had been removed so that we had nothing of our past. I was upset because my colouring book and crayons were in there along with my teddy bear. "Time for prayers," shouted Miss Cook, and once the lights were switched off, the room became pitch black. A bit later on Yvonne got into the bed and like the night before wrapped her arms round me. "Here Rose, I kept him safe for you," and put my teddy in my hands. "Oh thank you Yvonne. Where did you hide him?" She replied she would show me in the morning, and to go to sleep, which I did. In the morning Yvonne showed me a loose floorboard under my bed. "Hide teddy in there so they won't find him." It turned out most of the girls had items hidden away.

"As the weeks went by, I learnt more of the orphanage from Yvonne. I hadn't seen it yet, but there was a large yard at the back of the building, again with a high wall, dividing males from females. Under no circumstances were the males allowed to mix with the females. At the front, where I had seen a little bit, there were extensive gardens, but these were out of bounds. On the ground level were the dining room, kitchen, sickroom, toilets and a storeroom where all the numbered clothes were kept, along with the laundry room. When girls left, the numbers were unstitched and then restitched onto a uniform for a new girl. The first level had the governess's office, Infant 1 and Infant 2 dormitories, ages from two to seven, bathroom, two teachers' rooms, and two classrooms. The second level the same but for Junior 1 and Junior 2 dormitories, ages eight to twelve, and level three had Senior 1 and Senior 2 dormitories, all girls over thirteen. Above the last level was the attic. Once you went up to the Junior dormitories, but only when there was a bed available, in the bathroom was a bath. You were then allocated a bath night. Anyone who decided it was a good idea to be bad was put into a punishment book, which was then read out at the beginning of a day before breakfast in the dining room. Those numbers called had to stand in front of the governess on the raised platform so everyone could see them. They had to drop their briefs, bend over, and depending upon the severity of the punishment, were given the equivalent caning. Some girls then had a problem with sitting down. About three times a year, some of the girls would just vanish, to where nobody knew.

"One day we were taken out into the yard, to watch a girl being caned. Her crime - she had wet the bed. Then she had to sweep and wash the whole yard until it was clean, which in windy weather was never ending. It was that day I heard screams coming from the male section, and whatever was being done to him it sounded horrific. Other punishments, depending upon the severity, were you had your mouth rinsed out with soap and water; no food all day; solitary confinement; stand barefoot on the slabs, day and night, with a notice saying "Ignore this child", and if you cried you were humiliated at breakfast and then those who wanted to could push that girl around all day. Sometimes the whole dormitory was punished for one girl's stupidity. The daily routine was get up and wash, make the bed and dress, breakfast, bed check, lessons with a small break, more lessons, supper and then bed. We were woken at 6am and bed was 8pm. Hair was cut and washed in rotation every month. During the morning some of the older girls had to wash and clean all the stone floors. In the summer months we were allowed to play in the yard for a short while, but told what to play. We could also talk in the yard. The winter months you stayed inside unless you had a punishment and then you would see girls stood in the yard in the rain and snow, all day. This time of the year some of the girls died.

"About six months later, Yvonne disappeared and I was heartbroken. She had been my friend since day one and I really missed her. I never found out where she went, and she never said goodbye. She had shown me what to do and what not to do, how to stay out of trouble, and steer clear of the senior girl gangs. From then on I kept myself to myself. I was polite to everyone but learnt to depend on only myself. I more or less obeyed the rules and life was just about bearable. My first punishment was for dropping a bowl in the dining room and I had the ruler whacked over my knuckles four times. The back of both my hands came up in black bruises. I witnessed some horrific punishments over the years, which I would rather not remember or talk about. Many years later, I'm not sure how many, I was in the junior section, and our teacher Miss Rowman, told us we could go into the garden grounds and pick flowers for our lesson. This was the only time I ever went into the gardens. They were lovely, with various flowers, trees and bushes. I saw paths leading to other places, but these were closed off, and I wasn't going to be stupid enough to investigate. I made my way up towards the gate and found various flowers, which I carefully picked and put into my basket. I saw a patch of wild bluebells, but when I went to pick one, I heard a scream. I looked around and saw no one, so picked the bluebell, then heard the scream again and followed the direction of it. I saw a small gap in the wall that separated the building. Afterwards, I wished I'd just gone straight back to my class.

"I looked through the gap and saw a naked boy tied to a tree. Four other boys had hold of his arms and legs and were pulling them hard. I could see the boy was in agony. "This'll teach you to snitch on us you little weasel," said the tallest boy. The four boys looked like they were fifteen/sixteen years old, the one tied to the tree younger. "I'm sorry, I didn't mean to, but the governor threatened to flog me in front of everyone." One of the other boys said, "Well Pete, we've stretched him, now what?" Pete replied, "We haven't stretched everything," and took hold of the boy's private part and yanked it hard. The boy screamed again. "Go on Pete keep pulling him till he gets hard and comes." Pete looked at the boy who had spoken and said, "If that's what you want Mickey, I'm happy to oblige." I should have left straight away, but I was petrified of making a noise. I watched as Pete pulled and pulled and the boy's private part became bigger and hard. Then he was groaning and I saw something spurting out of it. One of the other boys then took hold of the boy's part and pulled again, stretching it, but this time the tall boy kept whacking it with a thick stick. The boy was screaming in agony. "Enjoy that did you snitch? Now I think it's time you got thrashed." I turned my eyes away from the brutal scene taking part, and watching where I put my feet, quietly tiptoed away, and then ran like the wind back to the class.

""Where have you been 16?" asked Miss Rowman annoyed. "Sorry Miss, I thought I heard someone shouting, but I was mistaken. I did manage to get these flowers though." Miss Rowman replied, "Hands out," and I had the ruler six times. It didn't matter what I did, I couldn't get that poor boy out of my mind, so a week later I decided there was only one thing to do. "You are absolutely sure of this 16?" asked the governess sternly. I replied I was and told to wait. The governor then entered the office and I repeated what I had seen. "Now 16, I warn you to think before you answer, or else the consequences, FOR YOU, will be dire. You are one hundred per cent sure that you heard the names Pete and Mickey, as two of the boys there?" asked the governor seriously. "Yes governor, I'm sure." The governor looked at the governess, who looked at me and said, "You can go now 16 and say nothing, or else. Do you understand?" I replied I did, and left and returned to the dormitory.

"Some weeks later, I had a pain in my side and was sent to the sickroom. On the way there I saw a gang of five girls talking, and had to pass them to get to the sickroom. I didn't want to pass them and so stood hidden quietly behind a section of the wall. I heard one of them say, "If I ever find out who grassed my brother's up I will personally kill her." One of her friends replied, "What did they get?" "Three bloody months solitary, and then prison for three months." "Come on Lucy, they did commit an assault on another boy, who's had to leave to go god knows where." Lucy replied, "Well, some friend you turned out to be Elaine, so now you can bugger off and you're not part of my gang anymore. Say a word and you're dead as well. Got it." I heard footsteps moving away. "Don't worry Lucy, we'll find her," said one of the other girls. I then heard the rest of them walk away and peered round the corner. It was clear, but now I was very scared. In the sickroom the nurse told me it was just a muscle strain.

"Over the next couple of weeks, some of my dormitory started having "accidents". I heard from another girl that word was out it was one of us that had snitched on the boy's assault, as we were the ones in the garden that day. I had no idea what the girl I had overheard looked like, I only saw her back, and so I was wary of all the older girls. On the way to class one day, I was "accidentally" pushed down the steps, and landed at the feet of the governess. "What is the meaning of this 16?" she asked annoyed. I apologised and said due to my own stupidity I had slipped, and was sorry for causing a problem. I was made to scrub the dormitory floor, at mealtime, so no food or water, for a week. Everyone in the dormitory now started not trusting each other. If a girl wasn't picked on, she was the snitch, but none of us were going to do the dirty and tell the governess. Over time, all the girls had an "accident." Then some of the senior girls were having "accidents." One day at breakfast the governess said in a rage, "It has been bought to my attention about all these so called "accidents". I will find out who is behind this and god help you. You will see a punishment I have never done here before. So, if anyone knows who it is, I will be in my office. Whoever it is, be warned, everyone will be punished for your actions." I looked round the room and most of the girls had gone white with fright. The "accidents" stopped, but two weeks later I was called to the governess's office. As I entered I saw a man and woman sitting at the side of her desk. "Ah, come in 16. I would like you to meet these people, with a view to going to live with them. Both you and I know what has been happening, and I feel it's only right to get rid of you." I looked at the couple in stunned silence, and then said in a hushed voice, "Please governess, I know I don't have the right to ask, but what if my family wants me back?" "What family?" asked the man. The governess put her hand up, and looking at me said, "I thought you had been told 16. A couple of years ago there was a huge explosion at the pit where your father and brothers were working. Everyone lost their lives, and that included your family. Your Aunt Jean is also dead." Tears sprang to my eyes, but I made sure they didn't fall down my face. Suddenly I felt very alone. "Do you think 16 will suit you? I can see she is now nine years old," asked the governess. "She'll do," said the man. Looking at me the governess said, "16, you will go to your dormitory where you will find different clothes for you to change into. You will leave everything else on your bed. You take nothing from here. When you are ready, sit outside my office." I replied, "Yes governess." Back in the dormitory I saw the change of clothes. There was a skirt, blouse, cardigan, socks, shoes, briefs and a coat. I changed quickly and was about to put teddy in my pocket when one of the teachers passed. "Oh no you don't 16, that stays here," and taking it off me she threw it on top of the wardrobe. I glowered at her as she left the dormitory. No way was I leaving my teddy. I looked down the corridor and saw it empty. I knew there was a chair outside the classroom, so I quietly tiptoed down, picked the chair up and put in front of the wardrobe. I felt around and then my hand landed on teddy. I grabbed him, got off the chair, again looked in the corridor and put the chair back. Now how was I going to smuggle him out? I opened a cupboard in the corridor quietly, and saw a piece of string hanging down, and grabbed it. Back in the dormitory I tied teddy round my waist. I made sure he was at the side of me, so if the governess did check me she wouldn't see him, unless she lifted my cardigan up. I put the coat on and went and sat down outside the governess's office, to see what fate awaited me."

CHAPTER 5

"As I was sitting there waiting, the gang of girls I had seen by the sickroom walked past. "Going somewhere are we 16?" asked the one called Lucy. I recognised her voice. I just shrugged my shoulders. Lucy looked at me through narrowed eyes and said, "Good riddance to bad rubbish." As she went to walk off, she stopped dead in her tracks. Rounding on me she spat, "It was you wasn't it? That's why you're going. You're the bitch." I felt the colour drain from my face and replied, "No I'm not. I thought I would stay here forever." "You're a liar and I can tell by your face. Well don't worry ... Rose Clark .... from Hayleigh, yes I know your real name, and so will my brothers and his friends. Remember the names Pete and Mickey Cooper. They'll find you one day, so keep looking over your shoulder you low life bitch." "What's going on here?" snapped the governess. Quickly I replied, "Nothing governess. 12 and her friends were wishing me luck." The governess raised her eyebrow and said, "In here 16," and pushed me through the door. I heard her speaking to the girls but couldn't hear what she said. Back in the office, looking at me the governess said, "Now then 16, the paperwork, including your adoption, has been signed and you now belong to Mr and Mrs Brambles. They have decided to keep your given name and so you will now be known as Rose Brambles. I hope you realise what a lucky girl you are, and if you don't behave yourself, you will be returned here, with a severe punishment. You may now leave." I stood and thanked the governess and followed my new guardians out of the orphanage to start whatever life I was now going to have. I put my hand on my side and thought, *If I don't have anyone else, I've always got teddy.* Outside the rain was pouring and I was put into their car.

Slowly we drove down the steep hill that I remembered from when I arrived, but this time driving away from the orphanage.

"It was nearly dark when we arrived at their house. "Take her in the back way Nancy so you won't be seen," said Mr Brambles. Mrs Brambles grabbed my arm and virtually dragged me to a door at the back of the house. The door led into a kitchen, and she quickly drew the blinds and then put the light on. The kitchen was small, but everything was neat and tidy. I was told to sit down on one of the chairs, and watched as she put the kettle on and got three mugs out of the cupboard. "Now Rose, would you like tea or coffee?" I didn't answer. "Rose, I'm talking to you, please answer me," she snapped. I looked at her and said, "I apologise Mrs Brambles, I'm used to being called 16, not Rose, and I've never had tea or coffee." Mrs Brambles looked shocked. "Oh, I see. Well what would you like to drink?" I replied, "Water please." Mr Brambles came into the kitchen and said, "I'll light the fire in the sitting room and draw all the curtains, and then the three of us can talk." I wondered what he wanted to talk about. Had I said or done something wrong already? After the drinks had been made, I was shown into the sitting room. It was a large room with lots of packed boxes. I remembered what carpet looked like and bent down and untied my shoes and took them off. The last thing I wanted to do was make it dirty and receive a punishment. Mr and Mrs Brambles just looked at each other. "Please Rose, sit down and make yourself comfortable," said Mr Brambles. "As you can see, at the moment we are packing as the day after tomorrow we are leaving to move down south. Perhaps I should explain."

"First of all my wife is Nancy, and I'm Hugh. I work as a banker and my company are promoting me to take over a new branch down south. Nancy does all sorts of charity work, and that's how we found out about you. We know what you saw and did, and I think it was very brave of you to tell the governess. Alas, the sister of these boys, and her gang, were causing trouble and you had to leave. We have always wanted a girl, and with us leaving the area, this was the perfect opportunity for us to have you. Believe it or not, the governess does have a caring side to her. No one will be able to trace you with a new surname. Until we leave you will have to stay in the house so you won't be seen. Once in the new house, we thought we would say you were our daughter, but we think it better if you became our niece, and nobody will be any the wiser. You will call us Aunt Nancy and

Uncle Hugh. Does this make sense to you?" I wasn't sure how to reply, so I just nodded my head. Mrs Brambles then said, "You must be hot in your coat Rose, here let me help you take it off." As she touched me, for some reason I stepped back. "It's alright Rose, I'm not going to hurt you, I promise." As my coat came off, teddy fell to the floor, and I froze. Mrs Brambles picked it up and said, "What a lovely teddy," and handed him back to me. I took him gingerly and just stared at her. I didn't know what was going on. Why were they being nice to me? It was all too much and I wanted to go back to the orphanage. Mr Brambles looked at his wife and said, "Nancy, I think all of this is confusing Rose, as she looks bewildered. Why don't you show her to her bedroom and then she can rest?"

"Mrs Brambles held her hand out and cautiously I took it. She took me upstairs and showed me my bedroom. There was a big bed, a wardrobe, chair and the floor had a thick carpet with rugs on it. I put my foot on the carpet and it felt strange, like I was walking on a sponge. "Which side of the bed do I sleep on Mrs Brambles?" She looked at me and kneeling down so she was my height said, "Wherever you want Rose. This is your bed in your room. I know you're use to sharing, but now it's all yours. There are clothes in the wardrobe, but we will buy new later on. I have put a nightie under your pillow. Now if you need the bathroom it's across the way. If you need to use the toilet in the night, it's alright to do so. I have put a towel, toothbrush, toothpaste, flannel and some soap here on the dresser for you. If you feel scared at all, just call out and I will come to you. I hope you and teddy have a good night's sleep." With that she left. I sat down on the bed and it sank. I stood up straight away. Had I broken it? I looked in the wardrobe and saw other clothes either hung up or in piles on the shelves. I stood there not knowing what to do with myself and burst into tears. I cried tears I had held back for years. The next thing I knew Mrs Brambles was cuddling me. "It's alright Rose, please don't cry. Here blow your nose and dry your eyes," which I did. Looking at her I said, "I'm sorry Mrs Brambles but I'm lost. I don't know what to do."

"She smiled, but I noticed she had tears in her eyes, and said, "What would you do at the orphanage?" I told her I would have a quick wash, brush my teeth and hair, and then go to the toilet. Change into my nightie and then lights out. "Then that's what we'll do," she said. She took me to the bathroom and filled the basin with water. When I put my hands in, I pulled them out quickly. "That's hot," I said. "Can I have cold water please?" Mrs Brambles said it was only warm and washed my face, neck and hands for me. There was a nice smell and I realised it was the soap. I brushed my teeth and then she brushed my hair and sighed saying, "The first thing we must do is get your hair seen to. Did you use to have it long?" I nodded, and then I surprised myself by yawning. The toilet was separate to the bathroom, so once I'd used it, I went back to the bedroom, undressed and put my nightie on. "In you get Rose." I looked at her and said, "I'm sorry, I sat on it and I broke it." She laughed and replied I hadn't, it was just the way the mattress was made. Carefully I climbed in and she pulled the sheet and blankets round me, and then handed me teddy. I took him and cuddled him into my chest. "Rose if you need to put the lamp on in the night, see this button, you just push it, and then push it again to switch it off. Remember if you need me, just call for me." As she went to leave I said, "Mrs Brambles ... thank you." She smiled and closed the door. I noticed a clock on the bedside table and it was showing 10.30pm!! I laid there looking at the ceiling, thinking it was all a dream, but not for long as my eyes slowly closed. The next thing I knew the sun was streaming through the windows.

"I jumped out of the bed thinking I would get a severe punishment for sleeping so long, and then remembered I wasn't at the orphanage. There was a knock at the door and Mrs Brambles popped her head round. "Morning Rose, I hope you and teddy slept well?" I replied I did and apologised for being late. "It's only 8am Rose. Come down to the kitchen when you're ready, no rush. Here is a pair of slippers for you, so you don't dirty your socks. I hope they fit." I was stunned. 8am, so I had overslept two hours. I used the toilet and then went into the bathroom. I turned on the tap and the water got hot. I turned it off straight away and turned on the cold tap. I washed, brushed my teeth, brushed my hair, and then dressed in the same clothes from the day before. I found my way to the kitchen to see both of them sat at the table. Mr Brambles looked up as I walked in. "Morning Rose, how are you today?" I replied I was well. He smiled and asked what I would like for breakfast. Mrs Brambles put her hand on her husband's arm and said to me, "What are you used to Rose?" I said awkwardly, "Nearly cold porridge, bread and dripping, and gristly meat." "Well you won't be eating that anymore. I will do you some toast and a boiled egg," said Mrs Brambles. "Please may I have a mug of water?" I asked. "Would you like to try a hot drink?" she asked. I thought I'd better do what I was asked, and replied I'd try. I watched as she poured browny coloured water into a mug, and added some white liquid, called milk. I took a sip and found it to be nice and so I drank it. The toast and boiled egg was put in front of me. The egg was in something and I didn't know what to do. Mr Brambles took the spoon and hit the eggshell on the top, and then sliced it off. "Cut your toast into long pieces and then dunk it into the egg." I did as I was told, and it was the best thing I had tasted for a long time. Mr Brambles told me to eat the white of the egg as well. When I finished, all that was left was the eggshell. I could have eaten that all over again, but that would be greedy.

"Mr Brambles explained he had to go to work, but his wife would look after me. I was quite happy to stay indoors as it was still pouring with rain. "Would you like to help me pack up this crockery?" asked Mrs Brambles. I nodded. She showed me how to take a piece of tissue paper and wrap it round the item, then take two pieces of the large newspaper and wrap it again. We spent a couple of hours doing that, and then stopped for a drink. I noticed my hands were black, and didn't understand why. "It's alright Rose, as it's just the print from the newspaper. Let's wash them." I watched how she filled the small bowl up with some hot water and then cold. "See if that's too hot," she said. Slowly I put my hands in the bowl and it wasn't cold - in fact it was nice. "Here use the soap Rose," and she handed me a small piece. I cleaned and dried my hands and sat at the table, whilst she made some tea. "Rose, I hope you don't mind me asking, but I need to know what you were taught in the orphanage. For example do you know the days of the week?" I repeated them and she smiled. I then told her we were taught reading, writing, doing sums, and spelling. If we were all good we were allowed to do a bit of drawing. Later on we were taught a bit of history and geography, which I hated as it was boring. I had just started learning about different flowers.

"Afterwards we carried on with the packing, until it was time for her to start the evening meal. Mr Brambles returned and asked if we'd had a good day, to which we replied we had. When the meal was put in front of me, I just looked at it. On the plate were a couple of thin pieces of meat, a small amount of round white things and some vegetables. "Rose, do you not like it?" asked Mr Brambles. I looked at him and said worriedly, "What is it? I've never had anything like this before." I saw the look between the two of them. "I'm sorry Rose, neither of us realised how hard this would be for you," said Mr Brambles kindly. "It looks like we have a lot to show you, so hopefully you'll bear with us, and then together we can give you the life you should have had. So what we have here is meat called Spam, and it's fried. The white things are potatoes. Try it, if you don't like it we will find something else. How does that sound?" I replied, "I'm sorry to cause you trouble. Perhaps I should go back." Mr Brambles took my hand in his and replied, "You will never go back there Rose. I promise you we will help you all we can." I sort of smiled and half believed him, and tried the food in front of me. I ate everything, as I had been taught, not knowing if there would be a punishment if I left anything. Later on when I was in bed I cuddled teddy and told him of my day, and thought of my family who were now all lost to me.

CHAPTER 6

—————～————

"The day arrived for us to move. A large furniture van arrived and everything was loaded into it. A large food hamper was placed in the car for the journey, along with other essentials. "Nancy, have a look and see if the coast is clear, so we can get Rose in the car." Nancy went outside and looked around and said it was clear. Quickly I was put in the back of the car. "Cooee, Nancy, thanks heavens I thought I'd missed you." Mrs Brambles quickly threw a blanket over me and put her finger to her lips. "Oh, hello Mildred. Yes we are just about to go. I did come over earlier but you were out. I was going to pop a note in your post box." "Mildred lovely to see you," said Mr Brambles. Mildred replied, "I really am going to miss you both, but I wish you all the best, and good luck with the new job Hugh." I heard them thanking her and then saying they really must be going. I heard the car doors close and then we were driving away. After a short while Mrs Brambles said, "Rose you can sit up now. So sorry about that. It will never happen again." Later on in the morning, we pulled in at a picnic place and had some food and a drink. Back in the car I fell asleep, but had a horrible dream. I was on my way back to the orphanage. When I got there, Lucy and her friends were waiting for me. They beat me up and then she took teddy and ripped him to shreds. I woke up crying. "Hugh, pull over." The car stopped and Mrs Brambles got in the back, and put her arms round me. Eventually we got to the village of Rilford, and drove round until we found the house.

"This time we all walked in the front door. We had a look in the empty rooms, which already had new carpets on the floors. In fact, apart from the kitchen and bathroom, which had something called lino, the whole house was carpeted. We went to the back where the kitchen was, and much to Mr and Mrs Brambles' surprise there was a large dish with food in it and a note. It read,

Welcome.

I am Stella and live across the road at No 22. I have left you a chicken casserole, which just needs heating up, about 15 minutes. Hope you like it. I have put milk, butter, cheese, bread and eggs in the fridge. In the cupboard there is tea, coffee, sugar, along with bowls, mugs, and some crockery. I have laid a fire for you in the sitting room and the matches are at the side. I knew the old occupants hence me having a key, which I now leave for you. Look forward to meeting you. Please don't hesitate to pop over if you need anything.

Stella

""Well, what a lovely welcome," said Mrs Brambles. Mr Brambles replied, "Very nice indeed. You see to the meal and I will bring in everything from the car, light the fire and set up the camp beds in the sitting room." A short while later we had eaten the casserole with bread, and it tasted good. We then had a look around. By the front door, on the right, was what was called a cloakroom, with a basin to wash in and a separate toilet. Opposite, on the left, was a large room, which was decided to be the dining room when entertaining. Next to that was the sitting room, and next to that another room, which was to be used for us to eat in, instead of the kitchen. Upstairs there were two bedrooms, both a large size, bathroom, separate toilet and two large cupboards, of which one was called an airing cupboard. Back in the sitting room, Mr Brambles said, "Well Nancy, what do you think?" Mrs Brambles replied, "I think we will be happy here. Rose, I'm sorry, but just for tonight we will all have to sleep in here. The furniture will arrive tomorrow and the first room to be sorted will be your bedroom. Once that's done you can sort your room out, whilst we sort out the rest. It's going to be a bit of a shambles for a bit, but we'll get there." I just nodded, but felt a bit awkward, as I had never slept in a room with a man! I washed and brushed my teeth in the cloakroom and changed into my nightie and put on something called a dressing gown. Mr and Mrs Brambles did the same. Soon I was cuddled on the camp bed, and as usual clutching teddy, with lots of blankets over me. The bed felt like the bed at the orphanage, and I still thought I would be sent back. I closed my eyes and knew nothing until I was awoken the following morning.

"After breakfast, Mr Brambles told me to go and have a look at the back garden. I went out the kitchen door, and just stood and looked. To me, it looked huge. There were a couple of small buildings to the side. One was going to be the laundry room, and the other was the coal shed. The garden had a large grass area, trees, plants and shrubs all round, and all this was enclosed by a brown fence. Hanging from one of the trees were two ropes, attached to a piece of wood. I went up to it and pushed it. It moved, and I jumped back. "It's alright Rose, it's called a swing. Here, come and sit on the wood," said Mr Brambles, which I did. "Hold on to the rope, both sides, and lift your feet of the ground. Now I'm going to push you, so don't be frightened." Soon I was swinging backwards and forwards. It felt funny at first, but then I liked it, and for the first time, in a long time, I felt myself smile. Suddenly there was a loud sound, and I was told it was the furniture van. I stayed in the sitting room, watching the men bringing in the furniture, out of the large window. I could see there was a small garden at the front, either side of a wide path, which led down to the main road. At the side of the house was another building, which I was told was a garage, and that's where the car was. After some time, Mrs Brambles came and got me and we went to my bedroom. I had a wardrobe, a dressing table, a bed already made up, some chairs, and lots of shelves. In the corner of the room was what looked like a small house, which had me curious. Large boxes were in the middle of the room. "Rose, these are all your things now, and I hope you like what we have got for you. Over here is what we call a doll's house, and it opens like this." Inside were all small rooms with small bits of furniture and toys. I couldn't believe my eyes. "In these boxes are some clothes, shoes etc, and I thought you might like to put these in your wardrobe, either on the shelves, or on these which are called hangers. The rest of the things in the boxes, you can put them where you want. I will bring you something to eat and drink shortly," and with that she left.

"Slowly I unpacked the clothes and thought how nice they were, until I came across a green dress. I just sat there and looked at it. *So they are sending me back,* I thought. I grabbed teddy and sat in the corner of the room, and that's how Mrs Brambles found me. "I've brought you ... Rose, what's wrong?" I just pointed at the dress and said, "When am I going back?" She put the tray of food and drink down and came to me, and taking my hand helped me up and we sat on the bed. "How stupid of me Rose. I had totally forgotten what clothes I had bought for you. Just because it's green, doesn't mean we are sending you back. We are over four hundred miles away now. You will see lots of girls wearing green dresses, sometimes it's a school uniform. I will take it away, so don't worry. Now eat your sandwiches and drink your tea." She went to take the dress, but I stopped her, and said, "No it will remind me to be good, and ... thank you ... aunt." Her whole face lit up as she smiled at me, and went back to her work. It sounded funny saying "aunt" but I had to start saying it now. I finished putting the clothes and shoes away. Upon opening a small box, again I was stunned. Inside were various toys, including dolls, another bigger teddy, and other soft animals. I placed all these on one of the shelves. "It's alright teddy," I said, picking him up and cuddling him, "You will always be my favourite." In another box there were books on various subjects, which again I put on the shelves. I went to look out the window and saw the furniture van driving out, just as it started raining.

"Rose, can you come down please?" shouted my aunt. Immediately I thought I was in trouble, so walked down the stairs and towards the kitchen gingerly. My aunt took one look at me and said smiling, "I wondered if you might like to know what some of these items are, to help you." I nodded, and so she pointed out the toaster, kettle, fridge/deep freeze, oven, crockery, cutlery, utensils and various other things. She had put a calendar up so I could see the day, date and month. Then we went into the sitting room and again she pointed out the pieces of furniture. "Rose, do you like your bedroom?" asked Mr Brambles. I replied, "Yes thank you ... uncle." He gave me a hug and said, "Welcome to our family Rose." For the first time I believed him. It was another four weeks before my aunt and uncle had the house exactly as they wanted it. My uncle only had two days helping and then had to go to his new job in the town of Fracton, about five miles away. He told me he was the new bank manager, which was a very responsible job. He had twelve staff, and explained what they were and what they did. I didn't understand most of it, and I think he knew. We met the neighbour Stella, and I was introduced as their niece. I sat quietly on one of the large armchairs, and only spoke when I was spoken to. Stella seemed a nice lady, but unfortunately she and her family were moving to somewhere called Australia. Uncle showed me on a map and it was a long, long way away.

"That night after I'd been to the bathroom and toilet, and changed into my nightie, I decided to put the empty boxes into another cupboard in my bedroom. As I opened the cupboard door I saw someone standing there looking at me and screamed. Dropping the boxes I went and hid in the wardrobe. Both my aunt and uncle came rushing in. "Rose where are you?" "In the wardrobe," I said. Uncle opened the door and looking concerned said, "What happened and why did you scream?" Pointing at the cupboard I said, "There's ... there's a ghost in there and it frightened me." My aunt opened the cupboard door slowly and looked in. "There's no ghost here Rose, you must have imagined it. Come and have a look." My uncle just said, "Nancy," and pointed to something. My aunt turned to see where he was pointing and paled. Looking at me she said softly, "Rose have you never seen a mirror before?" I shook my head. "Nancy stand in front of the mirror, so we can show Rose there's nothing to be frightened of." My aunt did as my uncle said, and he took my hand and slowly took me to it. I looked and could now see two of my aunt. My aunt moved her arm and so did the one in the mirror. "What's it for?" I asked. My aunt explained that when people got ready to go out, they would look in the mirror to make sure they were presentable, or their hair was perfect, or to put a hat on properly. "Have a look," she said and moved away. I went and stood in front of it and saw a very sad-looking girl, with brown eyes and black hair just below her ears looking back at me. She was very pale and thin and looked like a ghost. I stared and then tears started to fall down my cheeks. "I look horrible," I said and ran to the bed, got in and covered myself with the blankets. I heard muffled voices and my door being shut. Someone sat on the bed and my aunt said, in a funny voice, "Rose it's teddy. I want to cuddle you, please." I pulled the blanket down slowly and grabbed teddy, but before I could grab the blanket my aunt put her arms round me and said, "Rose you are not horrible. Once we've got you on a good diet, and you start to fill out, you will grow up to be a beautiful woman. It will take time. I don't want to over feed you and make you ill. How about tomorrow we go to a hairdresser and get your hair sorted out. That always makes me feel better." I nodded as I didn't know what a hairdressers was. There was so much I had to learn.

"The following morning my aunt and myself went into Rilford, where we found a hairdressers. The lady looked at my aunt and said, "Good morning, what can I do for you today?" My aunt replied, "It's not for me, it's for my niece. Is there any chance you can tidy her hair up?" The lady ran her fingers through my hair and said, "Well if a hairdresser cut this, she should be bad-mouthed. I'll wash it and then see what we can do." I was given a towel to put in front of my face so the stuff she washed my hair with didn't get in my eyes, as I bent over the basin. Once washed, she rubbed something else on, but it had a nice smell. Then I was sat on a chair and a cape wrapped round me. She pumped the chair up, and to my horror I saw myself in a mirror. She got the scissors and started doing things, and then got a machine that dried my hair. I looked everywhere but in the mirror. When she'd finished my aunt was delighted. "Oh Rose, you look so pretty. Have a look." Slowly I lifted my eyes to look in the mirror to see a different girl looking back at me, and I looked a lot better than before. I sort of smiled and thanked the lady. Afterwards we went shopping in one of the stores and I was bought some more clothes that I liked. We went to a cafe and had a cup of tea and a piece of cake. Afterwards I felt a bit sick, but kept quiet. My aunt held my hand whilst we were walking, but I felt like everyone was looking at me and knew where I had been. Naturally they didn't. When my uncle arrived home, he said what a lovely girl I looked, and I smiled.

CHAPTER 7

"Over the next couple of months I slowly started becoming use to my new way of life, but there was still lots of things I had no knowledge of. It was decided that I should go to school, but first of all a plausible story had to be invented for me being with my aunt and uncle. After several ideas it was decided that my uncle would have a brother called Ernest, who lived in a remote cottage on the Lancashire moors, and they had had a huge falling out, but years later he received a letter saying Ernest was dying and wanted to make amends before he met his maker. He went to see Ernest and found him and myself living is squalor. Ernest's wife had died three years before. They made their peace and my uncle agreed he would take and raise me, as he was my next of kin. Later that day Ernest took his last breath. My uncle took me home and then we all left to move to Rilford. Uncle told aunt and me, if any one questioned us further, just to say it was a private matter. We both agreed. My uncle went to look at a few schools but the standards, for me, were too high. One school said they would take me, but I had to take some test to see where I would be best placed. Due to lots of things my aunt had taught me, I was enrolled to join after the Christmas holidays, which was about two months away.

At home I asked my aunt what Christmas was. She looked at me stunned and said, "Rose, did you not celebrate Easter and Christmas at the orphanage?" I replied, "No aunt, one day followed another and that was all we knew. Every day was the same, and we certainly didn't have days off. None of us knew the day, date, month or year. One girl had a hidden notepad and would mark a day and when she had seven we knew a week had gone by; four weeks a month. We were taught them, but that's all." Aunt made a pot of tea and we went into the sitting room. Aunt was looking through her books and pulled a couple out. "Rose, come sit next to me on the settee, as I have something to show you." She showed me a couple of books that told all about Christmas with pictures. I was amazed. "Will we have that this year aunt?" "I don't see why not Rose, and it will be a lovely Christmas for all of us." Whilst I was waiting to go to school, my uncle decided it wouldn't hurt to have a private tutor, which he arranged. A lady arrived one morning, and was shown into the dining room. My aunt then took me in and introduced me to her. She was called Mrs Higgins. She explained her timetable to my aunt, and then gave me a copy so I would know what to revise for each lesson. Visions of the orphanage crept back into my mind. She came three days a week at 9am. The order of those days were to get up and wash, breakfast, lessons 9am to 11am, then a small break, more lessons from 11.30am to 1.30pm. I then had something called homework to do. At least in the afternoons, I could go and play on the swing, or play upstairs in my bedroom. The two months went quickly, and I felt better now at going to school. Mrs Higgins told my uncle she was impressed with how quickly I had taken all my lessons on board.

"A couple of weeks before Christmas my aunt and I went into Rilford and bought decorations to go on the tree. Uncle was going to pick a small tree up a couple of days before Christmas Eve. We went to the butcher and greengrocer and aunt gave them a list of what she wanted. Again it would all be collected just before Christmas Eve. Then we passed a shop, which had lots of boxes in the window, but there were people in them. I tugged my aunt's hand and whispered, "What are those?" She told me they were called televisions and one was being delivered to the house the following week. I was mesmerised by them and she had to drag me away. Back at the house, in the back room, aunt laid out different coloured papers on the table and gave me a pair of scissors. She showed me how to cut them into long strips. Once that was done I was given a pot of glue. "What you do now Rose, is glue the ends of this one only," which I did. "Now take the next coloured strip and put it through that one, then glue it. Do that until you have use up all the coloured paper. This is what is called a Christmas paper chain." By the time I'd finished the chain was very long. Aunt then put it in a box so the chain wouldn't get damaged. The next couple of days I made four more paper chains.

"Now Rose, whilst I think of it, what would you like for a Christmas present?" I looked at her blank and replied, "Nothing, thank you." She didn't seem upset at my answer, so I thought nothing more of it.

"The following week the television arrived, which apparently was rented, and was set up in a corner of the sitting room. I just glared at it, wondering how people got inside it. Then different things were on it, so I just sat and watched. Uncle tried to explain to me how it worked, but it was confusing. I soon got used to it though. One night my uncle said, "One thing we must know Rose is when is your birthday? I hope we haven't missed it." I replied, "I'm sorry uncle, as I don't know. I know my mam gave me teddy on my birthday." He looked at his wife and said, "Nancy, where's the paperwork we signed. There must be information on it." My aunt got up and went out and then returned with a folder. Looking through the papers she eventually found it. "Oh, your birthday is the 25th December and this year you will be ten years old. Double celebration every year then." That was when I realised I had been at the orphanage over four long, long years. My uncle must have noticed I'd gone quiet and said, "Well, shall we see what's on this box then?" I smiled and then later on we had our meal in the back room. Slowly my aunt was giving me different foods to try so my diet would be more varied, and I would help her. She made things called "toad in the hole" (sausages cooked in a batter which rose up when being cooked); fish pie, corn beef hash, something called a stuffed marrow, with minced up meat in it, and lots of different stews, and some had dumplings. Every Sunday we had a roast dinner. It was either beef or chicken but always with roast potatoes, vegetables and gravy. If it was chicken we'd also have stuffing. My aunt always baked her own cakes and they tasted wonderful. Mine not so good!!

"Christmas Eve arrived and I helped my aunt decorate the tree uncle had brought home the night before. Then we went into Rilford and picked up the meat and vegetables that aunt had ordered. The weather had turned very cold and aunt said it might snow. I remembered we had huge snowdrifts at the orphanage. Everyone was wishing everyone a "Merry Christmas" and soon as I was saying it. Back at home; my uncle had arrived, as he had finished work early. The rest of the day we just relaxed and either played card games or watched the television. When I went to bed I told teddy the following day was my birthday and so it must be his as well. In the morning I hugged and kissed teddy and wished him "Happy Birthday." I went downstairs to the back room, where aunt and uncle were having their breakfast. "Morning Rose, Happy Birthday and Merry Christmas," they said. Aunt had made me my favourite breakfast, toast soldiers and two boiled eggs. Afterwards we went into the sitting room. I had forgotten about the paper chains I'd made, and these now hung round the top of the room. There was a long piece of paper with "Happy Birthday Rose" written on it, and it stretched across the room, and underneath the tree were lots of different sized parcels wrapped in various coloured paper. "After lunch Rose, we will open the presents. Now we thought we'd go for a walk and see what's there is around here," said uncle. We put our coats on and set off.

"We were on the outskirts of the village, and so we turned left out of the driveway. We passed other houses and a little way down we saw a sign that said "Park Entrance." We followed the lane and came to some large open iron gates. We followed the pathway and soon came to a huge playground. I knew what the swings were and uncle told me the others were single slides, a large slide that could seat ten children and swung backwards and forwards, a merry-go-round, which if you spun too quickly you could feel sick, see-saws and saddle mates which were various animals on springs held in the concrete. I tried all of them apart from the large slide. It was fun. We walked further on and found a large open round building, which was called a bandstand. Suddenly it started snowing, and so we turned round and headed back home. I enjoyed walking in the snow, holding one hand of my aunt and the other with my uncle. Aunt went into the kitchen and started cooking the Christmas meal. About an hour later she called to my uncle and me and we went into the back room. The table had dishes of food, and at the side of our knives were long shiny things. There was a large chicken which uncle carved, roast potatoes, stuffing, peas and carrots, and two other vegetables, which were brussel sprouts and roasted parsnips. I didn't like them at all. A large jug of gravy and Yorkshire puddings. "Grab hold of the end of this," said aunt, "and then pull as hard as you can." I did and there was a pop and the shiny thing ripped in two and some things fell out of it. "It's called a Christmas Cracker. Now here's your hat, so put it on. What did you get for a present?" It was a small plastic ring. The meal was lovely, but I ate too much and felt very full afterwards.

"After we had washed up and put everything away, we went to the sitting room to relax. Aunt and uncle passed my presents to me. They had bought me everything I needed for school, which included a pencil case, pencils, rubber, sharpener, small satchel and writing books. "This is your birthday present from us," said aunt. It was a lovely warm coat with a hood. "With winter now here, the coat you've got won't keep you warm, but don't worry, if you don't like it, we can change it." I hugged them both and said it was lovely. I then did something I thought I never would. I took it upstairs to my bedroom, and put it on and then slowly opened the cupboard door and looked at myself in the mirror. I had changed over the months. I was slowly putting weight on and my hair was growing. I actually looked a different girl, and then I realised I was. I went back downstairs to tell them what I'd done, but they were both asleep, so I watched the television and eventually my eyes closed. Later on we had chicken sandwiches and a small piece of Christmas pudding. After a good night's sleep, the following morning I asked if we could go to the park, but overnight the snow had fallen heavily, but we did play in the back garden throwing snowballs at each other. Aunt fried up all the leftovers from the day before and said it was called "bubble and squeak". The rest of the week flew by and then it was New Year's Eve. I heard my aunt telling my uncle this would be the first year they hadn't attended a party with their friends. I felt sad for them. A week later it was time for school.

"The school was a fifteen minute walk from the house, but if it was raining or snowing, Aunt would take me in her car. Just after we arrived in Rilford, uncle said it would be a good idea for aunt to have her own car, and so she got one. The first day I was scared and stayed on my own, but by the end of the week, I had made some friends, boys and girls. I wasn't too bad at the lessons, but loved playtime. We would go out in the yard and play games in small groups. I learnt hopscotch, skipping, and playing marbles. One of the girls showed me how to play cat's cradle, and noughts and crosses. I liked skipping as I could either do it on my own, or two girls would turn the skipping rope, and one by one we would jump in and out saying, "All in for a bottle of gin, All out for a bottle of stout." I watched as the boys played games of conkers, and football. One of the school lessons was called P.E. and we played rounders, or used various objects in the school hall. They were benches we ran along, a hobby horse you had to try and jump over, hula hoops, and we'd end up with a tug of war between the boys and girls. I actually enjoyed being at school. When the nights were lighter, my aunt and uncle let me go to the park and join my friends. The first couple of times they took me, but soon I was going on my own. I also walked to school and back.

"After I'd been there for nearly a year, I found out that the following year I would have to leave to go to a senior school. As I got home one day, I heard my aunt and uncle talking in the sitting room. "Hugh, I want us to have our lives back, to how they were before Rose arrived. I want us to go on holidays again, go out and have fun. I've started my charity work again, but I have to be home at a certain time every day for Rose. You work all day and we hardly see each other. Remember when we use to meet at lunchtimes and go off somewhere." My uncle replied, "So what are you suggesting Nancy? There is no way I'm abandoning Rose." "Good heavens Hugh I would never suggest that. I was thinking about Rose going to a boarding school for young ladies, and we would still see her over the holidays, and …" I didn't listen to anymore. I went to my bedroom and cried. They didn't want me any more. I'd heard of boarding schools, and to me, it was like them sending be back to the orphanage, but at least I'd have the weekends to look forward to.

CHAPTER 8

———————— ∼ ————————

"About a month before I finished school I had to sit my exams. I did well and passed five of the subjects. My aunt and uncle were delighted, and took me out for a celebratory meal. The last day of school, for me, was sad. I'd enjoyed being there, and wanted to stay, but knew I couldn't. A couple of weeks into the holidays, my aunt drove me to Watchford Boarding School, where I sat and did more exams. A couple of weeks later, uncle received a letter saying I'd passed and they wanted to arrange a meeting. When we arrived the headmistress and her deputy met us. We were taken on a tour of the school, and I was told what to expect, and that made me not want to go. I wouldn't be going home at the weekends as I thought. I was only allowed home for Easter, Summer and Christmas holidays. I had to share a dormitory with twenty other girls, so no privacy whatsoever, and it was taken in rotation for baths, hair washing, etc. I felt like I was going straight back to the orphanage, although the building was better. The headmistress told us that the day started at 7am and lights out varied between 8 and 9pm. There would be four lessons in the morning, an hour's lunch break and then three lessons in the afternoon. A bell would sound for us to move to the next classroom. Some of the lessons were Arithmetic, Geography, History, Art, English including Literature, and Religious Education. Running in the corridors was strictly forbidden.

"The dormitories had a colour theme and there was roughly a hundred girls boarding. After school finished, prefects were put in charge to make sure our homework was done. Once finished it was our time to do what we wished. There was a library, playing fields for hockey and rounders, netball and tennis courts. The uniform would consist of blue vest and briefs, white shirts, yellow and purple ties, grey pleated skirts, grey and also white socks (knee and ankle length), purple cardigans and purple blazers with yellow edging, and blue shorts. Like the orphanage everything had to be labelled. My aunt and uncle were told how many items of each clothing were required and where they could be bought in Fracton. I would also need sport shoes. They were also given a list of books that also had to be bought. We were allowed to write home but all letters would be censored. By the time we left I already hated the place. Back home my aunt and uncle worked out roughly how much everything was going to cost and were stunned. It was very expensive, but they went ahead and bought it all. On top of all that they also had to pay for me to stay at Watchford.

"I went off to the park to drown my sorrows. I got on one of the swings and swung high, very high and a couple of my friends were getting concerned and shouted to me to slow down. Eventually I did, and they asked me what was wrong. I just told them I didn't like my new school. "Don't go," said one of them. I smiled and said, "How can I not go?" The answer was, "Run away from home." To me that sounded like a really good idea, but where would I go? and my aunt and uncle didn't deserve that for everything they had done for me. I knew I would just have to put up with it, and that's when I started to misbehave. Through the holidays I would just go off and not tell them where I was going. I got in with a gang and started doing bad things. I argued mainly with my aunt, and then just before I was due to go to Watchford, I snapped and said, "Well at least you're happy I'm going. Yes I overheard your conversation with uncle, so now you will have all the time you want to spend with your friends. I'll be out of your way. Why don't you just send me back to the orphanage." She paled and the next thing I knew I was over her lap getting my backside slapped hard. "You ungrateful wretch. How dare you speak to me like that, and after everything we have done for you? You wait until your uncle hears of this. Now get out of my sight before I say or do something I will regret." I ran to my bedroom, clutched teddy to my chest and sobbed into my pillow.

"After a couple of hours, I had had time to think about what I had been doing and what I had said. I deserved the spanking. All I had to do now was apologise for my behaviour. Quietly I crept down the stairs. The house was empty. I went and sat in the sitting room and felt dreadful. A bit later I heard the key in the door lock. I jumped up and rushed out, but it was my uncle. "Rose, what's wrong?" he asked. I told him everything, and he replied, "I'm disappointed in you Rose, but I can see remorse in your eyes. I expect your aunt has just gone for a drive to cool off." At that moment the kitchen door opened and my aunt walked in and I went to her and put my arms round her waist and said, "Oh aunt, I'm so sorry for what I said. I didn't mean it. I have so much to thank you and uncle for. I behaved like a very ungrateful brat. Please forgive me." My aunt just patted my head and said, "Best we don't talk about it anymore, so will you lay the table for dinner. I didn't feel like cooking, so I went to the chip shop." After that my aunt and I were never the same again.

"I started school and hated it. It brought all my orphanage memories back, not that I had forgotten them. Some of the older girls started picking on me, and would get me into trouble, hence I had the ruler about once a week. Then one day I sat next to someone who saved me, and that was you Ruby."

Ruby and her parents had sat quietly whilst Rose told them her story. Ruby put her arms around Rose and said, "I'm glad I saved you, and we will be friends forever, and that's a promise." Monica and George both hugged and gave Rose a kiss on the cheek.

"Why didn't you tell us last Christmas was your birthday?" asked Monica.

Rose smiled and replied, "There was no need. You made me feel so welcome." George took Rose's hand in his and said, "That's taken a lot of courage for you to tell us your story Rose, and I promise none of us will breathe a word of your past. Tell me how old are your aunt and uncle?" Rose replied, "I'm not sure, maybe early/middle thirties." Monica said, "Well there's one thing, if you're with us or not this year, we will celebrate your twelfth birthday." Rose smiled and then said she was feeling tired. They all decided it had been a long day and so they all retired for the night.

Once back at school, after the summer holidays, Rose and Ruby were inseparable. They were nicknamed "The Two RR's." They helped each other with their homework, spent a lot of time in the library studying, and it didn't go unnoticed by the teachers, who didn't like the close bond that had been formed. Along with the agreement of the headmistress, it was agreed that they were not to sit next to each other in class, at P.E. one would do netball, whilst the other one played tennis. They would sit at different tables for their meals, and one would be moved to another dormitory. It was Rose that was moved. The prefects were told that under no circumstances were the two girls ever to be together. Rose wasn't stupid and knew exactly what was happening. She decided she would have a good look around the school on her own. A couple of days later, she passed a note to Ruby which said, "After lunch meet me at the changing room, but make sure you're not followed." As Ruby walked towards the changing rooms, she saw two girls behind her. Quickly she nipped into the toilets. The two girls waited and waited, but Ruby didn't come out. They went in and the toilets were empty.

"Psstt," said Rose quietly to Ruby. "Follow me." They went out into the grounds, making sure no one was around, and went down a path that led to a shed. "When we can, we can meet here and hopefully we won't be missed. How did you get here?" asked Rose.

Ruby replied, "I saw two girls and went into the toilets. The cubicle at the end has a larger window than the rest, and once I stood on the toilet and then the ledge, I climbed out." Both of them laughed.

Rose said, "They think they can split us up, not a chance." Ruby agreed.

One weekend, Rose was sitting in the library when Ruby walked in, and straight away she noticed she was limping. Quickly she wrote a note, and then beckoned to the prefect watching guard.

"I need a book from one of the shelves over there, can you get it for me … please."

The prefect replied, "Get it yourself, I'm not your slave." Rose smiled to herself and went to get it. As she passed Ruby she dropped the note discreetly. Ruby waited until Rose had sat back down and read it. It just said 4pm. In the shed Rose asked Ruby what had happened. Ruby told her, when she was playing netball, another girl had a fall. The teacher was treating her, when a girl pushed her to the ground and kicked her in the leg, and said, "A message from Janet." Janet Swithers was one of the prefects. Rose felt her temper rising. Janet was the biggest bully in the school, and had got her into trouble on more than one occasion.

"Are you sure you're alright Ruby?" she asked. Ruby said she was fine and had gone to the nurse to check it out. "Ok, we'd better go," said Rose and they hugged each other, and left separately.

One morning Rose woke up with dreadful cramps in her stomach. When she went to the toilet she saw she had a little bit of blood in her briefs, and it worried her greatly. She went to class, but the teacher could see she was in pain and sent her to the nurse.

"Well Rose," said the nurse, "This is what is called "your periods." This will happen every month for many, many years." She went to a locker and came back and put the items on the desk. "This is a sanitary belt and a sanitary towel. The belt obviously goes round your waist and you attach the sanitary towel to the clips. Then you cover it with your briefs. You will need to change at least three times a day and the period will last five to seven days. Here are two belts and two packets of towels and some brown bags, which you put the soiled towel in, and place it in the bins provided in the toilets. Make a note of today's date and then next month you will know what it is. You can come to me for more towels and I will inform the headmistress, who will ask for payment from your uncle." Rose felt embarrassed about that! "As to the tummy pain, take these tablets and have two each morning and that should help. Anything else come and see me. I will inform your P.E. teacher, so you will be relieved of games." Rose now understood why some girls sat and watched. She went to the toilet and put the items on, which felt most peculiar. As she walked she felt like she had a huge wedge between her legs and it was uncomfortable. The next five days, to Rose, were disgusting. She hated this thing her body was doing. It soon passed and she was back to her normal self. Ruby had been concerned, but Rose managed to pass a note explaining.

Before winter set in properly, the headmistress told them at assembly that competitions were going to be held. The school would be split up into groups and then tennis, netball, hockey and rounders would be played to see who came out on top. Rose hoped she would be in the same group as Ruby, but she wasn't. Her group actually had nice girls and she got on well with them. As she watched Ruby playing hockey, she saw Janet tackle her hard and Ruby went down in agony. Rose went to go to her, but a prefect stopped her and told her if she didn't want a punishment to sit down. She sat down. Ruby was carried off on a stretcher. Rose was fuming. Her group didn't win any of the competitions, but when they played tennis, Rose ended up playing against Janet in the final. Rose was determined to beat her. The match was close and it came down to the last serve. Rose aimed for Janet's face, but lobbed it too high and lost the game.

Janet laughed and when they went to shake hands over the netting, Janet grabbed Rose's hand hard and said, "You seriously think you can beat me, you pathetic excuse for a human being? Well I'm on your case Brambles, so look out." How Rose didn't swing her tennis racket at Janet's head she'll never know, but she was determined on revenge for Ruby. The nurse told Ruby she was lucky her leg hadn't been broken.

Rose started watching Janet and made notes of her movements. One day she watched as Janet disappeared behind the school garages. Rose waited a couple of minutes and went and peered round the corner. What she saw had her smiling. There was Janet, back up against the wall, cigarette in hand, kissing one of the builders, who had been brought in to build new classrooms. Rose could see his hand was up Janet's skirt. She now had her ammunition, but would use it wisely. She noticed Janet would meet him on Tuesdays and Thursdays. Rose wasn't really into gym work, but now she was and started strengthening her arms.

After a couple of weeks, she waited until she saw the man leave Janet and walked round the corner and said, "Well, well, look what "Miss Goody two shoes" has been up to. Wonder what the headmistress would say?"

Janet hastily pulled her briefs up and replied, "You breathe a word Brambles and I'll throttle you." Before Janet could say anything else, Rose had her left hand round her throat and lifted her slightly off the ground.

"Really?" said Rose. "Strange it's ME who's got her hand round YOUR throat." Janet was struggling and gasping for air. "Now you bully, you leave Ruby and me alone. You will stop your "guard dogs" following us, and you will tell the headmistress you think her plan has worked. DO I MAKE MYSELF CLEAR, YOU NASTY BITCH?"

Janet who was slowly going blue nodded her head and Rose removed her hand. Janet fell to the ground trying to catch her breath. Rose looked at her in disgust and then walked off smiling to herself, but boy did her left arm ache, but it had been worth it.

CHAPTER 9

Janet and her friends never bothered Rose and Ruby again. For a couple of weeks afterwards, Janet wore a scarf around her neck, saying she had had an accident. Rose just smiled. She told Ruby the whole story and they laughed so much, especially as Rose was mimicking Janet's actions. They played the headmistress's "game" and stayed apart during school time, but afterwards they would meet up and talk about their day. Soon winter set in, but this year Rose was going home for the Christmas holidays, and not to Ruby's. A taxi was sent for her, as her aunt and uncle were busy. When she arrived home the house was locked, so Rose sat on the swing until one of them arrived. Darkness was falling and Rose was freezing.

Eventually her aunt arrived and looking at Rose said emotionless, "Oh, was it today you were coming home? I thought it was tomorrow. I suppose you'd better come in then." Rose sighed and wished she was at Ruby's.

Her uncle greeted Rose more cordially. "Rose, lovely to see you. I hope school is going well?" Rose replied it was and told him what lessons she was having, and what she had learnt. Her aunt called them for their meals, which were fish and chips with mushy peas. Rose asked them politely if they were both well and had they been anywhere interesting.

Her aunt replied, "We are both well and where we go is of no concern of yours." Rose was taken aback and lowered her eyes. "As to the arrangements for Christmas, your uncle and I have been invited over to the Brown's residence for Christmas Day. They are very influential people, with friends of the same calibre, and we are honoured to have been accepted as friends of theirs now. We will spend some time with you over the week, but New Year's Eve, we will be entertaining here, and I would prefer it if you stayed in your room."

Rose said very politely, "Aunt would you prefer it, and I mean no rudeness, if I went either to my friend Ruby's or back to school so I won't be of any trouble to you? I certainly don't want to spoil your lovely plans in any way at all."

Her aunt glowered at her and replied, "No you will NOT embarrass us by doing either of those. You will stay in your room."

Rose replied, "Of course aunt. May I please be excused and retire for the night?" Rose was dismissed by a flick of her aunt's hand. She looked at her uncle, who had his head down looking at the table. Up in her bedroom she unpacked her case, and wondered how far it was to walk to Ruby's. She had no way of getting in touch with Ruby as her aunt would not have a telephone in the house, and as far as she could remember, there wasn't a telephone box anywhere near. She saw teddy and cuddled him. At least he was always there to welcome her.

In the morning, after washing and dressing, Rose went down to the back room to find her uncle on his own.

"Good morning uncle," she said.

"Morning Rose," he replied. "Your aunt has gone out and won't be back until later. I have to go to work this morning, but should be back mid afternoon, unless any problems arise. What would you like for breakfast?"

Rose replied, "It's alright uncle, as I can make myself something." Rose just made herself some toast, which she had with butter and marmalade.

"What are you going to do today Rose?"

Rose replied, "I will maybe go for a walk round the park, weather permitting. I would also like to buy you and aunt something. Are there any jobs I can do for you to earn some pocket money? (Ruby had explained to Rose about pocket money.)

Her uncle raised his eyebrow and said, "Rose I never gave pocket money a thought. How remiss of me. Here take this and spend it wisely. Your aunt and I need nothing," and with that gave her a ten shilling note.

"Oh uncle, that is a lot of money. I can't take that. I thought maybe a shilling or a florin."

"Nonsense, it's yours. Now I am leaving in about ten minutes if you want a lift into Fracton." Rose, as a thank you, gave him a small kiss on his cheek, and went to get her coat and bag.

As they were just about to leave Rose said, "Uncle how will I get back in?" He went to the kitchen drawer and gave her the spare key to the kitchen door. Whilst they drove to Fracton her uncle told her how her aunt had now taken up embroidery, and was doing a peacock, which gave Rose an idea.

"You will have to catch the bus back Rose. There is the bus station," he said pointing it out to her, "Just ask for the bus to Rilford." He pulled up outside the bank. This was the first time Rose had seen it and was surprised how big it was. They said their goodbyes and her uncle said if she had any problems to go to the bank and ask for him.

Rose walked round the town, looking in most of the shops, enjoying herself. She noticed the sky was getting dark and wondered if it was going to rain or snow. It rained heavily. Rose dodged from shop to shop and found what she wanted to buy. Back at the bus station, for the first time, she got on the bus. She just hoped she knew where the stop was! The journey was long, but at least she was in the dry. Some time later she recognised her road, and saw somebody had already gone to the front to get off, so she decided to do the same. Alas, she had a ten minute walk in the rain until she got home, absolutely soaked. She unlocked the kitchen door, but didn't go in. She went to the laundry room where she took off and hung up her coat, skirt and socks to dry. Back in the kitchen she saw some newspapers by the bin, and put three sheets on the floor and put her shoes on them, with a couple of pieces crumpled up inside her shoes. Her uncle had taught her that. She had left her slippers by the kitchen door, which she now put on. In the bathroom she wrapped a towel round her head to dry her hair, and then put it on the back of her chair, in her bedroom, to dry. She put her purchases away, smiling as she did. She would wrap them later. Back downstairs she made herself a hot drink and a sandwich, and took it into the sitting room. She put the radio on, but not too loud. She saw what looked like an easel in the corner and went to look. It was her aunt's embroidery and it looked wonderful. It was then she realised there wasn't much in the way of Christmas decorations. The mantelpiece over the fireplace had Christmas cards on it, and by the television, on a low table, was a small silver tree with red baubles on it. Rose thought back to her first Christmas with them and thought in the morning it would all look different. She had eaten her sandwich and drunk her drink and went back to the kitchen to wash, wipe, and put the plate and mug back where they belonged. She didn't want to upset her aunt in any way.

Later on her uncle arrived back, and minutes later her aunt. As they sat eating their dinner her uncle said, "Did you get drenched Rose?" Her aunt looked back and forth at both of them.

"I did uncle, but I have put my coat, skirt and socks in the laundry room to dry, and my shoes on the newspaper as you showed me."

Her aunt said annoyed, "Who told you, you could go out?"

"I did," replied her uncle. Her aunt stood up and looking at her husband said, "I will speak to you later Hugh ... in private. Rose you can wash, dry and put the dishes away, and don't break any of them." With that her aunt walked out of the back room and went upstairs.

"I'm sorry uncle. I didn't mean to cause trouble." Her uncle took her hand and replied, "You haven't and leave your aunt to me."

The evening went by silently with only the sounds of the television. Rose decided to go to bed and said her goodnights. A couple of minutes later, as she went to go to the bathroom she heard raised voices, and crept down the stairs.

"... care Hugh. Whilst she is under this roof she will do as she is told. She will only go out when I say so."

"Nancy please, surely after all this time you can forgive Rose for her one and only outburst. She was immediately sorry. Look how well she's doing at school. Her results are beyond expectations, and she's polite and keeps herself well groomed. Can't you cut her some slack?"

Her aunt replied, "There you go, sticking up for her all the time. You need to remember where she came from, and I don't trust her."

"For god's sake Nancy, that wasn't her fault. You're treating her like some criminal, not a niece. I'm not arguing any more, but I will ask one thing. Please try and be cordial towards her, as she's only here for another ten days, and then she goes back to school." Rose tiptoed back up the stairs and quietly closed her door. She wrapped the two presents up she had bought and more than anything hoped her aunt would like her present.

When Rose woke in the morning, the clock was showing 8.30am. Her aunt would be annoyed as they had breakfast at 8am. Very quickly she washed and dressed, grabbed the presents and rushed downstairs and into the back room.

"Merry Chri … The room was empty as was the house. In the kitchen was a note saying they had left and might be back later, unless they were asked to stay the night. Rose was so disappointed. She looked at the two presents in her hand. She had bought her uncle his favourite tobacco, as he smoked a pipe. For her aunt she had bought, at great expense, four different coloured threads for her embroidery. She went into the sitting room. Nothing had changed. There was no Christmas or birthday presents for her. Rose sat down and sobbed until she ached. Once she calmed herself, she had some breakfast of toast and boiled eggs. She decided she would go for a walk round the park as the sky looked favourable. After washing her dishes, she went upstairs and changed. She put her shoes on, which were still in the kitchen, and had dried out. Now she needed her coat from the laundry room. She went to the kitchen door but found it locked. She had given the spare key back to her uncle and saw him put it back in the drawer. She opened the drawer - no key. She went and tried the front door - locked. Rose then realised her aunt had locked her in, and she was furious. She felt like going into the kitchen and smashing up every piece of crockery, slashing her aunt's embroidery, but knew that would only lead to more trouble. Instead she decided she would have a nice long bath, and put the immersion on.

About an hour later Rose was lying in the bath with bubbles up to her neck. She had found something called "Bath Foam" in the cabinet and squirted some into the flowing tap water. A mass of white foam started to appear. The more she squirted the more foam she got. When she noticed how much she used, she knew her aunt would notice, so she took the top off and added cold water and then carefully tipped it up and down. Now it looked the same as before. She opened the two small windows to let the steam and smell out.

Never in her life had she stayed so long in a bath. She ducked her head under the water and washed her hair at the same time. She was very careful though to make sure none of the water went over the top of the bath. After she had wrapped a large towel round herself and one round her head, she let the water out and then cleaned the bath thoroughly. In her bedroom she rubbed her hair until it was drier. She went to the cupboard and opened the door and looked in the mirror. She dropped her towel and looked at her naked body. She twisted and turned looking at it from every angle. Luckily she had filled out in the right places. She had a small waist and hips. Her legs were long and looked athletic. Her stomach was flat and not sunk in as it was before. She put her hands on her breasts, which were also now developing, and soon she would need what was called a brassiere. Her bottom was rounded, but again small, and her hair now was well below her shoulders, and was black. She decided her face was pretty. All in all she felt she looked good, and today she was twelve years old.

Afterwards she dressed and went to make herself something to eat. She ended up with cheese sandwiches, two of them!! She watched television for a bit, but found it boring, so she decided to have good look around the house. She did the downstairs, but found nothing of interest. The only room upstairs she had never been in was her aunt and uncle's bedroom. She opened the door and peered in. She was surprised to see two single beds and not a double. Like her room there was wardrobes, a dressing table, etc. She opened one of the wardrobes and saw all her uncle's suits hung up, along with various coloured shirts. On the shelves were socks, underwear, ties, handkerchiefs and other items. The other wardrobe had all her aunt's clothes in. Some of them were very posh. Rose never knew her aunt wore such clothes. She took some of them out and held them up to her, looking in the big mirror on the wall. She started pretending she was a glamorous film star, and twirled round watching as the dresses flowed out. Then she tried on her aunt's hats, laughing as she put them on her head one way and then another. Making sure she put everything back in the right place, she closed the wardrobe door. Next she looked at the dressing table. There were various small bottles of perfumes, which Rose smelled. Some were awful, others lovely. There were a variety of trinket boxes and lots of makeup. Rose was tempted to try the lipsticks and eye shadows, but thought the better of it. As she looked round the room she noticed a large piece of furniture, with a rolled top that came halfway down. Rose tried to push it up but it was locked. Curiosity got the better of her. She looked in the trinket boxes and found some small keys. Taking one by one so she didn't put them back wrong, she tried them in the lock. The last one fitted and the lock clicked open. Rose slowly pushed up the rolled part and it revealed it was a desk.

CHAPTER 10

The desk had lots of papers and letters strewn over it. In the middle at the back were two long oblong drawers, and down each side were smaller drawers. Rose looked in the small drawers but found nothing but bits of jewellery, some old postcards, and more letters. In the two oblong drawers were official looking letters. Rose chewed her lip, knowing it was wrong to look, but she couldn't resist. She pulled one out and carefully scooped up the letters and laid them downwards. As she looked quickly at each one, so she laid them back in the drawer face upwards. There were letters about her uncle's promotion, a marriage licence, a small birthday book, and a small bible. In the second drawer however, Rose saw an envelope with "Blackthorn Orphanage" in big bold letters. How long she stood and looked at it she had no idea, but slowly she was transported back there. She was like a ghost wandering through the building. A loud bang outside brought her back to the present. She rushed to the window to see a car driving out of the driveway. *Must have come to the wrong house,* she thought. She went back to the desk and looked at the rest of the contents. There were three bank books. One in the name of her uncle, her aunt and her. Rose was astounded at the amount in each of them. There was only one entry in hers, but it was for a hundred pounds, but it was in the name of Rose Clark!! Suddenly Rose didn't want to look anymore. She put everything back in, until she came to the orphanage envelope. She decided to look. Everything on the sheets was about her life there. One sentenced at the end stood out. She was to be taken on as a "charity case". There was nothing in writing about her being called Rose Brambles. She was still Rose Clark.

Rose made sure it looked like nothing had been moved, pulled the roll top down and relocked it, and then put the key back where she found it. Questions were going through her head. Why did the governess tell her she had a new surname when she didn't? Why did the Brambles confirm that was her new surname? Why was the bank book in her old name? So many questions that she would never have an answer to. The evening was now drawing in and so Rose closed her bedroom curtains. When she got to the bottom of the stairs she saw a white envelope on the floor. She picked it up and went to put it on the hall table, when she saw it was addressed to her. She opened it and saw it was a birthday/Christmas card from Ruby and her parents. She let out a small scream and said to herself, "No, no. I missed them because I was being so nosy. They could have got me out of here."

Rose went and sat in the sitting room deflated. A bit later she sighed, got up, drew the curtains and put the lights on. She did the same in the back room and drew the kitchen blinds. She looked in the fridge, but apart from eggs, cheese and butter there was nothing else. She looked in the cupboard and found a tin of spam. She had watched her aunt slice it and fry it, so it was time for her to try it. She found the oil and pan, and a little bit later on she had a fried spam sandwich. She made a pot of tea and drank two mugs. When she washed everything up, she remembered to wipe the top of the oven down to clean up any splashes she'd made. Turned out she'd made quite a few. She looked around the kitchen and made sure it was clean and tidy. Satisfied she went and watched the television until 10pm, then went to bed.

The following day her aunt and uncle returned about 11am. For something to do Rose had dusted, polished and vacuumed the house. She hoped that would please her aunt. It did, a little bit, until she heard her aunt saying she'd only done it because she'd made a mess. Rose resigned herself to the fact, that whatever she did, she would never please her aunt.

"Please would it be alright if I go to the park for a couple of hours. It would be nice to get some fresh air in my lungs."

Her uncle replied, "Did you go to see if any of your old friends were around yesterday?" Rose was about to explain when she saw her aunt glower at her.

"No uncle. I decided to stay in and read some of my books for when I go back to school."

"Off you go then, and be careful," said her uncle. She went and changed, got her coat from the laundry room, and walked briskly out of the drive. There was a cold wind blowing but Rose didn't care. She virtually skipped to the park. There were lots of people around, but she didn't see any one she knew. She sat on the swing and swung, not too high, but could feel her hair flowing out behind her. She pushed herself round on the merry-go-round, as fast as she could and then stood and watched the park whirling round and round. Afterwards she heard music, and headed towards the bandstand. Lots of people were there, either listening or dancing to the band. Standing there she started to feel cold, and decided to go back home.

When she got back, her aunt was cooking. "Do you need any help aunt? I could maybe wash up as you go?"

Her aunt replied, "No. Your uncle wants to see you in the sitting room." Rose felt the colour drain from her face. They must have found out what she had done.

"Aunt said you wanted to see me uncle?"

He was reading the newspaper, and peering over his glasses replied, "Yes Rose I do. Sit down."

Rose did as she was told, and held her breath. "Rose, first of all where did those two presents come from?"

Rose replied, "They're from me uncle to you and aunt."

"Oh, your aunt thought somebody had come round yesterday. Well thank you, can I open mine now?"

"Yes uncle," and so Rose got up and took his present to him. He was pleased. "May I ask what you got for your aunt?" Rose told him, and he smiled. "Secondly, I have received a letter from your school. After the Easter holidays, which I'm sorry to say we will be away, you will be allowed to go on various trips. Now one thing I know you don't have is funds. I decided that a savings account be opened for you. Here is your savings book and I have made an entry in there of five pounds. This five pounds I have sent to the headmistress, so when you need funds to pay for the trips, she will deduct it from the total. That way you will know what you have left. The last thing is the new classrooms at your school are soon to be finished. One is to be domestic science, where you can learn to cook properly. Another one will be a language classroom, and you will be taught French. The last one will be for Drama. I need to know if you want to attend these, as naturally I have to pay for them." Rose thanked her uncle for her savings account, and said she would like to take the three classes but was concerned about the expense. Her uncle told her education was the most important thing to learn and not to worry.

The rest of the week went by quickly. Her uncle was back at work, and her aunt back to her charity work. Rose was given the spare kitchen door key so she could come and go as she wanted to. Next it was New Years Eve, and her aunt reminded her what to do in the evening. Rose offered to help but was told to go away. About 6pm her aunt gave her a plate of various sandwiches and a mug of tea, and told her to go to her bedroom. Later on Rose could hear people arriving, and wanted to see the ladies in their dresses, and so she decided to go and peer over the bannister. Some of the dresses were so elegant. She heard her aunt speaking differently. More la de da.

"Of course one does what one can do for these poor unfortunate orphans. Alas Hugh and I are far too busy to entertain one of them in our home. Oh darling do you have a moment? May I introduce my husband Hugh. He has the influential position of being the bank manager at Stocks Bank in Fracton." Rose went back to her bedroom. So that's why her aunt didn't want her to be seen - heaven forbid they had a "charity case" in their house. The downstairs party went on until the early hours of the morning. On the stroke of midnight, Rose wished teddy a Happy New Year.

Three days later, it was time to go back to school. Rose had her breakfast and then changed into her uniform. She brushed her long hair back and then plaited it into a pigtail. She packed her suitcase, but this time she decided to take teddy. Her satchel had the books in she'd brought home for revision.

"Rose, I'm going so if you don't hurry up you can either walk or catch the bus," shouted her aunt.

"I'm ready aunt." Rose took a last look round her bedroom to make sure she hadn't forgotten anything, and went downstairs, feeling relieved she was going. She couldn't wait to see Ruby. Her uncle gave her a hug and a kiss on the cheek, much to his wife's disgust. The ride to school was in silence. Once there, Rose thanked her for the lift, but before she could say anything else her aunt drove off.

"Rose, Rose," shouted a voice she knew well. She turned and saw Ruby running towards her. They hugged each other tightly. "Come on Rose, Mum and Dad want to see you." Both girls walked over to Monica and George, who gave Rose a hug. "Rose, it's lovely to see you. Did you have a lovely time at home?"

Rose replied, "Not really. Thank you all for your lovely card, and I'm sorry I didn't open the door, but I couldn't - it was locked."

Ruby looked at Rose and said stunned, "You were locked in, but why?"

"My aunt didn't want me going out. I'm so pleased to see you Ruby. I have missed you so much." Monica noticed Rose had tears in her eyes and went to her.

"Easter holidays Rose, and I don't care what your aunt and uncle say, you're coming to stay with us for the week, and that's a promise."

Rose replied with a smile, "I was going to ask you, as my uncle has already told me they will be away."

"We'd love to have you Rose," said George. "Now you two had better go in or you'll be late. Hope you both have a good term, and Monica and I will see you both at Easter." Hugs and kisses were given all round.

As they headed towards their separate dormitories, one of the teachers stopped Rose and told her she was back in the same dormitory as Ruby. Both girls were elated. The rest of the girls had left the two beds at the bottom empty, so Ruby and Rose would be side by side. There was lots of talking until a voice shouted,

"Assembly Hall NOW." Quietly and quickly they all made their way to the hall, where everyone else was assembled. Shortly afterwards, the headmistress walked in with the teachers. Rose noticed there were some new ones.

"Good morning girls," said the headmistress.

The girls all replied back, "Good morning headmistress."

The headmistress continued. "I am delighted to tell you all that five new classrooms have been completed. One is for domestic science, one for languages, and one for drama. The other two classrooms will now accommodate all the girls who want to stay and go on to higher education, which means this will be for girls aged fifteen upwards. This will depend solely on your parents, and these classes will start after the summer holidays, when the new term starts. To that end, you will see we have three new teachers who have joined us, and I would like you to show your appreciation." The whole assembly clapped. "We have also changed your curriculum, for Class 3 and upward," said the headmistress. "The board has decided it would be to your advantage to visit memorable places, for example, museums. I have a list from your parents who have already agreed to these trips. You will behave as young ladies at all times. Anyone, who decides to disobey, will be severely reprimanded, so you have been warned. These trips will start after Easter. Now, I believe the dining room is ready for you. As I always say, anyone who decides it's a good idea to be disobedient, think about the repercussions, not just for yourself, but the whole school. Thank you girls," and with that the headmistress and teachers left.

After the meal, Rose and Ruby went to the dormitory to finish unpacking. Rose then told Ruby everything that had happened, including looking in her aunt's desk. Ruby was confused.

"I don't understand Rose. Why would they tell you that and it not be true?" Rose replied she had no idea. As she started to unpack her satchel a small parcel fell onto the floor. Rose picked it up. "What is it Rose?" asked Ruby. Rose untied, and unwrapped it. Inside was a box, which held a delicate necklace with "Rose" in the middle. "Oh Rose it's beautiful. Is it from your aunt and uncle?" Rose saw a small piece of paper tucked in the lid of the box. It was from her uncle, and along with a pound note, said,

Rose, I hope you like it. It's your birthday present, but just from me. I'm sorry about your aunt. Write to me, but to the bank address above, not home. If you need anything, you only have to ask. Thought the funds might come in handy. Love, your uncle xx

Rose was stunned, but delighted. Her aunt might not want her anymore, but her uncle did. Tears sprang to her eyes, and she wiped them away.

"Oh isn't he cute," said Ruby. Rose looked at her and saw she had teddy in her hands. "I felt like I didn't want to leave him at home, so I brought him. It was the last thing me mam gave me." Ruby hugged

Rose and told her to remember to lock the drawer in her locker, so teddy or the necklace didn't go missing. They spent the rest of the day, chatting to the other girls, going for a walk in the grounds, had their supper and then bed. School started properly the following morning. Now Rose sort of enjoyed school, the following three months flew by, and soon it was Easter. As promised she went to Ruby's and had a great time. This time however, when they went to the shops, Rose had her own money. Rose had also packed some of her normal clothes, so as not to go in her school uniform. Ruby's parents had bought Ruby a record player and a radio, so both of them spent a lot of time dancing round Ruby's bedroom to the various pop tunes. They used hairbrushes as microphones, and sang badly. Both of them couldn't sing at all, but it made them laugh so much. Rose also found out that Ruby's parents were a doctor and nurse. Rose wrote to her uncle about once a month, just to update him on what she was learning. Once every month she had to put up with the dreaded stomach cramps, and Ruby had now also started having her periods. As the biology teacher said, "It's all part of growing up."

CHAPTER 11

As promised after the Easter break, Rose's class were told they were going to go to London, to visit historical sights, and they would be gone for two nights. Accommodation in a hostel had been arranged to save money. Rose had written to her uncle asking if it would be possible to have some pocket money. He sent her five one pound notes. Petrified in case she lost any of it, she asked the teacher going with them, if she would look after it for her. The teacher took out a notebook and wrote Rose's name in it, along with the other girls who had done the same thing, including Ruby. The day arrived and the twenty girls were loaded onto a small coach, just after breakfast, and settled down for the journey. Rose knew all of them had to behave, because if they didn't, all future trips would be cancelled. The trip to London took about three hours, with a couple of stops for toilets etc. As they were driving round, the teacher pointed out buildings and bridges of interest. The driver pulled up outside Buckingham Palace, but only for a minute. Soon they arrived at the hostel, which was clean, and were shown to their rooms. Each room had ten beds, but nothing else. However the doors could be locked. The bathroom and toilet were down at the end of the corridor. The manager of the hostel assured them nobody else would be using them. After a quick turn around, they were back on the coach. After only a few moments the coach pulled up outside the museum.

"Now girls," said the teacher, "if any of you should get lost, and I hope you won't, this is where the coach will be, but not until 5pm. Those of you who have watches it's now 1.30pm." The teacher did a head count, and then said all excited, "Right let's go on our adventure." Rose and Ruby looked at each other and giggled.

Once inside the museum, they had a tour guide, but his voice was soooo boring. After an hour, the guide left them and the teacher told them to look around on their own, but to behave at all times, and to be back at the entrance by 4pm. Ruby and Rose walked round, but Rose found it all a bit boring. There were rooms filled with old antiques, medals, coins, and things from archaeological digs. She did however like looking at all the different coloured stones, in particular the blue ones, and decided that was going to be her favourite colour and told Ruby. Ruby loved all the red stones. Rose also liked looking at the masses of books, all in glass cases. As agreed, all the girls met at the entrance ahead of time. The teacher understood why, but she was not going to tell them what she had planned for the following day. As it was still light, the teacher walked the girls down to the Thames, and again, pointed out various famous buildings. Soon they were in the coach and back at the hostel. A large room had been set aside for them. Once they had assembled the tables and chairs, they were served with a hot meal of shepherd's pie and vegetables, followed by jam roly-poly and custard. Back in their rooms, the girls chatted about the day and the general consensus was - boring. They dreaded where they might be going the following day.

Breakfast was served in the large room again, and soon they were stood outside the next museum. However, once they walked inside, they couldn't believe their eyes.

"What is that?" exclaimed one of the girls. The tour guide told them it was called a Diplodocus. It was one of the biggest dinosaurs, along with the Brontosaurus. It would swallow leaves whole along with stones called gastroliths. These stones stayed in their stomachs and helped with digestion.

Rose turned to Ruby and said, "I like this museum. Wonder what else there is?" Once they had all eventually left the dinosaur, they went into another room where there were large models of Pterodactyl's, and the great Palaeotherium. The guide told them the Pterodactyl was a prehistoric flying mammal, which had a wingspan of three feet, a long beak and roughly ninety teeth. It had good eyesight, and ate mainly insects and fish. Sometimes they would be seen eating dead dinosaurs. Pointing at the Palaeotherium, they learnt it was a mammal that ate vegetation either from the ground or leaves off the trees up to four foot high. It use to like forests, but once the forests started turning to grassy plains, slowly they became extinct. In other rooms there were made up displays of oceans, forests, grassy plains, with exotic animals and plants in them. This time the girls were reluctant to leave. Back they went to the hostel to have a meal and a rest. The teacher told them to be downstairs for 2pm, as she had a surprise for them. The girls met as arranged and were curious as to where they were going next. The teacher arrived and was pleased the girls were prompt, and were behaving extremely well.

"We are going on a small walk to our next venue," she said, "so pair up into twos and follow me. Please be courteous to other people walking." After a five minute walk they stopped outside a large building which had a sign saying "Madame Tussauds".

Most of the girls had never heard of Madame Tussaud. Another girl told them it was statues of people, dead or alive, made from wax. This had Rose curious and she couldn't wait to get inside. As they went through the door a guide stood either side. Neither of them moved. The teacher went up to the booth and got the tickets.

"Bit rude of them not to come to us, isn't it?" said Rose.

Ruby looked at them more closely and said, "That's because they're statues." Rose was amazed, as they looked so lifelike. The teacher called them to one side.

"Now girls, as you can see, this place is very busy. We have to wait a couple of minutes for this school in front of us to clear the first two rooms, and then we can go. Do not touch any of the statues. Here are pamphlets telling you about Madame Tussaud, and a map of each of the exhibits. Now I have a word of warning. In the basement is the Chambers of Horrors. This exhibit is quite gruesome, so if any of you do not want to visit, may I suggest you have a look around the gift shop."

Rose looked at Ruby and said, "We going?" Ruby just nodded. Soon they entered the various rooms. There were two rooms, which had royalty. The present Queen and family; Queen Victoria and her family; Queen Mary and family; Henry VIII and his wives; Charles de Gaulle; JF Kennedy and his wife Jacqueline and Abraham Lincoln. All had plaques saying who they were. Another room had all the Cabinet Ministers along with Prime Ministers. Other rooms had models of which some were, Shakespeare, Gandhi, Florence

Nightingale, Kenneth Moore, Stirling Moss, David Bailey and Christie Shrimpton, Admiral Nelson and Elizabeth Taylor. In a corner of one of the rooms was a lady laying on a chaise longue.

"Look, she's breathing," exclaimed one of the girls. True enough her chest was rising and falling slowly. It was a waxwork called "The Sleeping Beauty." The last room the girls found the best. It had Tommy Steele, who was the first popular singer to be done as a waxwork, and The Beatles, with a separate Paul McCartney. Most of the girls had eyes wide looking at their singing heroes.

Only half of them went down to the Chamber of Horrors. As soon as they walked in the lights were dimmed slightly to give it an eerie feeling. THUD. THUD. They all looked towards the sound to see a guillotine being drawn up and then crashing down. Every now and then a bloodied head would roll past the guillotine. One side of the wall in a glass case was a large guillotine, with a plaque that read that the guillotine was from the French Revolution and was used to behead Marie Antoinette. On the other side, on spikes were some of the bloodied heads of those who had been beheaded. Next there was scenes of murderers and criminals and their victims, some chopped up in bits, other with horrendous wounds and covered in blood. For extra effects blood curdling screams were echoing round the room. As they passed a cell, a hand shot out and touched one of the girls, who screamed. The teacher noticed the girls were all staying close together, some were even holding hands. Lastly there were wax heads made from the death masks that Madame Tussaud had been instructed to make. Once they had been beheaded they were given to her, with the blood still dripping from their necks. Rose asked Ruby if she was alright. Ruby replied she was glad they were going back upstairs. Up in the light, Rose noticed some of the girls were very pale!! Once they met the rest of the girls though, it was all talk about the gruesome scenes. The teacher pointed out another couple of glass cases that had old catalogues that Madame Tussaud had printed as she toured the UK. There were also books opened showing a list of expenses. The teacher did a head count and led them outside, after they passed a waxwork of Madame Tussaud.

"I hope you all enjoyed Madame Tussauds?" she asked. The girls replied they had thoroughly enjoyed it. To finish the day off, they were taken to a shopping centre.

"Girls it's now 4.30pm and you have until 6pm. This is my thank you, to you all, for being so responsible and well behaved whilst you have been here, so please don't any of you let me down now. Those of you who have funds with me, make a line and I will give you what you require. Don't forget, back here at 6pm. Now go and enjoy yourselves." Rose and Ruby both got three pounds, out of their five, and went off to explore. They found lots of clothes shops. Ruby bought trousers and a jumper, whilst Rose bought a skirt and blouse.

Rose said, "Ruby, where do you get a brassiere from? I'm getting big and I think I need one." Ruby grabbed Rose's hand and took her to a lingerie shop.

Once inside the assistant looked down at them and said, "And what can I do for you two young ladies?"

Rose replied going red, "I think I need a brassiere, but have no idea what to get."

"Go into that cubicle and strip to your waist and I will come in and measure you. Your friend can go in with you." They went into the cubicle and Rose removed her blazer and shirt. She didn't mind Ruby seeing her, but felt self conscious about a stranger seeing and touching her. The assistant came in with a handful of brassieres.

"Can you put your arms out to the side for me please?" Rose did as she was told, but flinched when the woman went to put the tape measure round her. "It's alright, I'm not going to hurt you," she said gently, "but I need to measure you properly." Rose was measured across her breasts and underneath. The assistant explained that was how you found the right sized bra and cup size. After Rose had been measured the assistant helped her into some bra's as they were now called. Eventually Rose got one that felt comfortable and bought three.

Once that was done, Ruby spotted a large Woolworth shop. "Oh Rose, come on. Let's see what sweets they've got." Rose had never been in a Woolworth's before, and her eyes were everywhere. As to the sweets, there were things called sherbert flying saucers, aniseed balls, gobstoppers, love hearts, sweet cigarette sticks, sugar mice, liquorice chewing sticks, bubble gum, barley sugar, refreshers, lollipops, opal fruits, spangles, fruit pastels and gums, pear drops, honeycomb, caramac, milky way, mars bars, spacedust, dolly mixtures, humbugs, cherry lips, sweet bananas, jelly beans, and all sorts of other sweets. On the shelves were rows of large bottles that contained hard boiled sweets. They were weighed by the quarter pound on the scales and put into a white bag. They each bought a bag of pick 'n' mix and then went to the other side of the shop to look at the comics. Along with various newspapers, for the boys there was The Beano, The Dandy, Eagle and Desperate Dan. For the girls there was Bunty, Diana, Jackie and Princess. Ruby bought Bunty and Jackie. Rose had never seen comics before, but kept her ignorance from Ruby quiet. She would learn. Soon they realised the time. Walking very quickly, they just managed to get back for 6pm.

Back at the hostel, they had a meal of steak and kidney pie with vegetables, and rhubarb and custard. The following morning, after a hearty breakfast, they were back on the coach and heading back to school. Once back, the teacher told them to stay on the coach until the headmistress addressed them. About five minutes later the headmistress, along with the teacher, came marching towards the coach, with her arms swinging. Once on the coach, she looked at all the girls and then said, "Well done girls. I have had a glowing report from your teacher. I hope you all found it interesting. In your next history lesson, your teacher is going to ask you all various questions, so I hope you took good notice of what you saw and were told. Off to your dormitory, and back to lessons after lunch." With that she left the coach. All the girls thanked the driver for safely getting them there and back. When they all went for lunch, they were surrounded by the other girls wanting to know all that they did. Silly as it was, Rose had never felt so wanted. As told, the next history lesson many questions were asked, but the teacher was impressed with their answers. The weeks went by quickly and soon it was time for Rose and Ruby to go home for the summer holidays. It was also time for some of the older girls to leave.

Summer championships were held, but this time Rose and Ruby's class won quite a few events. Rose won all the tennis matches and, again, ended up in the final against Janet Swithers. Janet had left Ruby and herself alone, but was bullying other girls. Standing on the tennis court she looked at Janet and smirked. Janet won the first two games, but Rose was toying with her. Unbeknown to Janet, Rose had been having extra lessons. Rose came back with a vengeance and won the first set. Janet won the second set by a whisker. Then it came down to the last game of set three. They had the same points, until Rose slammed three aces down the court. She was one ball away from winning. Rose served and could feel the tension in the air. Janet responded with a low lob, but Rose just got to it and popped it over the net. There was no way Janet could get to it. The cheers went up - she'd won. Rose had got her revenge at last.

As Janet went to shake hands Rose said, "As someone once said to me, "Good riddance to bad rubbish." Rose walked off the court feeling so proud. Ruby hugged and congratulated her, as did a lot of other girls. Rose had written to her uncle asking him what was happening for the summer holidays, as Ruby and her parents were going away to the seaside for the first two weeks. Her uncle told her that he had booked out holidays for the two weeks Ruby was away. At least she wouldn't be on her own with her aunt. Then, and only if Ruby's parents agreed, she could spend the rest of the holidays with them. Naturally, George and Monica had agreed. Secretly they loved Rose like another daughter.

CHAPTER 12

Rose was determined this time not to take any notice of her aunt's behaviour towards her. She would be polite at all times and try to help. Her uncle arrived to pick her up, and Rose was delighted, as she could also introduce Ruby's parents to him. Hugh, George and Monica got acquainted, whilst Rose and Ruby went to get their suitcases. They hugged and kissed each other's cheeks and couldn't wait to see each other in two weeks time. Just before they left, Monica called to Rose.

"Take this," she said and pressed a key and pound note into her hand. "If it's get too much, get a taxi and just let yourself in. There's plenty to eat, so make yourself at home. Promise me." Rose kissed Monica's cheek and promised. Quickly she put the key and money into her trouser pocket, and went back to her uncle.

As they were driving home Hugh said to Rose, "I decided to go home the scenic way, and thought we might go into Fracton first and have a meal somewhere. Is that alright?"

Rose replied, "That would be lovely uncle." About three miles from Fracton, Rose noticed a lot of ugly buildings going up and asked her uncle what was going on. Her uncle told her a farmer had sold all his lands to the government and specialised army barracks were being built. It should all be finished by Christmas.

"Hopefully it will mean more money will be spent in Fracton, and maybe more bank accounts opened." Rose just smiled, but thought what a blot on the countryside it looked, and then thought no more about it.

Once in Fracton, Rose and her uncle had a lovely meal in one of the cafes. After that her uncle had to pop into the bank and so Rose went with him. Inside the bank it was quite big. Her uncle pointed out the cashiers and explained they either took money from their customers, or gave them money. Everything had to be recorded and signed. Then other staff updated the people's bank accounts. There was about twenty staff in all. Her uncle's office was quite posh, and had nice leather chairs for customers to sit on, who needed to talk to him about various circumstances. Ten minutes later they left and went home. When Rose walked in, her aunt was in the kitchen, so she went up to her and hugged her saying,

"It's lovely to see you aunt. I hope you're well and had a lovely Easter holiday?"

Her aunt, a bit taken aback by this polite encounter replied, "I'm quite well thank you. I'm glad to see your manners have improved."

"Nancy," snapped her uncle. Rose said she would go upstairs and unpack. In her bedroom she looked for a secret place to hide the key and money. She put them in a sock and tying it up in a specific way, stuffed it right to the end of one her shoes. As it turned out Rose hardly saw her aunt, as she now had a high position in a charitable organisation, which kept her very busy.

Rose and her uncle had a lovely two weeks. They would go off to different places, which Rose had never been to before. She loved being out in the countryside, and walking through the woods and forests, and listening to the songs of the birds. They stopped at a country inn one day, and to Rose it was idyllic. The car park was at the side. The front of the inn had trails of rambling roses growing all across the walls, and there were two beds of different flowers growing either side of the pathway. The inn had a separate building with a waterwheel, with the water going round and round. The innkeeper told them he still ground his own flour. The river was quite wide and fast flowing. Swans and ducks swam by, but some of them were on the grassy walkway alongside the river. Inside the inn it was like going back to another era. Thick brown wooden beams with beige walls. All the seating was either in booths or separate tables, again in brown, with a jug of small flowers on each. Old pictures were on the walls, with some going back to the Victorian era. Others were painted landscapes of the area. At the back of the inn was a large grass area with tables and benches, which is where they sat down. They both had gammon and pineapple with chips, which was delicious. Rose sat there and thought she could live somewhere like this.

The day before she was due to go to Ruby's, she had to ask her uncle something, but felt slightly embarrassed.

"Uncle, I'm sorry but I need to ask you something." Her uncle looked at her and said,

"What is it Rose, you know you can ask me anything?"

Rose blushed slightly and said, "I know it's very expensive uncle, but I seem to be outgrowing my school uniform. My shirts are ... um ... tight across my chest."

"Oh is that all? Come we'll go into Fracton and get what you need. Can't have you "bursting out all over" now can we?" Rose actually laughed. Later on, she had new shirts, cardigans and bras. The assistant who checked her measurements said her bras were slightly too tight. Again Rose was embarrassed, but the assistant soon put her at ease. The following day her uncle drove her over to Ruby's. Her aunt never even said goodbye to her. Ruby and her parents all looked to have caught the sun. George and Monica invited Hugh in, but he apologised and said he really must get to work.

He hugged and kissed Rose's cheek and whispered in her ear, "Don't forget, if you need anything, you know where I am. Now take this to tide you over for any more trips or whatever. Good luck with your new classes, and don't forget to write to me. I do so love your letters." Rose thanked and promised him. They all waved as Hugh drove off.

Straight away they all wanted to know what each other had been doing for the last two weeks. For once Rose had a good time and George, Monica and Ruby were pleased. The next four weeks went by quickly. Ruby's parents did shift work, so on the days when they were both off, it was into the car and driving out to the countryside or the seaside. They actually managed to spend a weekend at the seaside. Monica took Rose to a store and bought her a swimsuit. Rose was extremely embarrassed at how much of her body was on show, but when she saw other girls were on the beach in them, she didn't feel so self conscious. When George and Monica were at work, Ruby and Rose would lie on large bath towels in the back garden and sunbathe. Within a couple of weeks Rose had a lovely brown tan. She had to smile though when she undressed, as it looked like she still had her swimsuit on, but it was white!!

One day as Rose and Ruby were sitting in the garden Ruby said, "I think next year we will have to wear bikinis."

Rose frowned and said, "Bikinis?" Ruby showed her one in a magazine her mum had bought.

"Good heavens Ruby, we can't walk round in those. Why it barely covers our bits," she exclaimed.

Ruby burst out laughing and replied, "Rose, you have a wonderful figure, and you are very attractive. You must try and stop being so self conscious. You're my soul sister and I wouldn't let you dress in anything that would make you look stupid. I know you would tell me if you didn't like me in something." Rose chewed her bottom lip as she let what had been said sink in.

"I'm sorry Ruby. I don't mean to cause you any trouble."

Ruby looked at Rose stunned, and replied, "Rose, you have never, ever, caused me any trouble. Perhaps I was a bit insensitive, so I should apologise."

Rose said, "Neither of us need to apologise. I'll start by looking at myself in my bra and briefs." Both of them laughed. Soon it was time to return to school, to a new class, and new lessons.

Now they were both in Class 4, with only a year to go before they sat their GCE exams. After that, if they passed, they would have to decide whether to stay on for another two years. Rose had already decided. She would rather be at school than at home, so she had a lot of studying to do. The three new classes they had were drama, French and cooking. Rose and Ruby loved all three. The drama classes helped Rose a great deal on dealing with different emotions, and situations. The French lessons were interesting, mainly because the teacher was from France, and she made sure that the pronunciation was correct. As to the cooking classes, all the girls looked forward to it. They started off simply by learning to boil an egg, and progressed from there. Rose wasn't too good at making cakes, but she tried her best. One morning their cookery class was at 8am. They had to cook their own breakfasts. The teacher told them she wanted to see plates with two sausages, two rashers of bacon, black pudding, fried bread and an egg. Tomatoes and/or mushrooms were optional. The teacher watched them and pointed out any mistakes, but on the whole she was pleased with their efforts.

Rose and Ruby carried on studying and learning. The holidays came and went, and before they knew it, they were in Class 5. For some of the girls this would be their last year. Rose knew of eight who were going to stay, and that included Ruby. This was a hard year for Rose's class. If they wanted to secure good jobs, they needed qualifications, and that meant study, study, and study. Just before the start of the summer holidays, the exams took place. They were all nervous.

The teacher looked round the room and said, "First of all girls, let's take three deep breaths. In, out, in, out, and in, out. Feel better now?" The girls all nodded. "The exams, as you know, will take a week, with one exam in the morning and one in the afternoon. During your exams you will not speak or write notes to anyone. If you do, you will be asked to leave the class, with a failure for the test. This morning in front of you is the exam for Geography. This afternoon it will be History. Each exam varies between two and three hours. It's now 9am, so turn your exam papers over and good luck." Rose looked at the exam, read it through, and her mind went blank. *Think Rose, think. You can do this. Now relax and read it again,* she said to herself. Suddenly she was writing and before she knew it the teacher said, "Stop, your time is up."

The teacher walked round and collected the papers. "Time to relax girls. Off you go for lunch. Back at 2pm please." Rose and Ruby compared how they'd answered the questions, and decided they'd done their best. After lunch they sat the History exam, and so it continued for the rest of the week. At last it was time to relax, and the summer holidays were only a week away.

Rose had already spoken with her uncle about staying for another two years, and was delighted when he told her he was pleased she wanted to further her education. Of course it all depended on her results. Like every summer now, Rose spent two weeks at home, mainly with her uncle, and the rest with Ruby and her parents. This year all of them went to the seaside for two weeks. They stayed in a small guesthouse, and had three rooms. Breakfast was served every morning, and if they wanted an evening meal they had to book. Rose and Ruby had both bought bikinis, and Rose wasn't so self conscious anymore. She had watched as her figure had developed and, like Ruby, she had a good figure.

As they were walking down to the sea, Monica said to George, "I think our girls are attracting quite a bit of attention." George looked up from his newspaper and saw five or six lads eying the girls up.

"Well," he said, "If I was one of the boys and saw them walking down the beach, I'd be eyeing them up, but of course I'm not, so I'm going to keep an eye on them. First sign of trouble and I'll be down there." Monica kissed George on his cheek.

"What was that for?" Monica replied, "Because like me you've taken Rose to your heart, and see her as Ruby's sister."

George smiled and said, "Want to know a secret. I couldn't have asked for a better best friend for our Ruby, and yes she is a sister to her. Rose is a delight, but I still feel for what she's been through."

Monica replied, "I really don't understand her aunt, but still that's nothing to do with us."

"Well I can assure you Monica, no harm will come to Rose as long as she's with us. I have admired her since she trusted us and told us her story. I think life is good for her now, and at the end of the day, that's all that matters, and that goes for our Ruby as well."

Rose and Ruby had noticed the boys watching them, and giggled. The boys had started playing football, and the ball got kicked nearer and nearer to them. Both of them were knee deep in the sea, when the ball splashed down next to them. Rose got most of the splashes, and turned to see a couple of the boys wading in towards them.

"Sorry about that. Told my friend not to kick it so long."

Rose picked the ball up and threw it at them, saying, "No problem, but I didn't appreciate getting splashed. Maybe you could play further down the beach. I would hate it if the ball accidentally hit a child." The boys got the ball and walked off.

Ruby looked at Rose and said gently, "That was a bit rude wasn't it?"

Rose laughed and replied, "Let's see what happens shall we?" and winked at her. Both of them went swimming and when they came back, the boys were at the water's edge, just kicking the ball between them.

"You two lovelies fancy a cold drink?" asked one of the boys.

"No thanks," replied Ruby nicely.

"Oh come on, it's our way of saying sorry about the ball." Rose replied, "No apology needed, but thanks for the offer of a cold drink, but I think our parents are beckoning to us. Nice to have met you," and with that both girls ran back up the beach to George and Monica.

"Problem?" asked George. Both girls smiled and shook their heads. The rest of the day, all of them sunbathed, had a picnic Monica had prepared and swam in the sea.

Four weeks later Ruby received her exam results. She had passed with flying colours - all 'O' level passes.

"Rose you must go home and get yours," said Ruby. "Ring your uncle and you and I can go on the bus to Fracton and get them."

"Nonsense," said Monica, "I'll drive you over there, it's not far." Rose phoned her uncle but he told her there was no post for her yet, but would look out for it. What none of them knew was that Rose's aunt had seen the letter, opened it and then torn it into bits.

CHAPTER 13

Another week went by and still Rose had not received her results.

"Ruby where's your letter?" asked Monica. Ruby gave her the letter. Monica saw there was a phone number and contacted them.

"Mrs Smith, I can confirm that Rose Brambles' results were sent out with everyone else's. I'm sorry but I cannot divulge what her results are. May I suggest you see the headmistress at Watchford, as she has copies of all the results?"

Monica thanked the lady for her help. "Get your coats girls, we're going to the school to get Rose's results." A short while later Rose was smiling. She had passed all her exams just like Ruby. "Celebration time," said Monica. That evening they dressed up and went to a posh restaurant. Rose and Ruby had the young men's heads turning. With their makeup and hair done, they could easily have passed for eighteen. They all ended up with steak, chips, mushrooms and onion rings. This was followed by Black Forest gateaux, and coffee. The next day Rose phoned her uncle and told him the good news. He was absolutely delighted, but was concerned that the letter had not arrived. That evening Hugh asked Nancy if she had seen the letter. She said she hadn't, but Hugh knew she was lying. He kept quiet to keep the peace. A couple of days later Rose and Ruby met Hugh, and he too, took them for a celebratory meal. These days he kept quiet about seeing Rose, but that day, Nancy had seen him with Rose and another girl, and was absolutely furious, as he found out when he returned home.

Summer was over and it was back to school. Over the school

holidays two new dormitories had been built, and it was one of these that Rose and Ruby now occupied with eight other girls. They were furnished for young ladies, and had their own bathroom, with bath, and a separate toilet. Hairdryers were also supplied. At the side of each bed was a small wardrobe, with lock and key. Their lessons carried on from their exams, but a lot more in-depth. Not only that, the girls could now pick which lessons that wanted to continue with. Rose and Ruby carried on with Maths, English and English Literature, French, Domestic Science and Drama. The new classrooms were spacious enough for the twenty girls, but they only needed one. The other one was used as a study class, where the girls could go if they weren't taking the planned lesson. Again the terms flew by, and soon they were in their last year. As usual, just before the summer holidays, they sat the very last exams. On the last day of terms, the twenty girls, with the headmistress's permission, had a small party in one of the dormitories. All the food was what they had baked that week. The drinks were water and pop. They were allowed to have a transistor radio, and they all danced, laughed, some cried at leaving their friends, and had a thoroughly good evening. The following morning, Rose, Ruby and the rest all said their goodbyes to the teachers and other girls. The headmistress thanked them for being outstanding pupils, and wished them all the luck in gaining good employment.

This summer however, Rose went to Ruby's first and then home. Both of them were now looking for jobs, but there wasn't a lot to choose from. It was Monica who came up with the suggestion.

"Have either of you thought about going to secretarial college? You can learn shorthand and typing, along with office procedures, which I'm sure will help you gain better employment, especially in offices, and you can stay at the college." Rose and Ruby talked about it and decided to make some enquiries. There was a secretarial college at Wrinkton, halfway between Rilford and Birn. If they didn't want to stay, they would have to get a bus each, there and back. On her way home one night, Monica went to the college and got some leaflets, about costs and courses. They both decided to go, and after Rose had asked her uncle's advice, booked a six month course, starting in September, and also sharing a dormitory. In August, Ruby celebrated her 18th birthday. Rose would celebrate hers on Christmas Day. That year was also the year that the age of consent dropped from twenty-one to eighteen. George and Monica had booked a large hall, to celebrate both Ruby's and Rose's birthdays, and invited girls from the school, along with other friends. On the night over a hundred people attended. Most of the boys danced with Rose and Ruby, but one got rather frisky with Rose, and she replied by accidentally kneeing him in his privates.

A couple of days before secretarial college was due to start, Rose went home. Her uncle picked her up and they had a lovely talk. Her aunt was still out, so Rose went upstairs to unpack. She got a box from the cupboard and carefully folded up all her school uniform, as she wouldn't need it again. Thanks to her uncle, he had given her some money so she could go shopping to buy new clothes, which she now hung up in her wardrobe. Teddy went back on her bed. She heard her aunt drive up and gave her a few minutes to come in. As she walked down the stairs she heard her aunt saying,

" ... I'm not staying home. She'll have to get herself a job and earn some money for a change. I'm sick to death of the way you mollycoddle her."

Rose felt her temper rising and stormed into the kitchen. "Nice to see you again aunt, but I think you need to listen to what I have to say, and I apologise if you think I'm being rude. You don't need to change anything to do with your life, as the day after tomorrow I am going to secretarial college in Wrinkton, and will be staying at the college for six months. After college I will be looking for a job and hopefully somewhere else to live. I'm sorry I've been such a big disappointment to you. Now, if you don't mind I'm going out for a walk," and with that Rose grabbed her coat and slammed out the kitchen door. She walked into Rilford and ended up getting fish and chips from the chip shop, and sat on the bench in the small park.

Back at the house, Nancy was having a real go at George. "Where the hell did she get all those clothes from? Yes I've been in her bedroom and looked around. I suppose you've paid for this college as well. You seem to forget you have a wife to clothe and feed, but more important that money grabber is NOT your niece. I want her gone from this house as soon as possible. Do I make myself clear Hugh?"

Hugh, for once in his life, rounded on Nancy. "When the hell have you ever wanted for anything? I've worked my backside off to give you everything, including this house, which in case you've

81

forgotten, I've bought from the bank. When we agreed to have Rose, be honest, you loved her like a daughter, until the day she overheard you slagging her off. How did you expect her to respond? You were shouting so much, the whole bloody street must have heard you." Nancy paled at this outburst, but replied with venom, "Don't you ever swear at me again. I could leave you tomorrow and not need you." To Nancy's stunned surprise Hugh replied, "That's fine by me, off you go." Hugh then put his coat on, got in his car and drove off.

Rose started to feel chilly and walked back home. Once she entered the house she felt the tension in the air. She saw her aunt in the sitting room doing her embroidery. Her uncle was nowhere to be seen. Rose knew they'd had another argument over her, and went to her bedroom. About an hour later she heard her uncle's car drive in. The house stayed silent. Rose started reading her favourite book *Pride and Prejudice* and went off into a trance thinking about her own Mr Darcy. The following day Rose caught the bus into Fracton and went to see her uncle, as she was concerned. Alas, he was in a meeting and couldn't be disturbed. She went to the shopping centre and bought things for college, and some more clothes, along with two pairs of boots for winter. One pair of black and one of brown. Whilst Rose had been in Fracton, she had the strange feeling she was being watched, but saw no one, until she was about to come out of the shopping centre. There sitting in her car was her aunt!! Rose back tracked and found a back entrance. Making sure her aunt didn't see her, she quickly rushed down the road to the bus station, and caught the bus home. Once back she went to her bedroom and started to pack her suitcase for college, putting her new purchases in it first, followed by the one's she had bought with her uncle. After she had finished, she locked her case and put it in the cupboard. By the time her aunt arrived back, looking furious, Rose was sitting on the settee with her legs curled up under her, reading a book and drinking a mug of tea.

"Hello aunt, can I make you a pot of tea?" Her aunt totally ignored her. Rose shrugged her shoulders and carried on reading.

The following morning her uncle said he would take her to the college. Her aunt just raised her eyebrow. Rose got her case, and then packed a smaller case with toiletries, her radio, hairdryer and other bits and pieces, including teddy. Once they were in the car Hugh said,

"Sorry about yesterday Rose. My secretary told me you had called in. Is everything alright?"

Rose smiled and replied, "I was concerned about you and aunt, as I seem to cause her great distress when I come home, and I'm sure my outburst didn't help."

Hugh replied, "I don't understand her these days. She now mixes with highbrow people, who are fine, but she is turning into a real snob, and I don't particularly like it. You know me Rose, I like the quiet life, but now I'm dragged to dinner parties, which we then have to reciprocate. Sometimes I find it all too much."

Rose felt sad for him and replied, "Have you tried to tell her how you feel uncle?"

"Yes, and no," he replied. "I suppose I go along with it because I do love your aunt very much. Ah, here's the college. Now before you go here is your old savings book and I have put five pounds in it for you, and no, your aunt knows nothing of this. If you need more, give me a ring and I can either send it, or better still you can come and see me. I do miss you Rose, and I've never said it before, but I love you too." Rose had tears in her eyes and leant over and kissed his cheek. At that moment they saw Ruby with George. The girls hugged each other, and then hugged Hugh and George. As they went to leave to go into the college Rose called to her uncle and ran back to him. She hugged him again and whispered in his ear,

"I love you too uncle."

Rose and Ruby settled into college life quite quickly. This time however, it was a mixture of males and females. The men took the business studies, and only a few took shorthand and typing. The dormitory they had been given was spacious and they shared the bathroom facilities with six others. There were only forty students staying at the college. On site was also a small canteen where you could buy various meals and drinks, along with a library and small study rooms. After a week Rose and Ruby were enjoying themselves, and especially the attention of the young men. Three in particular had decided to be their "saviours". They were called John, Will and Steve. They were all nineteen. The five of them attended the same classes and slowly became good friends. After being there about a month, John told them there was an insurance office, in Wrinkton, looking for temporary part-time filing clerks. The men went and were given the jobs. The job entailed putting files in year and alphabetical order. They had mentioned two ladies might be interested. Rose and Ruby went for an interview one lunchtime. Inside the office was a long counter and a young lady attended them.

"Good afternoon ladies. Can I help you?" she asked cheerily. Rose explained why they were there.

"What are your names please?"

"Rose Brambles and Ruby Smith."

The lady replied, "Take a seat, and I'll see if Mr Tribble is available." Ten minutes later the girls were sitting in front of Mr Tribble.

"So young ladies, I understand you're interested in the positions. Would you care to tell me a bit about yourselves," and they did. "Well, I'm more than happy to take you on. I will need to contact the college to ask them. I have already asked about three gentlemen and they said it wasn't a problem. If you would both like to wait outside." About five minutes later he called them back in. "The college is happy for you to take the positions, and suggest every morning, from 9am to 12.30pm, you attend college and then start here at 1.30pm until 5.30pm. It will be Monday to Friday, and on Saturday it's 9am until 1pm. The pay will be two pounds a week. The young gentlemen are starting on Monday, so may I suggest you start at the same time?" Rose and Ruby were delighted. Now they could start saving.

On the way back to the college Rose said, "Do you think we should go and see the principal and thank her?" Ruby agreed. They went to the principal's office and asked her secretary if they could see her.

"Please Rose and Ruby come in," said the principal. "My apologies for not meeting you before, but I have been rather busy. How may I help you?"

Rose replied, "Ruby and myself just wanted to thank you for allowing us to get employment. Will this cause problems with our tuition?"

The principal smiled and replied, "If all my students were as good as yourselves, I would be delighted. You have both excelled so far in your lessons. Do you know how long this temporary job will be for?"

Ruby replied, "We're not sure, until we see what is required of us."

"That's alright," replied the principal, "but I would like to let you know that after Christmas is when the real study work starts. Hopefully you will be finished by then. If not you can extend your course for another three months. We will also reimburse the funds you have paid if you do leave in March, which I think you will. In the meantime the typing pool is open until 8pm every night and on Saturday. Sunday it's closed. You have your shorthand books, so you can test each other. I see you have our "Three Musketeers" looking after you. At least I know you will be accompanied on the dark nights." Rose and Ruby frowned at each other. "Ah, I see you have not heard of them. It's a book written by a Frenchman called Alexandre Dumas. I suggest you read it, if you have time. There is a copy in the library, in French and English. I thoroughly enjoyed it." They both thanked her and left. Ruby said on the way to the canteen,

"Isn't it nice to be called by our first names and not surnames?" Rose agreed, and said, "I think I'll call our three escorts "The Lads." Ruby was fine with that. Later that evening Rose went to the library and got a copy, in French, of *Les Trois Mousquetaires*.

CHAPTER 14

When the five of them arrived on Monday afternoon, they were taken to a large room at the back of the office.

Mr Tribble said, "Here are all the files that need sorting. I'm sorry to say but at the moment they are all in numerical order. Our head office has now decided they need to be in their correct years, and the names in alphabetical order. I will leave it up to you how you do it. The toilets and kitchen are at the bottom of this corridor. We do ask that you clean any mess up that you make, as we don't have a cleaner. If you need anything, please see one of the staff." The five of them stood there and looked around. There were six separate cabinets with at least fifty files in each!!

"This is going to take forever,'" said Ruby. The lads started debating how to arrange it all. Rose whispered in Ruby's ear and Ruby said, "That's a good idea Rose."

The lads turned and Steve said, "How?"

Rose replied, "Just a suggestion. If we get five large boxes, like the Kellogg's boxes, we will have one for each year. We put all the paperwork in the correct year box. Once that's done, we take the first year, and with the shelves being empty, we put everything in alphabetical piles. Then we take a pile each and put them in order, and back into the files, which will need to be labelled."

Will smiled and replied, "Not just a pretty face are you?" Rose blushed slightly.

"Where are we going to get the boxes from?" asked John.

"The shopping centre. Try the large Co-op," replied Ruby.

"Hang on," said Rose, "we can't walk through the office with these boxes. Let me see if there's a back door," and with that walked towards the office. She saw one of the ladies, who spotted her and went over. "Sorry to bother you, but we need to get some large boxes and don't want to bring them through the front door. Is there by any chance a back door we could use?"

She replied, "Yes there is. Come with me." They went right to the back of the building, and Rose saw the door. "The key is hung up here, but whatever you do make sure you remember to re-lock it. Mr Tribble seems likeable, but believe me when I say he has a really nasty temper." Rose promised she would lock the door when the lads went out, let them back in and then lock it again. The lads went off and Rose and Ruby started undoing some of the files. About twenty minutes later, Rose went to the back door and saw the lads waiting and let them in, then re-locked the door and put the key back. The boxes were broken down, but it didn't matter. They made them up again, marked the year, and started putting the paperwork in the correct year. Just doing that took them two weeks. The whole room was now covered in dust. One day one of the ladies came in to give them some birthday cake.

"Good grief folks, open the windows. You'll all have sore throats."

Steve replied, "We weren't sure if we could. Didn't want any alarms going off." Will opened the two small windows, and the room soon cleared.

"Brought you all some of my birthday cake, hope you like it. Don't forget to close the windows." They all thanked her, and she got a kiss from each of the lads.

At the end of the second week, John suggested they all went out and had a nice meal, and then maybe go to a disco. Rose and Ruby had never been to a disco and were a little concerned. Will picked up on their looks.

"You've never been before have you?" Rose and Ruby both shook their heads.

"Don't worry we'll look after you," said Steve. They all met up by the college entrance at 7pm. John had booked a table for five at one of the restaurants. The meal was lovely, and they all got to know each other a bit better. Rose didn't know why, but she actually felt safe with the three of them. Then they walked to the other end of town and went into a place called "Dance Disco". It was now 10pm.

John said, "It won't be too busy at this time, so we'll just stay for an hour and then go back to the college." Inside it wasn't big, but it was dimly lit. Hanging from the ceiling was what they called a glitter ball, and two lights were trained on it. As it spun round so different coloured lights went round the room. There was a small bar, and a dance floor. About twenty girls were dancing round to the music being played by a DJ (disc jockey), operating from a corner of the room.

"Come on you two, let's sit down and people watch. Two soft drinks?" asked Steve. Rose and Ruby nodded. Slowly the disco got busier, and Rose and Ruby watched as lots of ladies and men were dancing. To Rose some of the dancing looked indecent. Ladies swaying their hips up and down the men. True to their word, after an hour they left, and it was 11.30pm when they got back. They said goodnight to the lads and thanked them for a lovely evening, and then quietly tiptoed to their dormitory, so as not to wake anyone up.

The following day, being a Sunday, Rose and Ruby met up with some of the other ladies, mainly to see what they'd missed on the Friday afternoon lesson. Eight of them got together in one of the small study rooms, and started testing each other's shorthand. Soon it was lunchtime and the ladies walked over to the canteen. The cook looked at Rose and Ruby, and then behind them.

"Where's the three musketeers today then?" Rose replied they hadn't seen them.

One of the girls said, "If you're talking about Steve, Will and John, we saw them in Dance Disco about 1am, dancing with three leggy blondes."

The cook replied, "Hangovers then. Serves them right. Now what can I get my lovely ladies." A couple of hours later, Rose and Ruby were back in their dormitory.

"Fancy some fresh air Ruby?" They put their coats on and walked towards the small park, arm in arm. It was a chilly day, but the sun was sort of shining through. They passed children playing in the playground, with parents watching their every move. "What do you think of the lads?" asked Rose.

Ruby replied, "I think all three of them are cute, but I really like Will. Which one do you fancy?"

Rose replied, "None of them really. They're good company and we have a laugh with them, but I don't have feelings in that way for them, and yet I feel safe with them, if that makes sense?"

"You ever kissed a man Rose, properly I mean?" Rose replied she hadn't.

"Wonder what it's like?" asked Ruby. "Hopefully one day we'll find out," replied Rose. They carried on walking round the park and then made their way back to the college.

When they went down later on to the canteen, they saw John, Steve and Will in a corner, looking rough.

"Well gentlemen, I'd say you all look the worst for wear," said Rose.

John replied, "Ooh, don't shout Rose, our heads are cracking."

"Serves you right," said Ruby. Both of them laughed.

"Three glasses of water and six headache tablets," said the cook banging the glasses on the table. "Should be ashamed of yourselves. If I was your mother..."

A bleary eyed John looked up and said, "Sorry cook, we get the message," and with that the three of them took their tablets with the water.

"Now my lovely ladies, what can I get you?" Rose and Ruby decided to have some sandwiches and a slice of cook's homemade walnut cake. "May we also have a large pot of coffee, for all of us?" asked Ruby. Rose and Ruby paid the bill between them. Slowly the lads started to feel human again.

"So we hear you went back to the disco. You should have stayed. Rose and I could have walked back to the college," said Ruby.

Will looked at her and replied, "You must be joking. If anything had happened to you, we would never have forgiven ourselves. Safety of our two beautiful ladies comes first."

Ruby blushed slightly and replied, "Flattery will get you nowhere," and they all laughed. Rose and Ruby decided to leave the lads, and went to their dormitory. Separately they went to the bathroom and had a strip wash, changed into their nighties and got into their beds.

"What are you reading now Rose?" Rose replied, "The Three Musketeers in French. Not sure about it at the moment, only time will tell." About an hour later they said goodnight to each other and turned the lights out. Ruby dreamt about Will, and Rose dreamt about Musketeers.

At the insurance office, all of them had got into a rhythm and a month later all the paperwork was being filed alphabetically. Mr Tribble decided to see how they were getting on.

"Well ladies and gentlemen, I must say this is looking excellent. Tell me how you went about it," he asked looking at John. John explained and Mr Tribble asked whose idea it had been. John replied it had been Rose's. Looking at Rose he smiled and said, "Brains as well as beauty. I'm impressed young lady." Looking at the table he saw a stack of plastic cups. "Where did these come from?" he asked. Steve replied they had got them from the college, so as not to use their cups, and it saved by not using the hot water. Every night they took the used ones back to the college and put them in the bin. Again Mr Tribble was impressed. "How much longer do you think you will be?" John replied it would all be done before Christmas, so probably another two/three weeks. "Very well, I will inform my head office. Thank you for all of your hard work." With that he left them. Two weeks before Christmas they finished. It had taken them ten weeks to get it all done, but at the end of the time, they had all been paid twenty pounds. The lads had more or less spent theirs, but Ruby and Rose had saved most of their wages. On their last day, Mr Tribble called them into his office, and congratulated them on a job well done. He had got his secretary to type out a reference for each of them, which they accepted with gratitude. He gave them their last wages and wished them well. They all went back to the college happy. Back in their dormitory Ruby opened her wage packet.

"Oh heavens, Rose open your wages." Rose did and was surprised when five pounds fell out instead of two pounds. There was a note saying, "Merry Christmas and thank you for a job well done. Mr Tribble." Rose was delighted. Putting the five pounds with her other savings, she now had eighteen pounds to bank. A fortune that she would need soon.

With Christmas just around the corner, Rose phoned her uncle to see what was happening. He told her if she wanted to come home, she would have the house to herself for four days at least, as they had been invited to friends, or if she wanted to go to Ruby's that would be fine, but he did want to see her. Rose decided, as much as she loved Ruby and her parents, she quite liked the idea of being on her own for a while. She had plans to sort out. Ruby understood, but insisted she stayed with them for the New Year, and Rose agreed. The last weekend of college all five of them went out for a meal and then headed to the disco afterwards. Rose and Ruby had been quite a few times with the lads, and would now get up and dance with them. The lads were old enough to drink alcohol, as was Ruby, but the pair of them stuck to soft drinks. Both Rose and Ruby were good dancers, and lots of lads came up and asked them for dances. They accepted a few, but John, Steve and Will kept their eyes on them in case of any trouble.

Whilst Rose and Ruby were dancing, John asked Will and Steve, "Either of you two think we'll be lucky enough to get Rose and Ruby in the sack? Personally I don't want to. I enjoy their friendship too much." Both Will and Steve agreed.

"As much as I'd like to get to know Ruby a lot better, I now look on them as sisters I never had," said Will.

Steve then said, "I respect them too much to do that to them. It's an absolute pleasure to take them out for a meal and then come here, and none of us expecting anything when we say goodnight." John said, "I'll drink to that, and another great term with them next year. Going to miss them like hell when we say goodbye at the end of March." Both Steve and Will agreed, and the three of them toasted Rose and Ruby.

The college broke up two days before Christmas Day. Ruby's dad picked her up, and Rose's uncle picked her up. The lads were introduced to them both, and they had about a fifteen minute chat. Then Rose and Ruby hug and kissed Will, Steve and John on their cheeks, as they went their separate ways to go home. Rose and Ruby hugged each other and Rose said her uncle would drive her over to them a couple of days after Boxing Day.

Once in the car Hugh said, "You seem to have made some nice friends Rose in those young men." Rose replied, "They are uncle and, in a roundabout way, protect us. All three of them are gentlemen and we have a good time together, and nothing is expected of Ruby and myself, if you know what I mean."

Her uncle smiled and said he understood. "Rose if you don't mind me asking, what have you been living on, as you've never asked me for any money. I hope you haven't been depriving yourself?" Rose told him about the job they had all got and how the college had helped, and neither herself of Ruby had dropped behind in their subjects. She also told him she needed to go into Fracton to bank her savings. Her uncle was well impressed. Soon they were home, and Hugh unlocked the door.

"It's alright Rose, as Nancy isn't here. She's gone ahead to the Blooms and I will join her tomorrow, so we have the rest of the day to ourselves." Rose was delighted at that bit of news.

CHAPTER 15

That evening Rose said she would cook them a meal, but her uncle insisted that they went into Fracton, and that's what they did. In the morning Rose made breakfast for both of them, having her favourite - boiled eggs and toasted soldiers. Soon it was time for her uncle to go, and he gave her the key to the front door.

"I hate to leave you on your own Rose, especially as it's your eighteenth birthday tomorrow." Rose assured him she would be fine. She was going to look at the jobs available and also somewhere else to live. Her uncle was sad about this, but understood. "Well in that case your Christmas present just might help." He produced the savings book Rose had seen in her aunt's desk. "There is two hundred pounds in here for you. I can always move your other savings into this account, if you wish. I knew one day you would move out, and this is to help you get somewhere decent."

Rose threw her arms round his neck and said, "I really don't know how to thank you. You have done so much for me, and I promise I'm going to do everything possible to make you always be proud of me."

Hugh, who had a tear in his eyes replied, "I'm already proud of you Rose," and kissed her cheek. "Now I must go or else your aunt won't be happy, and we don't want that do we? Be back two days after Boxing Day." Rose smiled and watched as Hugh drove out the driveway, waving as he went.

Rose saw a stack of newspapers by the kitchen door and took them into the sitting room. She knew this time of the year there wouldn't be many jobs around, and she was right. She went and checked the cupboards with regards to food for the next couple of days. Typical, her aunt had bought nothing. Looking at the clock she saw it was midday. The shops in Rilford would be closing soon, so she quickly got changed, grabbed a shopping bag and walked into Rilford. She managed to buy some fresh vegetables, and a couple of potatoes, two chicken breasts, a tin of spam, four slices of ham, a small Christmas pudding and a packet of dream topping. Rose knew there were eggs, cheese, butter, milk and bread in the fridge. Happy with her purchases she walked back home. Just as she got to the door, it started to snow lightly. She put her purchases away, made a drink and went into the sitting room. She turned on the television, but didn't find anything to watch, so switched the radio on instead. Again she looked through the newspapers and this time an advert caught her eye. "Temporary Trainee Librarian required. 1st week of April for approx six months. Apply in writing to Langmoth Library." Langmoth was about an hour's bus ride away from Rilford. Rose loved books and decided she would write to them immediately. Later on she made herself a couple of fried spam sandwiches, and a drink. She curled up on the settee and watched the television until 9pm, then went to bed. She picked up the savings book and hid it in her suitcase, as she wouldn't need to touch any of that money yet.

The following day, as always, Rose wished teddy happy birthday. She was now eighteen and was of age. The one thing she wanted to do was to learn to drive. As she went to make her bed, she noticed something under her pillow. It was a box wrapped in birthday paper.

"Is this from you teddy?" she asked laughing. Inside was a lovely watch, and it was from her uncle. A little note said, "Hope you like it. Happy Birthday Rose xx." She had a quick wash and brushed her teeth. Her hair was always in a pigtail, but she was debating whether to change it. She put her watch on and admired it. Her uncle certainly had great taste. So as not to damage it, she took it off and put it on her dressing table. Another thing her aunt must not find. After breakfast, she went into her aunt and uncle's bedroom. It had been changed around, and now there was one bed either side of the room. Rose looked for the desk key and found it. She pushed the roll top up and looked for the orphanage papers. Once she found them, she took them downstairs and read them again. First thing, the day after Boxing Day, she was going to get the document copied, but where? The only safe place she could copy it was at the college. She knew the college wasn't closed, as some students were staying there. For some unknown reason, she just wanted a copy. Perhaps it was just a reminder of how lucky she had been.

As she went to put it back in the envelope she saw another piece of paper. What she read stunned her. It was a certified copy of a letter, dated six months previous. It read,

I, Nancy Brambles, of 4 Lennic Street, Rilford, England, do hereby declare the following information to be true and legally binding.

With regards to one Rose Clark, now known as Rose Brambles, and of the same address, I hereby confirm that myself, or my husband Hugh Brambles never adopted the said Rose Clark, and the attached document from Blackthorn Orphanage is in fact a fake document. The said Rose Clark was forced upon us, mainly due to an assault she had witnessed between four boys and their victim, and needed to be got rid off as soon as possible, and we were threatened beyond our control if we did not take her. We took her in and fed and clothed her, and gave her everything she required, including expensive schooling. This child has now turned into a nasty human being, and is taking us for every penny we have. I cannot prove it, but I am convinced that this Rose Clark might be blackmailing my husband. Upon our demise's, I hereby declare that no funds or the house is to go to the said Rose Brambles. The house will be sold and along with our funds, after funeral expenses etc have been deducted, will go to any charitable organisation. More information will be in my Will.

The said Rose Clark, now Rose Brambles, was born in Chattle Street, Hayleigh, Lancashire, daughter of Doris and Robert Clark, and her birth date is 25th December. This year she will reach her eighteenth birthday. She was deposited at Blackthorn Orphanage at the age of five years.

Her aunt had signed the document, and her signature witnessed by the solicitor and his secretary, in Fracton. Rose actually felt sick. She knew she'd fallen out with her aunt, but to do this was beyond belief. The worst thing was her uncle didn't know, and she couldn't tell him. Rose also felt betrayed, as somebody else out there now knew her true identity. Tears slowly fell down her face and she had never felt so unwanted.

Rose knew it was wrong to go through her aunt's desk, but at least she now knew her aunts hatred of her. She carefully put both documents in the envelope and threw it on the armchair. Rose got herself into such a state, and went through every emotion possible, and then felt totally drained. Eventually she dragged herself upstairs and drew herself a bath. As she laid in the bath she started to relax, and then thought of all the good things that had happened, like Ruby and her parents, friends she had made, and the Three Musketeers. She started to laugh at that, as they were nothing like the Musketeers she was reading about. Feeling better she dried herself off and went into her bedroom, and looked at herself in the mirror. Rose could see she now had a woman's body. Her breasts were now full and round, and her stomach had a very slight curve, but she knew her periods were due. At the top of her thighs she now had dark hairs, which covered her womanhood. Her bottom was more curved, but not big. Her legs were still long and lean. Her hair was in her usual pigtail, and so she undid it and let her hair fall loose over her shoulders and down her back. She started to pretend she was a model and made all sorts of poses. Then she did laugh, good and hearty.

Quickly she got dressed and went downstairs, as she was feeling hungry. She put the oven on, and put some dripping in the oven pan and put it in the oven to get hot. Next she cleaned and washed some vegetables and put them in a saucepan. She peeled a potato and cut it up into four pieces, and got the chicken breasts from the fridge. Carefully she got the oven pan out, and put the chicken and potato pieces in the hot fat. Half an hour later, she had her Christmas dinner, and it tasted good. She only had one piece of the chicken. She'd have the other in a sandwich later. Now feeling full and content, she went into the sitting room and put the television on. She watched a couple of films, and laughed at the comedy shows. About 7pm Rose made herself a chicken sandwich, and steamed the small Christmas pudding she had bought, and made the dream topping. She was enjoying being on her own, and doings things when she wanted, and not being told when. She couldn't wait to find somewhere else to live, but knew it wasn't going to be easy. First of all she had to get a job.

Boxing Day passed much as the day before. The following morning Rose was up early and walked into Rilford and then caught the bus to Wrinkton. There was a cold wind blowing, and the sky looked like it was either going to snow or pour with rain. It did the latter. Once in the college she went to the business study room and copied the documents.

"Oh hello Rose, surely you're not back already?" Rose jumped and immediately felt guilty, and turned to see Angela stood in the doorway.

"Hi Angela. No I'm not back yet, but I forgot to take my shorthand book and notes home, so just jumped on the bus to get them. Thought it better if I copied my notes. Hope you had a nice Christmas." Angela replied it was alright, but quiet. "Fancy a trip to one of the cafes?" asked Rose, who felt a bit sorry for Angela.

"Love to Rose. I'll just grab my coat." Rose and Angela dodged the rain as they made their way to one of the cafes that was open. They had a pot of tea and some cake. Both of them talked about this and that for about an hour, and then Rose said she must get back. It would be just her luck that her aunt and uncle came back early!! Rose went to the bus station, and Angela went back to the college. As Rose passed the Post Office, she went in and bought a stamp and posted her letter. Soon she was back home, and put the documents back in the desk. She put the copies in her suitcase with her watch and locked it. The key she hid. For something to do, she cleaned, polished and vacuumed all the rooms, except her aunt and uncle's bedroom.

Her uncle arrived back the following day.

"Where's aunt?" asked Rose. Hugh explained her aunt had been taken ill, and would return in a couple of days. Rose raised her eyebrow and replied, "Oh I hope it's nothing too bad. I don't like to think of either of you being ill." Hugh replied he was sure she would be fine in a couple of days. He had had a dodgy tummy and they blamed the turkey casserole!! Hugh asked Rose how her days had gone, and she told him about the advert at the library, and that she had applied. (She had kindly asked the library to reply to her at the college. She didn't want her aunt seeing the letter.) She even told him about going back to the college, but not the real reason. Rose hated lying to him, as she desperately wanted to tell him what she'd found.

"Right let's go out for lunch to a country inn. Are you going to Ruby's tomorrow?" Rose replied she was. They drove to Fracton and took the road out to the countryside. Rose noticed the new barracks, that had now been completed, had two soldiers on patrol at the entrance. There seem to be lots of soldiers exercising.

Looking at her uncle she said, "Did you get any new accounts from the barracks?" Hugh replied they had. Soon they arrived at the country inn, and had just got inside when it started pouring with rain. It was warm and cosy inside and a huge log fire was burning. They both decided on the Christmas menu. Hugh asked Rose what her intentions were after she finished college. Rose replied she wasn't sure. It just depended on what employment became available.

Hugh replied, "I could try and find you a job at the bank. It would be good pay."

Rose replied, "Thank you uncle, that's very kind of you, but I would like to try and make my own way. I have to learn as they say, "to stand on my own two feet." I know you will always be there for me, but you must look after aunt."

Hugh smiled and replied, "Your aunt treats you like dirt, and yet you worry about her. You have a good heart Rose."

When they got back home, Rose went up and packed her suitcase. She put her savings book in the envelope with the copies of the documents and sealed it. She put her clothes on the chair ready for the morning. The last thing to go in her case would be teddy. No matter how bad things got, she still had the teddy her mam gave her all those years ago. Rose and her uncle spent a pleasant evening, talking, and watching the television. The following morning they drove over to Ruby's. This time Hugh accepted the kind offer to stay for a drink, and talked to George and Monica, whilst Rose and Ruby went upstairs.

"Ruby, any chance we can go shopping tomorrow? I need to get some of those horrible towels, and get a new dress for the party."

Ruby said, "Hang on a minute," and went to her bedroom. When she returned she gave Rose a box. "Try these instead, so much more comfortable and discreet. My mum and I had a talk about me now being eighteen, and I might fancy a lad and taking it further - I don't think so. Embarrassing, but then she's a nurse. These are called Tampax, and not being crude, you insert them inside. I've tried them and no problem. You can also flush them down the loo. Mum also told me, because like you, I have dreadful period cramps, if you see your doctor, you can get something called the pill. It regulates your periods so you know when you're due on. It also helps you to not get pregnant." Rose was a bit taken aback by what Ruby was saying, but she'd try anything to get rid of those horrible towels.

Monica called up to Rose that her uncle was leaving. Both of them went downstairs and they all said their goodbyes to Hugh. Rose watched until he had driven out of the drive.

"Rose, fancy a cup of tea?" called Monica. Rose went into the kitchen and joined them.

"How was your Christmas, Rose?" asked George.

Rose told them everything she'd been up to, except the documents. "If you get the employment at the library, that's going to be a long way to travel every day," said Monica.

Rose replied, "If I get it, then I will look for somewhere to stay in Langmoth, and I want to learn to drive."

George said, "Your aunt no better then?"

Rose replied a bit sharply, "I never want to see her again unless I have to." George and Monica looked at each other, but said nothing.

CHAPTER 16

———⁓———

"Well, don't the three of you look absolutely beautiful? I am going to feel so proud escorting you tonight," said George. Rose, Ruby and Monica had spent the day together. They started off at the hairdresser's, and for once Rose had her hair styled down, in long curls, and not in a pigtail. Whilst having their hair done, they also had their nails done. Another first for Rose. Afterwards they went to what Rose called a "posh" shop and got new dresses etc for the New Year's Eve party. Once the shopping was done, they took everything back to the car, and then went to a restaurant for a meal. They eventually arrived back late afternoon. George had just been to the barbers, and done the shopping for New Year's Day and the day after. Everyone then relaxed until 7pm. Rose and Ruby did each other's makeup, and got dressed together. Rose's dress had a V-neck, with small capped sleeves, and was fitted at the waist and fell to just above her knees. It was in a light blue colour. Her shoes and bag were in beige, and she wore her Rose necklace. Ruby's dress was in satin brown with a square neck and no sleeves, but had lace across the top part. Like Rose's it fell to above her knees. She wore a pearl necklace, and brown shoes and clutch bag. Monica wore a light yellow chiffon dress, with a high neck and no sleeves. There were two small bands of silver just above her waist. She wore silver shoes and had a silver bag. When they arrived at the venue, they were stunned to see it was a massive hall, and there must have been at least a hundred people.

"Heavens, Joan told me it was a quiet affair," said Monica. Quite a few of the guests were from the hospital, and naturally George and Monica knew them. Rose and Ruby knew no one. They found a table by the dance floor and sat down. A waiter attended them and got them all some drinks.

"Monica, George, so glad you made it," said a lady. This turned out to be Joan.

"I thought you said it was only a small party Joan?" said Monica.

Joan laughed and said, "This is only a small gathering, as it's usually two to three hundred people. Now, who are these two beautiful young ladies?" Monica introduced Ruby and Rose. "I think you two will be having lots of admirers for the evening. Wonder who will be in your arms at midnight? Well must mingle, so I will see you later. Oh, please help yourselves to the food, there's plenty," and with that Joan left. Rose and Ruby had already caught the eye of some young gentlemen. Two of them came up and asked them for a dance. To be sociable they agreed. Monica and George watched them, to make sure nothing untoward happened. It didn't. Rose and Ruby danced with quite a few men then had something to eat and drink with Monica and George. The party was now in full swing, and the drinks were flowing. It was coming up to midnight, when two men came up and asked Ruby and Rose to dance. Rose didn't particularly like the man she was dancing with, mainly because his hands were all over her. Before she realised what was happening he had grabbed her and was kissing her, but when she went to say something, he tried to stick his tongue in her mouth. His breath was foul. He had one hand on her breast and the other had pinned her arms behind her. Rose struggled to free her arms, but unsuccessfully.

"Come on girl, let's go and screw. I bet you're good at it. Can't wait to see you naked."

Ruby and her young man had seen what was happening, and went to her aid. "Mark let her go." Mark released Rose's arms and as he moved she swiftly brought her knee up to his groin. He groaned in agony, and other dancers moved away. Within seconds George was at her side.

"Get off her you lout. Go and cool off somewhere, and then you can apologise."

The man looked at George and said slurring his words, "She led me on. She's a tease, and she's gagging for it." Monica saw George's right arm go up and stopped him.

"I'm sorry, so sorry Rose, and my apologies for my brother being an idiot, and a drunk. Are you alright?" Rose shakily replied she was fine. Joan had now arrived and asked what was going on. Jim told her.

"Why do you always disgrace our family Mark? Now get out of my sight." Jim grabbed Mark and marched him away. "Monica, George, Ruby and Rose, please accept my profuse apologies for my son. If he was like Jim I'd be a happy mum. Is there anything I can do?" Monica told Joan they would look after Rose and to celebrate with her friends.

Ruby held Rose close and asked her if she was alright. Rose, who had now recovered, whispered, "If that's what kissing is like, I'll give it a miss in the future." They all went and sat back at their table. A waiter came over with four fluted glasses and a bottle of Champagne.

"With sincere apologies from our host," he said.

Suddenly over a microphone came a voice saying, "Ladies and gentlemen, we have a countdown of ten starting from now." George popped the champagne cork and poured out small amounts in each glass. A church clock chimed it was midnight. "Happy New Year everyone." Everyone clapped and cheered, and hugs and kisses all went round. Monica, George, Ruby and Rose all hugged and kissed each other.

George said, "I'm sorry Rose that your evening was spoilt."

Rose smiled and said, "It wasn't, because I'm here with my special family, and that's all that matters."

George handed each one of them a glass. "You two just take a sip," which they did.

Rose laughed and said, "The bubbles went up my nose," and they all laughed. They stayed at the party until 1.30am, and Rose and Ruby still danced with some of the other young men, but Rose was wary. They found Joan and Jim and thanked them for a wonderful party. Joan hugged and gave them a kiss on their cheeks, as did Jim who again apologised for his brother, who nowhere to be seen.

Someone tapping on her door woke Rose in the morning. She looked at the clock and was stunned to see it 11am!!

"Come in," she replied. It was Monica with a mug of tea. "Morning Rose. How are you this morning? I was concerned after last night."

Rose smiled, took the mug of tea and replied, "I am absolutely fine." At that moment there was another knock and Ruby popped her head round the door.

"Morning Rose," and sat on the other side of the bed. Ruby looked at her mum and then Rose and said, "Is everything alright?" Monica explained she was just making sure Rose was alright after the incident. "Mum, why are men like that?"

Monica replied, "Take it from me, not all men are like him. Once some men start drinking, not all, they take on a different person. They get drunk and senseless and think they can do what they want. I bet if you saw Mark today, he would be mortified."

Rose replied, "Well if that's kissing, I have no intention of kissing any man at all."

Monica realised it was time to talk to the girls. "Believe me girls, it's not like that. When you start courting, you get to know each other a little bit before the kissing comes in. A kiss on the cheek is fine. I'm sure this will sound old fashioned, but George asked my permission when he first wanted to kiss me. A kiss, on the lips, is supposed to be gentle, sensual and enjoyed."

Ruby asked, "What comes after the kissing?" A while later Rose and Ruby knew all about how to behave with a man, how a man should treat them, petting, lovemaking and how their bodies will respond. She also told them about the man's side of things as well. She also explained about periods, the pill, condoms and having a cap or diaphragm fitted, and the withdrawal technique. She also went into details of how infections could be caught. Being a nurse, Monica told them both everything in full detail. Better they knew, than not. "Well I don't know about you two, but I'm famished. Fancy breakfast?" Both girls nodded and then Ruby said, "Not sure I can look at a sausage again." All three of them burst out laughing.

When they got down to the kitchen George said, "Thought you'd all hibernated."

Monica kissed his cheek and said, "Birds and bees."

George flushed slightly and just said, "Ah." George volunteered to do the very late breakfast and soon bacon, sausages, eggs, fried bread, tomatoes, mushrooms, and baked beans, along with toast and jam/marmalade and a large pot of coffee, were on the table. Everything was eaten and drunk. After they had washed up and dried everything, they all went into the sitting room and watched the television. The rest of the day was spent just being lazy, as were the following two days. Then it came time for Rose and Ruby to pack to go back to college. This time Monica drove them back. Waiting at the gates for them were John, Will and Steve. They all hugged and kissed each other and Monica was introduced to them.

As Monica said goodbye to Ruby and Rose, she said, "Cor, wish I was attending."

Ruby replied embarrassed, "Mum!!" They waved as Monica drove off. Rose and Ruby arranged to meet the lads in the canteen at lunchtime. They quickly went to their dormitory and unpacked and then down to the hall. The principal greeted them all and told them the curriculum had now changed. Those taking both subjects would now attend shorthand and typing in the mornings, with business studies in the afternoon. However, those only taking one subject would take it for the full day. Rose and Ruby were taking both, whilst the lads were only doing business studies. At lunchtime they all met in the canteen.

The cook saw them and said, "Ah my lovely ladies with their three musketeers. Lovely to see you all back. Now what can I get for you?" They had a selection of sandwiches and cake, with coffee. They all caught up with each other's news, and the lads hoped Rose got the library job. Due to the workloads they now had, the five of them rarely saw each other during the week, but every Saturday it was out for a meal and then the disco.

One night at the disco, after they had all been dancing for some time, Rose was thirsty and took the glass with the water in it.

"Rose are you alright?" asked John.

"Oh bugger, Rose has accidentally drunk my vodka," replied Will.

"Here Rose, drink this coke, and it will help."

Rose took the coke and drank it down, feeling the burning sensation getting duller. "Heavens, what was that?" asked Rose.

Will replied cheekily, "Your first alcoholic drink. You could have waited until I diluted it with the coke. You feeling alright now?"

Rose nodded. "What does it taste like as it should be?" asked Rose. Will got another vodka and put the coke in it. "Try it now, but don't gulp it down in one go." Rose tried it and liked it. She then gave it to Ruby to try. From then on the girls would always have one vodka and coke, but it lasted them the night.

At the beginning of February, Rose received a letter from Langmoth Library. They wanted her to attend an interview a week later. All of them were pleased for her. Rose went to the principal and showed her the letter. The interview was at noon on a Friday. The principal said that would be fine, as she could check with Ruby what she had missed. The day of the interview arrived, and it was pouring with rain. Rose was going to get the bus, but decided to arrive looking smart, so she had to get a taxi. It was a fifteen minute drive. Once she arrived, she was shown to a small room, where a panel of three librarians were seated. They soon made her feel at ease. The interview went well, as far as Rose was concerned. The position was temporary because one of the ladies had given birth and was due back in six months.

One of the librarians took her to the part of the library where she would work, if she got the job. It was a large room with lots of tables with lamps on them, and nearly all of them were taken.

"Just watch," whispered the librarian. There was a lady sitting at her desk watching. As soon as she saw a hand go up, she went to that person, who gave her a list of the book/s they wanted. She then went and got them, took them to the person, and then back to her desk, and wrote in a book the title and the name of the person. Rose and the librarian walked round the cabinets, which held the books and their categories. Outside the room the librarian said, "It can get quite busy getting the books, and there is a button by the desk, and when pressed another lady will come to help. Fifteen minutes before the library is due to close a bell is rung. The books then need to be ticked off and replaced in the cabinets. This can take up to one maybe two hours. The hours are from 9am until 5pm with a break for lunch. Your wages will be fifteen pounds a week. One thing I would like to know is how do you intend to get here every day from Rilford?" Rose replied that if she was accepted she would be looking for a room to rent in Langmoth. The librarian shook her hand and thanked her for coming, and gave her directions to the bus station. As Rose walked back, she had a look in some estate agents' windows, and made a note of some lodging houses. An hour later she was back at college. Ruby arrived just after Rose had finished changing.

"Rose how did it go?"

Rose replied, "I think it went well and I would like to work there. I should know in a week." The letter arrived offering Rose the job, and she was delighted. Now she didn't have to go home, but she had to find somewhere to live, in five weeks!!

A couple of Saturdays later, Rose went to Langmoth to look for a room. Ruby and the lads wanted to go as well, but she politely declined their offer. She had to do this by herself. The first four she went to were disgraceful for the money they wanted. She had a rest in a cafe where she had a meal and a drink. She decided to give up and went back to the bus station. Just before she got there, a notice in an estate agent's window caught her eye. "Room to let, ladies only, clean and tidy house." Rose wrote down the address and went there. It was literally just around the corner from the library. It was a small detached house, with a small garden in the front, and a car parked at the side. There was fencing dividing it from the house next door. Rose liked the look of it, and went and knocked on the door.

CHAPTER 17

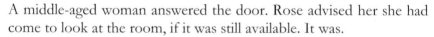

A middle-aged woman answered the door. Rose advised her she had come to look at the room, if it was still available. It was.

"Come in and I will show you," said the woman who was called Mrs Rothers. They went up a flight of stairs and into a room at the end. The room was a decent size and furnished with a bed, wardrobe, settee, television, fire, table and two chairs. There was a large window that overlooked the back garden, which was full of small shrubs and flowers, along with a washing line and prop. "The bathroom and kitchen are across the way. I have two other young ladies staying and they are both nurses, and do shift work. Now the television is rented and has a slot in the back, which takes shillings. Here is the meter for the electric, which again takes shillings. I will provide clean linen every Sunday. There is a laundromat round the corner for your other washing. In the cupboard at the top of the stairs you will find dusters, polish, carpet sweeper, iron and ironing board. I'm not a nosy person, and only when you are in, I do like to check that the rooms are clean and tidy. The dustbins for your rubbish are at the side of the house. The rent for the room is three pounds, and I will need a month's deposit. You will have a letter confirming all of this, which you and myself will sign. A couple of rules are, the door is bolted at 10pm every night, but unbolted at 6am when my husband goes to work, and under no circumstances are men to be brought back. I would also like the noise from the television or radio kept to a minimum. Naturally it would be appreciated if you kept as quiet as possible, especially after 6pm, as we have two young children. I never know when the other two ladies are in. I'll show you the bathroom and kitchen." Both rooms were small but adequate. Mrs Rothers advised her that if she needed a bath, to put the money in the meter to heat the water, but to make sure one of the other ladies didn't nip in. The toilet was separate to the bathroom. The kitchen was fully fitted, with cabinets, a gas oven and fridge. There was crockery in the cabinets along with cutlery. Again there was a meter for the gas. "Might be an idea to talk to the other two ladies about sharing the gas. Well my dear, let's go to my sitting room and you can tell me what you think."

Mrs Rothers and Rose went back downstairs. Rose noticed the house was spotless and quiet.

"Well Miss Brambles, would you like to move in?"

Rose replied, "I would like to Mrs Rothers, as I have just gained employment at the library for six months, but at the moment I am attending secretarial college in Wrinkton and don't finish for another two weeks. Would this cause you a problem?"

Mrs Rothers liked this young lady and replied, "I think we can come to an arrangement. If you have three pounds on you now, I will keep the room for you." Rose was delighted and did have three pounds, as she had taken some of her savings out, just in case. Mrs Rothers produced a contract and wrote Rose's name on it, and confirming she had paid a three pound deposit. Rose would pay the month's rent when she moved in.

"I hope you will be happy here Rose, and I look forward to seeing you in two weeks. Here is my telephone number in case you think of anything once you've got back to college." Rose thanked her and they shook hands. As Rose went to leave Mrs Rothers said, "Oh Rose, good luck with your college exams." Rose smiled and again thanked her. Rose walked back to the bus station with a smile on her face. The first person she saw back at the college was Will.

"Well, you look like the cat that got the cream," he said flashing her a lovely smile. Rose told him her news. "I'm so pleased for you Rose. I can't believe in two weeks we will be saying goodbye for ever."

Rose felt sad, but replied, "I know Will, but we do still have two weeks together. Are we all going out tonight?"

Will replied, "Of course. See you and Ruby at 7pm."

Ruby was in the dormitory revising when Rose walked in. "Rose, any luck?" Rose told her everything.

"Are you sure you can afford it Rose? Once you've paid your rent, electric, gas etc, that's not going to leave you much to live on."

Rose smiled and replied, "I have nearly twenty pounds saved, and I have the other savings book my uncle gave me, although I would rather not use any of that just yet. I can make sandwiches for my lunch instead of going out every day. Ruby I'll be fine, and if I'm not, well I'd rather not think about that. One thing I won't do is go home again." Ruby noticed the tone in Rose's voice and asked her what had happened. Rose went to her suitcase and got the envelope with the documents. "You know I told you I had been in my aunt's desk. This is a copy of the document from the orphanage." Ruby read it. Rose then said, "Yes I went to her desk again, and this time, along with that document, I found this."

Ruby paled as she read it. "That conniving bitch," she said. "Obviously your uncle doesn't know of this. Oh Rose, I really don't know what to say. I hope I never meet your aunt. Rose, what's wrong?" Rose had looked at the savings book her uncle had given her, and had totally forgotten it was in the name of Rose Clark. She showed it to Ruby. "I'm sure your uncle will change it for you. He thinks the world of you and must have forgotten."

Rose agreed and said, "Come on, we need to get changed, as it's nearly 6.30pm. The lads will wonder where we are."

The lads were all delighted for Rose.

"Ruby, you got anything lined up yet?" asked John. Ruby said she'd seen a couple of office jobs in the Birn newspaper and had applied. One was at a bank, the other a solicitor's office. As always they enjoyed a lovely meal and then went to the disco, and danced the night away. The next two weeks flew by, and they had sat their exams, and all passed. They had gone out and celebrated. At the disco that night, it was like the whole college was there, and it was one big party. The day came when they had to say goodbye to each other. It was a sad parting, and all of them had tears in their eyes. George had come to pick up Ruby and Rose, as Rose had a couple of free days before she went to Langmoth. She had phoned Mrs Rothers to let her know when she would arrive. She had also spoken to her uncle to let him know her news. He was pleased, but sad, as he wouldn't see her for six months. Rose told him she would see him some Saturdays.

"The three of us are going to miss you two so much," said Steve. "We have had an absolute ball this last six months, and now it's going to be ..."

Rose laughed and replied, "The three of you live in the same town. Are you seriously telling us that you're not going to get up to your usual antics after today?"

John replied, "Of course we will, but like you two, we have to find employment. Fun is great but not without money." The five of them hugged each other tight, and gave kisses on their cheeks, and wished each other well. The lads stood and watched as Rose and Ruby drove away, waving until they were well out of sight.

"Well I suppose we'd better catch our train home," said Will, and the principal who been watching them, saw three very upset young men walk away from the college.

The two days Rose spent at Ruby's, she hardly saw George and Monica, as an emergency was keeping them at the hospital.

"Rose, you will stay in touch, won't you?"

Rose took Ruby in her arms and hugged her, saying, "Ruby, of course I will. I won't come up every weekend, but I will come up as much as I can. I promise to ring you at least twice a week. There is no way in this world that I am going to neglect my "special" family. I love you all and that's a bond that will never be broken." Both of them ended up with tears running down their cheeks.

The day arrived for Rose to go to Langmoth. Alas, George and Monica were working, and Ruby had an interview at the solicitors in Birn. Rose only had a couple of suitcases, and George had booked and paid for a taxi for her. A little while later she was at Mrs Rothers. "Rose, lovely to see you. Your room is all ready for you. Here let me help you with one of your cases, oh and this came for you." Together they went up the stairs to her room. Suddenly two children, a boy and a girl, came running in.

"Hello," said the boy, "I'm Charlie and this is Katy."

Rose smiled and replied, "Hello, and I'm Rose."

Mrs Rothers collared the pair of them before they went to jump on the bed. "Downstairs, the pair of you. You know you're not allowed up here. Sorry about that Rose, let's just say it's one of those days." Rose replied it wasn't a problem.

"As promised Mrs Rothers, here is my month's rent," and handed over her twelve pounds.

"I will pop a receipt under your door Rose. If you need food, which I'm sure you do, there is a supermarket about two minutes down the road. In the kitchen the ladies have left you an empty cupboard for your use. If you need anything, please don't hesitate to pop down. Here are the keys to your room and the front door. Now I will leave you to unpack etc. Good luck at the library tomorrow," and with that Mrs Rothers left.

Rose unpacked her cases, but anything personal she left locked up in one of her cases. She didn't need to shop that night, as Monica had made sure she had the essentials. In a shopping bag were tea, coffee, sugar, carton of milk, bread, butter and cheese. In one plastic container were various sandwiches, and in another one, pieces of cake. Rose smiled to herself, and was already missing them. George had given her a bag of shillings, just in case she ran short!! She went into the kitchen to put her goods in the fridge. There was a note on the counter top, which said, *"Hi Rose. Middle rack in fridge is yours, as is middle cupboard. Welcome. Sara and Savannah."* Rose thought how nice that was. Once her things were put away, she made herself a drink and went back to her room. Sitting on the settee she opened the letter. She knew it was from her uncle as she recognised his writing. Inside were three five pound notes. Her uncle had written, *"I know I promised to let you find your own way, but I want to make sure your rent is at least paid for a couple of months. You can always pay me back when you're flush. Lots of love, Uncle xx"* Rose could only smile, as she couldn't be mad at him. She hid the money in her case, as hopefully she wouldn't need it. Time was getting on and she was feeling tired. She went and washed her mug up, dried it and put it away. Then she looked in the bathroom. The meter was nearly empty, so she put a shilling in, hoping the water wouldn't take ages to get warm. It didn't. She had a quick wash, went to the toilet, and then locked her door. She hadn't noticed it before, but there was a small cabinet at the side of the bed with a lamp and clock on it. She got into the bed, which was actually quite comfortable, read another couple of chapters of *The Three Musketeers*, and then turned the light out and slept.

Rose woke about 7am, washed, dressed and made herself a meal. She could faintly hear the children downstairs running around. About 8.45am, she left, locking her door, and then quietly went down the stairs and out of the front door. The sky was cloudy and it looked like rain, so she walked briskly to the library. Once inside she was met by a lady called Elsie Tuthers, who was going to show Rose what to do. Elsie was a small, plump lady, and dressed rather dowdy, but had a lovely personality. Rose spent the morning getting herself familiar with all the different categories of books, and where they were. In the end she drew a diagram and kept testing herself. There were lots of categories. As people arrived, their names were written in a book and a table allocated. There were thirty tables. A list of books were then given, and she would go with Elsie to get the books, and was then shown how to write them in the book, next to that person's name. As the books were returned, they were ticked off and only then replaced on the shelves. At lunchtime, another lady or gentleman came and took over. Elsie showed her the staff room, where she met other librarians. She had half an hour for lunch. Elsie pointed out various places to her, where she could buy sandwiches, have a quick meal, or shop. There was a park about five minutes away.

After lunch Rose was surprised to see so many books that needed putting away. Elsie explained most people left at lunchtime, and others would come in after lunch. Late afternoon students would arrive and then they were busy. At the end of the day, as long as all the books taken out had been returned, depending on the time, they could be stacked on a trolley to be put away the following morning. Rose had enjoyed her first day, but was worn out. On the way back to her room, she went and bought some groceries, and other things she needed. Back at the lodging house, there was another note for her in the kitchen from Savannah. *"Hi Rose. Not sure when we'll see you, as at the moment we are doing shift work - 6pm to 6am. With regards to the gas oven, we both put in two shillings a week. When it's emptied, if there's any over, we just put it back in. Hope you're happy with that. Seems to work fairly."* Rose was fine with that. Now she knew she would have the kitchen and bathroom to herself in the evenings. Tonight she was weary and couldn't be bothered to cook, so just had a drink and some of Monica's cake. She put five shillings in the television and sat down to watch whatever was on. The next thing she knew it was dark and 9pm! She washed up her dishes, had a quick wash and went to bed.

Over the next two weeks, Elsie stayed with Rose, and saw how quickly she was learning. The third week Elsie left Rose to it and only helped if she got really busy. After a month, Rose was on her own. She had telephoned Ruby and was delighted to hear she had been offered the employment in the solicitor's office. She had also spoken to her uncle at the bank, and he was pleased she had settled in so well, but if she decided to give it up, there was definitely a job for her in the bank.

CHAPTER 18

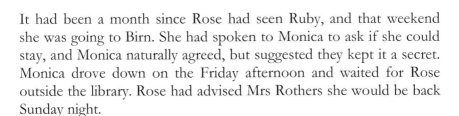

It had been a month since Rose had seen Ruby, and that weekend she was going to Birn. She had spoken to Monica to ask if she could stay, and Monica naturally agreed, but suggested they kept it a secret. Monica drove down on the Friday afternoon and waited for Rose outside the library. Rose had advised Mrs Rothers she would be back Sunday night.

"Rose, Rose," called Monica. Both of them hugged and kissed each other's cheeks. "Let me look at you. You look a bit tired, are you over doing it, or are you not eating?"

Rose smiled and said, "A bit of both, but honestly I'm fine. I can't wait to see Ruby."

"Then let's go," said Monica. Twenty minutes later they drove up to the house. "Stay in the kitchen Rose, and I'll see what's going on." George and Ruby were talking in the sitting room. Monica beckoned to Rose.

"Ruby you alright? You seem a bit down," asked George. "I'm fine Dad. I'm just missing Rose."

Rose put her head round the door and said, "Good job I'm here then."

Ruby jumped up and hugged Rose so tightly. "I have missed you so much. Are you here for the weekend?" asked Ruby. Rose replied she was. "Any chance of a hug for me?" said George. Rose naturally hugged him and kissed his cheek. Then Ruby and Rose went upstairs.

Both of them spent time telling each other what their jobs were like. Ruby also told Rose that a lad called Jake had asked her out.

"Oh Ruby, when are you going? Is it tonight or tomorrow?"

Ruby told Rose he had said he was busy this weekend, so the following Saturday, and they were going for a meal and then the cinema.

Rose raised her eyebrow and said cheekily, "Back row?"

Ruby playfully slapped her arm and blushed slightly and said, "Any good looking librarians?"

Rose laughed and replied, "You must be joking. Their all fuddy duddys."

Monica called up the stairs, "Girls, dinners ready." As they all sat round the kitchen table, Rose felt part of a family again. She hadn't realised how much she'd missed them. Monica, however, was watching Rose eat. She could see how much Rose was enjoying her meal and knew that she hadn't been eating properly. She would have a gentle word later on. After the meal they all sat in the sitting room discussing this and that.

"I know it's not warm enough yet, but do you two fancy a drive to the seaside tomorrow, and then no doubt some shopping afterwards?" asked George. Rose and Ruby said they would love to go, and so they did.

George and Ruby decided to go for a paddle, whilst Monica and Rose walked arm in arm along the promenade.

"Rose, I'm worried about you. You look tired, and you've lost weight. Is everything alright?"

Rose smiled at Monica and said, "I know, and you're right. I like the job but sometimes, especially after the library has closed, it's so busy, getting everything done, and by the time I get back to my room, I'm shattered. Most nights I sit down and fall asleep. I'm getting into a routine now, and things are changing. Thank you for caring," and Rose gave Monica a kiss on the cheek. They stood and watched George and Ruby running in and out of the sea, and laughed. Later on they were all enjoying fish and chips, in newspaper, sitting on a bench on the promenade. George then bought four hot coffees. The rest of the day they visited the shops, and then went home. Monica had to go grocery shopping. Rose and Ruby decided to go to a new disco that had opened in Birn. It was quite large inside, with plenty of tables and chairs, and the dance floor was bigger than the one in Wrinkton. The DJ was in a corner, and the glitter ball spun round and round. They both ordered a vodka and coke, and found a table. Within five minutes of them getting their drinks, two lads came up and asked them to dance. As it turned out, they spent the rest of the evening with them. The lads were called Clive and Paul, and both worked at an insurance company in Birn. They asked if they could all meet up the following weekend. Rose replied she was sorry but she wouldn't be there, and explained why. Ruby said she'd already made arrangements. As Rose and Ruby walked home, they were slightly tipsy, and they talked, laughed and giggled all the way.

The following morning, both of them had a slight headache, so out came the painkillers!! All of them had a late breakfast, and then relaxed until early afternoon, and then a late lunch. Soon it was time for Rose to go. Monica had offered to drive her. Rose packed and then said her goodbyes to George and Ruby.

"I want full details of your date," she whispered to Ruby, who blushed.

Monica drew up outside Rose's, and said, "Would you mind if I came in and had a look at your room?"

Rose replied, "No, of course not." Rose got her case, and Monica picked up a large box from the boot. Rose looked and raised her eyebrow. She was just about to ask Monica what it was when Mrs Rothers opened the door.

"Hello Rose. Did you have a lovely weekend?"' Rose replied it had been wonderful, and then introduced Monica. "Nice to meet you," said Mrs Rothers. Rose and Monica went up the stairs, and Rose unlocked her door.

"What a lovely room," said Monica, and Rose smiled, pleased that Monica liked it. "Now where's your kitchen?" In the kitchen, Monica put the box on top of the unit. "Which is your cupboard Rose?" Rose showed her, and then looked stunned. In the box were tins and tins of different things. "Heavens above ..." Rose stopped and looked at Monica. "I don't know what to call you now. Mr and Mrs Smith seems so formal, and George and Monica too personal." Monica smiled and said, "You have our blessings, if you want to, to call us "adopted" Mum and Dad. After all we look upon you as our second daughter. What do you think?"

"I think Mum and Dad, as long as Ruby's happy?"

Monica replied, "Ruby suggested it." Once the tins and other things had been put away, Rose and Monica went back downstairs. They hugged and kissed each other and Rose promised she would eat properly, and ring them.

"Bye ... Mum, and drive carefully." Monica waved and drove away with a happy tear in her eyes.

At the library the next day, Rose was introduced to a newcomer called Cliff. He was a handsome lad, slightly taller than Rose, and he had a lovely smile. Elsie said, "Cliff is going to be with you Rose for a couple of weeks only. After that he will be going to various parts of the library as he is studying to be a librarian." Over the next two weeks Rose and Cliff got on really well, and Cliff asked her out for a meal. Rose accepted, and phoned Ruby on the way home. Ruby's date with Jake had gone well and he had been a perfect gentleman, and now they were "dating." Rose was pleased for her. She hoped Cliff would be the same.

When she got home, she had the pleasure, at last, of meeting Savannah and Sara. Savannah was cooking, and asked Rose if she would like to join them. Rose said she would love to. They went into Sara's room, which Rose loved, and it gave her some ideas. The three of them got on really well, and before they realised it, it was midnight. Savannah told Rose they were back on nights the following day, so it would probably be another month or so, before they met up again. As soon as Rose's head hit her pillow, she was firm asleep. Rose and Cliff had made arrangements to meet at a restaurant at 7pm on the Saturday. Elsie had noticed Rose had a spring in her step and was happy for her. She had turned out to be a hard working young lady, and deserved something nice. On the Saturday Rose must have changed about four times. In the end she wore her flowery maxi dress, which showed her figure off. When Rose got to the restaurant she saw Cliff was already there, looking very handsome.

Cliff saw Rose and waved to her, and watched as she looked like she was gliding along the floor. To him she looked absolutely gorgeous. He stood up and gave her a kiss on her cheek, pulled her chair out for her and made sure she was comfortable. They had a lovely meal, and left about 9pm.

Walking along the pavement towards the centre of town he said, "Rose do you fancy going to a disco?"

Rose looked at her watch and replied, "I'm sorry Cliff, as much as I'd love to, the front door is bolted at 10pm, so I need to be back."

Cliff replied, without thinking, "That's not a problem, as you can bunk up with me at my place." Rose was taken aback.

Suddenly Cliff realised his mistake and said, "Oh no, no. Sorry Rose, I didn't mean together. I have a two bedroom flat on the other side of Langmoth. Naturally you would have the spare room. Please forgive me, as that came out all wrong."

Rose smiled and said, "It's alright Cliff, don't worry." They walked back to Rose's and Cliff asked if they could go out again. Rose said she would love to. As she went to go in, he caught her hand and said,

"May I kiss you goodnight?" Rose blushed slightly and said yes. Cliff took her in his arms, and gently kissed her lips. Rose had never kissed a man before, but remembered what Monica had told her, and parted her lips slightly. Cliff kissed her again, but this time with a slight urgency. Rose broke the kiss and moved away.

"Goodnight Rose. See you at the library. Enjoy the rest of your weekend." Rose kissed Cliff's cheek, and went inside. In her room she touched her lips, and they felt fuller. She liked the kiss, and hoped Cliff would give her more. That night she went to bed with a smile on her face.

Rose and Cliff saw each other every weekend. They would go for meals, have a picnic, the cinema, or take long walks along the riverside. They would spread a rug out on the grass and lay down. When Cliff thought nobody was looking, he would sit up and bend over Rose and kiss her. Rose would kiss him back. One day, Cliff borrowed his friend's car, and they drove out to a secluded picnic area. Cliff had brought a bottle of wine with him, so as they ate, they sipped a glass of wine. It was a hot sunny day, and Rose had put on shorts and a long loose blouse. Cliff had shorts and t-shirt on. Rose laid back on the rug and stretched, feeling contented. Cliff took all of her in and wanted Rose badly. He bent over and kissed her, and Rose responded, linking her arms round his neck. Cliff could feel her breasts rise up as she linked her arms round him. Cliff kept kissing her, and slowly pushed his tongue into her mouth. Rose jumped but only slightly. Rose was in another world, and hadn't realised Cliff had undone her bra and was kissing and kneading her breasts. His thumb went over her nipples and they went hard. She was enjoying his touch. Slowly Cliff moved his hand down over her stomach and started to put it down her shorts. Rose stopped him straight away.

"No Cliff. I haven't known you long enough. I'm sorry." Rose sat up, re-clipped her bra, and pulled her blouse down.

"It's alright Rose. I understand. I have no intentions of rushing you. I need to pee, so I'll just pop behind that bush." Rose saw the bulge in his shorts, and knew he wasn't going to pee. He was going to relieve himself. When she heard him groaning, she knew she was right. She packed up the picnic stuff, and put the basket back in the car. When Cliff returned she looked at him, and said gently,

"I'm sorry you had to do that Cliff, but we've only been seeing each other for about a month. I hope you're not upset with me?"

Cliff responded by gently kissing her lips, and said, "Some things are worth waiting for."

Rose had now done three months at the library and had got to know who the regular ones were. They would nod and smile and mouth a silent "morning" or "goodbye." With it now being summer, the library got quiet. Rose found she was getting bored. Some days only one or two people would turn up, and consequently the days dragged. She still saw Cliff at the weekends, and she knew he wanted to take their relationship further, but Rose didn't want to. She had phoned Ruby every weekend, and Ruby had told her she had finished with Jake. He had started getting possessive and she didn't like it. As luck would have it, Jake had decided to move to London and wanted Ruby to go with him, but she said "No". Rose had written to her uncle every month, but was missing talking to him, so one lunchtime she rang him.

"Oh Rose, it's so lovely to hear your voice. How are things going?"

Rose replied, "I've enjoyed the library uncle, but now I'm getting bored," and explained why.

"Rose, are you going to Ruby's at the weekend?" Rose replied she wasn't. "Can I come and pick you on Saturday, about 10am, as I have something to show and discuss with you?" Rose said she would love to see him. Saturday arrived and Hugh picked her up, and they drove back to Fracton. Rose noticed new shops had been built and Fracton was expanding as a town. A thought went through her head. Maybe she could find a job and accommodation in Fracton.

First of all they went to the bank, and Rose noticed that the building had been expanded. Hugh drove past the bank and then turned right up a lane, which was wide enough for a small van to drive up. At the top was a large area, where any vehicle could turn around or be parked. High brick walls, and no windows, surrounded the whole area, but outside the back of the bank, there were two doors. Hugh unlocked one of the doors and took her to one of the offices that was stacked high with files.

"As you know Rose, three months ago we started the age of decimalisation. Some of the coins became currency ages ago, like the 1 and 2 shilling coins which were replaced by the new 5p and 10p, and the new seven sided 50p piece replaced the ten shilling note. The large banks in the cities coped by closing for five days, but small towns like Fracton were left to fend on their own. We were doing well until a month ago. I received a letter from Head Office, saying that two small village branches were being closed, and all the accounts were being transferred here. Hence the bank has been made bigger, as we needed more space. I need someone I can trust, to take charge of all the accounts. All the cheques cleared in pound shillings and pence need to be converted to decimal. All coins need to be checked, and those that are now obsolete need to be put aside, to be sent to London. The only old coin being kept at the moment is the sixpence. Rose, if you want the job, it's yours." Rose was surprised at this offer, but it would mean moving back to Rilford, which she didn't want to do, so she thanked her uncle and asked if she could think about it. She didn't want to let the library down. Hugh smiled and replied, "Of course my dear, but there is something else I need to show you."

CHAPTER 19

They went out of the bank, and Hugh locked it. Then he unlocked the other door. After they had gone up some steps, he unlocked another door, which to her amazement opened up into a large airy one bedroomed flat. There was a sitting room, bedroom, separate furnished kitchen, and separate bathroom. The kitchen and bathroom had lino on the floors, whilst the sitting room and bedroom had blue carpet. The kitchen and sitting room overlooked the high street, whilst the bedroom and bathroom overlooked the back lane. In the sitting room was also a telephone.

"This comes with the job Rose. I know you have another three months to go, but if you're getting bored, please promise me you will think about it. I would love to see you every day. Should you want the telephone connected, let me know." Rose was seriously thinking of it, now she'd seen the flat. They went back down the stairs, locking the doors. "Now my dear, how about lunch at that nice little country pub we have been to before?" Rose replied she would love it.

After lunch, they went for a walk and chatted, and then Hugh drove Rose back to Langmoth. "Don't forget to think about my offer Rose. Enjoy your day tomorrow." Rose kissed Hugh's cheek, and promised she would. Back in her room it was the only thing she thought of. A flat all to herself, and she knew the bank wages would be good. It would also mean she would be near Ruby and her mum and dad.

On the Monday, the chief librarian called Rose to her office. "Please Rose, come in and sit down. I have some news to tell you, but first of all I must say how well you have fitted in here, and your work has been excellent. Alas, the news is that Mrs Turnball, who you have been standing in for, has contacted me and wants to return to her position as soon as she can. This means, and I'm sorry to say, I will have to let you go, but not for five weeks. I hope this will give you time, if you decide to stay in Langmoth, to gain other employment."

Rose replied, "Thank you for telling me, and my uncle has a job for me, for when I leave. Would Mrs Turnbull like to come back at the beginning of next month, as that would be fine with me, but I am more than happy to stay on for the extra five weeks?"

The chief librarian replied, "I'm happy to do whatever you decide Rose. I just didn't want to see you out of a job. Have a word with your uncle and your landlady, and let me know your decision soon." Rose thanked her left. There was nobody in the room, and all the books had been put away. At lunchtime she had made her mind up. Now all she had to do was tell Cliff.

When she got home that evening, she tapped on Mrs Rothers door.

"Hello Rose, everything alright?"

"May I have a word please Mrs Rothers?" Mrs Rothers showed her into the sitting room. Rose then explained she would like to leave at the end of the week, but was more than happy to pay the following month's rent, so Mrs Rothers wouldn't be out of pocket.

"Bless you Rose, that was nice of you to offer me a month's rent, but it won't be needed. You have been an excellent tenant, and I will give you a reference for the future. I will be sorry to see you go, but I wish you all the best for the future." Rose would be sorry to leave, but in a roundabout way it had worked out well, as she wanted to finish with Cliff. At work the following day, she told the chief librarian her decision, who accepted her decision. Lunchtime, she went and phoned her uncle, who was delighted, and said he would pick her up Saturday morning. Rose had looked for Cliff, but didn't see him, so she asked Elsie.

"Oh, didn't he tell you Rose. He's gone to a library in London for a couple of weeks."

Rose replied, "No he didn't tell me. Elsie I'm leaving on Friday, as Mrs Turnbull is returning earlier than expected. I have no way of contacting Cliff, so please could you say goodbye to him for me?"

Elsie replied, "So she's coming back, that's a shame. I was hoping she wouldn't and they would offer you the job. Oh well, never mind. Of course I'll tell Cliff. I know he's fallen for you and he'll be heartbroken." Rose felt guilty and Elsie saw it in her eyes. "Hey now, don't you go blaming yourself. He will be fine." Rose smiled and went back to her desk.

The week flew by, and each night she started packing things away. Rose decided not to tell Ruby, but keep it as a surprise. Saturday arrived, as did Hugh. Rose had put per cases and boxes down by the door. She stripped the bed, and folded up the sheet, blankets and pillowcases, and put them on the bed, cleaned and polished the room, and put the carpet sweeper over the carpet. She made sure her cupboard in the kitchen was clean as well. She hadn't seen Sara or Savannah, but left them a note. As Hugh put her cases and boxes in the car, Rose gave Mrs Rothers her keys back, and thanked her. Mrs Rothers actually hugged her. Rose had introduced her uncle, who also thanked her for looking after his niece. Mrs Rothers said it had been a pleasure. As Hugh said goodbye, he pressed something into her hand. Once she had waved them off she opened her hand, and was stunned to see it was twenty pounds. A small note said, "So you won't be out of pocket. Thank you." Soon they were at Rose's new flat, and they unloaded the car and put everything in the sitting room.

Hugh said, "I'm so pleased your here. Now one thing I didn't tell you about was your wages. You will receive twenty-five pounds a week, less five pounds for the flat. There are gas and electric meters in the cupboard at the top of the stairs. Your hours will be 8.30am until 5pm, with half hour lunch. Now we need to go furniture shopping, or else you'll be sleeping on the floor."

A couple of hours later, because Hugh was well known, the furniture men arrived with two single beds, two wardrobes, a dressing table, small tables and lamps for the bedroom, along with pillows, sheets, blankets and pillowcases. A settee, two armchairs, standard lamp, cabinets, small tables, net curtains, a larger table and four chairs, for the sitting room. Toaster, kettle, pots and pans, crockery and cutlery for the kitchen. Various other items had been bought as well, along with grocery shopping. Hugh had paid for all of it, as he knew Rose couldn't afford it all in one go, and it was his pleasure to do it. He loved Rose, and as far as he was concerned, Rose really was his niece. Rose told him she would pay him back out of her wages.

Hugh just smiled. "My dear, I will leave you now, as Nancy will be wondering where I am. I will see you Monday morning. If you look out of your bedroom window I usually arrive between 8 and 8.15am. Come down and I will let you in the back door. Here are the two keys and a bag of change for the meters."

Rose hugged Hugh and said, "I really don't know how to thank you uncle, but I will work really hard, and won't let you down. I assume aunt doesn't know I'm here?"

Hugh just replied, "I'll tell her when I'm ready," and with that he left. Rose looked round the flat. In the kitchen, under the work surface, she saw something and pulled it out. It was a twin tub, and it looked brand new. *Uncle,* she thought. Rose then started sorting everything out. When she'd finished she was shattered, but the bed was made, the net curtains and normal curtains up at the sitting room and bedroom windows. She had filled up the meters and decided to have a relaxing bath, before she cooked herself a meal. Before any of that though, she was going to phone Ruby.

After a good night's sleep, Rose had her favourite breakfast of toast and boiled eggs. About 10am she rushed down the steps, out of the door and round the corner, where Ruby was stood outside the bank.

"Ruby," she called. Ruby turned and went and hugged her. "I have a surprise for you, so follow me," said Rose.

"This flat is yours?" said Ruby stunned. Rose made them both a drink, which they took into the sitting room, and she told Ruby everything. "So you're here permanently. Yes, I've got my sister back. Mum and Dad are going to be so pleased."

Rose said, "I have another surprise for you. Come and look." She took Ruby into the bedroom. "You can stay overnight as well, so if we go out, you don't have to get a bus or taxi back home."

Ruby replied, "This is the best day ever." Later on Rose made a meal, which they enjoyed, whilst listening to the radio. Rose was going to see how much it was to rent a television. Time came for Ruby to return home. Rose promised she would ring her in the week. Rose walked Ruby to the bus station and waved as she left. On the way back Rose noticed a doctor's surgery. She really needed to go and get the pill to help her stomach cramps. Then a name above an office made a chill go through her. It was her aunt's solicitors!! She shrugged it off and carried on. She saw the shop where she could rent a television, the grocer's, butcher's and other shops. Back in her flat, she relaxed on the settee and finished her book *The Three Musketeers*, which she had enjoyed.

Rose was up washed, dressed and had eaten when she saw her uncle drive in. She went down the stairs, locking both doors. "Morning uncle."

Hugh smiled and kissed her cheek. "All settled in Rose?" he asked. Rose replied she was. "Rose, whilst we are in the bank, I'm afraid you will have to address me as Mr Brambles, and I will have to call you Miss Brambles. Head Office ruling. There is also a dress code. The men have to wear grey suits, with white shirts, grey ties, socks and shoes. The ladies have to wear grey skirts, which must not be above the knee, white blouses, grey cardigans, grey shoes and umm ... grey stockings."

Rose replied, "I will go and change uncle, but I don't have a grey cardigan or stockings."

Hugh replied, "For today you are smart enough my dear. Now it's coming up 8.15am and I must let the staff in and introduce you." Hugh and Rose walked through to the front of the bank. Rose looked round whilst Hugh opened the side door. As people entered, there was a long counter in front of them, split into divisions with a separate teller behind a glass division. The money and coins were passed underneath the glass. There were large ledgers at the side of each teller. Rose counted eight positions. There was a reception desk, some large settees and armchairs for the clients. At the side were four private offices, of which one belonged to the deputy manager. To get to the other offices, including her uncle's and hers, you had to go through another door between two walled off partitions. There was also a staff room, kitchen and toilets. The bank's vault was down some steps by the back door, to which her uncle and the deputy manager had to unlock together.

Rose watched as her new colleagues walked in. There were twelve men and eight ladies. They all looked at Rose. Rose lowered her eyes, not sure where to look.

"Good morning ladies and gentlemen," said her uncle.

They all replied, "Good morning Mr Brambles."

Hugh then said, "As you can see we have a new employee, called Miss Brambles. Yes she is my niece, and will be helping to sort out the client accounts. Miss Brambles has also taken over the flat above the bank. Any questions?" Everyone shook their heads. "Very well, five minutes to your positions. Miss Fothers will you please show Miss Brambles what she has to do?"

"Yes Mr Brambles." Everyone went to the staff room and put their handbags or whatever in a numbered locker. They then all put name badges on. Rose felt better seeing that, as it would help her remember their names.

"What's your first name Miss Brambles?" asked Miss Fothers.

"It's Rose."

"Welcome Rose. I am Mary and you won't remember them all, but I'll quickly run through everyone's names. This is Kathleen, Deborah, Barbara, Irene, Lynda, Karen and Susan. These are Larry, Daniel, Peter, Michael, Thomas, Bruce, Terry, Chris, Brian, Walter, Philip and Donald. The deputy manager is Stanley Fanterton." A buzzer went and everyone left. "That buzzes at 8.30am so the bank is ready for the first clients. It buzzes again at 4pm for the bank's closure. Come and I'll show you your office."

Rose had an office opposite the kitchen.

"Did Mr Brambles explain what had to be done?" Rose replied he had. "Then I shall leave you to start. If you need me I will be next door, and make a drink whenever you want to. There are three of us in this section, and that's Peter, Chris, and myself. Lunch is from noon to 2pm, and we do it in rotation. What lunch would you like?"

Rose replied, "I will fit in with the rest of you, as I'm the newcomer."

Mary replied, "You alright to do 1pm to 1.30pm and I'll do 1.30pm to 2pm." Rose was happy with that. Mary left her, and Rose started looking through the files. *Well,* she thought, *let's get this into some sort of alphabetical order first.* By lunchtime she was only halfway through the "A's." Mary popped in to see how she was getting on. Rose explained what she was doing.

"One good thing is that all the cheques are now in alphabetical order. Let me know when you need them. May I make a suggestion?

Once you have all the "A's" in order, start changing those accounts, instead of waiting to do it all at the end. Less boring." Rose thanked her and went off for her lunch. Firstly she went to the doctor's surgery to make an appointment. The receptionist gave her a form to fill in, and an appointment was made with Doctor Kerris, a female doctor, for lunchtime on Wednesday. Then she rushed up to her flat and made a sandwich and a drink. Spot on 1.30pm she was back at her desk. Soon it was 4pm and she heard the buzzer go. She found out that the next hour all the tellers had to add up their ledgers, and make sure what they had in their tills agreed to their ledgers. At 4.55pm, Mary told Rose it was time to pack up and go, as Mr Brambles locked the bank up at 5pm sharp. Rose tidied her desk and left with the rest of them. Her uncle said goodnight to them all, and smiled at Rose.

CHAPTER 20

———————～———————

Rose had enjoyed her first day. Instead of going to her flat, she went to the television shop. The assistant showed her various televisions, and Rose found one she liked. It was a twenty inch black and white television, and came with a four legged stand. It would cost seven pounds fifty pence for the first three months, which must be paid in advance. Afterwards it would be two pounds fifty pence a month. It would be rented on a minimum of twelve months, but if Rose decided to change it for a colour television, she could do so at anytime, but a lot higher rental. If she decided to keep it longer, the rental would drop slightly. Should the set breakdown, it would either be repaired or replaced at no charge to her. Rose was happy and it was arranged for delivery on Saturday morning about 10am. Next she went to the shoe shop to get some grey shoes for work. After they were bought, she went to a clothes shop and got white blouses, grey skirts and cardigans. Mary said the grey stockings were only needed in winter. Normal stockings were alright. Rose's funds were getting low, but she had enough food etc until payday on Friday. The rest of the week went by quickly for Rose. As everyone left for the weekend, the deputy manager gave them their pay packets. Rose only saw her uncle at the end of each day, as she decided it would be better if she entered and left the bank, the same as her colleagues. Friday night she phoned Ruby and asked her if she wanted to come over and stay. Ruby jumped at the chance, and said she would be there Saturday morning.

Ruby showed up about fifteen minutes after the television arrived. They decided to relax and catch up with each other for the rest of the day, and then later on they would go to the new disco that had opened about six months ago. For lunch they just had sandwiches, but for dinner they had fish and chips. About 9pm they made their way to the disco. Rose and Ruby had to queue to get in, which surprised them. Inside it was very much like the disco at Wrinkton, except it was twice as big, as was the dance floor. The only lights were those shining on two small glitter balls. The place was packed, but after eventually getting a drink, they found a table and sat down. Rose always smiled when she saw groups of women dancing round their handbags, which were on the floor. Rose and Ruby had small shoulder bags, and the strap went across their chests. Quite a few men asked them to dance and they enjoyed themselves. On the Sunday, they had a late breakfast, and Ruby told Rose how she was enjoying her position at the solicitors, plus the fact she was learning a lot about laws.

Rose smiled and said, "Who knows, one day you might be my solicitor."

Ruby replied, "Not a chance. It is a very man orientated business. Secretary would be as high as I could go, but who knows what the future will bring."

Soon Christmas would be arriving, and this would be Rose's first Christmas in her flat. She decided to ask Monica, George and Ruby over for Christmas lunch. Naturally, she asked her uncle, but he had to decline as Nancy had already made arrangements. Christmas Day arrived and about 11am, Monica, George and Ruby drove up and parked behind the bank.

"Oh Rose this is a lovely flat, and you've made it so cosy," said Monica hugging her and kissing her cheek.

George did the same and said, "If ever you want a flat sitter, I'm your man," and everyone laughed. Rose made them all a drink, and they sat in the sitting room catching up on each other's news. A bit later on, Rose started doing the lunch. Monica offered to help but Rose said she was her guest, and to just relax. Rose had already laid the table in the sitting room, and now she brought the meal in. One large dish had mixed vegetables, and another had roast potatoes. Each plate had a chicken breast with stuffing, and two Yorkshire puddings. Lastly she put a large jug of gravy on the table.

"Tuck in everyone, and I hope you enjoy it," said Rose. As they ate so they laughed and joked about various things.

"Rose, that was absolutely delicious," said George, and Monica and Ruby agreed.

"Hope you've left room for afters?" said Rose. She cleared the table and then brought in a large Christmas pudding, with a jug of custard, and a pot of cream.

"I can't eat another thing," said Ruby.

"Right," said George, "Rose cooked the meal, so we will wash and dry."

"Oh no you won't," said Rose, "I can do that when you've gone, hopefully a lot later on."

After they had all relaxed and watched the Queen's speech on the television, George went down to the car, and came back carrying a large box.

"This is for you Rose, and a Merry Christmas," said Monica. Rose undid the parcel to find a set of three casserole dishes.

"Oh thank you, it's just what I wanted. I was actually going to get some next week. I assume a little bird told you?' and smiled at Ruby. "We also have this for you as well Rose, and happy birthday from all of us." Rose opened a small box to find a dropped pearl necklace and matching earrings.

Rose welled up and had tears in her eyes, and said, "What on earth did I do to deserve such a wonderful family as you?"

Monica replied, "You have always and will always be our second daughter Rose, and all three of us love you very much." Rose couldn't hold back the tears that now fell down her face, and all of them hugged her.

"I have something for you too," said Rose, and vanished into her bedroom. When she returned, she gave each of them a present. She had bought Monica a sewing unit, which pulled out into various trays, and she could carry it around with her. George had his favourite tobacco, along with a new pipe, and Ruby a bracelet. They all loved their presents. Rose went and made a pot of coffee, and they settled down to watch the television again. Soon it was time for Monica, George and Ruby to go.

"Now we will see you New Year's Eve. Come as early as you like, as this year we are staying home. We can have nibbles and things and see the New Year in together. You will stay the night won't you Rose?" said Monica. Rose said she would, and so they all hugged and kissed each other, and Rose waved as they drove down the lane, until they turned onto the main road. Rose had had a lovely day, and once she had washed and put away all the dishes, she decided to have a nice long soak in the bath. The following day Rose just relaxed and did very little except read, eat and watch the television.

The following day Rose was back at work, but with it being holidays, the bank was quiet. The day before New Year's Eve, her uncle had advised everybody that the bank would close at 2pm. To their surprise, when they entered the kitchen there was food and drink laid out on the table.

Hugh arrived and said, "Just a little something to wish you all a Happy New Year, and here's to another prosperous year." Wine was poured out into plastic cups and everyone toasted to a new year. They all stayed for an hour and then left. Rose stayed on to tidy up and she could talk to her uncle. Hugh told her about his Christmas and Rose told him about her's. Hugh wished he could have been with her, and her family, as she called then now, but at no point was he jealous of this fact. He was in fact delighted.

"Rose I wasn't sure what to buy you for your Christmas and birthday presents, but I hope you will accept my gift when it arrives next week."

Rose replied, "Uncle you have bought me so much, how on earth can I repay you? I love you dearly but it doesn't seem enough."

Hugh took Rose in his arms and kissed her forehead, and said, "You are the light in my dull life, and to see you every day, is a dream come true. I wish I could do more for you."

Rose had never felt so humbled, and held him tightly in her arms, and said, "Don't ever forget uncle, I love you very much." Hugh asked her is she was off to Ruby's and she replied she was. At Ruby's it was just as Monica said. A lovely time just relaxing and enjoying each other's company. They toasted in the New Year and sang "Auld Lang Syne." Hugh's present arrived a couple of days after the New Year - it was a coloured television, and all paid for, so no more rentals to pay. Hugh had sorted it out with the television shop.

Over the next six months Rose finished changing all the clients' accounts. Now she would have to find another job, and flat. During these six months, Ruby had found herself a flat in Birn, and both of them had learnt to drive, so they took turns, not every weekend, to stay with each other. With George's help they both found a second-hand car they liked and George and Hugh paid for each one. Rose had a yellow mini, and Ruby a red mini. Rose parked her mini at the back of the bank. Both of them would spend one weekend a month with Monica and George. It now also gave them the freedom to drive to various other places, especially towns for different shopping. A couple of weeks before Rose was due to finish, she was called to her uncle's office. Hugh smiled when she walked in, and had noticed she had blossomed into a beautiful woman, as had Ruby.

"Please take a seat my dear. First of all a huge thank you for all the work you have done, which I must say is excellent. Even Mr Fanterton has praised your work. Secondly, as you know four of the staff have left, and I really need someone to take the position of Client Accounts Officer. It would entail double checking all the ledgers and tills after the bank closes, sorting out any discrepancies, keeping the clients' accounts up to date, and it would also take you into the world of investments. In other words you would be head of that section. You will have the office next to Mr Fanterton, so you can keep an eye on what's going on.

"Head Office has insisted that all the tellers must now have a buzzer installed by their tills, so if any problems arise, the buzzer will go off in your office, and you can hopefully help out. I wondered if you would like the position?"

Rose replied, "Oh uncle, oops, Mr Brambles, I would love to accept the position, but only if I'm not treading on anyone else's toes."

Hugh smiled and replied, "You can call me uncle when we are alone my dear, and as to the position, it would have been offered to Mary, who left last week. Your wages, after three months, would rise to thirty pounds a week less the five pounds for the flat. If you want to ask the staff if they have any objections please do so." Rose happily accepted the position. Now she knew she was staying longer, she asked her uncle if it would be possible to have the telephone connected in the flat. Hugh said he would see to it. "Rose, I don't like to pry, but are you alright for funds. I noticed you haven't taken anything from your savings book?"

Rose replied, "Sorry uncle, I haven't touched it because I can't."

Hugh raised an eyebrow, and said, "What do you mean you can't?"

Rose replied, "Because it's in the name of Rose Clark."

Hugh was mortified. "Oh Rose, I'm an idiot. Why on earth didn't you tell me earlier?"

Rose smiled and said, "I just wanted to keep it safe, until I really needed it, and so far I've managed." Hugh told Rose to bring the book to him and he would get it amended. Rose took it the following day, and Hugh had the name changed. When nobody was looking, Rose quickly kissed his cheek.

That morning, in the kitchen, she asked the rest of the staff if they were happy for her to take the position. She could see they were all genuinely happy for her, and thanked them. A week later, as she entered the bank Mr Fanterton spoke to her.

"Miss Brambles, I'm delighted you are joining us at front of office. This office is yours and if you need anything, please don't hesitate to ask me, especially when you start learning about investments. I will leave you to settle in." Rose thanked him and sat at her new desk. She had a clear view of all the tellers, and the general public. She decided she could sit and people watch all day, but she had work to do. A short while later teller number two's buzzer went off. Rose went immediately to Kathleen's position.

"Can I help Miss Brown?"

Kathleen replied, "This is Mrs Strocken, and she has advised me that there is a problem with her current account." Rose walked from behind the counter, and went to Mrs Strocken.

"Good morning Mrs Strocken, I am Miss Brambles. If you would care to join me in my office, I'm sure we can rectify the matter." Once in Rose's office, Rose excused herself, whilst she went to get the account. Back in her office Rose asked Mrs Strocken what the problem was. "You have deducted a cheque out of my account for one hundred pounds. I certainly did not write out a cheque to that amount. You have obviously taken someone else's cheque out of my account, and this is unacceptable." After looking through the account, Rose found the entry and then looked through the cheque folder. Much to her relief, she found the cheque, and presented it to Mrs Strocken.

"That is not my writing," replied Mrs Strocken. Rose asked her politely if it was her signature. Mrs Strocken confirmed it was, then after a couple of seconds said, "My apologies Miss Brambles, I seem to have wasted your valuable time. Now I see who the cheque is made out to, I will be having words with my granddaughter."

Rose replied smiling, "It has been my pleasure and I'm pleased we have resolved the problem." As Rose went to walk Mrs Strocken to the door, her uncle approached them.

"I hope everything is alright Mrs Strocken?"

"It is now thanks to this delightful lady. A credit to your bank Mr Brambles," and with that walked out of the bank. Back in her office Hugh explained that Mrs Strocken was a very wealthy woman, who had all her funds and investments at the bank. Alas, she had a very cunning granddaughter, who tried to take as much money from her as she could. "One thing Mrs Strocken is not, is stupid," said Hugh. About a month later, Hugh was in Mr Fanterton's office. "Tell me something Hugh, is it my imagination or do we seem to have a lot more gentlemen taking out accounts? They seem to have arrived since your niece came onto the floor."

Hugh smiled and replied, "Quite a good plan don't you think Stanley?" Both men just smiled at each other.

CHAPTER 21

Over the next two years, life carried on as normal for Rose, who was now twenty-one years old. She loved her new job, and got on really well with the other employees. Staff had changed over the years, and apart from a couple, new staff were now employed. There was one man, however, who had only joined about three months before, who seemed to have taken a dislike to her. Why she had no idea. One day as she was about to enter the kitchen, first thing, she overheard him talking to the others.

"Oh come on, are you all stupid? She's the boss's niece, and I think she spies on us, and if we make a mistake, she goes running off to uncle to tell him."

A female voice replied, "I think you're the stupid one. I've been here over a year now, and Miss Brambles has gone out of her way to show me how things must be done correctly. She certainly hasn't gone tittle-tattling to Mr Brambles. Stop trying to stir trouble Mr Cooper, or I will be obliged to say something."

The man replied nastily, "Oh yeah. Try it." At that moment Rose walked in.

"Morning everyone. I hope you all had a pleasant evening. Looks like we have a queue outside the bank, so if any of you need me, please just ask. Enjoy your day." Rose watched this Mr Cooper, who stared at her. Rose just carried on with her work, and didn't give him another thought.

Sometimes when Ruby stayed over, both of them would go to the disco. They had met and dated quite a few of the young men, but nothing serious. They had remained friends with them, and would often dance the night away with them. Nothing was expected at the end of the night. One night as Rose and Ruby were up dancing on their own, and keeping an eye on their jackets, which were on the seats by the table, Rose heard a female voice, at the side of her say,

"Now that's what I call talent." Rose casually glanced round to see five very handsome men walk in. She caught Ruby's eye, who looked and mouthed, "Phoar." They were all about six foot tall, short hair, and looked very fit. When the record finished, Rose told Ruby she needed the ladies, so Ruby went back to the table. In the toilets, there was a queue! Rose was worried Ruby would think she'd got lost. At last she got in the cubicle, and knew all the other ladies had gone.

She heard the door open and a voice started saying, "Now if we play our cards right Gloria, we can have all five of them. Hitch your skirt up a bit higher, and unbutton your blouse and show them great tits off. Just think what we can make. Now gotta pee."

Rose raised her eyebrow, and out of curiosity she had to see who these females were. As she was washing her hands, the two women came out of the cubicles. They were long legged blondes, and their skirts were so short you could just see the bottom of their buttocks. Rose came to the conclusion neither of them had briefs on!! Both were big breasted, and the blouses were undone to halfway down their chests, so their breasts were spilling out of their lift up bras. They were touching up their hair and make-up when Rose left. When she got back to Ruby she told her.

Ruby replied, "I bet they're prostitutes, and they're after those hunks." They watched as the women came onto the dance floor, and danced extremely provocatively at the five men, who were stood by the bar. Rose and Ruby giggled at their antics. The men didn't even bother looking at them, but two of them were looking at Rose and Ruby.

Rose had her back to the men, so when Ruby said, "I think we're being eyed up," Rose turned, and looked into the most gorgeous pair of blue eyes she had ever seen. It was like there was nobody else in the room, except the two of them. Suddenly she felt herself blushing and turned away, and her heart was beating so fast. She sipped her drink and looked at Ruby, who was also a deep red. It was coming up midnight, and time for the slow records to come on. The two leggy blondes were still trying to get these men's attention, and thought they had succeeded when the one with the blue eyes, and another, walked towards them.

"May we have this dance please ladies?" Rose and Ruby couldn't believe they were asking them. The one with the blue eyes held his hand out to Rose, who took it. Ruby went with the other one, who had deep brown dreamy eyes. "My name is Jean-Paul Pascal, but my men call me JP."

"I'm Rose ...... Rose Brambles. From your accent I take it you are French?" JP replied he was. Rose was all of a to do. She was dancing in this gorgeous stranger's arm and felt like she was melting. She had never felt like this before. It only seemed like seconds later when the DJ announced it was the last dance of the evening, and "goodnight."

JP took Rose's hand and kissed the back of it saying, "I hope I'll see you again soon Rose." JP and his friend returned to the others and left. Rose and Ruby sat down, both daydreaming.

"Come on ladies, you got no home to go to?" asked the barman collecting the dirty glasses.

Back at the flat, Rose said, "I think I've gone to heaven."

Ruby replied, "You and me both. Weren't they gorgeous, and they danced with us? Do you think we'll see them again?"

Without thinking Rose replied dreamily, "Oh god I do hope so. Did I just say that out loud?" Both of them burst out laughing.

"What was your dreamboat called? Mine was JP, short for Jean-Paul Pascal."

Ruby replied, "Antoine Gílle. Apparently they're over from Paris. He wouldn't say why, and I was too busy trying not to drool. He did say JP was their leader."

Rose said laughing, "Well JP can lead me any day. Come on, it's 2am, time to sleep."

Ruby replied, "You seriously think either of us are going to sleep?" They did and woke up at 10am on Sunday morning. Rose was up first, and after a quick wash, started cooking a late breakfast. Ruby woke to the smells of bacon, sausages, and coffee. After a wash, Ruby went into the kitchen.

"Need a hand Rose?" Rose shook her head, and handed her a tray.

On it was a plate with bacon, sausage, tomatoes and eggs. A mug of coffee and two pieces of toast, with butter and jam. Both of them sat at the table in the sitting room and chatted about the night before.

Ruby said, "Do you think they'll be at the disco next Saturday?"

Rose replied cheekily, "Ah does that mean you'll be staying next weekend?"

Ruby slapped her playfully and said, "If I know they'll be there, then yes I'm asking to stay next weekend." Rose laughed.

During the week Rose was busy in the bank, as that weekend it was Easter. Ruby was arriving late Friday afternoon, so that gave Rose plenty of time to get all her jobs done. On the Saturday they decided to drive to the town of Swethers, and found a great boutique, with all the latest fashions. Both of them bought plain and pleated mini-skirts, long coloured skirts, blouses, shorts and t-shirts, and button through shirt dresses. They then went to a shoe shop and with summer coming, bought sandals. Happy with their purchases, they found a cafe and had some lunch. Later on, in their new mini skirts and blouses they went off to the disco. Rose looked round but didn't see JP and his friends. On the dance floor they were joined by John and Jack, who they had dated, but nothing serious, and were busy chatting and dancing, that they didn't see JP and his men arrive. A couple of slower dances were being played, and John and Rose, Ruby and Jack were dancing closely.

Antoine spotted Ruby, and said to JP, "Look, there's Ruby and Rose."

As JP turned, so the smile left his face, and he said curtly, "They look to be busy with their boyfriends, so leave them be. After all we aren't here long, so better not to get involved." His men were surprised at that remark.

One of them said dryly, "There are more fish in the sea, take your pick." JP knocked back his drink and told them he was leaving. If they wanted to stay - fine. They all drank up and left. Ruby suddenly caught sight of Antoine as he went out the door. Looking at Rose she told her. Rose was disappointed but didn't understand. They could have said "hello."

Rose and Ruby carried on dancing, but deep down they were sad. *Oh well,* thought Rose, *no need to cry over spilt milk.* The following day they just lazed around, but on the Monday, as it was a lovely sunny day, they decided to drive out of Fracton to the countryside pub they'd found, and went quite often.

"Rose, Ruby," said Harold, the owner, "Lovely to see you both again. I assume you'll eat outside on such a glorious day?" They both nodded and walked out the back of the pub. Most of the tables were full, and they went to sit at one near the river when a voice called,

"Ruby, Rose."

They both turned to see Antoine, JP, and the other three men already sat at a table. JP didn't even look at them, but kept his head turned away.

"Ladies, please come and join us. There's plenty of room."

Rose replied, glancing at JP, "Thank you, but we don't want to intrude. There is a table ... Oh." The other table had been taken.

Antoine smiled and said, "Now you have no choice. Spread out men." Rose sat between JP and one of the other men, Antoine sat opposite JP, with Ruby next to him, and the other two men. "Apologies, I should make introductions," said Antoine. Pointing at each man he said, "This is Pierre Laroche, Jean-Paul Pascal, known as JP and our leader, I am Antoine Gílle, and these two are Andre Duval and Donatien Marcon. Gentlemen this is Ruby and this is Rose." All the men acknowledged them.

Harold had come out and spotting Rose and Ruby said, "There you are. Do I need to ask what you want to eat and drink?"

Rose smiled and replied, "No, the usual please Harold."

After Harold left, the one called Pierre asked, "What is usual?"

Rose replied, "Ruby and I always have gammon and pineapple with chips and peas when we come here. Then it's followed by apple pie and cream, and lastly a pot of coffee." Pierre nodded and the table went silent for a couple of minutes.

Antoine broke the silence and said, "We saw you at the disco with your boyfriends on Saturday night." Rose was taking a drink of water at the time, and it went down the wrong way, and she started coughing. Pierre gently patted her back, and Rose thanked him.

Ruby replied laughing, "You should have come over. John and

Jack aren't our boyfriends. They were years ago, but now we are just friends. We know we can dance and drink the night away with them and not be expected to do anything in return at the end of the night, if you know what I mean."

Suddenly JP said loudly, "Ouch." Antoine had actually kicked him under the table.

JP glowered at him. Rose looked at JP and said, "Are you alright?"

This time JP did look at her and replied, "I stretched my leg out and accidentally hit the table leg. I am fine thank you." At that moment Harold and two waitresses brought out their meals. The men had all gone for fish and chips, with mushy peas.

Andre said, "We have heard good reports about the English fish and chips, so we thought we try." Rose smiled and said she was sure they would enjoy it, and they did.

Whilst they were eating and talking, JP told them they were all from Paris, and had just been promoted as bodyguards to the President of France and his immediate family. They were only trained soldiers, and had been sent to Fracton, of which they'd never heard of, to get specialised training. The course was to last about twelve weeks. JP was senior to the others, but they all got on extremely well, and covered each other's backs. JP and Antoine were the only single ones, and at that bit of news, Donatien saw Rose and Ruby's eyes light up, as they secretly smiled at each other.

After the meal, Donatien said, "Why don't you four go for a lovely walk by the river, and us married ones will stay here and have another drink. You are driving aren't you JP?"

JP raised his eyebrow and replied, "Looks like I am now. Rose, Ruby, would you care to walk with us?" Rose and Ruby didn't need to be asked twice!!

As the four of them walked away, Andre said, "Well, if I were to have a bet, which with you two I'm not, I would say JP is totally taken with Rose. Did you see how he reacted at the disco when he saw her dancing with her man friend?"

Pierre replied, "It's not like him to fall straight away, but I have to agree he has this time, and soon he will have to leave her. That's when he'll need us, and Antoine too."

When the four of them reached the river, JP walked to the left with Rose. Antoine guided Ruby the other way. Rose turned to ask Ruby something and that was when both of them realised they were on their own. JP said, "This is lovely countryside. Have you lived here all your life Rose?"

"No JP, I was born in another county called Lancashire. I moved here with my uncle and aunt about eleven years ago. What about you?"

JP smiled and replied, "Born in Paris, became a soldier at the age of eighteen, and worked my way up. I'm now twenty-six and single. I have dated quite a few young ladies, but nothing serious as you say. That was until I first saw you. My apologies if this sounds, how do you say "corny", but when I saw you at the disco, it was like I had known you all my life. I have never felt like that before."

Rose blushed slightly and replied, "I have to be honest, when I danced with you I felt like I was melting in your arms, and like you, I have never felt that way either."

JP stopped and taking Rose's hands in his said, "I have an admission to make. When I saw you dancing on Saturday, I was jealous. I'm sorry."

Rose smiled and told him he had nothing to apologise for. "Rose can I ask you something?" Rose nodded. "Can I kiss you?"

Rose looked into his beautiful sparkling blue eyes, and whispered, "Yes if you want to." JP took Rose in his arms and gently and tenderly kissed her lips. Every nerve in Rose's body went into overdrive.

JP pulled way and said gently, "I could carry on kissing you all day."

Rose blushing said with a twinkle in her eyes, "Then why stop?" JP didn't need any more encouragement than that, and kissed her again and again. They walked back to the pub hand in hand. They spotted Ruby and Antoine, who were also hand in hand, and Ruby also looked flushed.

Andre, Pierre and Donatien had moved from the table and were sprawled out on the grass by the river. Andre spotted the two couples first and said,

"Well gentlemen, I think our love birds are returning, and JP is holding Rose's hand."

Pierre looked and said, "Umm, wonder why both girls looked so flushed?"

Donatien replied, "Come Pierre, do you not remember your first kiss with your wife, I know I do?"

Quick as a flash Andre said, "Mon Dieu, you kissed Pierre's wife?"

Donatien rolled his eyes and said, "You know what I mean."

Andre said, "Well gentlemen, if this is how they look after two hours, what on earth is going to happen after another ten weeks?" They all raised their eyebrows and wondered.

CHAPTER 22

All of them sat by the river for another hour and talked. Ruby explained that she didn't live in Fracton but Birn. Rose and Ruby told them what work they did, and all five men were impressed.

Antoine said cheekily, "So I can put my millions of francs in Rose's bank and if she won't return it, I can get Ruby's company to sue her."

Andre slapped Antoine's head playfully and said, "*Est-ce que quelqu'un vous a déjà dit, vous êtes un imbécile?*"

Rose and Ruby burst out laughing and Ruby said, "Ah, he's not an imbecile."

The men looked at them both surprised and JP said, "You understand French?"

Rose replied, "Yes. We both got 'A' level French, and I have read the French version of *Les Trois Mousquetaires*."

Pierre said jokingly, "I knew they were special, as they've read our story." Everyone giggled. JP then said it was unfortunately time for them to go back to the barracks. Andre, Pierre and Donatien kissed Rose and Ruby's cheeks, whilst JP and Antoine kissed them *au revoir* properly. They arranged to meet at the disco on the Saturday night. Rose had driven and so they followed JP's car, all the way back to the barracks, where they tooted and waved.

"Rose pull over for a moment."

Rose stopped and suddenly Ruby let out a shriek shouting, "I'm so happy. What a fantastic day. Is it Saturday tomorrow?" Rose laughed at her friend, but had to agree it had been an amazing day. Later on Rose waved as Ruby drove off, telling her to drive carefully. She drew herself a bath and laid there relaxing, thinking about her day. That night she dreamt of JP. About 7.30am Rose's phone rang, and it was Ruby.

"Please tell me I didn't dream what happened yesterday?" Rose laughed and said it wasn't a dream, and she would see her on Saturday.

At work her uncle called for her to attend his office. "Rose, I hope you had a lovely Easter?" Rose told him what had happened. Hugh was pleased but cautious, but would make no attempt to interfere. "The reason I needed to see you is that Head Office have advised me, due to so many people now going away to foreign places for holidays, we must have a foreign till. We will stock US Dollars, French Francs, Canadian Dollars and Spanish Pesetas. Any other currencies will need to be ordered from Head Office, with forms completed. For these currencies the public must give us at least a month's notice, and the maximum amount for any transaction is fifty pounds. We need to send a letter to all our clients advising them of this fact, and I hoped you would do it. I am expecting to take delivery of an electric typewriter today. Naturally type the letter, I will sign it, and then it can be photocopied. Alas all the envelopes will have to be done separately. Can I leave this with you?" Rose replied she would see to it. The letter was soon drafted and typed up, and then signed by Hugh. Rose spent most of the morning typing envelopes, and in the afternoon she got one of the juniors to place the letters in the envelopes and put stamps on them. It took her two days. Over the following two days the new foreign till was constructed. When Rose woke the following morning it was Saturday.

Ruby arrived early and both of them were excited. Ruby had half a car full of clothes, as she didn't know what to wear!! Rose just shook her head in despair.

"Ruby, to be quite honest, I don't think they care what we wear, as they're going to be there just for us." However as 9pm approached even Rose was getting the jitters. Both of them changed at least six times, did different hairstyles and eventually were happy with their outfit. By 9.15pm they were queuing outside the disco. Inside they got their usual table and waited. A short while later JP and Antoine turned up.

Rose looked behind them and said, "Where's the others?"

JP replied, "They decided we should come on our own." JP went to the bar and got some drinks. They chatted and danced and got on so well. The chemistry between the four was electric, and it didn't go unnoticed. As Rose and Ruby left the ladies, they bumped into the two prostitutes.

"Tell me something. How did you two pull those hunks? After all you're not much to look at," asked one of them.

Rose replied looking them up and down "Might help if you didn't put everything on show. Leave something to the imagination, and it doesn't do to be jealous when we are more attractive than you. Now if you'll excuse us," and with that Rose and Ruby walked off, heads held high.

Ruby laughed and said, "Nice one Rose, that told them."

JP had gone to get more drinks and was behind them when he heard Ruby's remark, and said, "Who told who what?" When they were sat down Ruby told them. JP and Antoine laughed, but then JP said,

"Looks like they took your advice." They looked over at the two women and smiled as they saw they had dropped their hemlines and done their blouses up.

After the disco finished, Rose asked JP where his car was. He said it was in the car park, which was just round the corner of Rose's flat.

"Please don't take this the wrong way, but would you both like to come back for coffee?" asked Rose. They both replied they would love to. Once in the flat, Rose made a huge pot of coffee and took it into the sitting room. Rose switched on the television and they watched a film. The four of them sat on the settee, with arms around each other, and kisses now and then, but JP and Antoine were perfect gentlemen. About an hour later JP said they must go. Ruby and Antoine went down the steps first, but JP caught Rose's hand and drew her into his arms and kissed her with a passion, and Rose kissed him back.

"Rose can I have your phone number?" Rose wrote it down for him, and then they kissed again. They went down to join Ruby and Antoine, who were wrapped in each other's arms. JP sort of coughed, and after Rose and Ruby received kisses on their cheeks, they said goodnight to them.

Back in the flat Ruby said, "I've just given Antoine my phone number. Do you think it was a bit soon?"

Rose laughed and replied, "I just gave JP mine." Soon both of them were in their beds and dreaming of their men. Alas they wouldn't see them again until Saturday, as their training was being stepped up, and that included Sunday training.

Sunday morning however, Rose and Ruby decided they would just happen to be passing the barracks to see if they could see them. They took Ruby's car, as they knew Rose's. Ruby pulled up a little way down the road from the entrance to the barracks, which gave them a good view of the training grounds.

"There they are," said Ruby. Rose saw where she was pointing and saw them. They were all stripped to the waist and in shorts.

"Oh my god, look at those fit bodies," said Rose. Some soldier was shouting orders at them and they were running up and down various obstacles, completely oblivious to the fact they were being watched.

After about fifteen minutes Rose said, "I think we should go. We don't want to get them in trouble, and that guard has been watching us." Ruby drove back to the flat. Meanwhile at the barracks, after JP and his men had finished training, a soldier said to them,

"Looks like you have some admirers." The men looked at him blank. "Two gorgeous looking ladies, both tall with great figures. One had long reddish black hair, the other brunette."

Andre said, "Now that sounds like Rose and Ruby. Probably on their way back from the pub and just happened to see us."

The soldier grinned and said, "Yeah, that's probably what it was, not," and left. Andre looked at his leader and then Antoine and said dryly, "Some men have all the fun." JP replied laughing, "We can't help it if they fancy us, and you're married." A pillow flying through the air, aimed at JP, followed that and then pillows were flying everywhere, and they all laughed.

On Friday night, about 6pm Rose's phone rang, and it was JP.

"Hi Rose, I wondered if I could take you out for dinner tonight, just the two of us, or is Ruby with you?"

Rose replied, "Ruby won't be here until tomorrow, and instead of going out why don't you come here. I've just put some chicken in the oven?"

JP replied, "Be there about 7pm, and I'll bring the wine." Rose quickly got a casserole dish out, and half an hour later had a chicken casserole in the oven. She quickly laid the table, and tidied up, went and had a quick wash and was just changing when she heard JP's car drive up. She checked she looked presentable, and went down the stairs to let him in. JP kissed her and gave her a bunch of roses and a bottle of wine.

"Come on in, and the roses are lovely, thank you."

JP said, "Mmm something smells nice."

"I hope you like chicken casserole?" JP replied he would eat anything, but loved home cooking. "Please sit and relax. I'll get a corkscrew for the wine and some glasses." In the kitchen Rose suddenly felt nervous, and then scolded herself. She checked the casserole and it would be at least another three quarters of an hour. When she went back in the sitting room, she could see JP was looking nervous as well. This was the first time they had been alone. She handed him the wine and corkscrew and he did the honours. He poured out two glasses of white wine, and they settled down on the settee.

"I understand you were at the barracks on Sunday. I hope we came up to your expectations?"

Rose flushed slightly and replied, "It was actually Ruby's idea. I think she quite fancies Antoine."

"I can assure you that Antoine fancies her as well, just as I do you."

JP took her wine glass and put it on the table and then took her in his arms and kissed her tenderly. He then let his kisses trail down her neck. Rose was on fire, and his kisses felt amazing. He then went back to her lips. Rose's t-shirt had risen up through no fault of either of them, and when JP's hand went on her bare skin, it was like a feather being brushed against her. She had never felt so wanted before. JP broke their embrace and just held her. Rose could smell the dinner and excused herself. She really needed a cold shower!! Carrying in the casserole, JP got up and sat at the table.

"Help yourself, and I hope it's alright. It was a question of just putting what I had into it." JP had already tasted it and replied, "You're beautiful, you speak fluent French and you're a great cook as well Rose, and if that's sounds "corny" I apologise." Rose blushed and thanked him for his compliments. Between them they devoured the chicken casserole. Unbeknown to JP, Rose had also put an apple pie in the oven, which she now put on the table. JP was stunned, but soon the pie and cream were gone. They also finished the bottle of wine. Later when they were about to settle down on the settee, and watch the television, Rose made a pot of coffee. JP stayed until about midnight, and then said as much as he didn't want to go, he must. Rose didn't want him to go either, but neither was she going to do anything stupid. They kissed each other goodnight and arranged to meet as the disco as usual on Saturday.

About a month later, the late May Bank Holiday was coming up. Ruby had told Rose she would be away with her parents for the week, and would she like to join them. Rose was sad to have to decline, but she was needed at the bank, but deep down she didn't not want to see JP. They had got very close to each other, and Rose knew she was falling in love with him. On the quiet Antoine had told her JP had fallen for her hard. Both of them knew they only had six weeks left, and Rose wanted JP to be her first lover. The Bank Holiday arrived and Rose went to the disco on her own, on the Saturday, knowing JP and his men would be there. It turned out only JP turned up. They decided to leave early and walked back to Rose's flat. Once inside Rose went to make the coffee, but JP stopped her.

"Come and sit with me," he said. They both cuddled up on the settee together and their kisses became more passionate. JP said, "Rose I want to make love to you, but first, and apologies for asking, but are you a virgin?"

Rose felt herself go bright red and with lowered eyes said, "I'm sorry JP, but yes I am. I understand if you need a more experienced woman …"

JP stopped her, and tilting her head up with his hand kissed her. "I asked Rose, because I want to treat you with respect. We will take things slowly and I want to show you how a woman should feel and respond before I actually love you properly."

Rose replied by kissing him. About midnight JP told her he had to go. To his surprise Rose replied, "You can stay if you want to."

JP replied, "I would love to, but only on the understanding that nothing will happen between us, but the thought of you sleeping in my arms is something I've wished for, for some weeks."

As they entered the bedroom Rose said, "I don't wear a nightie."

JP smiled and replied, "Neither do I." They both burst out laughing. JP took her in his arms, and as he kissed her, he slowly undid the buttons on her blouse, and then pushed it off her shoulders so it fell to the floor. Rose followed his lead and undid his shirt buttons and that too fell to the floor. Next Rose's skirt and JP's trousers also fell on the floor.

"Rose you are so beautiful," he said. Rose was taking in JP's firm athletic body, and put her hands on his chest. Her hands brushed over his nipples and she felt them go hard. "Can I take your bra off?" asked JP. Rose just nodded. Again he took her in his arms and kissed her. His hand unclipped the back of her bra, and her breasts were free. His hand roamed over them, and he heard a slight moan from Rose. "Let's get into bed," he said. Rose laid down and JP propped himself up on his side. He leant over and kissed Rose's lips and then trailed his kisses down her neck, but he didn't stop there. He took one breast and rubbed his thumb over her nipple, which hardened at his touch. Then he kissed her breast and took her nipple in his mouth and swirled his tongue round it. Rose felt every nerve in her body exploding, but not only that she felt her private place throbbing. JP then started kissing her other breast, whilst still caressing her other breast. Slowly he trailed his kisses back up to her lips and kissed her tenderly and passionately. "Roll onto your side môn amour." JP then cradled her into his chest, wrapping his arms round her and whispered, "Goodnight."

Rose, rather breathless replied, "Goodnight JP." Once JP knew Rose was firm asleep, he carefully got out of the bed and went to the bathroom to relieve himself, as he was as hard as a rock. Thank heavens they had both kept their lower underwear on. Back in the bed Rose had turned over and so he slipped in behind her, and pulled her close into his chest. His hand roamed over her flat stomach, but he went no further. Instead he laid his hand over her breast. Like Rose he then fell into a deep contented sleep.

CHAPTER 23

Rose awoke about 7.30am, and could feel JP cradling her. Carefully she moved his hand and got out of bed. She looked at JP sleeping, and took in all of his body. Unbeknown to Rose, JP had felt her wake and could feel her eyes roaming over him, and he hoped she liked what she saw. Rose thoroughly enjoyed looking at him, and then put the cover back over him. She put her dressing gown on, and went to the bathroom. After she had a quick wash, brushed her teeth and hair, she went to the kitchen and started preparing breakfast. A pair of strong arms encircled her waist and a kiss was placed on the side of her neck.

"Good morning môn amour." Rose turned and kissed him, noticing he only had his underpants on.

"Don't catch cold JP. Breakfast will be another five minutes." JP returned to the bathroom, had a quick wash etc, and then got dressed. Rose had put the breakfast on the table, and both of them tucked in, and drank the coffee. "What do you fancy doing today JP. We could pick up your men and go to the seaside?" JP smiled and replied, "I'd rather take you back to bed, but that will come later, so let's go to the seaside, but just the two of us."

Rose drove to the seaside town of Fete, about an hour's drive away. Whilst they were driving JP told her about the training they were doing.

"We are newly promoted to bodyguards, but do not have the intense training that is required these days. The Special Forces over here are the experts. We are covering things as counter-terrorism attacks, covert reconnaissance's, direct actions, and hostage rescues. Some of the president's bodyguards at present are leaving, due to other commitments. I know one thing, its damned hard work, but it will make us better soldiers. What about your life Rose, you haven't mentioned it at all."

Rose replied, "My life has not been all that good, and there are things I would rather forget." JP understood only too well. Soon they arrived in Fete, and Rose parked the car. Hand in hand they walked down the beach, after removing their shoes, and then waded into the sea, to just below their knees. Both of them were in t-shirts and shorts. JP always carried a change of clothes in his car. The beach wasn't that long, so they walked from one end to the other. JP would wrap his arm round her waist and drew her close so he could kiss her. "Come on JP, I'll show you a lovely tradition." Rose saw an empty bench overlooking the beach and told JP to stay there and she would be right back. She returned with fish and chips in newspaper. JP loved the tradition.

Later on back at the flat, when it was time for bed, again they both helped each other to undress, but leaving their lower underwear on. JP planted feather like kisses on her, but this time Rose did the same to him. Taking his nipple in her mouth and swirling her tongue round it, sent sensual feelings all through her body. Their kisses became more and more passionate, and as they were facing each other, Rose could feel his hardness against her.

Looking at JP she said, "This isn't fair on you. I think we should stop."

JP kissed her and said, "I'm fine, and all that matters is you, at the moment. Now let's kiss goodnight and sleep." JP had his arms round her, but he let his hand slowly slide under her briefs and caressed her buttocks. Rose felt her private part was on fire. JP rolled her over, and cradled her back into his chest, and they slept. In the morning, Rose was surprised when JP carried a breakfast tray into the bedroom.

"Your breakfast is served môn amour." They sat up in bed and ate their breakfast.

Once finished JP put the tray on the floor and taking Rose in his arms said, "Tell me your story Rose. I want to know everything about you." Rose was hesitant at first, but once she started the whole story came tumbling out. JP was stunned to say the least, and absolutely disgusted with her aunt.

"Rose, I'm so sorry for what you have had to endure, but am pleased you are now happy. You do realise both of us are going to be heartbroken soon, when I have to return to Paris."

Rose put her fingers to his lips and said, "Hush, I know, but I want to enjoy every moment I am with you, and I want you to love me. Why? Because I trust you."

JP held her tightly in his arms and said, "I would never hurt you Rose, because I love you."

Rose looked at him with tears in her eyes and said, "I love you too JP." JP wiped away her tears, and kissed her so tenderly, Rose felt like she was floating. Later on JP had to go, but said he would see her on Friday night. Rose kissed him goodbye, but when she went back into the flat she burst into tears. She dreaded the thought of never seeing him again. Ruby phoned that evening and Rose told her everything. Rose and Ruby had no secrets between them, or so Rose thought. Ruby admitted she had already slept with Antoine.

"Are you alright Ruby? Did it hurt?"

Ruby replied, "He was go gentle Rose, and yes it hurt a little bit at the beginning, but it soon stopped and I experienced the best thing in my life. I'm so glad it was Antoine, and he taught me things about my body as well."

"Just like JP," said Rose, "It must be a French trait, although we haven't loved each other yet." They carried on talking for about another hour, and Ruby said she would see her Saturday.

At work, Rose's thoughts were not on work, but JP, until Mr Cooper burst into her office and said nastily,

"Perhaps you should get your mind out of the gutter thinking about that French imbecile and concentrate on your job. I've been buzzing you for about five minutes."

Rose stood, walked over to her door and closed it, then turned to Mr Cooper and said annoyed, "I don't know who the hell you think you are, but you do not burst into MY office and shout abuse at me. And for your information, the bell on the foreign till isn't working yet, and obviously you weren't listening, as usual, when I told you all to send a junior to me if you had a problem. Now GET OUT." Rose calmed herself and then walked out of her office, to sort the problem. "Mr Cooper, I believe you have a problem. How may I help?" and she smiled at the client. Mr Cooper said, "The gentleman wants to change a hundred pounds into dollars, but I told ..." Rose put her hand up to stop Mr Cooper, and turned to the client smiling and said, "First of all my apologies for my tardiness. I'm sorry to say that the maximum you can take out of the country is fifty pounds, and the teller here would be quite happy to do that for you."

The gentleman replied, "Please ... Miss Brambles, no apologies needed. I require the funds of fifty pounds for myself and my wife, hence the hundred pounds."

Rose replied, "The best thing you can do is you withdraw your fifty pounds, and then your wife will have to withdraw fifty pounds. We have ledgers and paperwork to complete, to show we are not breaking the rules." Happy with her reply that was what the gentleman did. After he had gone, she turned to Mr Cooper and said, "I hope you listened so you know what to say if it happens again," and with that she went back to her office. It seemed every day Mr Cooper had a problem, and Rose was getting fed up with him. She didn't have these problems with the rest of the staff. Rose was glad when Friday arrived.

As she said goodnight to everyone, Mr Cooper said quietly, "You need a good Englishman between your legs, not a slimy frog." Rose was so taken aback, she didn't reply.

When JP arrived, he could sense Rose wasn't in a good mood. "Rose, do you want me to go, or can I help?" Rose went to him and kissed him and said, "You're not going anywhere," and told him about Mr Cooper. JP replied, "Sounds like jealousy to me. Come here and I'll make you feel better." After Rose had cooked a meal, they watched the television for a couple of hours and then went to bed. This time as they were kissing, JP slipped his hand under Rose's briefs, and whispered in her ear, "Spread your legs open a little way. I want to feel you." Rose did as he asked and JP's hand cupped her mound. He could feel Rose tense, and removed his hand, and started kissing her neck and breasts until he felt her relax. His hand wandered down over her stomach, and under her briefs. This time Rose stayed relaxed. Gently his hand went over her mound and down between her legs. Rose opened her legs a bit wider, and JP smiled. Very gently he parted her lips, and massaged his finger up and down. Rose moaned as her nerve ends became so sensual. JP didn't do it for long, as he didn't want her to climax yet. He had something else in mind for that. Slowly he removed his hand. He looked at Rose who was very flushed and breathing heavy. "Are you alright môn amour?"

Rose replied, "That felt wonderful. Can we do it again?"

JP smiled and kissing her replied, "Next time."

Rose asked, "Can I ... touch you?"

JP replied, "Probably not a good idea at the moment." Rose understood and blushed deeply. JP loved it when she blushed. They curled up together and slept.

The following morning JP suggested to Rose, it might look better if he wasn't there when Ruby arrived, and so he left saying he would see her later. Ruby arrived late morning and Rose noticed she didn't have her overnight case, and looked at Ruby frowning.

Ruby smiled and said, "Don't be mad, but Antoine's coming back to my flat tonight."

Rose replied, "Why on earth should I be mad, as that means JP can stay over? In fact he's only just left. He didn't want to cause you any embarrassment by being here."

"I know they'll be going soon, but I thank the day they came into our lives," said Ruby. "Rose one thing is that I'm going away for the last three weeks of July, but hopefully I'll be back for their last day." They had a "girlie" afternoon and then had a meal, and later got ready for the disco. Rose had bought a very sexy black bra and briefs set, which she put on. She then put on a buttoned through shirt dress, which was six inches above her knees. For once she decided to put her hair up. She joined Ruby in the sitting room.

Ruby went, "Wow Rose you look stunning."

Rose replied, "As do you Ruby." Ruby had a short black dress on, but with a low neckline. As Ruby now had short hair, she had backcombed it up into a small beehive, with a silver Alice band. At the disco JP and Antoine were waiting. As Rose and Ruby walked over to them, both JP and Antoine saw all the men turn their heads, but Rose and Ruby only had eyes for them. Antoine had already got them drinks, and so they chatted for a bit, and then danced. When the slow records came on, both couples melted into one. Later, Rose and JP kissed and said goodnight to Ruby and Antoine.

Rose and JP went straight to the bedroom. JP undid her buttons and as her dress fell to the floor, he looked at her with amazement. "You look absolutely beautiful," he said. He picked her up and laid her on the bed. Never taking his eyes off her, he stripped his jacket, shirt, trousers, shoes and socks off. Rose could see the bulge in his underpants, and wanted to see it.

JP said, "Tonight môn amour, I'm going to take you to heaven, and it will be so special."

Rose said, "I want to see you naked JP."

He replied, "Later." He bent over her and started kissing her lips, and her neck. He unclipped her bra and freed her breasts. He carried on kissing her, but now on her breasts and nipples. This time after he swirled his tongue over her nipples, he started sucking them and gently biting them. Rose was already in heaven. He was so gentle and his fingers always felt like he was trailing a feather over her. His lips left her breasts and he trailed kisses down over her stomach to the top of her lacy briefs. He put his hand under her buttocks and slowly lifted her, and pulled her briefs down. Rose was now totally naked and felt vulnerable.

"I won't hurt you Rose, I promise. Now spread your legs for me." Once Rose had done that, she felt JP spread open her lips to her entrance. Suddenly she felt his tongue licking between her lips, up and down. The sensations going through Rose were like tiny explosions going off. JP concentrated on sucking and nibbling her sensual nub, and soon felt Rose shaking. He knew she was going to climax soon, and spread her lips further apart to get more access.

Rose was grabbing the sheet either side of her, and she was breathing heavily, and moaning. JP then slipped a finger inside her, and she was so wet, so he slipped another one, and massaged her inside. Suddenly Rose let out a loud moan and was writhing in the bed. Her climax had hit her, and she saw stars. Her whole body was on fire and every nerve was screaming out in ecstasy. JP removed his fingers, and kissed her all the way back up to her lips. Her arms went round him, as his did hers and they held each other so tightly. Rose slowly came back down to earth, and kissed JP with such a passion he knew he was going to explode soon. Rose's hands went down his back and under his underpants and she caressed his buttocks.

JP said, "Rose I'm going to come, so give me a minute," and with that he rushed to the bathroom and climaxed. He then washed himself and went back, but this time he left his underpants off. He straddled Rose, and said it was now safe for her to touch him. Cautiously Rose took his manhood in her hand and massaged it. She was worried in case she hurt him, but he assured her, if she did, he would tell her. Rose watched as it grew in her hand. He was big, and she couldn't imagine him putting it inside her. JP stopped her and sort of pinched the top of his manhood, and it shrank. He slid down the side of Rose and rolled her towards him. "How do you feel?" he asked.

Rose replied, "Absolutely wonderful. You took me to heaven and it was so, so, special. I can't wait for you to love me properly." JP kissed her and then wrapped in each other's arms they slept. In the morning when Rose woke, her legs were tangled with JP's and she could feel his manhood pushing against her entrance, and moved slightly. JP woke and realised his body was responding to Rose.

He quickly pulled away and said, "My apologies Rose, but sometimes men wake up in a roused state."

Rose kissed him and replied, "It actually felt very nice."

JP kissed her back and said, "It's not time for that yet, but soon." Rose couldn't wait.

CHAPTER 24

———— ～ ————

At work, on Monday, Hugh called Rose into his office. Hugh had noticed a vast change in his niece lately, and knew she was in love with her Frenchman. He also knew another three weeks and he would be leaving, and he would be there to help her through the heartbreak.

"Rose, I must say you're looking extremely happy these days." Rose replied she was. "Rose, it's just to let you know that your aunt and I are off on a cruise. It will be the last three weeks of July."

Rose replied, "That's the same time as Ruby." Hugh raised his eyebrow, as that meant none of them would be there when the men left for Paris, and this worried him.

"Will you be alright Rose with them going?" Rose replied she would be fine, but Hugh noticed she was chewing her bottom lip. Rose then realised Ruby and her parents, and her uncle and aunt would be leaving that weekend. How quickly time had gone.

"Uncle would it be alright if I take off the last week of July, and the first week of August." Hugh said it would be fine. As she was passing the kitchen she heard Mr Cooper asking if they knew where Miss Brambles came from. They said they didn't know.

Rose walked in and looking at Mr Cooper said, "I come from a very small village in Lancashire called Thistlewoe. I doubt if you've heard of it. Does that satisfy your curiosity?"

Mr Cooper replied, "I apologise Miss Brambles, but seeing as I'm from that part of the world, I wondered if you lived near where I was, but alas not."

"Very well, now back to your till please Mr Cooper."

On the Friday night, Rose wished her uncle a lovely cruise, and then phoned Ruby and spoke to her, Monica and George. Ruby said they would be back late Friday night, and on the Saturday, she would arrive at hers early, so they could go and say their goodbyes. JP arrived about 8pm, and over the weekend took Rose to heaven, each night. Rose told him she had booked out the last week of July, so he could stay whatever nights he could. JP said that would be great, as the training was almost finished. They made plans on how to fill their week. If Rose had anything to do with it, most of it would be in bed, as she wanted many memories of their time together. Before JP left on Sunday night, they made arrangements for the weekend. Rose was going to pick him up at the barracks on Friday night about 6pm, and she would book a table at the countryside pub. Then when they got back, they had both agreed to go the whole way. Rose couldn't wait. Rose had a really busy week at work, especially with Mr Cooper!! Soon Friday had arrived and when Rose finished, she rushed up to her flat, and made sure everything looked special for when they came back. She put on her red strapless bra and briefs set, with a yellow shirtdress, and sandals. She did a last minute check on her hair and make-up, grabbed her keys and went down the stairs locking the doors behind her, and didn't hear the phone ringing.

Meanwhile at the barracks, JP had desperately been trying to phone her. After they had finished training at lunchtime, the colonel had sent a message for him to attend his office.

"Ah, JP, please take a seat. Tell me how do you think the training has gone?"

JP replied, "It has gone very well thank you Colonel. All of us have learnt a lot, and our gratitude is not enough."

"Excellent, that's excellent news JP, and we will be sorry to see you ago."

JP replied, "We still have a week yet Colonel."

"Alas you don't. There will be a helicopter picking you and your men up at 5.30pm prompt. I have received an urgent message that you must return today, at the president's wishes." JP's heart sank. The colonel noticed and said, "You don't seem happy to be returning. Got involved with a woman have you?"

"I have Colonel, and we had planned the weekend together. She is supposed to be picking me up at 6pm."

The colonel thought for a minute and said, "I will hold the helicopter until 6pm and at least you can say goodbye." JP thanked the colonel and left. First of all he went to the phone box and phoned Rose, but got no reply. He realised she was still at work. He wasn't allowed to phone her at the bank. Next he went to the billet and told his men. They were devastated.

Antoine said, "I can't say goodbye to Ruby, she's away until the end of the following week."

Andre said, "None of us can say goodbye. Rose and Ruby will think so badly of us. We'll have to leave them a letter.

JP then said, "Actually Rose is supposed to be picking me up at 6pm, so we can say goodbye properly."

Donatien looked at JP and Antoine and said, "You two going to be alright? We know how close you've both got to them. In fact I'm going to stick my neck out and say I think all four of you have fallen in love." Both JP and Antoine nodded. Andre, Pierre and Donatien knew they would be taking home two heartbroken men. They all started packing their bags, and JP was keeping an eye on the time. When it got to 5pm, he went and tried phoning Rose again, but she didn't pick up. Again half an hour later he tried, no reply. He thought she must be on her way.

Rose had left early, as she needed to fill up with petrol. The roads weren't too busy and she arrived at the barracks at 5.55pm. She saw a helicopter had landed and watched as the rotors started whirling round. She went to the guard and told him why she was there. Whilst she waited for him to phone through to JP, she watched as five men walked towards the helicopter. Then she realised who they were.

"JP," she screamed. JP heard her and turned, and ran towards the gate. "What's happening?" asked Rose.

JP took her in his arms and said, "We've been recalled back to Paris. I'm so sorry, we have to go."

Tears sprang into Rose's eyes and looking at him she said, "Please don't go JP."

"I have to môn amour. Please don't cry." JP now had tears in his eyes.

Rose was now sobbing and said, "I love you so much JP, and I was so looking forward to our becoming one tonight."

JP was kissing her with tears now falling down his cheeks. "I promise I will write, and hopefully one day I can fly back to you, or you could fly to Paris. I would love so much to show you Paris."

"JP we've got to go," shouted Andre. 'I have left you a letter, and one from Antoine to Ruby. I will never forget you Rose," and kissed her with such a passion. *"Je t'aime môn amour, je t'aime."* Rose, through her tears, watched as JP walked back to the helicopter, and then turned and waved. Rose waved back. She watched as the helicopter took off, and saw all of them waving to her, and she waved back until the helicopter was out of sight. She turned to the guard and asked if she could have the letters that had been left for her. He made a phone call and told her that the billet was empty, and there was no letters. It was only when JP unpacked his backpack he saw someone had put the letters in it.

Rose drove back to her flat slowly, as her vision was blurred. In the end she pulled over and her heart broke into two. How long she stayed she didn't know, but it was getting dark when she returned to her flat. Her world had shattered and she had no one to talk to. Back in her flat, she flung herself on her bed and sobbed into a pillow. Some time later she heard what she thought was someone banging on her door. She thought JP had returned to her and ran down the stairs. Flinging the door open she said, "JP you've come back."

A familiar voice replied, "Hello Rose."

***

Monica, George and Ruby returned from their holiday. Ruby phoned Rose, but there was no reply. She tried on the Saturday, but no reply.

"That's strange," said Ruby, "Why is Rose not answering?" Monica replied, "Perhaps she's already gone to the barracks." Ruby sort of agreed and said she would do the same. When Ruby arrived at the barracks, she was absolutely devastated when the guard on duty told her, the Frenchmen had left the Friday before. He also told her Rose had seen them go. Ruby thanked him and went back home.

"Ruby?" said Monica. "Oh Mum, they've gone. They went last Friday. I didn't even get chance to say goodbye to Antoine." Monica

161

took her heartbroken daughter in her arms and held her tight. She did wonder where Rose had gone. Ruby tried all weekend to contact Rose, but got nowhere. Ruby took Monday off, and drove over to Fracton. She noticed Rose's car was missing. She walked round and went into the bank. A man approached her and asked if he could help. Ruby asked if Mr Brambles was available.

"Ruby, how lovely to see you," and kissed her cheek. "Come into my office." Once seated Ruby said, "I'm sorry to bother you, but have you seen Rose?" Hugh replied, "Rose took this week off as holiday. She said she would need "alone" time, with JP going. Ruby, is there a problem?" Ruby told him about them going, and she was concerned for Rose. Hugh raised his eyebrow and said, "So they left two weeks ago?" Ruby nodded.

"Ruby, I'll give her another couple of days, and if I don't hear anything I'll contact the police. Whilst your here, let's go and see if she's in her flat and is just ignoring everyone." Luckily Hugh had spare keys to the flat. When he opened the top door, he called out Rose's name, but got no reply. The flat was empty. Ruby noticed the bread was going mouldy in the kitchen, and when she went in the bedroom, she could see the bed had not been slept in. There was something else wrong, but Ruby couldn't see what it was. They left her flat and Hugh promised he would call her, if he heard from Rose and not to worry. The following Monday, Hugh was convinced when he opened the doors to the bank, Rose would be there smiling as always. She wasn't.

"May I have everyone's attention please," he said. "Have any of you seen Miss Brambles at all?" They all replied they hadn't. Hugh thanked them and went to his office and phoned the police. Now he was very concerned. A policeman and policewoman arrived, and Hugh related what had happened.

The policemen said, "So to get the facts straight. Your niece met a Frenchman over here, and stationed at the barracks, with four others. They obviously fell in love, and now he's gone back to Paris, and she's nowhere to be seen. She has only been missing for a couple of weeks, and it's a bit early to start putting plans into action. She has just probably gone off to lick her wounds, and will come back soon. Give her another week or two, and if she hasn't returned then we will start investigating." Hugh was far from happy, but what else could he do. As they went to leave the policewoman asked gently, "Your niece wouldn't do anything stupid would she, like suicide."

Hugh was outraged and snapped back, "Certainly not." The policewoman apologised but said she had to ask the question.

Later on, before Hugh left the bank he phoned Monica and George.

George answered and said with concern in his voice, "Hello Hugh. Any news?" Hugh replied nothing and told him about the police.

"Typical. I'll have a word with Ruby and see if she knows where Rose and JP visited. Maybe she's gone there to reminisce." Hugh hoped he was right, and would stay in touch. Ruby visited Fete, the country pub, and other places, but nobody had seen Rose. That was when it hit her about Rose's flat. Her suitcase was still on top of the wardrobe. She phoned Hugh and told him. One morning as Hugh was passing the kitchen he overheard something he hadn't thought of. It was Mr Cooper saying,

"What's the betting she's run off with that Frenchman of hers? Upsetting us all like this isn't very nice, and poor Mr Brambles. I feel so upset for him." Hugh thought about this and thought, *has Rose gone to Paris, and how would she get there?* He knew Rose didn't have a passport, but there were ways and means. He phoned Ruby, but Ruby said Rose had never mentioned running away to Paris. Hugh waited another week and then called the police again. This time a full scale search was arranged. Everyone who knew Rose was interviewed. The police even went to the barracks and saw the colonel.

"How can I help you gentlemen?" he asked.

"I am Detective Bourtone and am in charge of this case. I would like to speak to the guard on duty on Friday 24th July."

The colonel made a phone call. A very short time later there was a knock at his door. "Enter," said the colonel.

A guard entered, stood to attention, saluted and said, "Senior Guard Timmoms reporting, colonel." The colonel looked at the detective and nodded.

"May I ask you to relate the events that took place, when I believe five Frenchman left here for Paris on the 24th July?" The guard told them of the events. "You are absolutely sure, the young woman got in her car and drove off?"

"Yes Sir. She was in pieces and I was concerned for her and watched as she drove off towards Fracton, until I couldn't see her anymore. She was driving a yellow mini." The detective thanked him and left.

The Fracton News soon picked up on the search, and Nancy was furious when she saw the headline, "Local Woman Rose Brambles Missing." It then gave a brief description of her and a short piece on the story. When Hugh arrived home, she demanded an explanation.

"Stupid slut probably asked for whatever she got, and now she's too embarrassed to face everyone. A Frenchman indeed!! What is this going to do for our reputations? I won't be able to hold my head up at the balls we attend anymore. Blasted girl."

Hugh had never hit Nancy, but now he was fighting not to. He walked straight out the back door and drove off. He went to Rose's flat and stayed there. He felt close to her being there, and he could shed his tears in private.

CHAPTER 25

Detective Bourtone went to the bank to see Hugh. "May I confirm your niece drove a yellow mini?' Hugh replied she did. "I'm sorry to tell you but we have just found her car. It was dumped at the back of the barracks, and had been hidden by lots of broken branches covering it. I'm sorry to say there was a lot of blood in the back seat. Do you know anyone who might have a grudge against your niece? An old boyfriend, someone who annoyed her, anything?"

Hugh said JP had been her only steady boyfriend, and as far as he knew, nobody had any malice towards her. "In fact everyone at the bank liked her, even Mr Cooper."

The detective picked up on this and said, "Was there a problem with this Mr Cooper?" Hugh told him that Rose and Mr Cooper had had a few run ins, but nothing that hadn't been sorted. "Can you point out this Mr Cooper for me, and tell me what you know of him?" Hugh looked for Mr Cooper but couldn't see him.

"He's probably on his lunch." The detective nodded, and then Hugh gave him Mr Cooper's personnel file.

"Can I have copies of this?" Hugh obliged, and the detective left.

Three days later the detective was back. "We need to talk Mr Brambles." In his office the detective said, "Now then Mr Brambles, I understand that you have been keeping information from me." Hugh looked at him perplexed. "It would have been helpful if you had told us your niece was in fact from Blackthorn Orphanage in Lancashire, and had witnessed an assault."

Hugh paled and said, "I need to protect her, but I will tell you the whole story, but I must ask for complete confidentiality."

The detective replied, "You have my word." Hugh told him of the events. "Thank you Mr Brambles, and this is between you and me. Tell me is Mr Cooper at work today?" Hugh went into Stanley's office and was told Mr Cooper had phoned in and apologised, but his mum had been taken seriously ill. "Hmm, how convenient," said the detective. "I will be in touch Mr Brambles."

Hugh kept Ruby, Monica and George up to date with what was happening. His curiosity got the better of him and he got Mr Cooper's file. Head Office vetted all employees, even though they didn't know it, and so Hugh had no reason to check them. He read the file and put his head in his hands and said, "Oh my God head office, what have you done?"

***

One afternoon, George received a phone call from a friend of his, who worked at Plark Hospital in Sanjers, which was twenty miles north of Fracton.

"Hi Martin, and what can I do for you?' asked George.

Martin replied, "I have a case I need to talk to you about. Some time ago a woman was found at the rubbish dump. She has a severe head injury and has been in a coma ever since. I think she needs specialised treatment, and I thought of you. Any chance we can transport her to Birn Hospital?" George told him to hold, and then contacted intensive care.

"Martin, you're lucky. The hospital has two beds available in intensive care, so we'll take her. Any idea who she is?" Martin said there was no identification on her, and nobody had reported a woman missing in the area. The police weren't really interested at this time.

Martin was just about to give George all the details when he said, "Sorry George got to go. I will make all the necessary transport and documentation reports. Her nurse, Nurse Barms will accompany her. She can leave in two days' time, but it will be late afternoon before she get to you, as the ambulance will have to drive very slowly." George replied that would be fine. Two days later the ambulance arrived and both George and Monica were there to take charge. Nurse Barms handed George all the paperwork, and said on the journey, she couldn't be sure, but it looked like the woman was trying to open her eyes.

In the ward, the patient was re-hooked up to all the drips and machinery needed. All they could see of her was her eyes and mouth. Nurse Barms explained her face had been battered to a pulp, but the skin specialist had done an excellent job, and if the woman was lucky enough to live, she would only have a few very faint marks. She also told them the bandages could be removed in two weeks' time. With that Nurse Barms said her goodbyes including patting the woman's hand and saying, "Good luck my dear."

Monica could see that the woman's body was covered in bandages. In fact she looked like an Egyptian mummy. Meanwhile George was reading the patient's notes, and felt physically sick. Once Monica had settled her patient, she went to George's office. "George you're as white as a sheet. What's wrong?"

George replied, "I can't believe this report, its horrific. This poor woman was repeatedly raped, and when she arrived at the hospital she was haemorrhaging so badly, they had to perform a hysterectomy. Every rib was broken, along with an arm and leg. She was battered beyond recognition, and then she was hit at the back of the head with a bar. What animals would do this to a poor defenceless woman?" Monica had no reply.

Over the next couple of days the woman had various scans and x-rays, and George was relieved to see her bones were knitting together nicely. Her head scan showed no permanent damage, but he was deeply concerned she was still in a coma after all this time. Monica, as a mother, felt for this woman, and spent as much time as she could with her. She would talk to her all the time, including talking about her daughters Ruby and Rose. The woman just laid there and never moved. A couple of times Monica thought she saw eye movement, but when checked there was none. A couple of days later, the woman thought she could hear voices, and tried to open her eyes, but they wouldn't work. She was in so much pain and made a noise. Suddenly a hand held hers and said gently, "It's alright. Please don't be frightened. You are in a hospital and I'm your nurse, Monica Smith. Can you try and open your eyes." She could see the woman tried but to no avail.

At that moment George came in. "Any change?" Monica told him the patient was trying to open her eyes, but couldn't.

George replied, "That's good. It shows she responding. Soon we can take the bandages off." The woman thought, *Bandages, what bandages, and what's my name?"* After two weeks, the bandages were carefully and slowly removed. The woman's face was black and blue, but both George and Monica could see the excellent work done by the skin specialist. Monica gently dabbed the woman's face with a warm cotton ball, and noticed the eyelids fluttering.

"It's alright. I'm just gently washing your face, as we have removed your bandages, and it's looking good. I have to go now, but will be back very soon. You just rest."

The woman could hear the voice clearly, and when she heard the door shut, she again tried to open her eyes. She only managed to open them a little bit. All she could see was black spots floating in front of her, with grey/white lines going up and down. She tried to lift her arm up, but it hurt too much. She could hear all sorts of beeping sounds and remembered she had been told she was in a hospital. She heard the door open and closed her eyes. She felt a hand take hers and squeeze it gently. She responded.

The nurse said, "Hello, can you hear me. Squeeze my hand if you can." The woman tried and Monica felt it. She went to the door to get George, when a quiet voice said, "Jeppa."

Monica turned and looking at the woman said, "What did you say?"

Again the voice said, "Jeppa." At that moment one of the other nurses came in and

Monica said, "Can you get Doctor Smith for me please?" George came rushing in and said, "What's happened?"

Monica replied, "She's trying to open her eyes and she mumbled something that sounded like Jeppa."

"Monica, gently wash her eyelashes with a cotton bud, as they might be sticking together." Monica did, and the woman slowly opened her eyes. Both George and Monica gasped. Monica said, "Oh my god George, its Rose." Rose was saying "Jeppa" over and over.

George said, "She's trying to say JP. I'll go and phone Hugh and Ruby." An hour later both Hugh and Ruby were sitting at Rose's bedside. Both of them were shocked at the state of her. Rose's eyes looked at these people, but who were they? She didn't know them.

Slowly she closed her eyes and everything went black.

Hugh looked at George and said, "What's happening?"

George put his hand on his shoulder and said, "She's unconscious, probably due to pain, but at least she's out of her coma, which is a good sign. I have to point out, that until Rose can speak, there is a possibility she won't know any of us."

Ruby replied, "But dad, she said, "JP."

"That's because it was her last thought," said George.

The next couple of days for Rose were hard. She still didn't recognise these people, but they all seem to know her, and this bothered her. They told her she had been saying "JP." What sort of stupid name was that? She had to put up with being poked and prodded, injections that made her sleep, and the beeping of the stupid machines. How on earth could she get out of this place? The one called Ruby had sat with her most of the day, telling her all the things they had got up to at school. Rose just looked at her blank. Ruby said she had to go, and would see her soon. *Thank heavens for that,* thought Rose. Ruby saw Monica and went to her.

"Mum I've lost Antoine, and now I've lost my sister. I don't know what to do."

Monica replied, "You need to give her time Ruby. You haven't been told the details of what happened to her, but it was a horrific assault. I dread to think of how she will be when the police start questioning her, and that's going to be any day now."

Ruby replied, "Tell me Mum. I need to know."

"Are you absolutely sure Ruby?" Ruby said she was, and if she knew she might be able to help, and so Monica told her. Ruby paled, and then ran to the toilet and threw up. Then she burst into tears. Monica held her whilst she sobbed.

True to form Detective Bourtone, along with a policewoman turned up the following day. George warned them she didn't remember anyone and not to push her too much. The three of them went into the room. Rose's bed was now raised at the back, so she could sit up.

"Hello Rose, I'm Detective Bourtone, and this is policewoman

Eve Huble. How are you feeling?" Rose shrugged her shoulders. "I'm sorry to have to ask but can you remember anything of what happened to you?"

Rose replied, "Why? What happened to me?" Bourtone looked at Huble and nodded.

Eve moved closer to Rose and said, "Do you remember, say, going to the army barracks, to see your friends off?"

Rose replied, "No." Eve gently asked her a few more questions but got nothing from Rose.

Bourtone said, "We'll leave you to rest Rose, but if you remember anything, you let Doctor Smith know."

After they'd left Rose said, "Who were they?" George noticed that Rose always replied to a question with a question. He knew this was a sign of deep-rooted shock. He decided that Rose should see a psychiatrist. After another four weeks Rose was getting physically better each day. Her bones had knitted back properly, most of the bruising was going, and she was having physiotherapy. She now remembered all of their names, as they visited often. She liked Hugh the best, but then he was supposed to be her uncle.

Between George, Monica and Hugh, they decided to send Rose to a convalescent home for her to get fully fit. As much as Hugh wanted her back at the flat, he was worried something might trigger a reaction and he wouldn't be there. Everyone at the bank asked after Rose and were very upset. Slowly Rose had got to know her psychiatrist who was called Marie Sávoire, and was French. Rose had surprised Marie when she answered a question in French. Hugh had paid for Rose to have a flat at the home, so she could have privacy. Marie saw her every day for a couple of hours. Very, very slowly, she would put Rose to sleep, and try and take her back to her past. Eventually after four months, Rose had remembered everything and everyone. However, she still had no memory of what happened to her, nor did she remember JP or his men. It was decided Rose was fit enough to go back to her flat, and her job. When she returned to the bank everyone welcomed her, but when she went shopping she felt like everyone was looking and talking about her. Naturally they weren't, they just wanted to make her feel safe again.

It was another three months, when one day Rose found a postcard from Fete, down the side of the settee. On the back, in French it said,

Môn amour

I will never forget the day I met you. I fell in love with you the moment our eyes met across that crowded disco. I have loved every minute of being with you, and when we love each other, I will take you to heaven and back.

The thought of leaving you is breaking my heart, but there are ways we can still be together. I promise to write to you as often as I can, and I will look forward to receiving your letters. I hope I can fly back to you soon, or maybe, you could fly to Paris. You will love it, and it's called the Capital of Love.

Je t'aimerai pour toujours, ma chère Rose.

JP xxxxxxxx

Rose sat and looked at it. She had flashes of a man, but no face. That night when she went to bed and closed her eyes, she drifted off into a dream. The man was stood there undressing her. She had her red bra and briefs set on, and he said she looked so sexy. He laid her on the bed, and then stripped and stood looking at her totally naked. His manhood was ready. He laid next to her, and started kissing her lips, gentle and tender. His hands roamed over her breasts and then he freed them from the confines of her bra, and as his thumbs went over her nipples they went hard. His mouth went down onto one, and she moaned as he swirled his tongue over it, and then sucking and nipping it. Then he changed to the other breast and did the same. Her arms were round his shoulders, caressing his back. His kisses went lower and lower. Slowly he removed her briefs, and his hand went between her legs, and Rose spread them slightly. He carried on with his kisses down over her mound, and then parting her lips to her entrance, his tongue flicked up and down. Rose could feel the muscles inside her clenching, and was moaning in ecstasy and saying "JP" in a raspy voice. He brought her to her climax, and then kissed her all the way back up. "I'm going to love you properly now môn amour." After he had put a condom on, he positioned himself on top of her, and she felt his manhood between her legs. He nudged her legs wider and slowly guided himself into her entrance.

CHAPTER 26

Even though Rose was wet from her climax, she was very tight, and he didn't want to hurt her. He pushed further into her, and stopped. He pulled out slowly and then pushed in again, going a little further each time.

He now knew he had to push hard and said, "Môn amour, this is going to hurt, but only for a moment. Are you ready?" Rose kissed him passionately and at that moment JP pushed into her. He felt her tense and remained still.

Rose said, "Don't stop JP. I'm fine, and you feel wonderful." JP carried on and soon Rose was writhing as she felt her climax hit her, and stars shone everywhere. JP also climaxed. Rose felt ecstatic and wanted JP to love her again. He said he would after a rest. He never stopped touching her or kissing her, and every touch was like little shocks of electric going through her body. JP let her take hold of his manhood and gently her hand moved up and down until he was hard for her. JP loved her three times that night, and then they slept. In the morning, they were facing each other and Rose felt his manhood was hard. Slowly she guided him into her, and JP responded. Soon Rose felt herself exploding into an orgasm along with JP. It certainly felt better without a condom on.

JP then realised and said, "I should have put a condom on Rose, as I can get you pregnant."

Rose kissed him and whispered, "I'm on the pill."

"How do you feel? Are you sore?"

Rose replied, "Only a little, but it was wonderful JP. Now I know the meaning of true love." JP kissed her and soon they were making love again.

Rose awoke with a start, and tears fell down her cheeks. She now remembered JP and his love for her. Her dream had felt so real, but she knew they had never loved each other. He'd had to go back to Paris, and now she was all alone. Ruby had already made arrangements to go over to Rose's, and so she put a couple of mugs on the kitchen counter ready to make a coffee when Ruby arrived. She then remembered making coffee for JP and she smiled. Other memories then flooded back, like making him meals, them going off out for the day. She put the postcard from Fete on top of her cabinet in the sitting room. Rose heard Ruby knocking on the door, and putting the latch up on the top door, ran down the steps to let her in. Halfway down, her last memory hit her like a ton of bricks, and she screamed, and screamed.

"Rose, Rose, it's Ruby, let me in."

Rose was screaming, "No, no, please no." In the bank it had been fairly busy, when all of a sudden they heard a blood curdling scream and everyone gasped. The bank staff knew it had to be Rose. Hugh ran out of his office and out the back door to find Ruby trying to get in. Rose was still screaming. Hugh went and grabbed the spare keys and unlocked the bottom door.

Rose was sitting on a step cradling herself and sobbing uncontrollably, saying, "I remember JP. I remember it all." Ruby went to her and wrapped her arms round her.

"Rose, it's Ruby. Let's go back upstairs." Rose went to stand but fainted.

Hugh carried her into the sitting room, and laid her on the settee. "What happened?" he asked. Ruby told him she heard Rose coming down the stairs and then she started screaming. Hugh frowned and said gently, "Looking at Rose now, I'm going to assume she's remembered the attack. Ruby, I just need to go back to the bank and advise Mr Fanterton what has happened, and whilst I'm there, I'll ring your parents and the police."

Rose, who had now calmed slightly, was sitting on the settee, drinking a strong cup of coffee, when Monica and George arrived.

George took her hand, and kneeling down said, "Rose, will you talk to me?" Rose nodded. Quietly she said,

"I remember my attack," and broke down again in floods of tears. George asked her if she was up to talking to the police. Again Rose nodded. Detective Bourtone arrived with the same policewoman, Eve Huble. Bourtone sat in the armchair opposite Rose. He could see how distraught she was, and decided to let Eve ask the questions.

Eve sat next to Rose and asked her gently, "Have you remembered something Rose, and do you think you could tell me what happened?"

Rose looked round and said quietly, "Can the men leave?"

Eve replied, "Of course. I'm sorry gentleman, but could you wait outside of this room."

Hugh said, "We can either stay in the kitchen or go to my office in the bank."

Rose said, "Kitchen, in case I need you." The men left. Eve moved over to the armchair and got her notepad and pencil out to write Rose's statement. Monica and Ruby sat either side of her, both holding her hands. Rose was glad they were with her.

Eve said, "Just start whenever you're ready Rose, and you can stop at any time for a rest, as I know this is going to be very difficult for you to tell us." Rose nodded and started.

"I left the barracks after saying goodbye to JP and waving to them. When I got back here, I felt so empty. Later on I heard someone knocking on the door. I ran down the steps thinking JP had come back. When I opened the door a voice said, "Hello Rose." There were four men stood there with balaclavas over their faces. I could just make out their eyes and mouths. I thought they'd come to rob the bank and said, "I don't have the keys to the bank." The one who had spoken laughed and said, "It's you we want." I was grabbed and something put over my nose and mouth and it went black. When I woke up, I was spread-eagled to a bed and my arms and legs were strapped wide. The four men were talking and looking at me. "Welcome back Rose. I hope you're comfortable?" "Please what do you want with me?" The man replied, "Tell me Rose, does this remind you of anything? I'll give you a clue. Think of a tree instead of a bed." For a couple of minutes I had no idea what he was talking about, and then it came to me, and my eyes went wide. "See brothers.

I told you she'd remember. I have waited twelve long years for you Rose Clark to get my revenge, and here we are. Now it's payback time." "Please don't hurt me. I was only a child when you did that stupid thing to that boy. I felt sorry for him. I honestly didn't know how badly you would be treated." I now knew the man talking to me was Peter Cooper. He came over and sat at the side of me on the bed. "You've got a lovely face at the moment Rose, but let's see what the rest of you looks like." I hadn't changed when I got back to the flat. He straddled me and ripped the front of my dress open, and worked his way down until the dress was completely destroyed. "Well, well. Look at these brothers. Red strapless bra, and briefs. Isn't red a sign for a prostitute?" They laughed and agreed. Peter told them they could remove their balaclavas, as I knew who they were.

"His rough hands roamed all over my body, pinching and squeezing in various places, and I flinched each time. Then he bent forward and kissed my lips. I tried to turn away but his hands held my head firm. "Open your mouth prostitute, as I want to put my tongue in you. Try and bite me and you'll suffer." I did as he asked and he rammed his tongue inside my mouth. He was licking the inside of my mouth and I didn't like it. I was trying to move, but I couldn't. He sat up and looked at my breasts. "Think this needs to go, don't you?" His hand went round my back and he undid my bra. Pulling it off, he tossed it to his brothers and said, "Feel how soft that is and still warm." One of his brothers said, "Come on Pete, you're straddling her, we can't see anything." Peter replied, "Your turn will come, but I'm sampling her first." Both his hands were on my breasts, kneading and pinching them, but hard. His mouth went onto my nipples and he bit so hard, I cried in out in pain. At the same time he was grinding his groin against me. I could feel he was hard and I was scared. Again I tried and pleaded with him to stop, so he gagged me. "Now for the unveiling to see what's under these briefs of yours." He yanked them hard and they ripped away. Now I was totally naked. "Just to let you lot know, she's as black down here as the hair on her head. Now I'm going to check how pink she is inside." I tried again to move, but couldn't." Rose had tears falling down her face and Eve said,

"Take your time Rose. I know this is bringing back bad memories."

Rose looked at Eve and said, "If I stop I won't be able to carry on." Rose continued. "His hands parted my lips and he rubbed his thumb over my sensitive part. He was rough, not gentle like JP. "Tell me Rose, was it good with a Frenchman. I understand their dicks are really small. Soon you'll have a real man inside you." I was shaking my head from side to side and trying to say, "No, No," but it was muffled. He watched me as he slipped his finger inside me, and I tensed. "Well, well, brothers. You'll never guess what I just found out. Our Rose here never did it. She's a virgin, and I'm going to be the first one to break her wide open. Time for the fun to begin brothers. You two take her breasts, you ram your dick in her mouth, and I'll show her a real good time this end." Pete stood up and dropped his trousers. His manhood was long and thick, and I was frightened. He put his hands under my buttocks and lifted me slightly. He eased his manhood in and out of me a couple of times, and then rammed it in so hard I screamed, but it was muffled. Pain ripped through my whole body. The one who had his manhood in my mouth, had straddled my face, and had his hands on the back of my head, and was bringing it up and down, and all I could see was his manhood going in and out of my mouth, and he smelled awful. "Hey bros look at her go, and she's got such a soft mouth. That's good baby, now faster, faster." My head was being pushed up and down so fast, that I was starting to feel dizzy. The next minute he groaned and said, "I'm coming, oh god I'm coming and this is so good. I've never raped a mouth before." He came in my mouth, and I had to swallow his stuff, and it was horrible. He pulled the gag back up and put it in across my mouth. Pete had kept ramming himself in and out of me, and I was hurting so much. Then he said, "While you're just lying there Rose, let me tell you a story. One of my brothers here worked in a solicitor's office in Fracton. Imagine my surprise when he phoned me and told me he had come across a document from a Nancy Brambles, naming you. Well, I just had to drive up from London to see you." One of his brothers said, "Hurry up Pete, I'm so hard it's hurting." Pete replied, "She's got a mouth." The next minute my gag was ripped from my mouth and as I went to scream, he rammed his manhood into it. He was so big I felt like I was choking. He rammed his manhood in and out of my mouth so hard, I felt like he was going to break my jaw. He didn't last long, and the gag was put back."

Rose was starting to shake and Monica and Ruby held her close to them. Through sobs she carried on. "Suddenly Pete started moaning and was ramming into me faster and faster, and it was hurting even more. "Here I come, my tight little prostitute." As he was coming, he grabbed my breasts and nipples and pulled them hard. After he climaxed he looked at me and said, "Now that's what I call a good virgin ride. I can feel you enjoyed yourself Rose, as you're so wet inside. All nice and ready for my brothers." As he withdrew his manhood, I felt something trickling down my legs. One of his brothers said, "She ain't a virgin anymore Pete, looking at the state of the mattress. Move over it's my turn now." Pete got off me, and his brother took his place, but his manhood was a lot thicker, and when he rammed it into me, the pain was so intense I blacked out." Rose was now sobbing uncontrollably and Monica said,

"Rose, please take a break and try and calm a little bit."

Rose, whose throat felt like it was closing up, and between blowing her nose and wiping her tears with tissues said, "I'm fine, honestly. I must finish this," and kissed Monica's cheek.

"When I came round the third man was in me, and as he was coming, he leant over and was biting my breasts and nipples so hard, I actually thought he'd bitten my nipples off. My insides felt like they'd been ripped to shreds. The fourth one was reluctant to take me. "Don't tell me you've got to like that bitch whilst working in the bank?" I was stunned when I heard that. "No Pete, just don't like the thought of rape, and anyway I'm not in the mood."

"I was made to watch as Pete yanked his brother's trousers down and got hold of his manhood and started pumping it up and down, until he got hard. "Remind you of anything Rose? Tell me did it turn you on watching me do this to that boy? Did your panties get all wet?" Looking at his brother he said, "Nice and hard now Mickey, so time to go a ramming. With all our sperm inside her, at least she's nice and wet, and still a little bit tight. NOW DO IT," he shouted. Mickey walked towards me, but I could see in his eyes he didn't want to do it. His manhood was near my entrance, but as he hesitated, Pete went behind him, got hold of hips and pushed his manhood into me. Pete kept pushing him in and out, until he groaned and came. "Told you you'd enjoy it. Now I'm hard and ready to go again. Don't forget her mouth brothers, just help yourself." At one point, I had all three of them on me. One in my mouth, one in my entrance, and the other one had his manhood in between my breasts and was thrusting away, until he came all over my face. I have no idea how many times they took me as I lost consciousness."

CHAPTER 27

"When I came round, I was in the back of a car, and in great pain and naked. Pete was saying, "... at the rubbish dump. Nobody will find her there, and then we'll kick the crap out of her." The car came to a stop and I was dragged out and thrown to the ground. Wherever we were it was dimly lit and stunk of rotten vegetables. Pete dragged me up by my hair and punched me in the face. I felt blood coming from my nose. Pete released me and I slumped to the ground. "Now Rose, haven't quite finished with you yet. This time I want better access so I can go deeper into that entrance of yours. I believe prostitutes love it." I was dragged over to something flat, laid down, and two of the brothers grabbed my legs and pulled them up to my shoulders. "Hey Pete, you gonna stick it in her ass. Now that will be tight." Pete replied, "Hang on and I'll find out," and with that rammed his thumb up. "She's tight alright, but I'm not into ass. I've seen a prostitute do it with two men. Want to try it?" His brother replied, "Sounds like a plan to me." Pete said, "We need to have her doggy style." They rolled me over and lifted me up. Pete dropped his trousers and went underneath me, and I was lowered on to his now hard manhood. When he checked he could thrust in and out properly, he pulled me forward so my buttocks went up, and every time he thrust my breasts were going up and down his chest. His brother spread my buttocks and rammed his thumb up and was pushing it in and out. "Oh she's so tight Pete." Then, I felt his manhood pushing in me. I was desperately trying to move, but I didn't have the strength. Then he rammed into me and I fainted.

"When I came to, both of them were ramming in and out and joking and laughing, about how tight I was in each entrance as they thrust in. My head had been lifted up and one of the other two had removed my gag and was thrusting his manhood hard into my mouth. Then one by one they climaxed. At that moment I just wanted to die. My body didn't belong to me anymore. I was like a limp rag doll and the pain was more than I could take. I vaguely saw Mickey standing to one side, looking sick. When they'd finished, Pete picked me up and threw me into a pile of what felt like slush. It was cold and slimy, but the back of my head hit something hard, and I saw stars for a moment. "Here put these gloves on and rub all that stuff over her," said Pete. I felt hands sort of washing me all over with stinking stuff. Pete then said, 'Well Rose, I really hope you enjoyed our little reunion, I know I bloody well did, and my brothers. Great fun all three of us having you at the same time. Now it's time to say goodbye. Pull her legs open." I felt my legs being pulled apart and then Pete kicked his foot right in my entrance. I screamed silently, and I doubled up with pain. "Hold her out straight," he said and proceeded to start kicking and stamping on me, and then they all joined in. The next thing I knew I woke up in hospital."

Rose totally broke down, and was having difficulty in breathing. Monica was talking to her gently, whilst Ruby hugged her. All of them felt so much for Rose, but Monica and Ruby were heartbroken. Even Eve couldn't believe Rose had survived such a horrific ordeal, and more than anything she wanted to get the Cooper brothers. Without thinking she said to Monica,

"Does Rose know all the details?" Monica shook her head.

Rose looked through very red blurry eyes and said, "What details?"

Monica looked at her and Rose could see she had tears in her eyes. "Rose, when you arrived at the hospital in Sanjers, you had something pushed up inside of you. When it was carefully removed, you started haemorrhaging badly. I'm so sorry Rose, but they had to perform a hysterectomy."

Rose went a deathly pale of white and said, "That means I can never be a woman again."

Monica replied gently, "Rose, when the time is right, and you meet the right man, you can be a woman again and feel all the emotions of love and you will be able to make love and feel all the sensual pleasures cursing through your body. You just won't get pregnant."

Rose said quietly, "I met the right man and now he's gone," and with that she burst into tears again. Ruby wrapped her arms round her and held her close, and Rose said, "Oh Ruby, I want JP back. I miss him so much and my heart is broken." Monica asked Eve if she needed anything else, as she could see Rose was now an emotional wreck and needed to rest.

Eve took Rose's hands and said, "Thank you Rose, and I'm sorry I had to put you through that. I'll go now, but we will see each other again." Once Eve left the room, she let the tears fall down her face.

Eve and Detective Bourtone left, but not before he had told Hugh he would be in touch with developments. George and Hugh came back into the sitting room. Rose looked at Hugh and held her arms out. Hugh went to her and wrapped his arms round her. Ruby went to the kitchen and made everyone a strong cup of tea, and then went to use Rose's telephone, only to find the line was dead. Later George and Monica said they had to go, as they were on a late shift at the hospital.

Ruby said, "If it's alright with Rose, I'm staying for a couple of days. I'll explain to my editor later."

Rose frowned and said, "Editor?"

Ruby smiled and replied, "Tell you later."

Hugh said he must get back to the bank. As he went to leave, Ruby told him about the telephone, and he said, "That's strange. Leave it with me Ruby." When he arrived back, all the staff were greatly concerned, and he told them Rose had remembered her attack and given a statement to the police. Within seconds a collection was done to buy her a bunch of flowers. One of the juniors went and bought a beautiful bouquet. Hugh took them up to Rose, but Ruby put a finger to her lips, and said quietly, "I persuaded her to go to bed and rest. She's firm asleep."

Hugh said, "Thank you Ruby. I know she's in safe hands," and kissed her cheek, and left. Ruby heard small moans coming from the bedroom. Rose was tossing and turning and saying "No," over and over. Ruby held her hand and Rose calmed. She couldn't believe what Rose had endured, but she knew one thing, when it came to the court case, she would run the story.

Rose woke up to wonderful smells wafting in from the kitchen. She already had her pyjamas on, so she put on her dressing gown and slippers. She sat on the bed taking in what Monica had told her - she would never have a baby. She put her hands on her stomach and sobbed for her loss. Ruby heard her and came in, and cuddled her.

Rose said, through her sobs, "I had a crazy notion to go to Paris and see JP, but what's the point now. No man wants a woman who can't bear his children."

Ruby looked a bit shocked and replied, gently but firm, "Rose Brambles, I will have none of that talk. You have been through a horrible, horrific ordeal, and if JP was here, he would still love you. He's not, and it's too early to talk about men at the moment, but in years to come I hope so much you meet someone and you love again."

"Do you still miss Antoine?"

Ruby nodded and said, "You never forget your first love."

Rose stopped crying and sort of smiled. "We had fun with them, didn't we?"

Ruby smiled and said, "Yes, we did, and it might help you for us to talk about them." Rose changed the subject and said, "Something smells good."

"It should it's shepherd's pie a la Ruby," and they both laughed. As they ate their meal, for the first time, they reminisced about JP and his men.

Rose said, "I found that postcard from JP. He promised me he would write, and yet I've received no letters from France. Have you?" Ruby shook her head and said, "I never gave Antoine my address."

Once they were sat on the settee, drinking tea, Rose said, "What's this about an editor. I thought you were at a solicitor's office?"

Ruby replied, "I was, but I was getting bored and there was no advancement. When we went on holiday, one day we were sitting on the beach, when a man came over and said, "Nice to see you relaxing doc." It turned out he was called Edward Missine, and he owns the *Birn Tribunal.* He didn't stay long, but Dad made arrangements for him to join us for dinner. He turned out to be quite a nice man, and I asked him what was involved in journalism. He invited me to go to the newspaper, and have a look around, and so I did. I had an amazing day, and he said if I wanted, I could start work being a typist, and if I wanted, climb the ladder to being a journalist. I finished at the solicitor's office, and started at the *Birn Tribunal* about a month later. I've been there four months now." Rose was delighted for Ruby, but then a thought crossed her mind.

"Were you involved in my disappearance?"

Ruby replied, "I asked to be, to make sure facts were not blown out of all proportion. Kevin was the journalist doing the report, and he was more than happy to let me help. I've done a couple of reports and Ed, as he likes to be called, said I had potential. So you know, I've asked to do the court hearing. Is that alright with you Rose?" Rose replied it was fine. Her mind started to wander and she wondered if they would ever catch the Cooper brothers.

***

Meanwhile at Birn police station, Detective Bourtone and Eve Huble were meticulously going through Rose's events of her attack. Quite a few times Bourtone had to stop reading it.

"How the hell did she survive Huble?" Eve replied, "I have no idea. It's only thanks to that woman's dog they found her, or else she would be dead. You know these Cooper brothers don't you guv?"

Bourtone replied, "You can say that again. When I was in London, we had all sorts of reports about them, but only Pete and Ronnie Cooper. They had their fingers in various pies, but we could never pin anything on them. I was then promoted to detective and sent here. Are the crew in the crime room?"

"Yes gov."

Bourtone and Eve went into the crime room, where there were twenty police, detectives and other people talking to each other. "Right you lot, listen up. I see we have some new faces so I'll do a quick recap. This," he said, pointing to a board with five photos on it, "is the victim Rose Brambles. These bastards are the Cooper brothers. This one is Pete, this one Micky or Michael, and both knew Rose from long ago. She witnessed them assaulting another boy and due to her actions, they both spent three months in solitary, and then three months at Tegra prison. Pete was less than co-operative, whereas his brother Mickey knuckled down and learnt a trade in carpentry. I didn't know of the existence of Mickey and Archie until recently. Ronnie moved to London to find Pete and worked as a garage mechanic. That's when the crimes with those two started in London. The other one Archie, who's the youngest, did various jobs and then gained employment at a solicitor's office in Fracton. As to Mickey, he found it hard when he came out of prison, but soon found various jobs. He fell in with a crowd of good men, and one of them worked at Stocks Bank in Sanjers, and got him a job as a runner. Slowly he made his way up the ladder and became a teller. As you know the bank was closed and Cooper was transferred to Fracton. Once he'd settled in Fracton, he met Archie, and they shared lodgings, but neither of them got into trouble until now. On the 24th July, Rose Brambles was subjected to one of the most horrific assaults I have ever seen. Nearly every bone in her body was broken, and due to severe internal injuries, she can no longer have children. Rose has just reached the age of twenty-two years old. Questions: "Why did Mickey Cooper stay at the bank for nearly two months, after the attack, knowing full well what had happened to Rose?"

"Where is he now? According to the bank he phoned in and said his mum was taken ill and had to leave. His mum's dead, and he hasn't been seen since."

"Where's Archie Cooper?" He was documenting certain files, when he came across some very useful info. What it was I don't know yet, but I will. I will deal with the solicitor in Fracton."

"Where are Pete and Ronnie Cooper? I think they've gone back to London, so one of you needs to get onto the London police stations and explain why there wanted."

"None of you, except Eve Huble and myself, talk to Rose Brambles. I will also converse with her uncle Mr Hugh Brambles, Manager of Stocks Bank in Fracton."

"Rose's yellow mini was found at the army barracks. It's been confirmed it was her blood in the back seat. Did they take this car with Rose to Sanjers rubbish tip? If they did they needed another getaway vehicle. Check with me first if you need access to the barracks and I'll speak to the colonel."

"I also want everyone in that bank checked out. Here's the list."

"Right I want all of you on this. I know after nearly six months most of the evidence will be gone, but there's always something, and we have a lot of loose ends to tie up." Banging his fist on the desk he said in an authoritative tone, "Find those bloody bastards, the Cooper brothers. I want them to go down big time, and it will be for attempted murder. My office door is always open. Right get to it."

Everyone replied, "Yes guv," and the search started.

CHAPTER 28

Ruby and Rose spent the following day, just chilling out. Ruby suggested they go for a ride out to their favourite country pub, but Rose was reluctant. She felt safe in her flat, but knew she must get back to her job. She still had bills to pay. Head Office had been very understanding about her attack, and told her uncle, until she returned to work, they would forfeit the rent. Hugh thanked them but said he would continue to pay the rent, but didn't tell Rose. He just wanted her to get better. He was furious though that Nancy had been nowhere near her.

After Ruby had gone back home, Rose decided to tidy the flat up. She spent the whole day cleaning, polishing, vacuuming, sorting the kitchen out and re-arranging her clothes. She made herself a meal, and sat eating it watching the television. Every now and then she glanced at JP's card. She went and got it and read it for about the hundredth time. "Goodbye JP," she said, "I will never love another like I loved you," and with that she put the postcard away in the cabinet drawer. After a couple of days, she was getting bored. *Time to go back to work,* she thought. Rose tried to telephone her uncle, but the telephone wasn't working. She watched for her uncle to leave the bank and opening the window called to him.

"Uncle, my telephone isn't working. Would it be alright if I return to work on Monday?" Hugh was delighted, and replied he looked forward to seeing her. As to the telephone he had reported it and an engineer was coming out on Monday. He had missed her at the bank, but would keep an eye on her to make sure she wasn't upset at all. Sometimes people accidentally said things they shouldn't. The first

186

thing Rose had to do was go down the stairs. She stood at the top of the stairs and walked down the first couple.

"For heaven's sake, it's only stairs. Walk down Rose," she said out loud. She took a deep breath and walked down to the door. She slowly opened the door, and felt the fresh air hit her. There was a cold bitter wind and she shivered. She looked round the yard, and there was nobody there. She smiled, closed the door and went back up to the flat. She walked up and down three more times and felt nothing.

On the Monday morning, she left the flat, walked down the back lane, and round the corner to the front of the bank.

"Oh Miss Brambles, it's so lovely to see you back. We have all missed you," said Miss Solden.

Rose replied, "Thank you, it's nice to be back. I'm sure I've got a stack of work to do." At that moment the bank door opened and once Hugh saw Rose, he gave her a huge smile. Rose went to her office and Hugh followed her. Once inside he hugged her and kissed her cheek.

"I'm so pleased to see you Rose. Alas, as you can see there is quite a bit to be done." Rose was looking round the bank, and Hugh realised what she was doing. "Rose, my dear, you're safe. He's not here and hasn't been for some time."

Rose turned and smiled and said, "I know uncle, but I just had to make sure. Now I'd better start sorting all this work out." There was a knock at her door, and Mr Fanterton popped his head round.

"Welcome back Miss Brambles. If you need a hand with anything please let me know." Rose thanked him. During the morning the telephone engineer arrived and Hugh took him up to Rose's flat. He checked the telephone and saw the cable went down to the bank. "Can you show me where this is linked in the bank please." Both of them went back to the bank and Hugh showed him. "There's your problem. The line had been cut. Won't take me long to fix it." *Cooper,* thought Hugh. The line was fixed half an hour later.

At the end of the day Rose was shattered, but she hadn't had time to even think about the Cooper brothers, and that was good. Over the next couple of weeks, Rose more or less got back to her normal life. She worked, shopped, but missed her car, so she asked her uncle where it was. He told her it was at Birn police station. She wondered if she could have it back. Hugh raised his eyebrow and asked her if she would like another car. Rose wanted her mini, so Hugh phoned Detective Bourtone and he agreed it would be returned, but after it had a thorough clean.

A couple of days later Rose had her mini back. Ruby was coming over for the weekend, so on the Saturday Ruby suggested they went to the country pub. This meant Rose would have to drive past the barracks. Another hurdle to deal with. Rose had only driven up and down the back lane, to get the feel of driving again. They set off late morning, and as soon as Rose saw the barracks, she pulled in. Memories of saying goodbye to JP came back, and Ruby thought of Antoine. No sooner had Rose pulled in, than she pulled out. Soon they were at the pub. As they walked in Harold spotted them and came rushing out from behind the bar.

"My two beautiful angels, how lovely it is to see you back. I have missed you both so much. Come, sit here by the fire and keep warm. Now is it the usual?" Both of them nodded. Ruby noticed Rose was quite relaxed, but like her, knew she was thinking this was where they had lunch with JP, Antoine, Andre, Donatien and Pierre. It was also the start of the four of them falling in love. Harold arrived with their gammon, pineapple, chips and peas, and they both tucked in. Afterwards they had their apple pie and custard, followed by coffee. Rose and Ruby chatted about work, and other things. JP and his men weren't mentioned. This was the first time they had actually gone out together, and both of them admitted it was great. When they left, Harold actually gave them a kiss on their cheeks and said he looked forward to seeing them again soon. Harold, like everyone else, knew what had happened to Rose, but no way was he going to ask if she was alright. He could see she still had pain in her eyes, and knew it would take time.

When they arrived back at the flat, Ruby braved a suggestion and said, "Rose do you fancy going to the disco later, maybe for just an hour?"

Rose replied, "Not yet Ruby, I can't. I'm sorry."

Ruby said, "No need to be sorry Rose. When you decide you're ready, we'll go." Both of them cuddled up on the settee and watched the television. After they'd gone to bed, Ruby heard Rose softly crying, but decided not to ask her if she was alright. After about fifteen minutes, she heard Rose sleeping soundly. She rolled over in her bed, pulled the sheet and blanket round her, closed her eyes and drifted off. In the morning Rose was up first and they had an early breakfast. Ruby suggested they drive over to Monica and George's. Rose thought that a great idea. They went in Ruby's car, and Monica and George were delighted to see Rose. They hugged and kissed her, and then went to the sitting room, where they talked and talked. Rose even talked about JP, without crying, and George said later that was a good sign. Monica however noticed Rose was holding her side quite a few times and turning pale. She knew she was in pain. A lot later on, Monica said she would drive Rose home.

On the way back Monica asked, "Rose, do you still have pain in your side. Sorry to ask but I noticed your hand kept going there?" Rose told her now and then a pain would shoot across her stomach, like a period cramp, but that wasn't possible now. Monica was concerned, and told her to see her doctor. Rose said she would. Once Monica had seen Rose safely into her flat, and told her to telephoned at any time if she needed them, now her telephone was working, she heard Rose lock the door, and she drove back home.

Rose went into her bedroom, and undressed. For the first time since the attack she really looked at her nakedness in the mirror. She now had a long scar that went across her stomach, which was now slightly rounded. *No more flat stomach or bikinis,* she thought. Even after six months, she could still see bruises that hadn't quite yet faded. She had a nasty one on her back. It had taken two to three months for her bones to knit back together again. The rest of her looked alright. She let her hand wander down over her stomach and cupped her mound thinking how gentle JP had been with her. Tears started to roll down her cheeks, and she brushed them away. He certainly wouldn't want her now. She looked at her face, and could make out three very faint lines, where the skin specialist had expertly patched her up. She sighed, and then went and drew herself a bath, and relaxed. Afterwards she went to bed and read for a short while, then slept. Again, she had another explicit dream of JP making love to her. In her lunchtime, the following day, she went to the surgery and made an appointment to see Doctor Kerris. The appointment was made for 9am the following morning. Rose informed her uncle she would be slightly late in the morning, and he told her not to worry.

"Rose, please come in and take a seat. May I ask how you are?" asked Doctor Kerris.

Rose replied, "I'm getting there thank you doctor. The reason I'm here is, over the last couple of weeks, I've been having a pain across my stomach, like a period cramp." Doctor Kerris told her to undress and she would examine her. Afterwards she told Rose she needed an x-ray, and could she go to Birn hospital, as they had all her notes. Rose said that would be fine. Doctor Kerris phoned the hospital and asked Rose if she could get there within the next hour. Rose replied she could. On the way back to get her car, she popped into the bank and told her uncle. He said he would drive her over, and that's what he did. Once at Birn hospital, they went to the x-ray department and bumped into Monica, who said she would stay with her. Rose was pleased she wouldn't be on her own.

"Rose, go into that cubicle and strip down. You can leave your bra and panties on." Rose went into the cubicle, undressed and put the gown on that Monica had given her. They then went down the corridor to the x-ray room. Monica had quickly phoned George, who came down to sit with Hugh. The radiologist helped Rose lay down, and after looking at her notes, decided an ultrasound would be better than an x-ray. Rose asked what an ultrasound was. The radiologist explained that a gel would be put over her stomach and then she would gently move the machine over her stomach, and she could see the results on the monitor's screen. Rose was fascinated, and watched. Afterwards she gave Rose some tissues to wipe her stomach, and then told her she could go back and change, and the results would be sent to her doctor.

Rose went and changed and then joined Hugh and George. Monica came along about five minutes later.

"I've had a word with the radiologist, and explained you are our other daughter, and she contacted Doctor Kerris, who we've met many a time, and she gave her consent for me to give you the results. You'll be pleased to know it's nothing serious. It's to do with your stomach muscles. Even after six months, they are still moving to go back to where they should be. You do have a bit of an infection, and George can give you a prescription. Doctor Kerris wants to see you again in a month." All of them were greatly relieved. Monica and George were coming up to their break time, and so they all went to the hospital canteen and had a meal. It was 2pm when Hugh and Rose arrived back at the bank. Hugh told Rose to take the rest of the afternoon off and rest and take her medication. Rose said she had work to do. Hugh replied it would still be there in the morning. He gave her a hug and kissed her cheek and waited whilst she went into her flat and locked her door. Detective Bourtone had suggested that Rose keep her doors locked at all times, as a precaution. That evening Ruby phoned Rose to make sure she was alright. Rose told her she was tired, but fine.

Over the next three months Rose gained her strength back, and her body had healed. Life was also back to normal. One Saturday night she suggested to Ruby, she would like to go to the disco. When they arrived, Rose hesitated, and once inside she had the feeling everyone was looking at her with pity.

"I can't take this Ruby. Everyone is looking at me, so I'm going."

Ruby replied, "Rose, it's not pity, it's concern. Don't take it to heart. Look, let's sit over there, and I'll get us some drinks." When Ruby was at the bar, the DJ came up to her and asked how Rose was, as he didn't want to intrude. Ruby told him she was getting there. The DJ said it was good to see them back and to tell Rose, which she did. Rose glanced at the DJ and he raised his glass to her. Slowly Rose relaxed.

A voice said, "Fancy a dance our gorgeous friends?" They both turned to see it was Jack and John. They hugged them and said it was great to see the two "RRs" back again. Rose didn't want to dance, so she just talked to John, whilst Ruby danced with Jack. Rose only managed to stay just over an hour, but now it was back to dancing the night away, but only with Jack and John, because she trusted them. Lots of good looking men asked Rose to dance, but she always declined nicely. John and Jack even walked Rose and Ruby home, and then went back either to the disco or their homes. Rose was busy at the bank, but every now and then she felt like she was being watched, not from inside the bank but outside. Ruby had now been promoted to a junior journalist, and would go with Kevin to report on various stories.

***

In a dirty squat, on the outskirts of Sanjers, Mickey Cooper was cold, thirsty and hungry. He had moved to the squat when the news filtered through that they had found Rose Brambles, and he quickly left Fracton. He was relieved she was alive, but knew her life was hanging in the balance. He still didn't know if she'd recovered or not. His brother Pete had found the squat by accident, and told him. He was lucky enough to find a room with a lock and key. He never ventured out in the day, but night time he would go out stealing food and drink. To survive he even ate raw meat. His lanky hair now hung down the back of his neck. He hadn't washed or shaved and now had a beard. He knew he looked and stunk like a vagrant, but Pete had told him to stay there until he could come and get him. That night, as usual, he went out and managed to scavenge some stale bread from round the back of a bakery, and found a half filled bottle of water. Back in the squat he ate and drank, and then crawled into his filthy sleeping bag. Suddenly the door burst open and torch lights shone in his face. A voice said,

"Mickey Cooper, you're nicked," and he was dragged roughly out of the room, and thrown into the back of a police van.

CHAPTER 29

———————～———————

Back at Birn police station, Cooper was literally thrown into a cell. One of the officers went to Bourtone's office, and said, "We got the bastard gov, he's in cell four."

Bourtone replied, "Excellent work. Let him stew for the night, and tomorrow we'll see what the little shit has to say." Bourtone had had a tip off from Sanjers police station. A woman had seen Cooper acting shifty and reported it to the police. Sanjers police station then contacted Bourtone and he sent officers from Birn to set up a stake out and watch. In the morning, Cooper was dragged up from the cells, and Bourtone could see he had had a beating.

"Fell down the steps did he constable?" asked Bourtone, but with a slight smile.

"Something like that gov." Cooper, who was handcuffed, was pushed down to sit in the chair opposite Bourtone's desk.

"Tell Dickiens and Bowkers to come in, just in case he decides to cause trouble, and I need you to write his statement down." Once the two officers arrived, Bourtone walked round to the front of his desk and sat on the edge of it looking at Cooper. "Right you bastard. I want a full detailed account of everything that happened on the night of the 24th July." Cooper shrugged his shoulders and said, "Nothing to do with me. You've got the wrong brother." At that moment Bourtone put his foot between Cooper's legs and pushed the chair so hard that Cooper and the chair went flying. Once the chair had been uprighted, and Cooper picked up and pushed back down on it, Bourtone said, "Start again shall we, but from the beginning."

Cooper decided to co-operate.

"I was brung up in Thistlewoe in Lancashire, wi me older brother Pete. I don't know what we did, but we ended up in Blackthorn Orphanage. Me brother Pete were out of control even then, and he ended roping me and two friends into assaulting a young lad who had squealed on him. We didn't know Rose Clark had seen us. Next minute we're hauled into governor's office, and told we were getting three months solitary confinement followed by three months in jail. Me sister Lucy had also been sent to Blackthorn. After Rose Clark left, Lucy broke into the governess's office and found the proof, and told us where she'd gone, and her surname was now Brambles. Pete vowed, if it were the last thing he ever did, he would find Rose Clark/Brambles and get his revenge. After we left prison, I went back to Thistlewoe, to find I had two more brothers, Ronnie and Archie. I never saw me sister again. I was also told the young lad Pete has assaulted had hung himself. There were no work, so I moved round counties, doing jobs here and there. Pete had buggered off and gone to London. Eventually I arrived in Sanjers and worked in a print shop. It were boring. I met some blokes in a pub, who worked at Stocks Bank, and one of them got me a job as a runner. I liked being there, and decided it was time to better me self. I worked hard and soon got to be a teller. Then we were all told Bank were closing. I was lucky, and got transferred to Fracton. It was there I met Rose Brambles, but didn't make the connection. I knew she were from Lancashire cause of her accent, but when she told me she was from Thistlewoe, I knew she were lying, and I realised who she were.

"I had lodgings in Fracton, and one day when I were in pub, I saw me brother Archie. He were going round solicitors, putting papers on something called microfilm. He too had lodgings, and to save money, I moved in with him. One day he told me, he'd found a document that he just knew Pete would love to know about. Archie said it were from a Nancy Brambles and saying things about Rose. I didn't know he had tracked Pete down, as had Ronnie, and stayed in touch. That night he told me he'd phoned Pete and told him. I were furious and said, "You bloody idiot. You've no idea what you've bloody well done. God help her." That weekend Pete and Ronnie turned up. "Where's that bloody bitch. I've waited so bleedin long to find her?" said Pete nastily. I said she were away for weekend, but she weren't. Pete and Ronnie rented a room where we were staying. He told me I had to find as much info on her as I could get. I chatted up one of juniors in bank, and she told me Rose was dating a Frenchman, but he were leaving last week of July. She were then going to take that week and the first week of August off as holiday. They had a holiday rota on wall in kitchen.

"On 24th July, Pete banged on door and told us we had to meet him in back lane behind bank at 9pm. I had no idea what were going to happen. When we got there, he made us wear surgical gloves, so no fingerprints would be found, and balaclavas, so she wouldn't recognise us. He banged on Rose's door and when she opened it, he said, "Hello Rose." She thought we'd come to rob bank. Pete put something over her face, and she went limp. "Get her in the car quick," he said. We drove out to some derelict buildings, and he picked her up, and we followed him into a basement, where there were a dirty mattress on a bed. He threw her on bed and then tied her arms above her to bedposts, and spread her legs and tied them to bed legs. She just laid there spread-eagled. "What you going to do to her Pete?" I asked. Pete replied, "Just have a bit of fun with her that's all," but I saw the look between Pete and Ronnie and knew something bigger was going on. Rose started to wake up, and Pete went and stood by her. Then he told her who he was and how he'd waited twelve years for his revenge. I saw Rose pale, and she started pleading with him. Pete then straddled her. The next thing her dress was getting ripped off her, with buttons flying through air. Pete looked at us and told us she had red bra and panties on, and wasn't that a sign of a prostitute. Pete said because she knew who we were, we could remove our balaclavas. I saw Pete bend over her and start groping her and then kissing her, and told her to open her mouth so he could tongue her. Next minute her bra came flying through the air and Ronnie caught it. Ronnie told Pete they couldn't see anything and Pete told him his turn would come, but he was having her first. It was then I realised they were going to rape her. I went to stand but Ronnie pushed me back down with a force. I honestly didn't want this to happen to her." Bourtone could see tears falling down Cooper's face.

"I could see Pete's hands roaming over her body, and Rose was flinching at his touch. He started biting her breasts and nipples and she screamed, so he gagged her with a hanky. I wanted to tell her to lay still, let them have her, and it would be over. Hopefully her

French lover had stretched her inside, so it might not be too painful. How wrong I was. I heard him rip her panties off and tell us she was as black there as her hair. Pete taunted her about her French lover, and she'd soon know how it felt to have a real man inside her. Then he turned and told us she were a virgin, and his grin was evil. I felt sick at what was going to happen, but I could do nothing. Pete told us to join in. Archie and I had to knead her breasts and tweak her nipples. Ronnie was going to put his dick in her mouth. Pete had dropped his trousers and lifting her buttocks slightly, thrust into her so hard, she screamed, but it was muffled because of the gag. Ronnie then straddled her face, and removed the gag and rammed his dick into her mouth, and pumped in and out until he came. Archie and I had moved away from her. I could see Archie touching himself up and he said, "Hurry up Pete, I'm hard and hurting." Pete told him she had a mouth. Archie was big, but soon straddled her, removed the gag and rammed into her mouth. Pete was still thrusting at her entrance, telling her how he had found her. Pete started grunting and came. Ronnie said, "She ain't a virgin anymore Pete, looking at the state of the mattress." I could see a mix of blood and sperm. If I thought Archie was big, Ronnie was now hung like a donkey. It was the largest dick I had ever seen. As he rammed into Rose, she passed out. He was riding her hard and fast, and soon came. Archie then took her, and as he was coming he leant over and started biting her breasts and nipples, which were now bleeding.

"Pete looked at me and said, "Now it's your turn Mickey. She likes it good, hard and fast." I replied I didn't want to rape her, and I wasn't in the mood. The whole room was full of sexual tensions and smells. Pete looked furiously at me and asked if I'd got feelings for her whilst working at the bank. I saw Rose's face as she realised who I was. Before I knew what was going on, Pete had yanked my pants down and was pumping my dick. I couldn't help it and got hard. He pushed me towards Rose, but I hesitated. He grabbed my hips and rammed me into Rose. Even though I didn't want to, she was so wet and still a bit tight. The more Pete rammed me in and out the more I enjoyed it, and then I came. I also felt Pete's dick hard between my buttocks and hoped he wouldn't put it up my ass. After I'd finished, I ran to a corner and threw up. The other three laughed. When I looked again, Pete was riding her entrance, Ronnie had his in her mouth, and Archie was thrusting between her breasts. I saw Rose had lost consciousness. When they'd finished with her, Pete told us to unstrap her and put her in the back of the mini. There was blood everywhere. Pete drove, with Ronnie at his side. Archie and I had Rose propped up between us totally naked. Archie kept sucking her breasts and nipples. We drove for quite some time and then I realised where I was. We were at the rubbish tip in Sanjers. "What the hell are we doing here?" I asked. Pete replied, "Dumping her body. No one will find her, but we're going to kick the crap out of her first." I couldn't believe the violence in my three brothers.

"Rose had started to come round, and Ronnie pulled her out and threw her to the ground. The place was dimly lit, and night time was now closing in, and the place stunk. I don't know why but Pete pulled Rose up by her hair, so she was standing, and then smashed his fist into her face. Blood started to pour from her nose, and he let her go, so she slumped to the ground again. I thought we were going to dump her and leave, but again I was wrong. Pete still had more revenge to inflict upon her. He dragged her to what looked like an old table and laid her down, and told her he wanted deeper access this time. He got Ronnie and Archie to pull her legs up to her shoulders. I stood back not wanting to be a part of it. Ronnie asked Pete if he was going to bugger her, but Pete said that wasn't his idea of fun, but rammed his thump in and told Ronnie she was very, very tight. He said he'd seen a prostitute taken back and front at the same time, and did he fancy it. Ronnie smiled and agreed. Pete said she needed to be doggy style. They turned her over and Pete positioned himself under her. Ronnie and Archie then bent her legs, so she was kneeling, and pushed her down hard onto Pete's dick. He made himself comfortable, and made sure he could thrust in and out, and then pulled Rose towards him, so her ass was in the air, and he could take her breasts and nipples in his mouth. Ronnie dropped his trousers, and when Pete said, "Go" they both rammed into her at the same time. Rose gave out a long curdling scream, which was muffled by the gag, and then passed out. They both rammed into her laughing and joking, saying how she tightened with each thrust, and it felt so good. Archie then decided to join in, and kneeling at the side of Pete's head, he removed the gag, and tilting her head back rammed his dick into her mouth. Pete looked at me and said, "Come on Mickey, take yourself in hand and you can jerk all over her. It'll be a foursome then." I just shook my head. One by one they all came and

Pete pushed her onto the ground, I actually thought Rose was dead, as she couldn't survive that horrific attack. I threw up again.

"Pete picked her up and threw her in a load of slimy stinking stuff. He went to the boot of the mini and came back and told us to put the thick gloves on, just in case there was anything sharp in the slime. Then he told us to rub the stinking stuff all over to get rid of any evidence, which we did. As I rubbed the stuff over Rose, without them seeing, I quickly pulled the thick glove off and I felt for her pulse and it was beating, but slowly, and at that moment she moaned and half opened her eyes. I put the glove back on. Pete told her what a great time they'd had with her, especially all three of them having her at the same time. He said it was now time to say goodbye, and told us to pull her legs apart. I couldn't believe what he did next. He kicked her hard right between her legs, and Rose doubled up with pain, and I could see she'd gone totally limp. Then he told us to hold her out straight, and started kicking and stamping all over her, and the other two joined in. "For god's sake Pete stop. You've killed her. What more do you want?" I shouted. When they'd finished, Pete told us to pick her up and take her to where a large pile of rubbish bags were stacked. Pete told us to carefully remove some of the bags, so she could be stuffed inside them. As we moved the bags, Archie came across a box. "Hey Pete, look what I found." It was a box with vibrators in it. "Bloody hell, look at the size of this one," said Ronnie. It must have been twelve inches long and had a very thick girth. Pete took it and said, "It's got three speeds. Low, Medium, Fast." He turned it on but nothing happened. "Archie, see if there's any batteries in the car," said Pete. After a minute Archie came back and said she had spare ones in the glove compartment, along with a torch. Pete got rid of the old batteries, and put the new ones in. He put it to fast. "Christ, feel that throbbing," and passed it round. "I didn't touch it."

CHAPTER 30

———————⌇———————

"Right, where's that torch. Shine it between her legs." Archie obliged. Pete pushed her legs open, and tried to push it inside her, but it wouldn't go. He went back to the slime and rubbed it all over it, and then came back and tried again. It only went in a little way, so Pete started thrusting it in and out of her. Eventually he got it all inside her, and closed her legs. "Put her in that space you've made, but put a rubbish bag behind her head, and another under her knees, with her legs dangling over the bag. That vibrator will be in her deeper then. Hark at it humming, lucky bitch. Never been jealous of a vibrator before. Right close the hole up with the other bags." What Pete didn't realise was, that as they were putting the rubbish bags back to cover her, I had pulled a couple away, from the other side. Again I took my glove off and felt for her pulse. I couldn't believe it, as she wasn't dead. Well not yet anyway. I moved four or five bags so air could get to her. "What you doing Mickey?" asked Ronnie. I replied I was making sure she couldn't be seen from any angle. Luckily he didn't check. We walked back to the mini. "Right," said Pete, "All of you strip, and put your clothes in a pile." We did as he told us, and Pete stripped as well. "Wipe your dicks on them towels, thoroughly." We did and then he gave us clean clothes and more surgical gloves. He picked the clothes, towels and gloves up and walked over to a rusted bin, put the clothes, gloves and towels in and set fire to them. He waited until the fire had finished and everything was destroyed." Micky went quite for a moment and then said, "I've just remembered something. The balaclavas were left in that basement with the bloodied mattress.

"We all got back in the mini, avoiding the blood on the back seat.

As we drove out I hoped Rose would be found soon. After driving for some time, I saw the barracks in the distance. Pete pulled off onto a dirt track. "Get out and stay here, as I won't be long." When he came back he was driving his black car, and we all got in. I asked, "Where's the mini Pete and how did you know to take her tonight?" Pete explained. "I watched and followed her everywhere, and last night she went to the barracks. Imagine my surprise when I saw her Frenchman take off in a helicopter. I followed her back home and then went and got Ronnie. I had already devised my plan and with luck was going to get the Frenchmen blamed for her murder, but that bit went wrong. Not to worry. Ronnie went to the back of the bank and broke into her mini, and steered it quietly down the lane, and then we drove both cars to the barracks. Not many soldiers were around, and I had already been up there and found the ideal spot. We parked my car there, and covered it with branches, and then we drove back to the bank and put her mini back. I found the derelict buildings by accident, and knew there were no squatters around. I was going to go to a rag and bone man to get a bed and mattress, but I saw one just left on a street, so I grabbed it, and took it to the building. Sanjers rubbish dump was ideal, as it's the biggest dump round here. With a bit of luck the diggers will scoop her up, and she'll be incinerated. Her mini is now covered with branches at the barracks, but I'm sure in time they'll find it. That's why I made you all wear gloves - no fingerprints.

"Now when we get back, Archie I want you to go up to her flat, turn out any lights and make sure both doors are locked so it looks like she has gone away. Don't nick anything. Mickey, you need to stay at the bank. Any news you ring me straight away. Ronnie and I are heading back to London, as I'm sure the police have had nothing to do in our absence. Archie how much longer will you be at the solicitor's?" Archie replied he had finished. "Then you'll come to London with us." Pete pulled up outside the back alley, and Archie ran round and did what he had been told. Pete then dropped me off at the lodging house. That was the last time I saw them. I know you won't believe me, but I regret so much what happened to Rose. I did as Pete asked, and phoned him and told him the police had started looking for her. He told me to stay put for the time being. Then I heard you'd found her alive, and relief swept through me. I phoned Pete and told him she had been found, but I didn't tell him she was alive. He told me to go to that squat in Sanjers and wait, and that's what I did."

Bourtone had listened quietly to Cooper's accounts of events, and it more or less matched Rose Bramble's account. He had also watched Cooper closely and he could actually see remorse in his eyes, and Cooper's tears silently falling. Also, if he hadn't moved those rubbish bags, he doubted if Rose would have been found in time. A woman, who was walking her dog, had let him off the leash. He had run round the dump and then found Rose's body and started barking. The woman ran to the nearest phone box.

He was curious though and said to Cooper, "Why didn't you tell your brother she was alive?"

Cooper looked at him and said, "Because she would never survive another attack. If he thinks she's dead, she's safe."

"When did you last talk to your brother?"

Cooper replied, "Last week. I found a 10p piece and phoned him. He said he was making arrangements to get us all to Spain, but he had loose ends to tie up first. He told me to phone him next week, but I know bloody well, they're going without me. What will happen to me now?"

Bourtone replied, "You'll stay here and be charged with kidnap and attempted murder. Take him back to his cell."

As Cooper went to leave he said, "Can you tell Rose I'm sorry for what I did, and her letters." Bourtone raised his eyebrow and said, "What letters?" Cooper replied, "One of my jobs was to get the mail every day. I saw a letter from France and took it. There were two, sometimes three a week. I told Pete and he told me to destroy them, and to cut her phone line, so she had no contact. Pete didn't want the Frenchman coming back to identify her, before we'd left England. I destroyed about twenty letters, and then they stopped coming." With that he was taken back to his cell.

Bourtone asked if Eve Huble was on duty.

"You wanted me gov?" she asked as she walked into his office.

"Yes, I need you to type this statement up." "Congrats on getting Mickey Cooper gov. Did he tell you everything?" Bourtone replied he had, and also filled in the gaps. Huble left, and Bourtone phoned his colleagues in London. He spoke with Hazellin, who was his partner before he moved. "Hazellin, I need your help," and he told him about what had happened. "You need to keep a tight eye on those bloody Cooper brothers. I want all of them behind bars."

Hazellin replied, "Believe it or not, we've got them staked out at the moment. Pete and Ronnie Cooper raped a prostitute a couple of nights ago, but this one lived, and has identified them as her attackers. We dragged them in, but they've got one hell of a solicitor, and were back on the streets within fifteen minutes. Word's out that they're trying to flee the country, hence the stake out. Any luck with Mickey Cooper?"

Bourtone replied, "Sung like a bird. Two things the brothers don't know is Rose Brambles is alive, and the other is that we've arrested their brother. Would like to keep it that way, if you get my drift." Hazellin said he would be in touch.

Bourtone called his team together, and told them of the events. "I must stipulate, that under no circumstances must word get to London about Rose Brambles being alive, or the fact we've got Mickey Cooper."

"Gov," said one of the officers, "couple of questions?" Bourtone nodded. "Instead of not saying Miss Brambles is alive, why not say she is. Surely this would make the Coopers come back to Birn, and we'd be ready for them."

Bourtone looked at the officer and said, "How do you feel about telling Miss Brambles that her attackers are on their way back, to finish the job?" The officer didn't answer. "Precisely," said Bourtone. "That poor woman has been to hell and back, and I have no intention of telling her that. Next question."

"We've got Cooper's statement. Can't we arrest them?"

Bourtone replied, "Need more evidence. Pete Cooper is far from stupid. He will blame everything on his brother."

Huble said, "What about a stand in gov?"

Bourtone replied, "That would take too long. These buggers could be on their bloody way to Spain within days."

***

At the bank, Hugh took a telephone call, and paled. He went into Stanley's office and said, "Stanley, may I ask a favour. If Rose should ask where I am at all, please can you tell her I've gone to see a new client."

Stanley raised his eyebrow and said, "Everything alright Hugh?"

"I've just taken a telephone call from Detective Bourtone. They've arrested Mickey Cooper, and he needs me to go over to Birn police station immediately." Stanley replied he would look after Rose. Hugh was soon sat in Bourtone's office.

"Thank you for coming Mr Brambles. May I ask how is Miss Brambles?"

Hugh replied that Rose was now back to being a normal woman again, but still had the odd wobble.

Bourtone said, "I needed to speak with you in private. As I said we have arrested Mickey Cooper, and he has given us a full detailed report. Here is his statement, which he has signed." Hugh read the statement, and felt physically sick, at what Rose had had to endure in her horrific attack. Bourtone opened his desk drawer and pulled out a glass and a bottle of brandy. He half filled the glass and pushed it over the desk to Hugh, who drank it in one go, but declined another.

Hugh couldn't speak for a moment, but then said, "What is this document he refers to from my wife?" Bourtone replied, "I had to get a warrant for this document, and I wasn't sure if you knew of its existence? Nobody else has seen this." He took the document out of the file, and gave it to Hugh. As Hugh read it he paled.

"This is absolute nonsense, and to answer your question, No, I have never seen this before. May I have a copy?" Bourtone got a copy for him. "Under no circumstances detective must Rose ever see this. Do I have your discretion?"

Bourtone replied, "I have to be honest with you Mr Brambles, there is a possibility the courts will want to see it, but I will do my damnedest to get it disallowed."

"What will happen to Cooper now?" "He will stay here until his brothers are caught, and then they will be escorted from London to here and stand trial at Birn Court. The charges will be kidnapping and attempted murder. If convicted, they will spend the rest of their lives at Alkin Prison, on the outskirts of London." Hugh thanked the detective and shook his hand. He needed to get out of there before he exploded. Bourtone said he would keep in touch.

Hugh needed to walk, and went to Birn Park. He was absolutely furious with Nancy. How the hell could she do that to Rose? But not only that, because of her stupidity, she had led Rose's attackers to her. He walked for about an hour and then drove back to Fracton. When he walked in the bank, Rose saw immediately that he was absolutely furious about something, and went to his office.

"Uncle what's happened? Is it to do with the Coopers?" Hugh replied it was just a private matter. Rose didn't believe him, but knew, later on, if he wanted to talk he would come up to her flat. Needless to say Hugh didn't go to Rose's flat. He drove home and waited for Nancy, who arrived about 7pm.

"Oh dear. You look like you've had a bad day," she said noticing Hugh was in a filthy mood. Taking her by the arm, he took her into the sitting room and pushed her down into the armchair.

"Hugh, what on earth is the matter with you?" she snapped.

Hugh rounded on her and snapped back, "Been to any solicitor's lately Nancy, and told a pack of lies, and then signed a document about them?" Nancy replied she had no idea what he was talking about. "Then please, explain this," he said and thrust the document into her hand.

Nancy paled and then said, "That little bitch. She's been in my desk." "No she hasn't," shouted Hugh. "One of her attackers worked at your solicitor's putting documents onto microfilm, when bingo, he comes across this. You led Rose's attackers to her, and I blame you for the horrific attack that she had to endure. The police have arrested one of them, so let me run through his statement, so you know exactly what she went through and the consequences. She was repeatedly raped, back and front, and they also rammed them in and out of her mouth. Every rib in her body was broken, along with her leg and arm, and kicked and stamped on her until she was unrecognisable. Then they had the gaul to thrust a twelve inch long vibrator up inside her, which had a wide girth, and left her naked, and hidden underneath rubbish bags to die. When they removed the vibrator at the hospital, she was so badly injured, that she had to have a hysterectomy. I presume you know what a vibrator is? I hope you're bloody well satisfied with yourself. Now you have a week to GET OUT of MY house. I never want to see you again, and I will start divorce proceedings."

Nancy broke down and begged for forgiveness and felt dreadful about the full extent of Rose's injuries. "Oh Hugh I'm so dreadfully sorry. Do you think Rose would see me?"

Hugh replied with venom in his voice, "You will NOT go anywhere near her. I will make sure you're adequately funded, and you can take whatever furniture you want. That's easily replaceable. Now I'm going out for a meal, and I will sleep in Rose's room from now on." Hugh and Nancy spent the weekend trying to avoid each other as much as possible.

CHAPTER 31

On Monday morning Hugh arrived at the bank looking dreadful, and all the staff noticed. Rose went immediately to his office.

"Uncle, please don't tell me nothing is wrong. You look absolutely dreadful."

Hugh looked at Rose, through sad eyes, which Rose noticed, and said, "I need to speak with you privately Rose. Can I see you after work in your flat?"

Rose replied that would be fine and she would cook him a meal. About 6.30pm Hugh went to Rose's flat. When he walked in, the smell of shepherd's pie wafted towards him, and he suddenly felt hungry.

"Uncle, what's wrong?"

Hugh replied, "Can we eat first, it smells delicious?" They had their meal and then sat on the settee.

Taking Rose's hands in his Hugh said, "Rose I have found something out, that I'm sorry to say relates to Nancy, which has led to repercussions. I have asked her to move out, and I'm filing for divorce." Rose looked at him absolutely stunned, and went to say something, but Hugh stopped her. "Let me tell you Rose, as it's to do with your attack. The police have arrested Mickey Cooper. He has been in Sanjers all this time in a squat. Anyway he has given his statement to Bourtone, who has assured me, that a certain document was acquired from a solicitor's where Cooper's brother worked. This document contained all your details, and ..." Rose put her fingers to his lips and stopped him saying anymore. Rose went to her bedroom and got the two documents she had photocopied years ago.

Rose sat back down and said shakily, "Is this the document uncle?"

Now Hugh looked stunned. "Where, how ...?"

Rose replied, "I'm so sorry uncle and I'm ashamed of what I did," and told him about going into their bedroom, twice, finding the documents and photocopying them at the secretarial college. Rose had tears falling down her cheeks, and said, "I understand if you don't want to see me anymore, as I have failed, and betrayed your trust so deeply."

Hugh wiped away her tears and held her tightly. "Don't be daft Rose, as this isn't your fault, but I do wish you'd told me. This document from Blackthorn is a fake. I have the original locked up in the vault at the bank. I can assure you were adopted by us, and ... Oh god, you've thought all these years you weren't ours. You are Rose, and I'll show you the document." Rose felt all the pent up hurt she harboured since the day she found the documents leave her.

"Uncle, I'm just as much to blame as aunt is. I didn't know how to tell you, and I was worried you might disown me for stealing. If I had told you, then I know you would have got the document from aunt, and the Coopers would have been none the wiser. However, I think I made an error when I told Mickey Cooper I was born in Thistlewoe. He wasn't the same to me after that."

"That's because the Coopers were born in Thistlewoe," said Hugh. "Please uncle, don't throw your marriage away. Both aunt and I are to blame. Promise me you will talk to her and stay together."

Hugh was always surprised by Rose and said, "I promise I will talk to her. She has asked to see you, but I told her to stay away. After everything she has done to you Rose, I can't believe you still care for her."

Rose replied, "I stopped caring for my aunt a long time ago, and she can't hurt me anymore. I have my own life now, and if she cared she would have come to me after the attack, but she didn't. That was when I needed her most. Thank heavens I had you, Monica, George and Ruby." Then a thought hit Rose. "You went to see Detective Bourtone on Friday didn't you, not a client?" Hugh nodded and asked her if she wanted him to tell her all of Cooper's statement. Rose took a deep breath and nodded. As he told her she went paler and paler, and Hugh thought she was going to faint, but she didn't.

When he had finished she smiled and said, "JP did write to me. He promised me he would and he did. What must he think of me? If he phoned he must have thought I was ignoring him. Not only did Mickey Cooper defile me, he took away the love of my life." Rose now broke down and sobbed in Hugh's arms. At that moment Hugh felt like killing Cooper himself. Once Rose had calmed, Hugh said he had better go home. Rose looked at the clock and it said 11.30pm. "Uncle it's very late. Why don't you stay here? You can either sleep in the spare bed or on the settee." Hugh said he would go home, as Nancy would be worried. Rose kissed his cheek as he left and said she would see him at work in the morning. Rose went to the cabinet and took out JP's card from Fete and kissed it. Then she put it back on top of the cabinet. It had been a long time since she had dreamt of JP, but that night she did.

The following morning Mr Fanterton opened the bank doors. Rose looked curiously, but then he told Rose, in her office, that her uncle had just been detained. Meanwhile back in Rilford, Hugh and Nancy were trying to sort things out. When Hugh arrived back the night before, it was to find Nancy pacing up and down, as she thought he'd had an accident.

In the morning as they sat at the table, eating breakfast, Hugh said, "Rose confessed something to me last night," and he told her. Nancy didn't say a word, and for once she just listened. When Hugh had finished he said, "So you see Nancy, Rose blames herself for her actions. I want to know something. You had one argument with Rose and then started treating her like dirt. Why?"

Nancy looked at Hugh and said quietly, "Jealousy. I was jealous of her. You and I had a wonderful life before she came. I tried my best to love her, but I couldn't. She wasn't ours. I saw the way you looked at her, and more or less gave her everything she wanted, and I felt pushed out. When I locked her in that Christmas, it was to teach her a lesson. I knew she'd been through my desk, and I knew she would again. I was so furious that I had the orphanage papers changed, and had that document done at the solicitor's. Again, I knew she'd read them because they were put back wrongly, and I didn't care. She had it coming to her … then. Now I dreadfully regret my actions. I should have gone to see her in the hospital, but I couldn't face her, and now that bridge is burnt forever. I don't want to lose you Hugh. Believe it or not, I love you as much now as I did when we were teenagers."

Hugh replied, "You can't even say her name can you, not even after all these years? I have to admit I still love you Nancy, and have decided you can stay, but things will change. As to what I don't know yet. Now I must get to work, as I have a bank to run." Nancy sighed a huge sigh of relief.

***

A week went by and Bourtone knew Cooper had to make a telephone call to his brother. Cooper was dragged up from the cells, looking slightly better. He'd been fed and watered.

"Right Cooper. Tonight you telephone your brother, but from here. I want to know where he is and what's happening. Do you understand?" Cooper nodded. Mickey had resigned himself to the fact that he was going to be locked up for the rest of his life. So why shouldn't his brothers join him? He was convinced they'd left him to rot in Sanjers. That night Cooper made the call, but from a payphone in the station by the front desk. Bourtone called for absolute silence, and gave Cooper a couple of 10p's. Pete answered and Mickey put his money in, and put the receiver between himself and Bourtone.

"When the bloody hell are you coming for me Pete? I'm cold, hungry, fed up of living in a squat, whilst you're in luxury in London."

Pete snapped, "Keep your bloody hair on. Archie is driving up at the weekend to get you. Everything is arranged."

At that moment a drunk walked into the station singing his head off, and made a beeline for Mickey. "Whhaars yyyoouu ddoooing mmaatte."

Mickey replied, "Bugger off you drunken bum."

The drunk carried on, "Wwhhoo yyoouu caallingg aaaa drruunnk?"

"Get lost old man, I'm trying to talk to me brother, and me money's running out." The drunk was forcibly removed.

"Where are you?" queried Pete.

"Phone box by The Battered Arms."

"Right, listen. Dump, Saturday, midday. Make sure nobody bloody sees you. Archie's in my car, then Friserton. Archie will fill you in," and with that Pete hung up.

Bourtone asked Cooper where Friserton was, but Mickey replied he had no idea. "Take him back to his cell, oh and Cooper, good acting" said Bourtone, who had been sweating with the arrival of the drunk. Mickey just shrugged his shoulders. Back in the main office he said, "Where and what is in Friserton. Find out, NOW."

Suddenly there was a flurry of activity in the office. About an hour later, one of the officers called Bourtone into the main office. Along with the photos on the board was now a map.

"Found it gov," Friserton is about fifty miles northwest of London. It's a derelict barracks, with a landing strip. Do you want one of us to drive down and have a look at the area?"

Bourtone sighed and said, "Not stupid is he? Where Friserton is situated, it's on the borderline of our's and London's jurisdictions. Crafty bastard. I need to know exactly where our jurisdiction line is. Whatever happens they must be in our jurisdiction. Right, call it a night for now, and see you all in the morning."

The following morning Bourtone said, "Right, you two go to Friserton and see what's there. Suss out this airstrip, and get back to me asap. Well don't just stand there." The two officers rushed out of the room.

Some hours later, one of the officers phoned, and said to Bourtone, "Not a lot here gov. Only half a dozen large billets, but we've checked them and nothing. We found the landing strip but it's covered with grass, and you wouldn't find it unless you were looking for it. What do you want us to do now gov?" Bourtone told them to return to the station. Bourtone phoned Hazellin in London and told him of the recent events, and Hazellin told him he had an idea.

Early Saturday morning, Bourtone and Hazellin and various officers, plus an armoured police wagon, arrived at Friserton. "Looks like somebody's been busy," said Bourtone. The landing strip had been cleared of grass, and was now visible.

"Gov, just found a refuelling tanker at the back of that billet," said one of his men, and pointed to it. Bourtone nodded.

"Need to fill you in about the Coopers," said Hazellin. "Three days ago Pete and Ronnie robbed a small bank, but got away with £10,000 in used notes. Luckily for us, there was on off duty policewoman inside. They grabbed her as a hostage, and was bundled into a car that Archie was driving. Not a good driver is young Archie, because as he rounded a corner too quick he had to slam his brakes on to avoid hitting a pedestrian. The policewoman pretended to hit her head on the window and they thought she was knocked out. When the car stopped, they dragged her out and threw her at the side of a garage. Slowly she opened her eyes and as Pete and Ronnie removed their masks, she recognised them. Next minute they drove out in another car." Bourtone asked if the policewoman was alright, and Hazellin said she was fine. Then Bourtone and Hazellin walked off talking to each other. Now all they had to do was just hide and wait.

Back in Birn, Mickey Cooper was driven to Sanjers dump. Four policemen with guns were carefully hidden. Mickey stood there, behind a shed, waiting for Archie. They all saw a black car cruising round the area two or three times. Mickey motioned to Archie, and Archie pulled up.

"Get in quick," said Archie. Mickey jumped in quickly and they sped off. At the end of the road a dustcart was reversing, accidentally on purpose, and Archie had to swerve to avoid it, but alas there was no room and he hit a lamp post. Within seconds the car was surrounded and both of them arrested, and put in a police wagon. Meanwhile, Pete and Ronnie were leaving London for Friserton, unaware various cars were following them. Pete was driving and keeping a watch for signs of the coppers, but he saw nothing out of the ordinary. Once they arrived at Friserton, they waited, and waited, and waited.

"Where the bloody hell is Archie and Mickey?"

Ronnie replied, "Could be an accident somewhere. Don't worry they'll be here. Can't say I'll miss this place, well apart from the prostitutes. Spain here we come."

Pete laughed and putting his arm round Ronnie's shoulder said, "I agree, but then we'll have Spanish prostitutes." There was a noise and Pete looked up. "Looks like our transport is here. Well Archie and Mickey have half an hour and then we go."

Ronnie asked surprised, "What you'll go without them?"

"If I have to," replied Pete. "You want to stay and serve life behind bars? Be my guest, but I'm off."

The plane landed on the strip. "Found it all right then Juan?"

Juan replied, "I wouldn't have done if you hadn't told me what to look for. You got the fuel and the money?" Pete nodded and walked over to the back of the billet and drove out the tanker. Whilst Juan refuelled the plane, Pete and Ronnie were getting worried about their brothers.

"Something's gone wrong," said Pete, "At least Archie's got the Spanish phone number. Have to set up another bloody pick up."

Juan said, "You ready to go, once you show me the money?" Pete opened the boot of the car and brought out a large and small holdall. He tossed the small one to Juan, who immediately checked it.

"Pleasure to do business with you Pete." Pete and Ronnie had a last look around, hoping to see Archie and Mickey, but nothing. They got on the plane. Suddenly from nowhere at least a dozen police cars drove towards the plane. "Get us the hell out of here Juan," shouted Pete. Juan started to turn the plane to take off, but two cars were blocking his way, and so he decided to turn and take off another way. As he started to get more speed for takeoff, gunshots rang out and they went into the fuselage. The fuel started to pour out, and he came to a halt. The police surrounded the plane and a couple of officers pulled Pete and Ronnie out.

CHAPTER 32

Once they had space, both of them started fighting like crazy and lashing out. It took six officers to wrestle Pete to the ground, and four for Ronnie. They were then handcuffed. Bourtone stood there watching the proceedings.

"Gentlemen," he said, "Now isn't this a nice surprise. You'll be pleased to know your two brothers are in Birn nick, and that's where you're going. Now be as good to spread your legs, so leg cuffs can be put on." Both men did as asked and the cuffs were put on. The two police officers at each side of them then held them still, so they couldn't move.

Pete laughed and said, "You think so? Well I'm delighted to tell you neither of us are going anywhere, as we are stood between two jurisdictions, and you can't touch us. Our solicitor will have us out within the hour."

Bourtone walked up to Pete, and looking him straight in the eyes said calmly, when he really wanted to punch his lights out, "You are actually, at this moment, stood in both jurisdictions. Did you seriously think I wouldn't work it out? Why the bloody hell would you come to a derelict place like this? Shall I tell you why? My friend Detective Hazellin here used to be a pilot, so when I overheard your conversation with your brother, he flew around the area. Imagine his surprise when he saw the yellow marks for the landing strip, but then he saw the thick green line marking out the two jurisdictions. Look where you are. You have one foot in each jurisdiction. The one thing you didn't think off was the fact your pilot had no idea what the green line was." Pete was absolutely furious. Bourtone continued,

"Pete and Ronnie Cooper, I'm arresting you for kidnap and rape."

Hazellin then said, "Pete and Ronnie Cooper I'm arresting you for armed robbery, murder, kidnap, attempted murder and various other crimes committed. You will be taken to Birn court first of all to stand trial, and then taken to the London Courts." Both of them were then placed in the armoured police wagon and chained to the inside rails. Just as they went to shut the doors Ronnie said,

"How did you know all this?"

Bourtone smirked and just said, "Extremely good police work. Oh nearly forgot in all the excitement, somebody tell them their rights."

Back at Birn police station, Mickey was put back in his cell, but Archie was put in one at the other end. Neither of them had spoken to each other all the way back. Some time later Pete and Ronnie were put in other cells. Upstairs, drinks were being handed round in celebration. Bourtone congratulated his officers on a "job well done."

Then he said, "Now the hard work starts. We need statements from these three bastards, and I know damn well Pete Cooper is going to deny any involvement, as I expect Ronnie Cooper will. Archie Cooper, not so sure. He's certainly not like the other two, and he's never been nicked before. Dickiens and Bowkers you interview him tomorrow morning, and keep him chained at all times. Rawthorn, Perkson and Whithers, you're with me interviewing the other two sods." At that moment the desk sergeant came in and said,

"Sorry to interrupt, but we badly need a hand in the cells. Pete and Ronnie Cooper are going ballistic." Bourtone went down and saw Pete and Ronnie injuring themselves on purpose.

"This is called "police brutality," said Pete. Bourtone asked someone to get a doctor to sedate them both. An hour later both of them were in straitjackets.

The following morning Hazellin and four of his detectives turned up. "Meant to say to you yesterday that life seems to be agreeing with you up here. I sort of noticed your waistline has got slightly bigger."

Bourtone laughed and replied, "At least I can relax. You can keep the Coopers of this world."

"Talking of them where are they?" Bourtone took Hazellin down to the cells.

"In those two," said Bourtone. Hazellin looked through drop down hatch and smirked.

"See they tried the police brutality routine. When you interviewing them?"

Bourtone replied, "I need to get the paperwork done, ready for the court to get a trial date. You're more than welcome to attend Archie Cooper's interview with Dickiens and Bowkers. We can interview those two bastards after lunch." Archie Cooper was brought up from his cell to the interview room, and pushed down onto a chair.

Bowkers said to him, "You've never been nicked before have you Cooper?" Archie just shook his head. "Well, let me give you some good advice, which will work in your favour. Tell the truth. What happened with Rose Brambles?"

Archie kept his head down and said quietly, "I didn't think Pete would be so violent. I know I raped her, but only because I got carried away with it all. I wish I'd been like Mickey and stood back. What's going to happen to me?"

Dickiens said, "Look at me Cooper." Archie raised his head and they could see he was crying. "You will be charged with kidnap and rape, and go to prison." Archie asked for how long. "That Cooper, will be up to the judge." Archie gave them his statement.

Hazellin returned to Bourtone's office.

Bourtone looked up and said, "Any joy?"

"His statement agrees with Mickey Cooper's," said Hazellin.

"Two down, two to go. Any luck with the judge?"

Bourtone smiled and said, "Trial in two weeks, but behind closed doors, and he doesn't want Rose Brambles to take the stand. Says she's suffered enough. He would, however, like Miss Brambles to ID the Cooper brothers, but unbeknown to them. I'll talk to her uncle about that."

Hazellin nodded in agreement, and said, "Pete or Ronnie first?"

"Let's take Ronnie first. If he coughs up, it's three to one." Ronnie was brought up, but just as they were about to interview him, their solicitor from London turned up.

"I believe you have my clients, Pete and Ronnie Cooper here. I wish to talk to them privately," he said rudely. Bourtone showed him into the interview room and closed the door, for all of two minutes.

"Sorry to interrupt, but thought you might like to read these," and gave him the two signed statements. He watched as he saw the solicitor pale, and then looking at Ronnie the solicitor said,

"You're on your own. I'm not defending you over this. You total and utter bastards. I hope you rot in jail," and with that walked out of the station. Ronnie was stunned.

"Whoops," said Hazellin smiling.

Ronnie scowled and said, "What did you give him?"

Bourtone replied, "Your brothers' statements, admitting kidnap and rape. So like your brothers you might as well give us your version of the truth." Ronnie took it that Pete had ratted on them all, so he told them what had happened. Like the other two, his statement was typed up and he signed it. As Ronnie went to go back to the cell, Bourtone shouted, "Bowkers, you can bring Pete Cooper up now." Ronnie turned and saw Bourtone and Hazellin smiling.

"You bloody bastards, you tricked me."

As expected Pete Cooper denied everything. Said he'd never been to Fracton, in fact he'd never heard of it. Hazellin looked him in the eyes and said, "We have a witness for the bank robbery. The woman you took was an off duty copper, and she wasn't knocked out. She saw who you were when you removed your masks. We have the prostitute you raped, who can ID you."

Cooper sniggered and said, "My solicitor will discredit them."

Bourtone smirked and said, "Well you just might have a problem there. We showed him your brothers' statements and he told Ronnie he hopes you rot in jail. He won't be defending you. So statement or not Cooper, you're going down big time. Take him back to his cell."

Hazellin said, "Well that went better than I thought. Thank god that twit of a solicitor turned up. For once he actually did us a favour. Well, my officers and I will go back to London. Do you want us back up for the court case? I know the courthouse is only over the road, but Cooper might have something planned."

Bourtone replied, "Let me show you something." They walked

back down to the cells, but Bourtone opened another door, which was the same as the rest of them. It was a passage, and Bourtone switched the lights on. As they walked Bourtone said, "Many, many years ago, Birn was the only town with a courthouse. One day as they walked two criminals across the street, they were shot. It was decided that a safer way had to be devised, so they built this." They had come to two other doors, and Bourtone opened one, and they walked up some steps. Hazellin was stunned, as he saw they were in the courthouse, but stood in the dock.

"Bloody hell, what a good idea," said Hazellin. When they went back down, the other door was opened and Hazellin saw the armoured police wagon along with two other police wagons.

"There is a back entrance to the court, with huge thick steel doors, and not many people know about it, as it's camouflaged." Hazellin was well impressed.

Back at the front entrance Bourtone said, "I'll ring you and let you know the outcome." Bourtone and Hazellin shook hands. Bourtone went to his office and phoned Mr Brambles.

A couple of days later Rose and her uncle arrived at the station. They were shown to Bourtone's office.

"Thank you for both coming. You remember Eve Huble, and may I introduce Judge Padges, who will be sentencing the prisoners? I thought it might help to have another woman at your side. You have nothing to fear Miss Brambles, as they will not see you. They are all in separate cells, and all you need to do is look through the small hatch, and tell us if you recognise them." Rose said she understood, but they could all see she was pale and shaking. As they got to the cells Rose stopped. She really didn't want to see them, and now everything came flooding back. Eve went to her and gently told her not to be frightened, and it would soon be over. Rose swallowed hard and nodded. She identified Pete, Ronnie and Archie straight away. Mickey she wasn't so sure. He now had long hair, and a beard. She whispered to Eve she needed to hear his voice.

Eve spoke to the sergeant. "You alright in there Cooper. You need anything?"

Mickey replied, "No thanks. When will I know my fate?"

"Very soon," and the sergeant closed the hatch. Rose confirmed it was him. They all went back upstairs and Hugh held Rose in his arms. The judge asked Rose to sign a document confirming that she had identified the Cooper brothers. Two witnesses then countersigned this. He also told her she wouldn't be needed in court. Rose and Hugh thanked them all for everything they had done, and left. Hugh drove Rose to the countryside pub she liked, where they enjoyed a lovely meal. Hugh noticed Rose seemed preoccupied.

"Rose, my dear, it's over. Please don't dwell on the past." Rose smiled and said, "It's not them uncle. It's a year today that I met JP," and tears fell down her face.

Two weeks later, the Cooper brothers were in court. All of them were hand and leg cuffed. Judge Padges had suggested to Bourtone that the sentences be passed separately. That way the brothers couldn't talk to each other, or know which prisons they were going to. Bourtone agreed. First one to appear was Archie Cooper. The judge could see he was shaking, and had his head down.

"Archie Cooper. You have been charged with kidnap, rape and attempted murder of the said Miss Brambles. How do you plead?"

Archie replied, "Guilty sir." Archie's head then shot up, and he said, "Please sir, are you saying she didn't die?" The judge confirmed she didn't die. He actually saw Cooper sigh with relief.

"Archie Cooper, as you have never been in trouble before, but due to the seriousness of this horrific attack, I hereby sentence you to five years in Corneat Prison. Take him away." Archie was taken back down the steps and put into a plain disguised police wagon and driven off. Next to appear was Mickey Cooper.

The judge charged him with the same crime but said, "Mickey Cooper, as you didn't actually perform the action of rape, you did pass on certain information to your brothers. However, certain information has come to my knowledge concerning your co-operation with the police. I hereby sentence you to three years at Glarith Prison. Take him away." Mickey, like Archie was taken down and driven off to Glarith prison.

Next to appear were Ronnie and Pete Cooper. The judge, at the last minute, decided to sentence them together. They were brought up separately and were made to stand at each end of the dock. They couldn't see each other as a panel had been put up to split the dock in half. Pete was full of self confidence, but when he appeared in the dock and looked around he froze. Apart from the judge, couple of court officials, and Bourtone and his officers, the court was totally empty. All week he had been planning what to say, hoping to plead with the jury that he was innocent.

Pete shouted, "What the hell's going on here? Where are the jury, the press and the public?"

"SILENCE IN COURT" said Judge Padges. "To answer your question Mr Cooper, this is a closed court. There is no jury as your brothers have all signed statements pleading guilty to kidnap, rape and attempted murder, and we have a witness implicating you in this horrific attack. As to the press and public, due to the excellent work of the police, and a secret joint police operation, they have no knowledge that you have been arrested." Looking at Ronnie Cooper, the judge asked, "Ronnie Cooper. You have been charged with kidnap, rape and attempted murder of the said Miss Brambles. How do you plead?"

Ronnie replied, "Guilty sir." Looking at Pete Cooper he asked the same question.

Pete replied, "Not guilty. I wasn't there and whoever this eyewitness is, they're lying." Judge Padges raised his eyebrow and replied, "Your brothers have signed guilty pleas, and you say you're not guilty? As to the eyewitness, I understand you think Miss Brambles died. Well I'm pleased to say she lived, but has had to have over six months' counselling. How on earth she survived, is only down to the excellent doctors, nurses, family and friends who have and still are helping her through this."

Pete was stunned and shouted in a rage, "You're lying. There's no way she survived that attack. I got my revenge. This is a trick."

The judge replied quickly, "How do you know if you weren't there?" Too late Pete realised what he had said and knew there was no way out.

Looking from one to the other, Judge Padges said, "I hope I never have to preside over a case like this ever again. The horrific attack you put that poor defenceless woman through was beyond comprehension. Peter Cooper and Ronnie Cooper, as the instigators of this horrendous crime, I hereby sentence you both to fifteen years imprisonment at Alkin Prison. You will leave this place and be taken to Alkin Prison, to await your appearance in the London court, where you will stand trial for murder, rape, armed robbery and other crimes committed. Take them away." Bourtone watched as Ronnie Cooper was put into the armoured police wagon first, which was disguised as a delivery van, and then a steel partition separated him from Pete. Next Pete Cooper was put in. Both of them were changed to the steel rails inside the armoured police wagon. For once neither of the Cooper brothers spoke. He watched as the wagon drove out of the entrance taking them to Alkin prison. Now things could get back to normal. Back in his office he phoned Hazellin and told him the news.

"Excellent," said Hazellin, "Now it's our turn. Neither of them are going to see the outside world ever again. I will do my best to keep Birn and Miss Brambles out of the press. Don't forget us down here, you know you're welcome any time." Bourtone replied he would keep in touch.

CHAPTER 33

Once the trial was finished Rose carried on with her life as normal. The bank was now very busy, and Rose was also helping Ruby writing her stories for the newspaper. Rose had also bought, at great expense, a camera. She was taking a great interest in photography. Rose only spent what she had to and had managed to save a lot. She still hadn't touched the money her uncle had put in her savings book. About a month later, Pete and Ronnie Cooper stood trial in London. They were both given life sentences, to be served in solitary, along with other associates of theirs. A friend of Ruby's, who had transferred down to a London press office, phoned her and told her. Ruby immediately phoned Hugh, who met her and together they went to Rose's flat. Rose was surprised to see them.

"Is everything alright?"

Ruby said, "It's to do with the Coopers. They've had their trial in London and it's in the newspapers. A friend has told me all their crimes were listed that had happened in London, but it printed that another attempted murder had taken place in another jurisdiction, with details. No names or places were reported. It's not headline news though. A tour operator has gone bust and thousands and thousands of holidaymakers are stranded abroad. The article of the Coopers only made page five."

Rose frowned and replied, "Everyone round here will know that's me. How can I face them?"

Hugh replied, "Rose, the Coopers will be chip shop paper tomorrow, and they're not even headline news. People here in

Fracton and Birn, more or less know already what happened, and I doubt if they'll take any more notice, and since when did we get London newspapers?" Ruby agreed with him.

A couple of weekends later, Ruby knew it was coming up to the year when JP and Antoine left with the others, and Rose's attack. Her boss at the newspaper noticed she seemed pre-occupied and called her into his office.

"What's up Ruby? Not like you to be down in the dumps." Ruby told him. "Then I have just the job and you can take Rose with you." Edward Missine, better known as Ed, had met Rose on a few occasions, and liked her. He felt sorry for what she'd endured though. "The Mayor of Whisley, which is a seaside town, has passed away. He was born and raised in Birn, and I thought it might be nice to do a piece in the newspaper to remember him. I was going to send Kevin, but perhaps you would like to go instead?" Ruby jumped at the chance, as this was just what they both needed. Ed said as a one off, he would book them into a hotel, single rooms if needed, and would pay for the petrol. He suggested they took a week, and then they could mix business with pleasure. Ruby telephoned Rose that night, and Rose said she would love to go, but first she must ask her uncle for the time off. Hugh agreed immediately. He knew the anniversary was coming up, and was going to try and plan something, but what he didn't know. This was a great idea.

At the weekend, Ruby picked Rose up and off they went to Whisley. It was a large seaside town and very busy. The hotel that Ed had booked was right on the seafront, and he had booked them two single adjoining rooms, en suite. The hotel manager, who was a lady, was lovely, and gave them a map of the town, and marked places of interest. The first thing they did, was to run down the beach, and paddle in the sea.

"Oh Ruby, this is lovely. The sun is shining, the sea is cool, the wind is blowing lightly, but more than that, it feels like freedom." Ruby noticed an immediate change in Rose, as all the past months left her. Silently she thanked Ed. They wandered round the town and found a nice little restaurant where they enjoyed a meal of fish and chips. On the Sunday they spend the day at the beach. Ruby wore a bikini, but Rose wore a swimsuit. They sunbathed, swam in the sea, had ice creams, and talked about this and that. Ruby was pleased because Rose actually spoke about JP and Antoine. It was a year, but neither of them had forgotten their feelings for them. Ruby had been out on a few dates, but nothing happened. Rose was now very wary of men. She would be polite, but gave them no encouragement whatsoever. She believed on the outside she was still pretty, but on the inside she was ugly. She felt dead from the waist down and knew no man would ever touch her there again.

On the Monday, Rose and Ruby went to the *Whisley Chronicle* offices. Ruby explained why they were there. The editor was really helpful, and told them what they wanted to know, and he even suggested calling on the mayor's wife, Mrs Higgith, as she too was from Birn. Ruby thanked him, and off they went. When they found the address, they drove down a long windy driveway, which had large trees on each side. When they reached the house, Rose thought it looked like they picked up the largest detached house, and placed it in the middle of a forest. There was a huge fountain in the front of the house, with landscaped gardens.

"Looks like the mayor was rather well-off," said Ruby. Rose nodded, as she was busy taking photos.

"Ruby look. There are squirrels in that tree." She photographed them. They walked up to the door and pressed the bell, which chimed inside. A maid opened the door and asked if she could help. Ruby explained, and they were shown into the sitting room. The room was huge, and had large paintings on the walls, and Greek statues stood by the windows. There was even a chandelier hanging from the ceiling.

"Good morning ladies. I am Mrs Higgith. How may one help you?" asked a very posh voice. They turned to see a lovely looking lady, maybe in her sixties and elegantly dressed.

Ruby replied, "Please forgive this intrusion at such a sad time, and our condolences at the loss of your husband. I am from the newspaper office in Birn, and with your permission, I would like to write about your husband, as I understand he was Birn."

Two hours later, Ruby had her story. Mrs Higgith turned out to be a wonderful, informative lady, and gave Ruby a full history on her husband and herself. They were brought refreshments, and the conversation flowed. It was obvious to Rose, after being married for forty years, that Mrs Higgith still loved her husband very much.

As they went to leave Rose asked, "May I ask if I can take your photo? It would be nice to put it alongside Ruby's story?" Mrs Higgith replied she would like that. After Rose had taken her photo, Mrs Higgith gave her a photo of her husband.

"Perhaps we could both go with the story," she said smiling, and Rose smiled back. After they left, Ruby thought it would be a nice idea to go for a drive. Rose said that was a great idea. They drove out into the countryside, and the views were spectacular. Rose had to change the film reel twice! Ruby pulled into a country pub, where they sampled the delights of home cooking. Steak pie, mashed potatoes and vegetables. The pub was busy and quite a few of the young men were eyeing them up. Rose felt uncomfortable when people stared at her. She immediately thought they knew what had happened. Ruby soon put her at ease. They drove back to the hotel and Ruby started re-writing her notes. Rose went off to a camera shop to have her films developed. She was told they would take two days. When she got back she tapped on Ruby's door.

"Come in Rose." Ruby had pieces of paper everywhere. "I need your help Rose. Tell me if this makes sense," and handed her two sheets. Rose read them, and suggested some changes. "That's great Rose. What would I do without you? Have you ever thought about leaving the bank, and joining the paper? You could be our photographer."

Rose replied, "As much as I would like that, it wouldn't pay very much, and I'd have to leave my flat." "Good point," said Ruby.

After enjoying a meal in the hotel restaurant, and a few drinks in the bar, Rose and Ruby left and went to their rooms. Once in her room, Rose saw the moonlight streaming through the window, and opened it. She could hear the waves crashing onto the beach and rocks. She looked up and saw the stars were twinkling. Rose knew what evening it was. It was the evening she had said goodbye to JP, and the attack. She put her hand on her stomach and felt the scar. She stood in the moonlight with her arms wrapped around herself and closed her eyes, and thought, *I wonder what JP is doing? It feels like he is here with me now, with his arms wrapped round me, and he's gently kissing the side of my neck.* When she opened her eyes it was to look at a bleary moon as her tears slowly fell for her lost love.

***

Little did she know, that at that same moment, in the president's palace gardens, four bodyguards were silently watching their boss. JP was sitting on a bench, by the River Seine, looking up at the moon. He knew what day it was. It was a year since he had to leave Rose so suddenly. He wished she was with him, and he had his arms round her. He brushed away the couple of tears that had fallen. One question always returned though - why did she never reply to his letters? His men knew his heart had broken when Rose never replied to his letters, and that bothered them, even after a year.

"Why do you think Rose never wrote to him? I can't get my head round it, as it's not the sort of thing Rose would have done," said Andre.

Pierre said, "I've known JP for many years, and I've never seen him like this. Even after a year, he's still broken. He throws himself into his work, like we all do, but when he gets time off, it's like he's lost."

Donatien said, "We've had him round for meals and introduced him to some lovely ladies, but he's just not interested. Antoine, did you ever write to Ruby?"

Antoine replied, "No, as we decided it was for the best. A long distance relationship wouldn't have worked. We just loved the time we had together."

Andre said, "Perhaps you should write to Ruby, as she'll know why. Once we know Rose's reasons, we can hopefully help him."

Antoine replied, "I would have written sooner, but I don't have Ruby's address. JP had left both of our letters, with our addresses, on the table in the billet. When he got back here, some idiot had put them in his bag. We will just have to keep watch over him."

Pierre said, "Move, now. JP's coming back."

***

Later on in the night, Ruby heard a scream. She was out of her bed like a bullet, and went straight into Rose's room. Rose was tossing and turning and saying, "No, no, please don't hurt me, please don't." As she went to scream again, Ruby put her hand over her mouth so it was muffled.

"Hush Rose, I'm here. Nobody is going to hurt you. I'm here," said Ruby cradling her in her arms. Rose started to calm, because she thought it was JP gently talking to her. There was a gentle tap on the door, and Ruby answered it. "Is everything alright? I heard a scream."

Ruby replied, "My apologies but my friend had a nightmare. I hope she didn't wake everyone up?" The lady manager replied not to worry, and she would say it was a cat brawl. Ruby smiled and thanked her. Ruby stayed with Rose until she saw she was sleeping calmly, and then went to her own bed. In the morning Ruby asked Rose if she was alright. Rose told her she had a nightmare about the attack, and Ruby then told her what happened.

"Oh how embarrassing," said Rose. "I must apologise." Ruby told her what the lady had said and Rose laughed. Whilst they were having breakfast, the lady manager came over and whispered,

"Sorry about the cat brawl last night, not a lot we can do about that," and she winked. Rose and Ruby smiled.

The rest of the week went by quickly. Rose and Ruby did all the things tourists did. Rose collected her photos and was delighted with them. Ruby loved the ones of Mrs Higgith, and the squirrels. Rose knew how to capture a story in her photos. Soon they said goodbye to Whisley and were on their way home. Ruby stayed the night at Rose's and left Sunday evening. That night Hugh phoned Ruby to make sure everything had been alright. Ruby told him about Rose's dream.

"I had a strange feeling that might happen. Do you think I need to get Rose more counselling?"

Ruby replied, "Honestly Mr Brambles, there is no need. Rose is fine. On the Friday night, we went to a disco, and we danced with various men, and two of them walked us back to the hotel, kissed our cheeks and said "goodnight." I checked on her later on and she was firm asleep." Hugh was relieved and thanked Ruby. On the Monday, Hugh noticed Rose had tanned slightly, and she looked so relaxed. Ruby had taken her story into Ed, and he was impressed.

"Ruby, did you take these photos?"

Ruby replied, "Heavens no, I'm useless. Rose took them." Ed asked Ruby if she had anymore.

"Yes, she gave me all of them, as there's some of the mayor's house you might want to use." Ed looked through them, and was more than impressed. "If Rose ever leaves the bank, tell her she's got a job here as a photographer. Look at the way she's captured those squirrels, it's brilliant." Ruby told Ed she had already suggested it, but it would mean her leaving her flat, and she didn't think the pay would be as good. Ed said, "I'm sure we could come to some amicable arrangement."

Rose and Ruby always got together at the weekends, and if Ruby was covering a story, Rose would help. Both of them would stay with Monica and George when they could. A big story was breaking in a large village, about twenty miles away from Birn, and Ed sent Ruby. A five-year-old boy had wandered off into a forest and hadn't been seen for two days. Ruby knew this was a very sensitive story, and treated it so. When she arrived she saw there were about twelve reporters and a TV crew. She couldn't believe how insensitive the men were, and decided to stay away from them. She spoke to the detective leading the search, and through him she managed to interview the parents. Ruby saw them later and showed them her report, in case she had misunderstood anything. She hadn't and they were happy for it to be printed. Ruby phoned Ed, and he took her report over the phone. Another two days went by and nothing. Ruby's heart had gone out to the family and friends. She was dreading having to end the story on a sad note. On the sixth day, the detective called everyone together.

"Ladies and gentlemen, I have news on the boy. I'm delighted to say he has been found safe and well. At the moment he is in the hospital, with his parents, undergoing checks. He has not been harmed in any way. He had found a derelict shack at the far end of the forest, and stayed there. Thank you for all your help, and I now ask that you all leave the area, so folks can get back to their normal lives." Ruby walked away to a quiet spot and cried, but they were tears of joy.

CHAPTER 34

———————∼———————

Over the next eighteen months, life changed for both Rose and Ruby. One day Hugh called Rose into his office.

"Rose, I wanted you to be the first to know. Head office wants me to move down to a new branch on the outskirts of London. I will be relocating in the next three months. Mr Fanterton, I'm pleased to say, will be replacing me. That's means a new deputy manager will be starting shortly. There is a possibility that he will want the flat. As he's senior to you, my hands are tied. I won't know until he arrives."

Rose replied, "Congratulations uncle, but I am going to miss you. If I have to move out, then I'll start looking for somewhere else. Is aunt going with you?" Hugh replied she wasn't, because of her work. Head office had a flat sorted out for him, and he would drive back to Rilford on Friday evenings, and return to London early Monday mornings.

"With the motorway, it's only just over an hour's drive. Now, I need to talk to Mr Fanterton and advise him of the new changes." Rose left his office with mixed feelings. On the one hand she was pleased for her uncle, but on the other hand she would miss him terribly. These days Rose only saw Ruby once a month if she was lucky. Ruby was now a fully fledged journalist, and went all over the counties on various assignments. The bank staff were told that afternoon. Everyone was pleased, but wary of the future.

Two weeks later, the new deputy manager arrived. Straight away Rose took a dislike to him, which was unusual. He strode into the bank like he owned it. He looked down his nose at the staff, and ran his finger over the furniture, checking for dust!! Rose was stood by the foreign till as she had just helped a client.

"You there, tell Mr Brambles, Mr Carnell Smetherson is here, and don't dawdle." Rose looked him up and down and replied politely but firmly, "I am Miss Brambles, and you will refer to me as such. Manners cost nothing. Please wait here," and with that she turned her back on him. Rose knocked on her uncle's door, and Hugh beckoned her in.

"Our new deputy manager, Mr Carnell Smetherson is here to see you uncle. Obnoxious excuse for a man." Hugh looked at Rose stunned. He had never heard her call anyone that before.

"Thank you Rose. I will go and inform Mr Fanterton. Is he really that rude? We've never met him, as head office appraised him."

Rose smiled and replied, "First impression, we will all be gone within six months." Hugh didn't like the sound of that, but once Stanley and himself had met him they agreed. Alas they were saddled with him. After work Hugh popped up to see Rose. "You'll be pleased to know that Mr Smetherson will not need your flat. I got the impression it was beneath him. In his words, he's looking for something more "up market.""

Rose laughed and replied, "He's going to be trouble. I hope Mr Fanterton can cope with him?" Now Hugh laughed and told her Stanley could more than cope with a little upstart like Smetherson. Rose hoped he was right, especially where the staff were concerned.

That weekend Rose drove over to Monica and George's. Ruby had phoned to say she would be late. When she arrived, they all knew something had happened.

"Okay Ruby. You look to be bursting at the seams. What's happened?" asked George.

Ruby said excitedly, "I've been offered a job down in London at *Gilmac News*, as a journalist. I have to attend an interview on Tuesday."

George said, "*Gilmac News*, isn't that one of the top London newspapers?" Ruby replied it was. Apparently the editor had seen her story on the missing boy, and had been following her stories. He phoned Ed and asked if he was prepared to let her go. Ed knew the editor, and told him only if she got a good deal, hence the interview.

Monica and Rose were both delighted, but Monica noticed Rose's smile didn't reach her eyes, like they always did.

"Rose you alright?"

Rose replied, "Oh I'm sorry. Ruby I am absolutely delighted for you, but it looks like I'm losing my best two friends to London." She then explained about Hugh, and the new deputy manager.

Ruby said, "Come with me Rose. There's always a need for photographers. Just think of the good times we'd have. Travelling all over the UK and maybe we might get to go abroad." Rose said she would think about it, but she would see how things went at the bank first. After Rose had gone to bed, she actually did think about it. She was only there, and in her position, because of her uncle. Banking was a man's world, and she knew she couldn't advance. Whereas if she went with Ruby, she could do her photography that she loved, and she could also see her uncle. Before she closed her eyes, she had decided to go to night classes and learn about journalism.

Two weeks later, Ruby had her interview in London, and was offered the job, and would start two weeks later. The pay was really good, but then London was expensive. She would be on a three month temporary contract, and if all worked out, she would then be taken on permanently. The editor recommended a good estate agent, for flats, bedsits and lodging houses. On the way back to her car, she popped into the estate agents and picked up some details of various places to stay. She wanted Rose to help her choose. On the Friday night, Rose stayed at Ruby's and they looked through and picked out some places to look at. Saturday morning they drove to London. One flat was in a seedy part of London, so that was out. The second flat was above a shop, so that was no good. They looked at another six places, but none of them were what Ruby wanted. Both deflated and tired, they drove back to Birn. Sunday morning they went to Monica and George's. Ruby showed them the ones they had a look at.

George said, "So who fancies lunch in London then? Let's all go, and have a look in other estate agents," and that's what happened. Ruby found a flat she wanted, so she wrote down the details. Monday morning Ruby phoned the estate agent, and made an appointment to go down again on Wednesday. It was a small flat about a ten minute walk away from the newspaper office, and she liked it, so a contract was signed for three months' rent. Rose was pleased for her.

Months later, Hugh had left and so had Ruby, but both telephoned as much as possible. One lunchtime in the bank, Rose walked into the kitchen to find one of the ladies in tears.

"What's wrong?" she asked.

Miss Antier replied, "It's Mr Smetherson. I accidentally made a mistake in my ledger book, and he's virtually accused me of stealing, and now I'm going to lose my job." Rose was furious and stormed off to Mr Fanterton's office, and banged on his door.

"Come in. Miss Brambles, are you alright, as you look very flustered?" Rose explained.

Stanley sighed and said, "Why on earth head office couldn't have promoted you is beyond reason. Between you and me I can't stand him. I have been watching him, and he's as nice as can be, when I'm around. The moment I leave, he's just downright nasty. Tell Miss Antier, that I have no intention of letting her go. Could you kindly check her ledger, and I'll have words with Smetherson."

Rose assured him she would sort it out. The staff knew if they had a problem, they just had to press the buzzer and she would go to them. Now Smetherson would come and butt in, and make a mountain out of a molehill. Instead of working in his office, he was always in the hall, looking at everyone and everything. One day Mrs Strocken turned up at the bank. Rose spotted her and went out of her office to greet her. Before she got there, Smetherson intervened.

"Good morning madam. I am Mr Carnell Smetherson, the Deputy Manager. How can I be of assistance?"

Mrs Strocken looked him up and down and said, "I have come to see Miss Brambles on an urgent matter. Is she here?"

Smetherson replied, "Oh she's around somewhere. I'm far superior to Miss Brambles, so if you would care to enter my office ..." Mrs Strocken had seen Rose walking towards her.

"Ah Miss Brambles, I'm so pleased to see you. May we talk in private?"

Rose replied, "Certainly Mrs Strocken. Would you care for refreshments?"

"No thank you my dear, but there is one thing you can do." In a rather loud voice she said, "Would you mind asking this sarcastic, stuck up baboon to get out of my way? His manners are diabolical." Everyone in the bank sniggered, and Smetherson walked off in disgust. In Rose's office Mrs Strocken said, "My apologies Miss Brambles, and forgive my language, but I can't stand bloody little upstarts like him. Who on earth does he think he is?" Rose could only smile, and then they sorted out her urgent business.

Rose had found a college that did tutorials in journalism, and attended three nights a week. It was hard work, but she persevered. She finished her course two weeks before Christmas, and passed her exams. Rose was going to drive down to London and stay with Ruby for the Christmas break, and she couldn't wait. The week before Christmas, the weather started turning bad. On the news she heard severe storms were due to hit all over the country. Rose only shopped when she needed to and didn't stockpile. That evening when she went to the supermarket, it was absolutely packed. She asked one of the staff what was going on.

"Scaremongering, if you ask me. The television and radio are telling everyone to get plenty of foodstuff, etc in, as it's going to be a very harsh winter. Look, we've even got boxes of candles at half price." Rose, for some unknown reason, also decided to do a big shop, although she didn't go overboard. Mostly she bought tin stuff, bottles of water, just in case the pipes froze, and she actually got two boxes of candles and matches. Luckily, when the bank had been refurbished, a new gas cooker and fridge/freezer had been installed in the flat. After Rose put the supermarket goods in her car, she went to the butchers and bought sausages, chicken, gammon slices, bacon, and other meats that could be frozen. On her way back she passed the ironmonger's, and saw a tent like thing that went over a car. Out of curiosity she went in and had a look, and ended up buying one. Back at the flat she put everything away, and for the first time the cupboards were nearly full.

Over the next couple of days, the winds picked up and they were icy cold. People didn't dawdle in the streets, which made them quiet. The bank was busy with Christmas just around the corner, and people would come in with red rosy cheeks. The snow started to gently fall the day before Christmas Eve. Rose now started to worry she wouldn't get to Ruby's. She decided to put the cover over her car, which took some effort, and managed to find some bricks, which secured the cover down properly. That night she heard the wind getting worse, but assumed in the morning all would be fine. How wrong she was. When she got up and drew her bedroom curtains back, it was to look onto a white scene. She looked out of the sitting room window, and saw the street was covered in about a foot of snow. Drivers were driving very slowly, but some were sliding. People were slipping and sliding on the pavements. She switched the radio on and heard that most of the country had been hit by a snowstorm and all transport was at a dead halt. People were told to stay inside, and not to drive, unless it was an absolute emergency. Lots of villages in Lancashire and Yorkshire had been totally cut off. Rose washed, dressed, had her breakfast and as she went to leave the flat, she saw Mr Fanterton slowly driving in.

"Rose, I'll let you in the back door," he called. Stanley only called her Rose, when nobody else was around. That morning only half the staff turned up, and Rose worked behind one of the tills. Even Mr Smetherson didn't make it in. The bank wasn't too busy, but outside the snow was falling heavily. About lunchtime, Mr Fanterton told the staff to go home, and Rose and himself would stay for the extra hour. At 1pm the bank closed and Rose helped Stanley take the money down to the vault, and then after checking everything was secure, they left by the back door, which Stanley then locked. They wished each other Merry Christmas, and Rose told Stanley to drive carefully.

Once in her flat Rose phoned Ruby, who told her under no circumstances, was she to even attempt to drive down. Rose had been so looking forward to seeing Ruby, and was upset, but there was nothing she could do. The weather had kept them apart for this Christmas. Rose then phoned her uncle, who was also stuck in London. Rose then realised Ruby, Hugh, Nancy, Monica and George, and herself would all be on their own for Christmas Day. By the following morning the snow had covered Rose's car. The whole country was at a total standstill, but worse than that, the winds had brought down power and telephone cables, so lots of counties had no electric and couldn't telephone for help. Rose was now glad she had got plenty of food in. Rose got telephone calls from Ruby and her parents, and Hugh all wishing her a happy birthday and Merry Christmas. They all made sure each other was alright. Later on Rose made herself a Christmas meal. Once she'd finished, she washed and put everything away, made herself a coffee, switched the television on for The Queen's speech, and then started to watch a film. Slowly she fell asleep. When she woke it was pitch black. She noticed the television was off. Strange!! She put her hand out and switched the lamp on - nothing. *Damn* she thought, *my meter must've run out*. She fumbled in the dark and found one of the boxes of candles, and lit one. She grabbed a bag of 50p pieces she kept by the meter, but when she looked the meter was nearly full. Back in the sitting room, she saw the streetlights were out, and then realised there was a power cut!!

"Oh no," she said to nobody but herself, "The fridge/freezer will start defrosting." Luckily she remembered someone telling her, if you covered everything with tea towels and newspapers, it would keep it cold, and not to open it. Rose covered everything. As there was nothing else to do, Rose went to bed.

CHAPTER 35

Around 5am in the morning, she was awoken by people talking, and they sounded like they were in the sitting room, and froze. Had somebody broken into the flat? Memories of her attack hit her, and she was petrified. The telephone was in the sitting room. Quickly she got dressed, and decided she would try and get out of the flat. She never shut her bedroom door, only pushed it to, and so she slowly opened it wider, and slipped out. As she neared the sitting room the voices got louder. It was two men and they were discussing how to rob the bank! Then she heard one of them mention explosives. They were going to blow the vault open. Suddenly the voices stopped and Rose stopped dead in her tracks. "Did you hear that?" said one of them. "Hear what?" asked the other gruffly. "I heard a noise, I'm going to look." Rose stood there, shaking from head to foot. Then she heard police sirens. *Oh thank heavens,* she thought, *the police are here. They must have set off the bank's alarm.* "Let's get out of here," said one of the men. Rose waited for the sitting room door to be flung open, but nothing happened. "You're nicked," said another voice. Rose thought, *what?* and slowly opened the door, and let out a very nervous laugh. It was the television - she had forgotten to turn it off. She sat down on the settee and let the relief sweep over her, and then said, "At least the power is back on." Rose went into the kitchen and made herself a mug of tea, went back to the bedroom and undressed, got back into bed and drank her tea. A memory surfaced of when JP had cooked her breakfast, so she snuggled down and with that thought, went back to sleep. It was 11am when she woke again. Looking out the window she could see it was still snowing. The severe winds had whipped up huge snowdrifts, and the one that covered her car must have been at least six foot high. Rose was now very pleased she'd bought the car cover.

The snow carried on until the following week, with more power cuts, and then Rose's telephone was out of action, and then the temperatures dropped dramatically, and lots of people had frozen pipes. The bank didn't re-open until after the first week of the New Year. The temperatures started to rise, albeit slowly, and then the frozen pipes started to thaw, causing some flooding in the houses, and other buildings. As much as Rose was comfortable with her own company, she was glad get back to work, well until Smetherson walked in. He was his normal pompous self, and Rose just couldn't abide him any longer. Sometimes he was even rude to the clients, and she received quite a lot of complaints. Stanley did what he could, but Head Office would not release him. After three months, Rose came to a decision. She phoned Ruby, and they made arrangements for Rose to go down that weekend. Rose asked Stanley if she could have the Friday and Monday off, so she could visit her uncle as well. Stanley agreed, but did wonder if Rose had an ulterior motive. She phoned Hugh who was delighted, and gave her directions to the bank. On the Friday morning Rose set off for London, and arrived about two hours later. Rose knew where Ruby's flat was and went there first and dropped her bags off, as Ruby had left a key in a hidden place. Rose would see Ruby later.

Rose made her way to Stocks Bank. It was a good half hour walk, and when she walked in the bank she stood in awe. The bank was as wide as it was high. Two large chandeliers hung from the ceiling, the wood was all medium oak. There were twelve teller desks and one foreign exchange. There were settees and chairs, tables with magazines and newspapers, and a large reception desk. The whole place was light and airy. She could see six private offices, but her uncle wasn't in one of them.

"Good morning Miss. May I help you. My name is Robert."

Rose was taken aback by him using his first name.

"Yes please," she replied, "I'm Rose Brambles, and I'm ..."

Robert put his hand up to stop her and replied, "You're Mr Brambles' niece. Nice to meet you. Your uncle told me to look for a beautiful lady with black/reddish hair. I recognised you as soon as you walked in. Please follow me." Robert took her through the bank, and a lot of the young men turned and looked at her. They went up some stairs where an office stood on its own. Robert knocked on the door and a voice said, "Come in."

Robert opened the door and said, "Excuse me Mr Brambles, I have your lovely niece here." Robert showed Rose into Hugh's office and left, closing the door behind him.

"Rose my dear, how are you? Let me look at you. As beautiful as ever," and hugged and kissed her cheek. "What do you think of the bank? Lot different to Fracton isn't it?"

"You can say that again uncle. It's so big. How many staff do you have?" Hugh told her there were forty staff. Apart from himself and his deputy manager John Soulfam, it was all first names. "Now let's go for lunch and you can tell me why you're really here." Rose just smiled at him. As they left his office, Rose noticed her uncle could see the whole bank below.

In the restaurant Hugh asked her how things were in Fracton. Rose told him. He already had a feeling Rose was fed up with Smetherson as Stanley phoned him now and then. He had asked Stanley to keep an eye on Rose. He still worried she might have flashbacks about the attack, and with Ruby and himself in London, he just wanted to know she was alright. Of course, he knew she still had Monica and George.

"I wish I could offer you a job here Rose, but at the moment there are no vacancies. For once, head office actually got me a good team, and they all get on with each other. Makes coming to work a lot better. If you're interested, as soon as a position becomes available, I'll ring you."

Rose smiled at him and said honestly, "Actually uncle, I'm thinking of a career change. I went to night college and studied journalism, and passed, but more than that I want to join Ruby as a journalist/photographer. What do you think?" Hugh wasn't surprised, and told her whatever she did, he would support her. If she decided to move down, he would look for a flat for her, as he now had clients who could help. Rose said that it all decided on how she felt in London. She had already noticed how busy the city was, people rushing here and there, along with men in pinstriped suits, bowler hats and umbrellas, and the women were all smartly dressed too. She knew there were seedier parts of London to stay away from, and crime was at a high level. Out of nowhere thoughts of the Cooper brothers came into her mind. Hugh noticed Rose had paled.

"Rose, what's wrong?" Rose told him, and Hugh took her hand. "It's only bad Rose if you get mixed up with a bad crowd. You have more sense than that, and you will always have Ruby and me. Now I'm really sorry my dear, but I must get back. Have a lovely weekend with Ruby, and come and see me before you go back to Fracton." Rose promised she would.

"Rose, Rose, I can't believe you're here," said Ruby throwing her arms round her. "I have missed you so much. Let me get changed and then we'll hit the town for a meal."

Rose replied, "Ruby can we just stay in, as I'm not that hungry. We could do all that tomorrow and maybe go shopping?" Ruby said that was fine by her. Ruby made herself a meal, as she hadn't eaten properly that day, and made Rose a ham sandwich. That night they told each other what had been happening since they parted, even though they had talked on the telephone. It was 2am before they went to bed. Ruby only had a one bedroomed flat, but had bought a sofa bed, which Rose found very comfortable. After a hearty breakfast, the following morning, Ruby said she had to pop a story into her editor, and then they would hit the shops. When they reached the offices of *Gilmac News*, Rose was surprised at how big the place was. Everything was done from there, including printing the newspapers. Rose watched in fascination at how the printing process was done.

"Ruby, what you doing here on a Saturday?" said a tall man, who looked to be in his late forties. He had a rugged face, but was good looking at the same time. He had a good physique and Rose assumed he worked out in a gym.

"Hi Marcus. You wanted my report on the opening of the new nightclub in Upper Kinton."

Marcus replied, "Right. My office." Rose and Ruby followed after him. In his office he looked at Rose.

Ruby said, "Apologies. Marcus this is my very best friend Rose Brambles. Rose this is my editor Marcus Cheffins."

Marcus extended his hand and Rose shook it. "So you're Rose, the great photographer, according to Ruby," he said with a slight sarcasm.

Rose replied, "I try my best and everyone likes my photos, but of course it's a matter of taste." *Touché* thought Marcus. He liked this Rose.

"Where's your report Ruby?" Ruby handed it to him and he quickly read through it. "Great report as usual Ruby, and it'll go in Monday's edition. How long are you here for Rose?"

"Only until Monday afternoon and then I return to Fracton." Marcus sort of nodded. As Ruby and Rose went to leave, Marcus said, "Did you bring a camera with you Rose?" Rose shook her head. Marcus went to a cabinet and the next minute a camera was thrown at Rose, which luckily she caught. This was followed by two boxes of colour film. "Show me what you got Rose. I'd be very interested." Rose looked stunned. "Ruby, bring the camera and films back on Monday, and I'll get them developed. That's all." Both of them left the office.

Outside Ruby said, "I've never seen him do that before. Well, looks like we're going sightseeing tomorrow." Rose was at a loss for words. Until midday Rose and Ruby went shopping. The fashions were so different in London. Rose saw lots of things she would like to have bought, but didn't. After a leisurely lunch, they went back to Ruby's flat. Ruby suggested they go to the new nightclub in Upper Kinton, which was a fifteen minute drive away. Rose agreed and after a rest, they got ready. First they went for a meal, and about 10pm went to the nightclub. The nightclub was huge, and very, very packed. As they made their way to the bar, Rose hated the way her body was being handled. Someone grabbed her buttock, a hand grabbed her breast, and she even felt a hand going up between her thighs.

"Ruby, can we get out of here? I don't like it." Ruby could see how pale Rose had gone, and grabbed her hand and steered her outside.

"I'm so sorry Rose, I didn't think it would be like that. Totally different from the opening night. Let's go back."

Rose felt awful, and said, "I'm sorry Ruby. I can't stand being manhandled, as it brings back ..." Ruby stopped her saying any more.

The last thing she wanted was Rose having nightmares.

On the Sunday they went sightseeing around the city, and Rose took photos. After a short while, they came across a procession of protesters.

"Wonder what they're protesting about?" asked Rose. Ruby said she thought it might be low wages. Everything was peaceful, but then one of the protesters threw a stone into a jeweller's window. Within moments all hell broke loose. The police arrived and for some it turned into a riot. Rose and Ruby got to a safe spot, but Rose was photographing everything she could. Once they saw the police making a move towards them, Ruby grabbed Rose, and they fled down some side streets.

"Phew, that was close," said Ruby. "I bet you've got some great shots Rose. I can't wait to see them." Rose just shrugged her shoulders. What she'd seen was quite upsetting, but it was how quickly it escalated that had worried her. "Come on Rose, I know a lovely pub we can go to for a meal. Are you alright?"

Rose smiled and said, "I'm fine. Let's go to this pub, as I could do with a vodka and coke." The pub was lovely, as Ruby said. It dated back to the 17th century, and had oak beams, the old fashioned tables and benches. It was like being transported back, and Rose loved it. She asked if she could take photos and the barman said it was fine. He even took one of the two of them. The meal was delicious, and later on some of the punters started singing and dancing. Rose and Ruby joined in the singing, and Rose took more photos.

"Damn," said Rose, "I've run out of film." After a great evening they went back to the flat.

"I can't believe you go back tomorrow. The weekend has gone so quick. Please Rose promise me you'll come back down again soon." Rose promised. On the Monday Ruby went off to work, whilst Rose packed and then went to see her uncle. Robert, again, escorted her to Hugh's office. Rose stayed with Hugh for a good hour, telling him everything that had happened.

"Thank heavens Ruby got you out of there. I read over fifty arrests were made. When do you think you'll come back down again? It's very difficult for me to see you at the weekends, as Nancy has us going to this or that." Rose told him she would let him know. One question Rose did ask was how much notice she would have to give the bank. Hugh said it would be one month, as she was paid weekly. They hugged and kissed each other, and then Rose went and got her car and drove back to the quietness of Fracton.

Meanwhile in the offices of *Gilmac News*, Ruby had returned the camera and two rolls of film to her editor. Marcus took them down to the development room and told them he wanted the pictures asap. Two hours later the photos were on his desk.

"Right," said Marcus, "let's just see how good this Rose is." As he looked through the photos he actually couldn't believe what he was looking at. The images she had captured were unbelievable. One of his photographers had taken photos of the protest, but came nowhere near hers. There was one photo that stood out. It was of a child and he assumed the parents. The boy about six-years-old, looked absolutely terrified and had tears streaming down his face, as his parents were desperately trying to get away from the police, to get to him.

Marcus couldn't take his eyes off the boy's face. This would be on the front page of the newspaper in the morning, but he had to get Rose's permission first. He went out and looking around saw Ruby.

"Ruby, in here now." Ruby wondered what she had done wrong. "Have I done something to upset you Marcus?"

"What? No, no. Has your friend Rose left yet?" Ruby said she probably had. "I need to contact her immediately. Look at this photo she took, and I want it front page tomorrow. Do you think she'll agree?"

Ruby replied, "I did tell you she was good. Rose will be delighted, I'm sure, but it might be better if I phone her." Marcus was happy with that.

"Tell Rose, for the protestor photos only, I'll pay her fifty pounds, and if she wants a job, she's hired."

CHAPTER 36

Ruby phoned Rose that night, and told her what Marcus had said. Rose was stunned and replied, "Fifty pounds. Wow, that's wonderful. Ruby, honestly, do you think I'd fit in?"

Ruby said, "Of course you will, and I'm here. Marcus was well impressed. Think about it, and as your uncle would say, weigh up the pros and cons, and see what you come up with." Rose replied that she would think very carefully, but she would have to give one month's notice. Ruby didn't think that would be a problem. Both of them talked for another hour, and then said goodnight. Rose made a drink and got a notepad, and made a list of pros and cons. The pros for London came out on top. This would be a huge step for Rose, but one of the main reasons she would move, would be because in London she could start her life over again. Here in Fracton, she still got looks of pity. Another reason was she couldn't advance any further in the bank, and she was getting bored. Hopefully, working for a newspaper would get her out of the office, and maybe travel to other counties, just like Ruby. Rose wasn't going to do anything rash though. There were still lots of questions to be answered.

On the Thursday night, Rose turned up at Monica and George's in a distressed state.

"Heavens Rose, come in. Who has upset you?" Rose was shaking from head to foot, and burst into tears, and so Monica held her in her arms. Through sobs Rose said she wanted her uncle and Ruby. George quickly phoned Ruby, who said she would contact Hugh. Two hours later, both of them arrived. Hugh had driven and picked Ruby up. When Rose saw her uncle she flew into his arms.

"My dear, what on earth has happened?" Rose hadn't spoken since she arrived. Monica and George were greatly concerned. Hugh sat Rose on the settee and Ruby sat the other side of her. Ruby took Rose's hands in hers and said gently,

"Rose, tell us what's wrong, and maybe we can help. Look Mum's made some tea, try and drink a little." Rose drank her tea and then started to calm down.

"Feeling better my dear?" asked Hugh. Rose nodded and then apologised to Monica and George for her abrupt arrival.

Monica raised her eyebrow at her, and said, "Rose you know we are always here for you, whatever the circumstances."

Rose smiled and then said with venom, "I hate that Smetherson."

Hugh said, "What has he done to you Rose?"

Rose replied, "I was busy concentrating updating the clients' accounts, when one of the teller's buzzers went off, and didn't stop. I looked up and saw Smetherson was at the till with Miss Woulder, and the bank's biggest client, Mrs Tuille. I immediately went to the till.

"Good morning Mrs Tuille. I hope I find you well?"

"No you do not Miss Brambles. I have just given your teller a cheque for one hundred pounds to be deposited into my account. The next thing I know is this imbecile has the audacity to say that my signature is not mine!!"

I replied, "I do apologise Mrs Tuille. May I introduce you to Mr Smetherson, our new deputy manager. Mr Smetherson has been very busy since he arrived, and has not had time to check the clients' file with regards to signatures." I was trying to defuse the situation, but I saw Smetherson looking furious. "Mr Smetherson. May I have your permission to go and get Mrs Tuille's file?"

Smetherson replied nastily, "I am quite capable of doing that myself. I have an intellectual brain, whereas women have brains the size of a small pea."

Mrs Tuille then snapped and said, "How dare you? I will be writing to your manager to have all my husband's and my accounts transferred to another bank immediately." With that she took her cheque, turned, and walked out the bank.

Smetherson looked at me and said, "Oh well done Miss Brambles. Now look what you've done. I will make sure Mr Fanterton blames you for this fiasco." I stood there stunned, and then I got annoyed.

"I walked straight into his office and slammed his door behind me. "Who the hell do you think you are?" I said. "Don't you ever insult me in front of a client, or my staff like that again. Perhaps the problem is you, and I'm now in the mood to tell you exactly what we all think of you. You are arrogant, a bully, self-opinionated, and have the manners of a rat sewer, and that's an insult to rats." I knew I'd overstepped the mark, but wasn't ready for his reply. "Oh hark at Miss Goody Two Shoes, who can't do a thing wrong. You only got this job because of your uncle. Well, you can't go running to him now. I am the deputy manager, and you will treat me with the respect I deserve. I suggest you watch your back, as you see, soon I will be the manager, due to my uncle being one of the directors of Stocks Bank. Tell me something, how does it feel to play the poor little rape victim?"

"WHAT?" said Hugh, Ruby, George and Monica, all at the same time. "I stood there and before I knew it, I had brought my right hand up and slapped him so hard across his face he nearly fell down. I rushed out of his office and into mine, and grabbed my bag, locked the door, then ran out of the bank. I went to the flat and tried to calm down but I couldn't. Memories of the attack played before my eyes, and I couldn't breathe. I must have fainted, as I woke up on the floor. Don't ask me how I drove here, as I have no idea."

"The bastard," said George, then apologised for his language.

"Right," said Ruby. "You are coming back to London with me until after the weekend, and I'm not taking "No" for an answer. Is there any chance Rose could stay longer Mr Brambles?" Hugh asked George if he could use their telephone. George nodded. After Hugh finished his conversation with Stanley, he came back into the sitting room.

"I've explained everything to Stanley, and he is going to say you have been called away on a private matter, and will be back shortly."

"Excellent, and thank you Mr Brambles," said Ruby.

Hugh smiled and said, "It comes at a price though. I insist on seeing my niece before she comes back here."

Both Rose and Ruby laughed, and Rose said, "That's a price I am more than happy to pay." Hugh said that before it got too dark, he must get back to London. George said he was more than welcome to stay, but Hugh declined. Half an hour later, he was on his way.

"I hope both of you are going to stay here tonight," asked Monica. Both of them nodded. Monica made a meal later on, and then they all cuddled up on the settee and watched the television. The following morning Monica and George waved them off, and told them to keep in touch. Rose drove back to the flat, packed a bag and then they left for London.

Once they got back, Ruby said she must go and see Marcus. Rose went with her to apologise for dragging Ruby up to Birn.

"Rose, nice to see you again. You taking me up on my offer?" asked Marcus. Rose replied she was thinking about it, but needed to discuss some things. "Ok. How long you staying?"

Ruby replied quickly, "Rose is here until next weekend."

Marcus thought for a moment and then said, "Idea. Why don't you join Ruby on a couple of her stories, take some photos, and then Ruby can show you how we link the photos with the story? I'll pay you for each day you come in. Deal?"

Rose shook his hand and said, "Deal." Ruby was delighted.

"Right to business. On Tuesday, the French President is arriving to see the Prime Minister. I want the story as to why he's here, and I want photos no one else has taken. Your first assignment Rose - interested?"

Rose nodded, and then said, "I didn't bring my camera with me." Marcus opened his drawer and handed a card to her. 'Don't worry about the expense, just go to the camera shop on the corner, pick out what you want, with a bloody good zoom lens, and tell them to book it to the account. Get it today, and you can practice over the weekend. Some of them can be heavy. You'll need the bags to carry it in, and get six colour films, plus whatever you need. In the meantime, I'll get a nametag done, so you can get access to the area. Enjoy your weekend ladies. See you Monday morning Ruby, and you too Rose if you're not busy."

Outside, Rose asked Ruby if Marcus was always this generous.

245

Ruby said he could assess people within five minutes of meeting them.

"He knows you're going to take the job, or else he wouldn't have given you the card. Now let's go camera shopping." Rose took over an hour in the camera shop, taking the cameras out of the shop to test them. When she was happy with the camera, then she had to choose a good zoom lens. She asked the assistant to attach the lens to the camera, so she could feel the different weights. Eventually she found one, got the bags and films, and handed over the card.

The assistant took it and said, "So you're the new photographer, and for a change, a lovely looking lady." Rose smiled, and thought how presumptuous Marcus was. After all, he didn't know her. Over the weekend Rose and Ruby had a great time. They went shopping, had meals, went to a disco, tried out Rose's new camera and zoom lens. Ruby showed her where they would be on Tuesday, and Rose walked up and down, picking out a good spot. Sunday evening both of them flaked out on the settee. Monday morning Ruby went to work, and Rose phoned her uncle. They arranged to meet for lunch, and Rose told him her news. He wished her luck as they parted. Tuesday morning arrived and Rose was surprised to see Ruby in trousers.

"Easier to run around in than a skirt, and Marcus is fine about it." Rose quickly changed and put trousers on as well. They made their way to where the French President was to arrive, to find he had already arrived. "Rose, I need to go and find out what's going on. You ok to stay here?" Rose said she would be fine.

Rose watched as Ruby mingled with the other journalists. Suddenly cameras started flashing and Rose saw the door open. Three men walked out first and Rose nearly dropped her camera. It was Andre, Donatien and Pierre. They stood looking around, and unbeknown to them, Rose took some photos. They hadn't changed one bit. Then she saw the French President come out. Quickly she got as many shots as she could, but then it looked like the was looking straight at her and waved. She had been concentrating on him, so that when she moved the camera slightly, she looked straight into a pair of blue eyes. A tourist at the side of her nudged her and before she realised, she'd taken at least six shots. When she moved the camera away, she saw JP and Antoine, but only for a second. They got in the back of his car, with his aide, and JP sat in the front passenger seat. The other four followed in another car behind the presidential car. They drove straight past her. Rose felt her heart beating out of her chest, and she was breathing heavily. When Ruby found her, she noticed Rose looked to be frozen to the spot, and was very pale.

"Rose?"

"Did you see them Ruby?"

Ruby frowned and said, "See who?" Rose shook her head and said, "I thought I saw somebody, but my mind must have been playing tricks. Did you get the story?" Ruby said she did.

Back at the office, Rose asked Ruby how to get to the film developing room. Ruby took her.

"Is there any chance I can have them first?" asked Rose, "Only there's a couple of personal ones I took." Ivan, who developed the films, said he would ring Ruby when they were ready. Ruby was busy typing her story up, whilst Rose paced up and down. Ruby knew Rose had something on her mind, but didn't push it. When Rose was ready she would tell her. Eventually the phone rang and Ivan said the photos were ready. Rose went down to get them.

"Hey Rose, here you go. Got some great shots." Rose thanked him, and as she walked back, she looked through them, and then stopped. She hadn't imagined it, as there were ten photos of JP and his men. There was one of Andre, Donatien and Pierre together, and one each of them separately. Two photos of Antoine, and four of JP. One photo of JP was a real good close up. All it showed was his face, and his beautiful blue eyes. Rose studied his face, and realised something wasn't quite right, but she couldn't work out what it was. She let her finger trace over his lips, and remembered his gentle kisses. She put the ten photos in her cardigan pocket, and went back to Ruby, to find Marcus was with her.

"That the photos?" Rose handed them over.

Marcus looked through them and said, "Bloody hell Rose, these are brilliant. Right we'll go with this one and that one. Rose do you want these under your name, or would you prefer an alias?" Rose hadn't thought about that. She looked at Ruby, and asked her what she thought. Marcus twigged something was going on here, and so he left to go to the gents.

"Nobody down here knows you Rose, and you deserve the credits. You should have your own name under them," said Ruby. When Marcus returned Rose told him - under her name. He seemed pleased.

Once everything was ready, Ruby and Rose went down to the printing room. Dennis and Walter showed Rose how everything was lined up, and then the process of printing. The report and photos were going on the front page. Rose watched fascinated at the process and then Dennis gave her a copy of the front page.

"Well done Rose and congratulations on your first front page," said Walter. Rose felt really good, and told Ruby she felt like celebrating. That night they went to a restaurant and celebrated. Once they got back to the flat, Rose looked at the photos she'd kept.

"Ruby, I've got something to show you. Do you remember I said I thought I'd seen someone I knew, well I did. You'd better look at these," and with that Rose laid out the ten photos on the table.

Ruby looked and said, "Oh my god, it's JP, Antoine, Andre, Donatien and Pierre. I didn't see them. Oh look at this one of Antoine, still as handsome as ever." Rose told her she could keep them, except the ones of JP. After they said goodnight to each other, Rose, again, studied JP's face. Then it hit her what was wrong. It was his eyes. The sparkle had gone, and she could now see a deep sadness, and she knew why. Her heart broke all over again for him.

CHAPTER 37

The rest of the week flew by and Rose went on a couple more stories with Ruby, but also spent time with her uncle.

"Uncle, can I ask you something?" Hugh replied she could ask him anything. "Now I've been with Ruby, I really like the idea of staying down here. How much rent do you think flats are, and what should I ask for wages?" Hugh said seeing as it was only Friday, he would make some enquiries, and ring her before he left for Rilford.

"Are you going to be alright at the bank for another month, if you decide to leave?"

"I will be fine uncle, because I have something else to look forward to." Hugh reminded Rose that when she gave the flat up, to make sure the telephone was cancelled, the meters emptied, and everything left clean and tidy. Rose smiled in reply. Early evening, as promised, Hugh telephoned Rose, and said he had found a flat for her, and one for Ruby if she wanted to move. They were both one bedroomed, and in a block with four others, but they were on the outskirts of London. Both flats were on the third floor. If they wanted to go and look, then they could pick up the keys from the estate agent in the morning. Rose said they would do that. Hugh told her not to worry about the rent, as until she was up and earning, he would pay the rent. Rose went to protest, but Hugh would have none of it. Hugh looked at it that he should be paying rent where he was staying, but that was covered by the bank, so he could happily pay Rose's rent.

Rose and Ruby loved the flats, which were on the top level, and there was parking for both cars. There was a small driveway off the main road, and a park was opposite. Shops, launderette etc, were just down the road. The rent would only be twenty pounds a week, as Hugh had done a deal, and both flats had gas and electric meters fitted, which took ten pences. The kitchens were fitted with cupboards and gas cookers, and lino on the floor. The bathrooms had bath, basin and toilet, again with lino on the floor. There was also a telephone in each sitting room, which would have to be connected. The rooms were all a good size, not too big, not too small.

"Your uncle is a diamond, finding these two flats," said Ruby. "All you have to do now is make a decision."

Rose replied, "I need to speak to Marcus first." Fifteen minutes later, Ruby pulled up outside *Gilmac News*. Luckily, Marcus was in his office, and Rose knocked on his door. Marcus beckoned her in, as he was on the telephone. Rose looked out the window whilst Marcus finished his call.

"Well Rose, you made a decision?"

Rose replied, "Yes, I have. I would love to work for you. I just wondered what the wages would be."

Marcus laughed and said, "Now what wage can I put on brilliance? I understand from Ruby you have passed a course on journalism, so I would like to see what story you can put to your pictures, and that way you'll get more wages. As just a photographer, I would usually offer twenty pounds a week, but with your talent, I would be happy to offer you thirty pounds a week. All your films will be developed here, so no expense to you. Again I will pay for films, and any camera costs. There's no uniform, but I do ask that when you're on assignments you look smart and tidy, and before you ask, I have no objections to you wearing slacks/trousers, whatever they're called these days. What do you say?"

Rose smiled and held her hand out and said, "Deal done. I do have to give a month's notice to the bank though."

Marcus shook on the deal and then said, "I'd forgotten you worked in a bank. I need someone to sort my ledgers out, you interested? More money, and something for you to do, if times are quiet?" Rose was agreeable. Marcus told her he would get a contract done outlining everything, and would send it to her address, for her to read and sign and return. "Welcome on board Rose. I think you and Ruby are going to be a formidable team." Rose thanked him and left.

"Well?" asked Ruby.

Rose replied, "Say hello to your photographer." Ruby was so excited and hugged Rose and kissed her cheek. Both of them left the building on a high. That night they went out on the town and celebrated. Sunday morning they had a late breakfast, and then Rose had to leave.

"I will ring uncle tomorrow and tell him of my decision, and we want to take the flats. Now all I have to do is give my notice in, but I think Mr Fanterton already has an idea of my intentions. I'll ring you to let you know I've got back safely." Both of them hugged and kissed each other's cheeks, and then Ruby waved as Rose drove away.

Back in her flat, Rose telephoned Ruby, as promised, then sat and wrote out her letter of resignation, plus another letter vacating the flat in four weeks' time. She saw JP's card and went and got the other photos. Again she studied the close up of his face, and understood what Marcus meant about a story being in a picture. Rose had assumed the sadness in his eyes had been for her, but maybe they weren't. He was a handsome man, and she knew women would want him. Perhaps another woman had broken his heart. After all, it was coming up two and a half years since they parted. Rose took the card and photos and put them away in a folder. She was starting a new life, and it was time to forget JP. She made herself a small meal, and a drink, then curled up on the settee and watched the television. In the morning she was determined not to let Smetherson upset her. The staff were pleased to see her back, and brought her up to date with bank news. Rose then went to see Mr Fanterton.

"Rose lovely to see you back ... or not?" he asked as he saw the letters in her hand.

Rose gave him her letters, and said, "I can't work here anymore Mr Fanterton, so I'm sorry to have to give you one month's notice. I will ensure all my work is up to date before I leave. I also wondered if I might ask a favour? I don't want anyone to know until after I've left."

Stanley understood, and said sadly, "I understand Rose. I, for one, will be very sad to see you go, and the staff won't hear it from me. Do you have a lot to catch up on?" Rose replied only what had come in last week.

"Well, I think you'll need time to sort out things with regards to your move. I suggest you take the next four weeks off, as let's say, paid holiday leave owed. At least you won't have to suffer Smetherson. May I ask what you're going to do?" Rose told him and then thanked him for his kindness. As she walked out of her office, making sure all was in order, for who ever took over, Smetherson walked towards her. Rose put her hand up to stop him speaking and said, "Goodbye," and walked out of the bank for the last time.

Back in the flat she phoned her uncle, and told him what Stanley had said, and the flats were great. Hugh was relieved, as she was getting away from Fracton. He had seen a much more confident woman in the last week, and it was lovely to see her smiling and laughing properly again. He gave her the name of a reputable moving company, and said he would send her the flat keys, once he had confirmed details with the estate agent. Ruby could pop round and see him when she could for her keys. She heard a noise downstairs and looked down the steps, and saw a brown envelope behind the door. She went down, picked it up and went back upstairs. It was from Stanley, with a short note saying, *"Dear Rose, here is your four weeks' holiday pay. I wish you all the luck in the world. Kind regards, Stanley Fanterton.* Rose put the money to one side, as she knew she would need the cash. Rose made a list of everything that had to be done. Both the meters were low, so she would only put the coins in when they were empty. The last thing she would do is have the telephone disconnected. At the end of the week, Rose received the new flat keys, and her contract from Marcus. She telephoned her uncle and asked if he could pop in on his way home on Friday night, as she wanted him to read her contract, to make sure all was in order. Naturally he agreed. Hugh was happy to confirm the contract was acceptable.

Rose had decided not to wait, and the following morning arranged for the removal van to arrive on the Friday. Hopefully, if all went well, she would be settled in London that night. Ruby had to give a month's notice where she was staying, so Rose would be able to help her move. The removal company dropped off three tea chests for Rose, so all her small items could be packed in them. That week, all she did was pack. She didn't think she had a lot, but once she started she was amazed at how much she did have. Of course, her uncle had paid for most of it. Early Friday morning, she put her suitcases in the car, along with various other bits and pieces, and in the passenger seat sat her teddy. Rose saw Stanley turn up and told him she would be another couple of hours, and would then like him to inspect the flat, and hand the keys back. At 9am the removal van arrived, and was packed an hour later. Rose had already cleaned the flat, so it was just a question of wiping everything over with a damp cloth. Stanley went up and checked everything, and then signed a document saying the flat had been left in a good clean condition. The meters needed emptying, but he would see to that. The telephone had been disconnected, and the fridge/freezer defrosted, cleaned and turned off. Stanley hugged Rose and wished her well. Rose actually had tears in her eyes. Stanley watched as she drove down the lane and waved.

"Well teddy," she said, "Here's to a new life for both of us."

That night Rose was in her new flat. When she arrived, it was to find a lovely blue coloured carpet had been laid in the hallway, sitting room and bedroom; the gas, water, and electric had all been turned on, and the meters filled; and the telephone connected with a note of her new number. In the kitchen a washing machine and a large fridge/freezer had been installed. Inside the fridge were eggs, butter, milk, cheese, various meats and bread. A huge bouquet of flowers was on one of the kitchen cabinets with a note saying, "Good luck Rose from everyone, except one, from the staff at Fracton." Rose felt sad, until the doorbell rang and it was the removal men. Large dust sheets were laid over the carpets to keep them clean. The men were wonderful. They gave Rose time to decide where everything was to go, and if she didn't like it, they moved it. One of them put up her curtain rails for her, whilst the other one made sure her television worked. Rose couldn't have asked for two nicer, helpful men. She gave them a five pound tip, to show her appreciation. Thank heavens there was a small lift. They wished her well and left. The first thing Rose did was find the kettle and the coffee. After a break, she set upon the kitchen where everything from the tea chests had been left. By midnight everything was done and she was shattered. She literally fell into bed and slept soundly. In the morning she woke up to the birds singing in the trees.

After her breakfast, Rose drove to the newspaper office. Everyone in the office said, "Morning Rose," and she replied "Morning" back. She went to Marcus's office first and knocked on the door. He told her to enter, and as she walked towards him she held out the contract.

"Rose, you didn't have to drive down from Fracton, you could just have posted it."

Rose replied, "Not a problem, and I don't live in Fracton anymore. I moved yesterday. I came in to tell Ruby. Here's my new address and telephone number.'

Marcus replied, "Does that mean you can start Monday?"

"Any chance I could leave it til Wednesday? I'm totally shattered and want to find my way around first." Marcus replied that was fine, and in London everyone just said, "phone". Rose thanked him and went off to find Ruby.

"Rose, what are you doing here? Heavens you look absolutely shattered."

Rose replied, "I moved yesterday. I'm here for good."

"Yeah," replied Ruby and hugged her. "Why didn't you tell me, I could have come over and helped?"

"Because you were working. Marcus asked me if I wanted to start Monday, but we've agreed Wednesday instead. Are you working all day?" Ruby replied she would be another hour and then she was free. Rose replied that she was going to go and look round the area, and be back later on. Rose found the camera shop, then the supermarket that was large, and some clothes shops. She also found a car park, which was about a five minute walk from the offices. At the moment she was parked out the office front, but assumed on weekdays it would be impossible.

She noticed the hour had nearly gone, and made her way back. Ruby was just packing up.

"Where did you go?" she asked. Rose told her. "Don't worry about the car park. I'll check with Marcus there's a space for you out the back." Minutes later she was back, with a car pass for Rose. "I'll show you how to get in. There is a back door, but if we walk round, you'll see better. Oh before I forget, when you start, we all call Marcus "Boss."" They left the offices and turned left, down to the end of the road, and left again. A short way up was a little lane, again on the left, and as they walked down it came into a small car park. There were spaces for twelve cars. "Number 12 is yours Rose, and I'm number 11," said Ruby. "Here's the back door. What have you got planned?" Rose said she needed to go food shopping. Ruby suggested they took Rose's car, as she could leave hers in the car park. They walked through the back door, into the offices, and out the front door again. Ruby gave Rose directions to a large shopping centre, where both of them did food and clothes shopping. Then they went back to Rose's flat, where Rose made a meal for both of them.

"Have you got your flat key?" asked Rose.

Ruby nodded. "Let's make a list of what you'll need for when you move in. I know you've got stuff already, but you might want a change." Ruby unlocked the door and said, "Oh Rose look at this." Everything that had been done in Rose's flat was done in Ruby's, except the carpet was a lovely shade of green. All the amenities were in, and Ruby spotted a note on one of the kitchen units. "*No doubt I will get told off, but I didn't think it fair, to do one flat and not the other. Hope it's to your liking, my "second" niece. Hugh Brambles.* Both of them were stunned.

CHAPTER 38

As a thank you to Hugh, Rose and Ruby took him to an expensive restaurant one evening. Rose, being crafty, had asked the restaurant manager under no circumstances was he to accept payment from her uncle. Hugh tried, but was politely refused payment. Rose and Ruby smiled at each other. When Ruby went to get her car, as she had picked Rose and Hugh up, Hugh said to Rose,

"My dear, when you next come to the bank, bring your savings books and I will update your address and other details. Now I know you're going to scold me, again, but I have paid your rent for three months."

"Uncle, this is too much, but thank you, and I really appreciate it. Now promise me you won't spend any more money on me."

Hugh just smiled and kissing her cheek said, "If I want to spoil my niece, I will, and that's an end to it." A car horn tooted, and they both got into Ruby's car. Hugh was dropped off first, and wished Rose "good luck" for the following day. When Ruby dropped Rose off, she said she would see her bright and early in the morning.

Rose frowned and said, "Marcus never gave me the working hours. What time do I have to be there?"

Ruby replied, "We meet in Marcus's office at 7.30am for a discussion on stories, then we have, when we can, an hour for lunch, and finish at 5.30pm." Rose nodded and said she'd be there. Ruby shouted out as she drove away, "See you "partner.""

Rose was up early and thought she had plenty of time, but one thing she hadn't reckoned on was the traffic going into London. She eventually got to the office at 7.45am. Quickly she made her way to Marcus's office, and saw they were all in there talking. Marcus spotted her and beckoned her in.

Rose said, "I am so sorry, I didn't ..."

Marcus stopped her and said, "Rose it's alright. My fault, as I should have told you a quick way to avoid the congestion. Right, everyone this is Rose, our new photographer who I'm putting with Ruby. Rose, this is Charlie, Harry and Malcolm, my other journalists. This is Noel, Patrick, and Reg, the other photographers." They all welcomed Rose, and Ruby handed her a coffee. Marcus then said, "All out, except Ruby and Rose." When everyone had left Marcus said, "Ladies, I have a story just right for you. A new shopping centre is to be opened today at 11am in the new town of Roltex. That's all I'm going to say. Now Ruby you do your story as usual, and Rose you do the photos, but Rose I also want you to write a story. No disrespect to you Ruby, just want to see what Rose can do. Back here I want two separate stories, and one story from both of you, with pictures. Understood?"

"Yes boss," said Ruby.

Rose replied the same.

"Get lost then," Marcus said smiling.

Ruby drove, but noticed Rose was quiet, and pulled in at a layby. "Rose, is something wrong?"

Rose said quietly, "I feel like a bit awkward. I've been here all of half an hour, and Marcus asks me to write a story. I feel like I'm treading on your toes. We're not going to fall out are we, because if we are, I'll look for another job?" Ruby could tell by Rose's voice she was worried.

"Rose, the only thing that would part us would be if you nicked my boyfriend, when I get one."

Rose laughed and said, "As if I'd want yours?" Then they both laughed.

"Marcus is interested in what we can give him. At the moment I give him stories, and you give him photos. Now if we can both do the same thing, we can put our stories into one and come up with a better one. Nobody sees the same thing, it's always slightly different.

It's those differences that really make a good story. Give you an example. When you looked at JP's photo, what did you see, and don't say great sex." Rose blushed deeply and replied, "The sadness in his eyes."

Ruby replied, "I just saw a handsome man. So our together story would be *Handsome man, but what lies behind those sad eyes*. Does that make sense?"

Rose nodded and replied, "One condition."

"What?" asked Ruby.

"I teach you to take great photos."

"Deal. Now we'd better going or we'll be late."

Once they reached the new shopping centre, both of them looked and couldn't believe what they were looking at. The whole shopping centre looked like it was made of glass!! You could see all the different shops inside, along with escalators, going up three storeys.

"Wow," said Ruby. Rose was already taking photos. They made their way to the entrance and waited for the Mayor of Roltex to arrive. Once he had arrived and given a rather long boring speech, the shopping centre was opened. Hundreds of people had turned up. Rose and Ruby walked through the large doors and stood and looked in awe. "How big is this place?" asked Ruby.

"Let's find out," said Rose. They found a plan that showed over a hundred shops, with four large stores that went up three floors. Every floor had large fans cooling the air. Planters were on every level with a variety of small shrubs and plants. Large paintings were on some of the walls. Ruby went off to find more information, and Rose took more photos. Rose got talking to some officials and found out the shopping centre covered fifteen thousand acres, and had a separate entrance for deliveries. Once the car park was finished, it would take over three thousand cars. Over the next year, a new direct road from London would be built. Rose thanked them and went to try and find Ruby. It took her over an hour.

"Ruby." "Oh there you are. What a place. You done?" Rose nodded. "Let's take all this back to the car, and then do some serious shopping." Some time later, they left the shopping centre loaded down with bags. Everything was so much cheaper than in the city.

Back in the office, they both typed out their stories, and then did one together as asked by Marcus. Once the films were developed they looked through them and picked out the ones they needed. Later on they went to Marcus's office.

"Couldn't have been much good if you two are back before nightfall. Did you leave any clothes in the shops?" Both of them frowned. "I saw the back seat of your car Ruby," he said, but he was smiling. "Right, stories." Marcus sat and read all three stories. "Your joint story is the one I'll go with, but with these photos. Ruby, great as usual. Rose, good attempt, but it was flat. Read Ruby's and you'll get the gist of what I mean, and by the way, I'm not criticising you. You bring your photos to life, whilst Ruby brings the story to life. You two are going be a great team, and that, as they say, is a compliment. Now the pair of you go home. See you in the morning. Oh Rose, here's a map to avoid the traffic congestion." The map worked and Rose turned up on time the following morning.

Over the next couple of weeks, Rose learnt a lot from Ruby, but Ruby was having problems taking photos. "Practice makes perfection," said Rose, and they both giggled. At the weekends, Rose helped Ruby move into her new flat. The small items were packed into both cars. On the last weekend of the month, Charlie and Patrick borrowed a van, and loaded all the larger items into it. To thank them, Ruby took them out for a meal, and the four of them joked and laughed all evening. All the men flirted with them, but Rose and Ruby knew they were harmless. This actually helped Rose, as it made her feel more comfortable around men.

Ruby was sent off to do an assignment on her own, so Marcus asked Rose if she could start doing his ledgers. He showed her into a small room, where there was a desk, with a lamp. On the floor were various piles of folders and files.

"Sorry about the mess," said Marcus, "but I try my best. This pile is the expense receipts and invoices, this pile is the bank statements, this pile is money received for advertising etc, and this lot is ... god knows what." Rose looked around and then smiled.

"I see you bank with Stocks Bank." Marcus replied he used to have to go into the city for the bank, but a new branch had opened which was nearer, so everything had been transferred there. "Got to meet the new bank manager next week. If he's anything like the other one, it'll be a really long boring meeting."

Rose laughed and replied, "I'll tell my uncle that."

"Uncle?" asked Marcus. Rose explained, and Marcus looked a bit embarrassed. Rose started to sort the files out into some sort of order. Looking at the ledgers for the last year, Rose just shook her head, as they were a complete mess. She went to see Marcus and suggested that she start the ledgers again, but only from when he transferred to her uncle's bank. Marcus said it was up to her to do it as she pleased, as long as he could understand what was what. Rose went out and bought new ledgers.

Whilst she was out, she popped in the bank to see her uncle, and gave him her savings books. He did whatever he had to, but only gave her one new book back. "I've transferred it all to one account, and that way you'll get better interest." Rose put the book in her bag, and told him about Marcus. "I'll have to be very boring then," laughed Hugh. Rose hugged him and kissed his cheek, and said she would ring him to arrange lunch one day. Hugh replied he would look forward to it. By the end of the day, all Rose had done was sort out the receipts. It took Rose another three months, between assignments, to get everything up to date. Marcus was delighted, as was Rose, as her wages had risen to nearly fifty pounds a week. One day she needed some cash, so popped to the bank to draw out five pounds. When the teller gave her the book back, Rose nearly dropped it. She had always been thrifty, and saved as much as she could. With the two hundred her uncle had given her years ago, and her savings, she had saved nearly five hundred pounds, but her uncle had rounded it up to a thousand. She was annoyed, but at the same time couldn't be mad at him. At least now, she was paying her own rent. She must try and think of a way to repay him, without him knowing.

Over the next year, Rose and Ruby covered a variety of stories, including a general election; the property boom; oil crisis; official states of emergency and the pop and youth cultures. Both of them were now capable of writing stories and taking photos, which helped Marcus out, as both of them could go to different events. Marcus never gave them stories to do where they would be upset. The other journalists would cover the rapes, odd murder, fires and unsavoury stories.

One day Marcus called them into his office. "Ladies, you're going on a trip. The very last coal face pit exploded yesterday, and I want both of you to report on it. Some people are saying it was done intentionally, others not, but over two hundred men, women and children died. This is big news, so don't let me down. Try and talk to the relatives and Rose you know what photos I want. Keep all your receipts for petrol, films, etc, and I'll reimburse you when you get back."

Ruby asked, "Where are we going boss?" At that moment the phone rang and Marcus said he would speak to them afterwards. Rose went off to the camera shop to get plenty of films. When she walked in, Steve, the assistant said,

"Hi Rose, you come for the box of films?"

Rose raised her eyebrow and said, "Box?"

"Yeah. Marcus phoned and told me to give you a box of twelve films. Something special is it?"

Rose replied, "Now you know Steve, I can't tell you." Steve laughed and handed her the box.

"Don't know if you're interested, but there's a new zoom lens arrived. It'll fit your camera. Here have a look." Steve attached it to a camera like Rose's, and she went outside to try it. Rose was surprised at the zoom, and what she could see.

"That's brilliant Steve, and I would love it, but I need to check with Marcus first." Steve said he'd put it to one side, for the rest of the day.

Back at the office, Rose saw that Ruby had packed her big bag with pads, pencils, and everything else she needed.

"Any idea where we're going yet?" asked Rose. Ruby shook her head.

"Fancy a coffee?" Ruby nodded and Rose went to the kitchen. As she was walking back to Ruby, Marcus came out of his office and said, "Coffee, just what I need," and took one. Rose looked at him.

"That Ruby's?" Rose nodded. "I'll take that, and you can go and get that new zoom lens."

Rose replied, "It's rather expensive boss."

Marcus smiled and said, "Since you've been here, you have really progressed, and I can now look at my ledgers and know exactly what funds I've got, so it's worth it. Now scoot before I change my mind." Rose grabbed her camera and was out the door in a flash.

"Knew it," said Steve, as she walked in the camera shop.

"Did you phone him?" asked Rose.

Steve looked so innocent and with a wink said, "Moi? Come on, let me show you how it works." Half an hour later Rose went back with the new lens, happy as could be. She was going to get even better photos now. As soon as she saw Ruby she knew something was wrong.

"Ruby, what's wrong?" she asked as she put her camera and lens on the desk. Ruby took a deep breath and told Rose it might be an idea for her to sit down.

"Why would I want to sit down?" Rose didn't notice but Ruby's hands were shaking.

"Rose, Marcus has told me where we are going. We have to drive up to Lancashire."

Rose replied, "That's alright, we can share the driving. Oh Ruby you'll love the countryside up there, lots of moors and wildlife."

Ruby said shakily, "Rose please let me finish. It's not just any pit. The pit explosion was at ... Hayleigh."

CHAPTER 39

Rose paled, and sat down on a chair and said quietly, "It can't be. I was told it was destroyed whilst I was at … I don't know if I can go back there Ruby."

Ruby hugged Rose and said, "I'll be with you Rose, and you won't be on your own. Maybe the other report they told you was another explosion that your family died in."

Rose had flashbacks of her family, but then took a really deep breath and said, "Yes you're probably right. We can't let Marcus down, so we'd better hit the road. Can I quickly phone my uncle to say we are going to be away, so he won't worry?"

Ruby replied, "Of course and give him my love." Rose phoned Hugh, who was quite concerned when Rose told him where they were going, but Rose assured him, she would be fine. They decided to take Ruby's car, as it was bigger. They drove back to their flats and packed a suitcase each, loaded them into the car and off they went. Ruby brought Rose up to date with what else Marcus had said.

"Marcus has booked us in at a pub called The Cross Arms, in Wheatfull, which is about halfway. He managed to get us two rooms, and it's paid for. In Hayleigh, we're staying at The Miners Lamp pub. He's booked us in for a week, but if we need to stay longer, to let him know. Do you remember it?"

Rose said, "No I don't, but I'm sure Hayleigh has changed. After all, it's twenty years since I left." With both of them driving, they made good time to Wheatfull, which was a small town. The pub was lovely and dated back to the sixteenth century. They had a great meal, and the beds were more than comfy. The breakfast, however, was wonderful.

The next day Rose drove, and Ruby fell asleep. Rose saw a sign that said Hayleigh, fifty miles, Blackthorn, two miles. Rose turned down the road to Blackthorn. They drove through the village, and then up the steep hill, memories coming back to her.

Suddenly Ruby said, "How much farther Rose? I need to stretch my legs." Rose replied, "Fifty miles the other way."

"What?" said Ruby. Rose was now at the top of the hill, and pulled the car over. In front of them was a huge area full of rubble, with some walls still standing, but covered in grass and a variety of wild flowers. A large rusty chain fence surrounded the area, and notices saying "Keep Out" were placed on the chain fence every now and then.

Rose got out and walked up to it, and turning said, "This is where Blackthorn Orphanage used to be."

Ruby looked at Rose stunned. "Rose, why on earth did you want to come back to this place?"

Rose replied, "To lay some ghosts to rest if that makes sense. It feels strange, like something happened here. Let's walk." They walked all the way round the area, with Rose pointing out where certain areas used to be.

Ruby shivered and said, "Can we go? This place gives me the creeps." As they got near to the car, Rose saw something glinting.

"Well, look at this," she said. Laid in the ground hardly readable was the large arch that had "Blackthorn Orphanage" written on it. The two signs for Males and Females still hung from their chains. Rose stood in a trance as memories flooded into her mind. Then she heard an anxious voice shouting, "Rose, Rose." It was Ruby. "Let's go," said Rose.

Ruby drove, and some time later they entered the now larger village of Hayleigh. Rose paled and said, "After twenty years it hasn't changed, it's just got bigger." As they drove through, Rose's eyes were everywhere. Soon they got to The Miners Lamp pub. It was on Chattle Street, where she had been born and raised for five years. A chill went through her. The street had obviously been demolished and rebuilt, and now had different shops and houses built on it. Ruby saw Rose shiver, but knew it wasn't from the cold. It was a hot, sunny afternoon.

"Rose, you ok?" Rose nodded and then told Ruby this was the street she lived on for five years. "Come on, Let's go and get settled in, and then we'd better get to the coal pit." As they walked in they noticed the pub was divided into separate areas. There was a small reception desk, a dining area and the bar.

"Afternoon lasses, what can I do for you?" asked a rather large man who looked them both up and down.

"We're from *Gilmac News*, and you have two rooms reserved for us," said Ruby.

"You're the journalists? Well, I would imagine every male will want to chat you two beauties up."

A woman's voice said, "For gawd's sake Arthur, put your tongue back in your gob, and take cases up to rooms. Sorry 'bout me husband, but you are good looking lasses. I'm Angie Turnbull, and that lump, as you've gathered, is me husband Arthur." Rose looked at the woman, as the name seemed familiar. "Follow me upstairs lasses. I gave you two rooms overlooking front of pub. Bathroom is between your rooms. Only you will be using it. T'others can use t'other one. Here you are." Both rooms were small but adequate. "Breakfast is from 7am til 9am. Lunch and dinner, order it in pub. You ever been here before?"

Rose replied a bit too quickly, "No," then asked, "which way do we go to get to the pit?" Angie shook her head and said, "That were dreadful, absolutely dreadful. All village is in mourning. Young bairns dead along with parents. Not nice for you two." Ruby assured her it was their job and they would be fine. Angie gave them directions and then left.

"Ruby, under what names did Marcus reserve rooms for us?"

Ruby replied, "It will be Miss Smith and Miss Brambles. Why?"

Rose replied, "I don't want to tell anyone I'm called Rose. Might sound daft but I have my reasons."

Ruby thought for a minute and said, in a not very good Lancashire accent, "Well lass, me Jenny, you Linda." Rose burst out laughing. Half an hour later they were at the coal face, or what was left of it.

Devastation was everywhere. There was only one road that led down to the pit, but at the bottom it was cordoned off, with police walking up and down. There were ambulances and fire brigades.

"Sorry lasses you can't go any further. It's too dangerous."

Ruby said, "Are people still down there?"

The policeman replied, "Ay lass. Fifty not accounted for." Ruby spotted about twenty journalists already there, and went to talk to them. Groups of people were huddled together, mostly crying. Ruby assumed they were the relatives of the missing. Rose started taking photos from different angles. Rose accidentally, on purpose, got photos of the people's faces, and her heart went out to them. Rose needed to get closer, and walked down the road. She spotted a gap in the fence and squeezed through. Making sure nobody else was watching, she ran towards a mound of scorched grass. Rose looked at the scene, and saw what was left of the pit - nothing. She could see rescuers working hard digging at the other end. The whole area was black and there was an acrid smell in the air. All the buildings were now rubble, and the tall steel shafts and wheels were mangled in heaps here and there. With her new zoom lens she got some really good shots of the scene. As she moved her camera along, she saw the rescuers stop suddenly. A couple of minutes later, three stretchers were carried out of the entrance. Whoever they were, they were dead. Her eyesight blurred, due to the tears falling down her face. That could have been her pa and brothers, if they hadn't already died.

Rose slowly walked back to find Ruby. "There you are Linda, you ok?" For a moment Rose was at a loss, and then remembered her change of name.

"Fine Jenny." Then she whispered, "They've just brought three more dead bodies out." Suddenly a huge scream rented the air, and both of them turned. They saw a policeman talking to one of the groups, and a woman screaming hysterically. It was really hard to watch, and both of them felt a huge loss for the family.

"Let's get back, as I need to phone Marcus with a short report," said Ruby. They drove back to the pub immersed in their own thoughts. Once in their rooms, Ruby told Rose what she had found out. She was told that there had been a huge explosion, about 1500ft underground, which caused fireballs. A build up of methane gas probably caused the explosion, but as of yet, they didn't know what had ignited it. The tunnels underground exploded, and the pit started to cave in, taking the shafts above ground, and the buildings with it. About a hundred and fifty men and boys were working in the tunnels, and fifty women and girls in the buildings. They had to wait until the HM Inspectorate of Mine and Quarries deemed that the site was safe, before a full investigation could be started. Ruby had spotted a phone box down the street and went and phoned Marcus.

"You two ok Ruby? You don't sound yourself?" asked Marcus.

Ruby replied, "We're fine, but this is so emotional, it's hard not to feel for the families."

"Want me to bring you back?"

"No boss, as I said we'll be fine. Ring you with more info when I get it," Marcus told Ruby if it did get too much for them to let him know and he'd send the men up.

When Ruby got back, Rose suggested they have a walk round Hayleigh, and so they did. Lots of places had changed. The school Rose went to, and the forest had gone. In its place was a busy main road. The corn mill with the water wheel was still there, but now it was a pub. Rose said, "I don't think much is going to happen at the pit, so why don't we drive out into the countryside tomorrow and I'll show you Hopa Apo Hill."

"Hopa what?" asked Ruby.

Rose replied, "It's Native American for Beautiful Dawn Hill. Before you ask I don't know how it got the name. I remember my mam and pa taking me up there once to see the dawn rising. It was beautiful." Tears filled Rose's eyes and Ruby hugged her.

Changing the subject quickly, Ruby said, "I don't know about you but I'm starving. We haven't eaten all day." Back at the pub, it was really busy. Rose and Ruby went to the dining room, where they had a lovely meal. Rose had her usual gammon and pineapple with veg and chips. Ruby had steak, onions, mushrooms and chips. Afterwards they had apple crumble with ice cream and then coffee. By 10pm, the pair of them were shattered and decided to call it a night.

In the morning, Angie saw Rose and Ruby coming down the stairs. "Morning lasses, hope you slept well?" They replied they did.

"Clean air, that's why. Not that smoggy stuff in London. Now sit and I'll get your breakfasts. Tea or coffee?"

"Coffee please," replied Rose. When the breakfast came, they couldn't believe their eyes. On a large plate were three rashers of bacon, two sausages, two eggs, black pudding, fried bread, mushrooms, tomatoes and baked beans. Along with that came toast, with jams and marmalades, and a huge pot of coffee.

Angie said, "If I know you lasses you won't eat til later. Get it down you, put some meat on them bones of yours." Rose and Ruby tucked in and ate as much as they could.

"I'm stuffed," said Ruby. "Never mind work, I want to sleep now."

Rose laughed and said, "We'll walk it off later. Come on, time for work." They went to the pit first. The news wasn't good, as they had found another ten bodies. The youngest was six. Afterwards Rose drove to Hopa Apo Hill. To get to the very top, they had to park the car and walk about two miles.

Once there Ruby said, "Wow, look at the views. You can see for miles. Oh Rose, you've got to take some photos."

Rose replied, "Here, you give it a go, and I'll take some afterwards." Ruby took the camera and took about six. Rose also took about six, but zoomed into various places.

Later on, back in Hayleigh, they started interviewing people about the explosion, being very careful not to cause more grief. Most of the ones interviewed use to work down the pit, and all said the same thing, "Bad for them left behind, but glad I weren't down pit that day." Back in the pub, Rose and Ruby collated their stories, and Ruby went off to phone Marcus. A couple of the local lads started chatting Rose up, and were asking her about life in London. Arthur had been watching the lads and could she was looking slightly uncomfortable.

"Oi lads, give the lass a breather. Ain't you got homes to go to for your dinner? Right bugger off then. Apologies for the language lass." Rose just smiled, relieved to be on her own until Ruby came back. She had noticed two other men looking in her direction, but as they made a move, Ruby walked in. They went back to the bar.

"Marcus is pleased with our reports so far. He wanted to make sure that we wanted to stay, and I said yes. I bumped into one of the other journalists, and he told me the Inspectorate are arriving tomorrow. They've also found the rest of the bodies."

Rose said, "These poor families. I feel like we're intruding on their grief."

"Marcus also told me we should speak to the locals and get knowledge of what the pit and pit life was like before the disaster." Rose nodded in agreement. They went up to their rooms, relaxed and then went down for their dinner.

After their meal, Rose and Ruby sat in the bar talking to various people. The two men Rose had noticed earlier came over to them.

"We hear you two lovely lasses are reporters from London." Ruby replied they were.

"Did you work down the pit?" asked Rose.

"Every man in Hayleigh worked at pit. Him and me been down pit since we were young lads. Our pa been down pit boy and man. You should meet im, and he'll tell you truth bout pit life. It were our day off, and it were raining. Thought it were thunder til we saw smoke rising from pit. Then siren went off, and we knew someut bad had happened. Can we buy you lasses a drink? Ruby said that would be fine. They talked for another hour, and then said they had to go, or their pa would be concerned. "Didn't catch your names"

"I'm Linda and this is Jenny. We'd really like to talk to your dad if he wants to talk to us."

One of them replied, "Talk to 'im tonight. Let you know tomorrow." As they were going out the door Ruby said, "Sorry we didn't catch your names."

"Oh sorry lass, this is me brother Frank and I'm Stephen, the Clark brothers, and our pa is Robert Clark."

If they had turned, they would have seen Rose go a deathly white and drop her glass, which shattered on the floor.

CHAPTER 40

"By heck lass, you look like you've seen a ghost." Rose apologised and said she would pay for the glass. "Don't be daft lass, we got plenty. Are you not well? Shall I fetch doctor?"

Ruby replied, "Thanks Angie, but no need for a doctor. I think all of this has got on top of her. It's her first big assignment. I'll take her upstairs so she can rest."

"Alright lass, just holler if you need us. Here take this, as she'll need it," and gave Ruby a glass with brandy in it. Ruby helped Rose to their rooms, who was shaking like a leaf. In Ruby's room, she sat Rose down on the bed.

"Drink this Rose, as it will help with the shock." Rose took a sip and put it down.

"That's vile," she said quietly. Then Rose burst into tears, and said through sobs, "I've just been talking to my brothers for over an hour, and I didn't know it was them. I thought they were dead."

At that moment she rushed to the toilet and threw up. Ruby was in bits, as she didn't know how to help her "sister" through this. Rose walked back in and Ruby thought she looked like a zombie from a horror movie. She went to her and hugged her, as she didn't know what else to do.

Rose then said with distress in her voice, "Why did the governess lie to me?"

Ruby took her hands and said, "Maybe she was given the wrong information. I'll try and find out if there have been any more explosions at the pit. I'm sure Angie would know. She told me she's been here all her life."

Suddenly Rose said, "Angie Turnbull, I knew that name rang a bell. She worked down the mills with me mam."

Ruby replied gently, "Rose, do you want to go back to London?"

Rose shook her head and said, "I need to find out more information. Sorry Ruby, but I want to be alone now." Rose left and went to her room, still in a daze. She undressed, washed and then got into bed. All sorts of things were going round in her mind, but within seconds she was firm asleep.

Ruby checked on Rose twice through the night, and was glad to see she slept. About 6am, she crept out and went to the phone box and phoned Monica and George. Monica answered, and knew immediately something was wrong. Quickly Ruby told her and asked for advice. Monica told her just to help Rose in whatever way she wanted.

"Just be there for her Ruby."

Ruby said, "Always Mum, always," and hung up. When she got back, she gently tapped on Rose's door.

"Come in Ruby."

"Fancy a cup of tea or coffee, or something to eat? I'm sure I could get you something on a tray."

"I'm fine Ruby. We'll have breakfast as normal, but not like we had yesterday. I'll have a wash and get dressed. Be with you in half an hour." A short while later they were in the dining room.

"Eh lass, you've gave us a turn last night. You look better this morning."

Rose replied, "I'm sorry about that. Would it be possible for me to have a couple of boiled eggs and toast? I really couldn't eat one of your lovely breakfasts."

"Ay lass, that's fine, and you lass?" Ruby asked for poached eggs on toast, and coffee. After they'd had their breakfasts, Angie said, "I hope Clark brothers didn't upset you. They've had such a sad life."

Rose surprised Ruby by saying, "In what way?"

Angie sat down and said, "When they were bairns they lost their mam in childbirth. Then their sister Rose and Aunt Jean went missing. They found Jean, and she'd been murdered. Never found lass though. Years later, their pa Robert told them he'd sent Rose to an orphanage. When Frank and Stephen went to get her, the place had burnt down and everyone living there died. Now their pa is dying. Got black lung disease, from long term exposure to coal dust."

"Now lass, you've gone pale again. Don't fret over Robert, as he's happy to meet his maker."

Rose replied, "They suggested we spoke to their dad, but maybe we should leave him in peace."

"Oh lass no. Robert would love to tell you his story." Ruby said they would think about it. Angie left them to get on with her chores.

"You alright Rose?"

Rose replied, "I don't understand. My Aunt Jean didn't take me anywhere. Ironic isn't it, all these years I thought them dead, and they thought me dead. Fancy a drive to Oswaldson? It's a town about twenty minutes away, but they have a huge library." Like the day before, they went to the pit first. Lots of activity was taking place, and Ruby asked a policeman what was going in.

"The Inspectorate is surveying the area to make sure it's safe to start the inspection." Ruby thanked him and went to talk to the journalists. Rose was taking a photo when a voice said, "Ne'er get a photo this far away lass." Rose turned to see Frank.

Keep calm, keep calm," she said to herself. "Have a look through there," she said and handed the camera to Frank.

"Bloody hell, that's close."

Rose sort of smiled and said, "It's what they call a zoom lens."

Frank shouted, "Stephen, get your backside ere." Stephen walked towards them. "What's matter with you. How do lass." Rose nodded and Frank gave him the camera. "Look thru that." "How the bloody hell does that work?" asked Stephen.

Rose explained. Ruby had now joined them and said, "Hello again."

They both replied, "How do lass."

Ruby could see Rose wasn't sure what to do or say, so she said,

"Sorry but we need to go to a meeting."

Frank replied, "Had a word with me pa. Not too well today, tomorrow?"

Ruby said, "We'll have to let you know, if that's alright."

Stephen replied, "No fret, whatever."

Rose and Ruby left. "Wow, you got through that better than I would have done," said Ruby.

Rose replied, "I saw them as strangers. Hard but it worked."

About an hour later they were in Oswaldson library. Ruby asked the librarian if they had any newspaper stories from twenty years ago. The librarian looked through her records and then took them to a small room.

"I'll bring the archive books for you." She came back with four large books on a trolley. Rose and Ruby thanked her and started looking through them.

Half an hour later Ruby said, "You need to see this Rose." The heading read:

SEARCH FOR JEAN AND ROSE CLARK

Robert Clark, of Hayleigh Village has confirmed that his sister Jean Clark, and five- year-old daughter Rose Clark, have disappeared. He told reporters that he had left his daughter in the care of his sister, whilst he went to work at Hayleigh pit. That night he discovered they were not at home and had disappeared. The police were called and an investigation had started. Searches of the immediate area have found no traces. He asked that if any one had seen anything strange to contact him, or report it to the police.

***

"That's totally untrue," said Rose. "Let's keep looking and see if the story continues."

Rose found the next story, and paled. "What is it Rose?"

"Read this," said Rose.

BODY FOUND ON TREEBURN MOOR

The body of a woman found on Treeburn Moor has been identified as that of Jean Clark, from Hayleigh, who was reported to have vanished with her niece Rose Clark. Treeburn Moor is twenty-five miles north of Hayleigh. It has been confirmed that Jean Clark was viciously assaulted, including rape, and had then had her life ended by having her throat cut, and thrown into a fast flowing river. Police have said this was a particularly horrific death, and are carrying on with their investigation to capture the culprits. Police have also confirmed there was no body or sighting of Robert Clark's daughter Rose.

***

"Looks like the Clark women were born to be raped," said Rose sadly. Ruby felt sick.

"Oh Rose, I'm so sorry. This must have brought memories back. I wish we hadn't started looking now."

Rose smiled and said, "Ruby, I have to do this. This is a puzzle, which I need to understand. What have we got so far? My pa said my aunt had taken me when she hadn't. He lied to the police and all the villagers. Why? Next question. How did Aunt Jean get all the way out to Treeburn Moor, seeing as she didn't drive? Something's not right. Let's keep looking." They found one more story about Rose's disappearance, and it was only two lines saying that the search had now been called off. An hour later they found the story of the orphanage, which was four and a half years later.

BLACKTHORN ORPHANAGE BURNS TO THE GROUND

Last night Blackthorn Orphanage was destroyed, with no survivors, except one, who was a boy. He told police he had lost his mind, after being assaulted by older boys. Late at night, about two months later, after he had got everything into place, he got the dormitory keys from the governor and governess offices. He found the key that unlocked the connecting door between the two offices. Firstly he went from bottom to top of the girl's side, locking every door, and pouring petrol around that he had found in the outside sheds, and hidden. Once that was done, he set fire to the torch he had made, and as he walked down he set fire to the petrol on each floor. Then he did the same to the boy's side. Once he was back at the front door, he locked this, and went round the back and locked that door. He then sat on the ground laughing as he heard all the screams from the people inside.

As the orphanage was well away from the village, and at the top of the hill, by the time the alarm was raised, and rescue teams arrived, it was too late. Fire and smoke was everywhere. Once the fire reached the kitchens, this caused a gas explosion. All that remains are a few walls, but the rest is now rubble, scattered with bones from the deceased. Over two hundred and fifty men, women, and children died. Most of these could not be identified as all the files and documents were also destroyed. The boy responsible was taken away to an unknown destination.

***

Ruby paled and said, "Look at the date Rose. It was six months after you left. Thank heavens your uncle got you, or I would never have my wonderful sister." They both hugged each other, more for comfort than anything else. They looked through all four archive books and did find a report about a small explosion at Hayleigh pit, when Rose would have been seven.

"That's what the governess must have read," said Rose. Rose put the books back on the trolley and wheeled it back to the librarian and whispered, "Thank you. We found what we wanted."

The librarian replied, "No, thank you for bringing the trolley back." Rose smiled and told her that she used to work in a library.

"I don't usually say this, but I need a drink," said Ruby, once they were outside. They found a cosy little restaurant and both of them had a vodka and coke. Looking at the menu Rose said,

"Lancashire Hotpot is what I'm going to have." Ruby said she would have the same, and both of them enjoyed it. Afterwards they had treacle sponge and custard, followed by coffee. They both discussed what they had found and Rose knew, there was only her pa she could get the truth from. It was late afternoon when they got back to Hayleigh. Rose told Ruby they needed petrol and so they went to the village garage.

"Fill er up lass?"

"Yes please," said Rose.

"You're them two lasses from London. You got your stories done?" he asked rather annoyed.

Rose raised her eyebrow and said politely, "I assume you have a problem with us?"

The man replied, "All bloody same you lot. Tell a load of lies."

Rose replied, "I can assure you sir, that before any story is written about the villagers, they will be shown the story first. This disaster needs to be treated with gentleness and compassion. How much do I owe you?" The man told her, and Rose paid, and then drove off.

Back in their rooms at the pub, both of them went over their stories, ready for the villagers to read them. So far they had ten. Later on, in the bar, a few of the villagers read their stories and were pleased. Rose spotted Frank and Stephen talking to Angie, and noticed they both looked sad. As Frank walked over, so one of the other journalists asked to speak to Ruby.

"How do lass. You still want to talk to me pa?"

Rose replied she did. "Doc says he ain't got long, so best if you see 'im tomorrow. Me and him will be at pit clearing th'area, but door be open." Frank told Rose where the house was.

"What time should I arrive?" asked Rose.

"Bout 11am. Pa no good first thing." Rose said she would be there. Frank left and then Ruby joined her.

"A meeting had been called at 10.30am tomorrow morning, about the findings of the explosion. Once that's done, we can then make our way back to London," said Ruby. Rose replied, "I've just made arrangements to see Robert Clark tomorrow at 11am."

"Oh Rose, I need to come with you."

"It's alright Ruby. I can go on my own. In fact it's probably better, as Frank and Stephen won't be there." They went and had their dinner, and met the rest of the families, who were also pleased at what they'd written.

The following morning Ruby went off to the pit, where the meeting was being held, and later Rose made her way to her pa's. She wasn't sure how she was going to be when she saw him. Would she tell him who she really was? Or keep quiet? She saw a note pinned to the door, which said their pa was upstairs in his bedroom. She still tapped on the door and opened it.

"Hello, Mr Clark."

Through a coughing fit she heard someone say, "Upstairs lass." Rose entered into a room, which wasn't exactly clean and tidy, but adequate, and went up the stairs. "In here lass." Rose went through the door and saw a ghost of her figure that was her pa, and took a sharp intake of breath.

"Mr Clark, I'm Ro ... Linda from the newspaper. I'm sorry to intrude, but are you sure you're well enough to talk to me?" Robert looked at this young woman and pointed to a seat for her to sit down, near the bed. His eyes looked into hers and said, "You got the eyes of me Mrs. She's dead, but soon be wi er." Rose froze for a moment. Robert started coughing and Rose saw a glass and a jug of water and poured him a glass and handed it to him.

"If you can, can you tell me about your life down Hayleigh pit."

"Ay lass, I'll tell thee."

CHAPTER 41

———————~———————

"Lass there's a bottle of medicine o'er yonder. Can I ave it?" Rose gave him the medicine, of which he drank half straight down. "Helps me chest and talk better. So you want to know what working down pit were like? Bloody hard back breaking work. I'll start at beginning. Me pa worked at pit, and I started age six. It were scary going down there, as it were dark in most places. Tunnels were dimly lit, and you could hardly see where you were going. Men and boys crushed together in lift cage. You went in clean, came out covered in black thick dust and soot. Me lads work at pit you know. Got coal by digging on me knees, in small cramped pitch black spaces. End of day me hands were blistered, and knees bloody. When I were twelve me pa died after shaft collapsed. Killed ten. Me mam were with bairn, and we had no money. Had to stay at pit so we could eat. Bairn died in his sleep. I use to have a lass you know. She were called Rose, but she were a bastard. She's dead cause of me." Rose stared at him, but her pa said no more, and she realised his memories were jumbled, but said nothing. Robert's breathing was getting bad but he carried on. "Lost me mam when I were fifteen. Had money comin in so could pay rent. Had to work ten hour shifts, six days a week. More coal you got, more money. I worked bloody hard. Sunday mornin went to church. In them days had to walk to pit, which were five miles. Working in pit had its dangers. Flooding, explosions, poor ventilation, gases and roof falls.

"When I were eighteen, met my Mrs. Doris she were called." A huge smile went across Robert's face as he said, "Now me Mrs, she were tasty. Big tits and bum. Good in sack as well. Nuff of that. She dead now. I'll be wi er soon. She saw wat I did. Me a murderer."

Rose looked shocked at that statement, and said, "Did you say murder Mr Clark?"

Robert replied, "Eh wat. Where were I? Oh ay. Me Mrs worked at mill and corn mill, plenty of money comin in house. Me sister turned up, had to share house. She were a pain, but when me Mrs had bairns, she looked after em. I'm sorry Jean for wat they did to you. She's dead an all. Me pa and mam, me Mrs, me sister, and the bastard - all dead. Morbid ain't it, but it's life. At pit I got offered another job. I were good at bad situations, and went to different pits to help em. Got more money and me and Mrs saved. Row of houses were to be sold, so we scrimped and scrapped and I got two next to each other. Me sister moved into one and paid rent, when she could, but she were a lazy cow, so didn't get much. Down at pit, another shaft collapsed and six dead. Poor pit ponies died an all. Poor buggers, they had a bad life, but we all looked after em as best we could. Me best mate got kicked by pit pony, brock his leg." Robert then had a very bad coughing fit, and Rose thought about leaving, but he'd mentioned her and Aunt Jean. Why did he think he was a murderer?

"Shall I come back tomorrow Mr Clark, so you can rest?"

"Nay lass, stay. More to tell you. In village most of men worked at pit. We all knew each other and all bairns. Lived in terraced houses with narro back streets, and outside bogs. At weekend some idiots went pigeon racing. Daft is you ask me. Others, like me, went whippet racing. Always bet too much. Me Mrs would go barmy. We had a club where we'd meet and drink, play cards and dominoes. Any one had problems they were told. Wished I done that. Too late now. Me Mrs were with bairn again, but both of em died. Had three mouths to feed, one had to go. Me lads started down pit and have been there since. They'll end up like me, black lung disease. Pits started to close all over country. Couldn't make targets set. I were in pit one day when an explosion ripped through tunnel. Bloody hell it were chaos. Men screaming in agony, and others trying to get out. Me and me lads were lucky. By heck that must be fifteen/sixteen years ago. Things changed after that. Pit were all re-shored up inside, and more lanterns to see in dark. No more pit ponies to drag wagons of coal out. Someut called a train pulled carts. It were only small, but a lad could steer it. Coal of course were used for the large steam trains, and heat houses and buildings. Now pits gone. End of an era."

Robert started coughing again, and drank the other half of his medicine.

Rose asked, "When did you become ill?"

Robert replied, "Since first day I started at pit. Got real bad last year. I'd finished at pit, due to bad health. Sold the old houses and got this. At least me lads will have somewhere when I'm gone. Don't know what they'll do now. Nought to keep em ere, well apart from a couple of lasses. Hayleigh will become a dead village." Suddenly Robert went pale and Rose could hear his breathing gurgling.

"I'll go and get the doctor Mr Clark?"

Robert grabbed her hand and said, "No lass. Me time is near, and I must confess to someut. You're a stranger so you'll do.

"When me Rose were five-year-old, I found out she weren't mine. She were a bastard, and I went loopy. I had er taken away to an orphanage, which later burnt to ground. She died in flames. For months I could ear er screamin. Me friend Angie told me about me Mrs, but me sister knew and I made er tell me everythin. Men owed me a favour and I asked them to take er away and deal wi er. Told em she were a virgin. They raped and murdered her and I were pleased at time. Over years I saw what I'd done, and so I'm a murderer." Rose had tears falling down her cheeks. "Eh lass didn't mean to upset you. Need to go to me maker with a clear mind." Robert studied the lasses face, and then he saw it. The face, the eyes, the dark hair, and the look of shock on his face had Rose realising he knew. "You can't be, but you look so much like her."

Rose took his hand and said gently, "I didn't die in the fire pa, as I was adopted six months before. Please don't think of yourself as a murderer. You didn't murder me and I'm sure you never told those men to murder Aunt Jean."

Robert was at a loss for words, but then said, "Don't tell your brothers. They grieved badly over you, and now I'm going to me maker. They probably won't believe you anyway. We ain't spoken about you for years." Rose promised. At that moment they heard voices as Frank and Stephen returned.

Quickly Rose kissed her pa's cheek and whispered, "I forgive you pa."

Robert smiled at her, and said, "Thank you Rose, and I did love you." Rose just smiled.

Rose went down and spoke with her brothers. Looking at them she was pleased she had made the promise to her pa. What good would it do, as she was going back to London, and would never see them again?

"I will have the story done properly by this evening for you to read."

Stephen replied, "No need lass. We know you'll do a good story." Frank had gone upstairs, and came rushing down.

"Need doc now," he said as he rushed out the door. Rose wanted to stay, but knew she couldn't. She said goodbye to Stephen. As Rose walked back, the time with her pa played on her mind.

"Linda," shouted Ruby. Rose smiled and went to her.

"How did it go?" asked Ruby.

"Can we drive to Hopa Apo Hill?" asked Rose. Some time later they were sitting at the top of the hill and Rose told Ruby about her pa.

Ruby listened, and said afterwards, "I can't believe it, but at least now you have the missing pieces. You sure about not telling Frank and Stephen who you really are?" "What good would it do Ruby? I tell them who I am, and then leave them. Better they think of me as dead, and carry on with their lives. At least I know they're alive, and well." Ruby agreed. "How did the meeting go?"

Ruby replied, "I'm starving. How about we go back to the pub and I'll tell you. I need my notes." Rose asked Ruby if she could give her five minutes alone. Rose sat and looked out over the view, again, remembering the time she was there with her mam and pa, and the tears fell silently. This had been a heart breaking journey for her, but she knew she would never come back to Hayleigh ever again. *Goodbye mam, goodbye pa, goodbye Frank and Stephen. I loved you all so much.* Rose dried her eyes and went back to the car.

Soon they were in the pub, having sandwiches and coffee. Ruby said, "The Inspectorate told us that as far as he could ascertain, the cause of the explosion was a build up of methane gas and coal dust, known as a fireball, which they think was ignited from a spark from a piece of equipment. It shot through the tunnel and everything in its path just blew up. The site is to be cleared with great caution, and an appeal has been launched for the victims and families of Hayleigh. Once the area is cleared, a monument will be built to honour the dead. The site will then be left to Mother Nature to take over."

Rose saw Stephen come into the bar, and say something to Angie, who came from behind the bar and took him in her arms.

Rose realised Stephen was crying. Her pa must have died. Then it hit her. Her pa had said Angie told him about her mam. Was she the Angie? Her blood ran cold and she felt angry. Ruby saw the change in Rose and looked in her direction. Ruby then realised what Rose was thinking.

"Rose, do you think she's the Angie?" Rose nodded. Stephen saw Rose and Ruby and walked over to them.

"Lasses. Thought you'd want to know our pa passed an hour ago."

Rose replied, "We're sorry to hear that Stephen, please accept our sincere condolences. Is there anything we can do?"

Stephen shook his head and said, "Pa's at peace now. Bye lasses." Stephen walked out the door.

Rose and Ruby went up to their rooms and wrote their stories out properly. Ruby then went and phoned Marcus.

"Excellent job ladies. You on your way back tomorrow?" Ruby said would it be alright if they stopped on the way back, just to relax a little. (She wasn't sure if Rose wanted to attend her dad's funeral.) "Sure, you both deserve it. See you when you get back. Can't wait to see the photos. Drive carefully." Ruby went back and told Rose.

"I'm not sure, as it might look a bit strange."

"We can always watch from a distance." The funeral took place two days later. Rose and Ruby watched the burial from the other end of the cemetery, making sure they weren't seen. The wake was in the pub, but Rose and Ruby stayed away. They drove into Oswaldson, and did some last minute shopping and then had a meal in one of the restaurants. When they returned the pub, most of the villagers had left, but Rose and Ruby slipped up to their rooms. On the stairs they saw Angie.

"You didn't ave to stay away lasses."

Ruby replied, "We did it out of respect for his family and friends. No one wants journalists at a wake. We will heading back to London tomorrow, after one of your lovely breakfasts."

Angie replied, "Be sorry to see you go lasses. You've been like a breath of fresh air." They all said goodnight. In the morning Rose and Ruby packed most of their stuff up, ready to leave later on. They had one of Angie's full breakfasts, and then Ruby went to phone The Cross Arms at Wheatfull to book two rooms, so they could break their journey. Rose brought her cases down and loaded them into the car, followed by her camera and films. "Well Rose, I thought you'd would ave stayed and come clean to your brothers." Rose turned and looked straight at Angie. "Don't fret lass, your secret's safe with me. When you walked in door, it was like Doris had come back. I worked with your mam at mills. Women notice, men don't, but then it's been so long since you seen your brothers, and you were dead to em any way."

Rose felt her temper rising and with venom in her voice said, "You'll keep MY secret, says the bitch that betrayed me. Yes my pa told me before he died. You told him about my mam. It was you who sent me to purgatory. It was you that had my Aunt Jean murdered. It's you who took me away from my pa and brothers, who I loved deeply. It's you that put them through the ordeal of me being burnt alive. It's all your bloody fault." Angie paled and said she didn't understand. "Because of you and your big mouth, my pa arranged for my Aunt Jean to be kidnapped and murdered. If you'd kept this shut," Rose said pointing to her mouth, "I would be here to console my brothers. So you tell anyone about me and I swear on the lives of my brothers, it will be the end of your life. Imagine what my brothers and those villagers left would say."

Angie who was visibly shaking said quietly, "I'm sorry." Rose just glared at her. At that moment Ruby came back and said the rooms on the way back were booked.

Looking at both of them, Ruby said, "Rose, what's happened?" Angie walked away and Rose replied,

"Let's just say, I don't like being told that my secret would be kept quiet, so I retaliated and swore at her. Let's get out of here Ruby. I want to go home - to London and my uncle." A short while later both of them walked out of The Miners Lamp pub. "Ruby, can we stop at the cemetery?" Ruby pulled over and Rose got out. Looking around to make sure she was on her own, she went to her mam and pa's grave. Rose said a prayer and blew a kiss to both of them and then left. Two days later they arrived back home.

CHAPTER 42

"Yes, my lovely ladies are back. It's been like a mausoleum round here, and you've only been gone just over a week," said Marcus, as Rose and Ruby walked into the office.

"Nice to know we've been missed boss," replied Ruby.

"Great stories, now I want to see your photos Rose."

"I've given Ivan the rolls to develop," replied Rose.

"Ok," replied Marcus. "Now follow me, as there's been a few changes." They walked past Marcus's office, and into the one next to it. "This ladies is now your office. These things are called computers, and take a bit of getting use to. It's like your typewriter, but it types on this screen, so you can make changes easier. I've got a computer guy coming in to see you in about fifteen minutes, so he can run through the basics with you. You can fight over which desk you want, but please, no blood." Rose and Ruby looked at him and sighed. "Leave you to it. Let you know your next assignment later on." Marcus left.

"Wow Ruby, our own office. We must be doing something right. Which desk would you like?"

Ruby replied, "Toss you for this one."

Rose laughed and sat down at the other one saying, "This one's fine for me." The computer guy arrived and left an hour later. Both of them now had a rough idea how to use them.

"Plenty of practice, I think," said Rose. "Ruby, I must go and see my uncle, so I'll see you after lunch."

"Rose, my dear, how lovely to see you back. Tell me how things went," said Hugh hugging her. Rose told him about Hayleigh. Hugh paled and replied, "I'm so sorry Rose, and if I'd known I would have made sure you went back to your family. I feel dreadful that we took you away."

Rose took his hand and replied, "Uncle, the best thing that has ever happened to me, well apart from JP, is that you took me away from that place. If my pa had wanted me back, he knew where I was. He's at peace now, and my brothers don't know I'm alive. You have given me such a wonderful life, and I just want to make you proud."

Both of them had tears in their eyes. "Rose, you make me very proud. Look at what you've accomplished. Now, I have some news of my own. Stocks Bank have wanted to go international for some years now, and have been in talks with buying out two smaller banks and consolidating them into one large bank in France. I'm pleased to say they have been successful, and have offered me the position of bank manager. This will be a huge bank. I've spoken to Nancy, and unfortunately, she will not go with me. If I go, I will let Nancy go. It's all quite amicable, and she doesn't know I know, but she's met somebody else."

"Oh uncle, that's so sad, but I suppose I understand. Will you take the position?"

"I'm not sure. A lot of things have to be taken into consideration. I have a month to think about it. If I went, would you come and visit me?"

"Of course. Both of us would come. Where in France would you go?" Hugh replied, "Paris."

"Paris," exclaimed Ruby, "Oh wow. Just think of all those Parisian shops. We'll have to get passports." Rose nodded, as a memory of JP surfaced, and she remembered him saying, "Paris was the city of love." What would she do if she bumped into him? *Who am I kidding? That would be like looking for a needle in a haystack, and anyway, if he's not already married or engaged, he wouldn't want spoiled goods.*

"Rose, Rose, you with us?" asked Marcus. "Oh sorry boss, I was just thinking about something."

"That was obvious Rose. These photos of Hayleigh are superb. I've decided to do a four-page pull out supplement and dedicate it to the villagers of Hayleigh. Naturally copies will be sent to Hayleigh. I want both of you to co-ordinate the supplement. I want all those stories in, and you sort out which photos are to be printed. When you've finished, let me know, and I'll just cast an eye over it. Well, what you waiting for? Get on with it," he said chuckling to himself, and left them to it.

"Let's look at the photos first Rose, as I'm dying to see them." Rose had taken nearly two hundred photos, but these included private ones. As they were taking the private ones out, Ruby said, "Do you remember taking this one," and handed it to Rose. Rose shook her head, as the photo was of her two brothers, and they were looking straight at the camera. Ruby said, "I think the photo should go with your dad's story."

Rose was studying the photo and replied, "Maybe."

The next couple of days Rose and Ruby matched some of the photos to the stories, to go on the first and fourth pages. The middle pages were all about the disaster with photos and Rose's pa's story. Rose decided to add the photo of her brothers. They asked Marcus to look over the pages, and his reply was, "Get it printed ladies." The following day, the supplement on Hayleigh went out with normal newspaper. Over the next two days, Marcus just let them get use to their computers. On the Friday night, they all went to Pizzaria, as it was Charlie's birthday. After the meal, Rose, Ruby, Charlie and Noel went to a nightclub, and danced away until the early hours. Rose and Ruby danced with lots of men, but two in particular, had taken a fancy to them. They introduced themselves as Marty and Gill, and said they were in a band. Rose and Ruby didn't believe them, but danced with them any way. At the end of the evening, Gill asked if they could take them home, but they thanked them and said they would be fine. Marty got annoyed and once they were outside asked why not. Luckily Charlie had been watching what was going on and went to them.

"There you are. I've been looking for you everywhere. Come on I've got a taxi to take us home."

Marty pushed him away and said, "Get lost, we saw them first, and they're coming home with us."

Charlie replied, "No need to get funny mate. They're my sisters and my responsibility, but let's ask them. Rose, Ruby would you like to go back with these two men?" Both Rose and Ruby shook their heads.

Marty replied, "What did I tell you Gill, just a couple of cock teasers."

Without any warning Rose grabbed Marty in his privates and said, "Well feeling this, it would have been a waste of time, little man. Now get lost." Ruby, Charlie and Gill stood there looking absolutely stunned. As Marty and Gill walked away, Gill said to Rose,

"Like your style Rose," and laughed.

Ruby looked at Rose and said, "Feel better?"

Rose replied, "I can't believe I just did that, but I felt insulted for both of us and saw red. Ugh, I need to wash my hand." Ruby and Charlie burst out laughing, and with linked arms, they went back to get their cars. None of them were drunk, as they'd been mostly drinking water or coke.

"You know who they were don't you?" asked Charlie.

"No," said Ruby, "but they did say they were in a band."

Charlie replied, "They are. They're in a group called "Stexiks" one of the worst bands for sex and drugs, and that's why I kept an eye on you." Both of them kissed Charlie's cheek and thanked him.

"We'll be more careful next time ... brother." They all said goodnight and made their ways home. Rose invited Ruby in for a coffee, and they sat and talked for another hour. At 3am they decided to call it a night. The following morning Rose was woken up by her phone ringing. "Hello," she said.

"Breakfast is served at my place in half an hour," said Ruby. As they ate breakfast they decided to drive to Roltex shopping centre. When they got there, they saw the car park had been extended, and the new road to London was over halfway finished. They enjoyed their day, going from shop to shop, trying this and that on, and giggling at some of the outfits. They had a break and went to a cafe, and by the time they'd finished, the back seat of Rose's was full of bags of clothes and food shopping. That night they stayed in and Rose cooked. On Sunday Ruby cooked dinner.

On the Monday, Marcus told them they were going to the south coast. A tanker had run aground, and oil was spilling out. Rose and Ruby set off and arrived two hours later. The beach was full of journalists, photographers and the public.

"I'm going up there," said Rose pointing to the top of a small hill. Ruby told her to be careful, and then went to join the other journalists. This was Ruby's way of getting to know more information. From Rose's spot, and with her zoom lens, she got photos behind the tanker, and was upset at what she saw. Seals and gulls struggling to survive all coated with oil. Lots of gulls had already been washed up on the beach, but they were dead. She saw people in overalls desperately trying to capture the ones flapping in the sea, and trying to clean them. Lots were put in boxes and driven away. This scene really upset Rose so much she didn't take any more photos. She made her way down the hill and went to find Ruby. Ruby was busy scribbling notes and laughing with two other journalists. When she saw Rose, she said her goodbyes, and they left. Back in the office Marcus sorted out the story and the photos, and they were published the following day. About a month later, Hugh phoned Rose, and asked if she would like to have dinner with him. Naturally Rose agreed.

Rose walked into the restaurant looking for her uncle. Hugh spotted her and stood up and waved.

"Hello my dear. How are you?" Rose replied she was fine, and hugged him. They talked about various things over dinner, but as they were having coffee Hugh said, "Nancy has asked me for a divorce." Rose went to say something, but Hugh stopped her. "It's alright Rose, as it's all very amicable. The house is up for sale in Rilford, and the proceeds will be divided in half. Nancy has told me she has met somebody else, and I'm happy for her. She is now looking for a flat. In a roundabout way, it has helped me come to a decision."

Rose smiled and said, "You're going to Paris aren't you?" Hugh replied, "I am. I have already flown over and seen the new bank, and talk about large and grand. Somebody younger could have gone, but because of my knowledge, they asked me. The new deputy manager, who has been appointed from head office, and I know, along with the French financial manager, who I yet have to meet, are holding interviews for another twenty or thirty staff. I fly over next week to sit in on the interviews, and go round and meet my new staff in the other banks, before they move. I will be gone for the week. Then back to London for the directors to cast their eyes over the successful applicants. I already have been told that five from here want to transfer with me, and luckily they all speak French. I don't think they realise though, that they will have to find their own accommodation. A huge flat is being built above the bank, which I will have. Don't suppose I can persuade you to come with me?"

Rose replied, "I'm really happy with being a photographer/journalist uncle, but if a Parisian newspaper had positions available for Ruby and myself, I might consider it. I can always fly over and visit you when I can. I will have to get myself a passport."

Hugh replied, "No need, as I will do it for you. I have the form for you, and one for Ruby, to complete in my office. You will need a photo, but it has to be taken in a certain way and a certain size." Rose told him she would pop into the bank the following day and pick them up.

"When do you think you will go permanently?"

Hugh replied, "Probably another month, as I have a lot of things to do here before then, and the flat should be ready by then. It would be nice if Ruby and yourself came over with me, as you know how good I am at picking out furniture, curtains etc, not." Rose said she would have a word with Marcus, and maybe they could take a week off. Hugh said that be wonderful. The following day, as agreed, Rose went to the bank, and Hugh gave her the passport forms.

"Uncle, according to this I have to send my birth certificate. I don't have one."

Hugh replied, "You do." He got up and unlocked a cabinet and pulled out a folder. "I don't like to bring up the past my dear, but may I ask if you still have those two documents you photocopied?"

"Heavens no uncle. I destroyed them, by burning them in a bin."

Hugh smiled and replied, "Good. I never told you, but Detective Bourtone sent me the copy he had, which I too destroyed."

"This document is the original, along with two copies of your birth." Rose looked at the long birth certificate and saw it had her date of birth, the fact she was a girl, her parents' name and the date the birth was registered and who by. The word "Adopted" was at the end of the entries. The smaller red certificate had her name, sex, date of birth and country of birth. It was a certified copy and was dated the day her uncle and aunt adopted her. She then looked at the document from Blackthorn Orphanage. Totally different to what she had found all those years ago.

"I will need the small one to send to the passport office, but I think you should keep these now," said Hugh.

Rose replied, "I only need the small one uncle. I would rather you kept the other two. At least I know they will be safe."

Hugh replied, "Very well my dear, I will do that. Now all you need to do is complete the form, get your photos, and along with Ruby's, I will get them done quicker than normal. Being a bank manager sometimes has its perks." Rose took the forms and kissed her uncle's cheek and promised she would get the forms back to him quickly. Back at the office she told Ruby.

"I don't have my birth certificate. Oh dear, does that mean we will have to go all the way back to Birn to see Mum and Dad?" she said smiling. Rose smiled and nodded. That weekend they drove up to Monica and George's, and were fussed over in a lovely, contented way. They had a great weekend, but soon it was time to return. Monday lunchtime, Rose took the forms etc back to Hugh. A week later they received their passports. They were blue and would last for ten years. The photo was laminated, and the paper was watermarked. Details of height, eye colour, hair colour and any distinguishing marks were included.

"All we have to do now is go to Paris and get them stamped," said Ruby. "I also owe your uncle five pounds. Will you give it to him for me Rose?" Rose said she would, but Hugh wouldn't take it.

"Tell Ruby it's a goodwill gesture." Rose raised her eyebrow, but smiled.

CHAPTER 43

Six weeks later, the house in Rilford had been sold, and Marcus had given Rose and Ruby the week off, making them promise to come back!! Hugh, Rose and Ruby boarded a plane bound for Paris. Hugh sat between them so he could hold their hands, as neither of them had been in a plane before, and he could see they were both nervous.

"Are you sure this is safe uncle?"

Hugh replied, "I assure you my "nieces" it is safe. The worst bit is taking off and landing, but I'm here for you both." As the plane took off and started to leave the ground, both Rose's and Ruby's ears popped.

"Can't hear," said Ruby louder than normal.

Rose replied, "What?" Hugh told them to take a deep breath, hold their nose and then blow out but keeping their mouths closed. It worked. The stewardess came round offering drinks. They all declined politely. An hour later, after a bumpy landing, in which Ruby thought the plane was going to crash into the airport building, the plane came to a stop. Once out of the plane, Hugh noticed both of them looked a bit pale, but was sure they were well.

"Do we get our passports stamped now?" asked Rose. Hugh explained once they got to immigration they would be stamped. Just after they'd left the plane and were walking towards the door to enter into the arrivals terminal, they were told to stop. A small jet, at the side of the runway, was getting ready to take off.

"Wonder what's going on?" asked Ruby.

Rose replied, "Must be someone important. Look there's about four gendarmes leading some men."

Hugh, who was taller than both of them said, "Well my dears, it's no ordinary man. It's the French President." As he said that the president walked past them. "Antoine," said Ruby. Antoine quickly looked and said "Ruby?" JP who was walking at the side of the president turned his head sharply round and looked straight at Rose. Rose stared at him for a couple of seconds and then lowered her eyes. They watched as the president walked up the few steps and into the plane, with JP, Antoine, Andre, Pierre and Donatien following him. Along with the other passengers, they were then ushered into the hall. It was then Rose realised if she'd put her hand out she could have touched JP.

Hugh noticed Rose had paled. "Rose are you alright?"

Rose replied shakily, "We come to Paris and the first Frenchman I see is JP."

Ruby linked her arm through Rose's and said, "They must have heard we were coming and decided to leave." Rose looked at Ruby, and then burst out laughing. Rose didn't dare say she was pleased. They got to immigration and had their passports stamped, and then collected their suitcases. As they entered the arrivals hall, Hugh spotted his name plaque and guided both of them to the driver.

"Bonjour Monsieur Brambles. Bonjour Mademoiselles."

Hugh replied, *"Bonjour* Pascal." Pascal loaded the cases onto a trolley and took them outside to where the small limousine was parked. The drive into Paris took about an hour. Rose and Ruby's eyes were everywhere.

"The architect of these buildings uncle is unbelievable. I think I will be taking lots of photos."

Hugh replied, "One thing you must remember, and this is very important, they drive on the other side of the road to England. You must look left, not right. I'm still getting used to it." Soon they pulled up in front of the bank.

"Good grief uncle, it's huge," exclaimed Rose. The bank itself was three storeys high, and the flat was on the fourth (top) floor. As work was still being carried on inside the bank, the three of them walked in. "This way," said Hugh showing them to the lift. Pascal was going to follow with their suitcases. When the lift stopped, they walked out into a hallway, and Hugh unlocked the door at the end.

Once in the flat, Rose and Ruby were stunned at how big it was. There was a huge sitting /dining room, two bedrooms, kitchen, bathroom and separate toilet room. Rose and Ruby looked out of the large windows and gasped at the view. On the other side of the road behind the buildings, was a large park that went down to the River Seine. They could see The Eiffel Tower in one direction, and Notre Dame Cathedral and The Louvre in the other. Rose had her camera out, and attached the small zoom lens she had brought, and started taking photos.

"Rose, you'll get better photos outside. I thought, weather permitting, tomorrow we could do the river tour, which lasts about two hours and you will see nearly all the attractions. Let me show you your bedroom."

"Wow what a bedroom," said Ruby. "I think I might need a map just to get round the flat." Hugh and Rose laughed.

"I'll leave you to unpack your cases, which Pascal has left outside in the hall. Then we'll go sightseeing and dinner." In the bedroom, as they were unpacking Ruby said, "I can't believe we saw Antoine, JP and the others. They still look as gorgeous ever, don't you think?"

Rose was silent for a moment and then said, "I suppose so. I only looked at JP for a few seconds and then looked away, when his eyes went ice cold. I could see the hatred Ruby, and I hope I don't see him again. I hope you see Antoine though, but if you do, please Ruby promise me you won't tell him what happened. I really don't want their pity after all these years." Ruby promised.

"You two gone to sleep in there?" asked Hugh.

"No, here we are uncle."

After walking round the centre of Paris for a couple of hours, they found a lovely restaurant and went in. It overlooked the Seine, and they watched the river cruises going up and down. Lovers were walking along hand in hand, and then stopping for some kisses. Workers were now rushing home, and very slowly the night was drawing in. They all enjoyed a sumptuous meal. Rose had coq au vin, Ruby had cassoulet and Hugh had boeuf bourguignon. For their sweets they had a variety of Macarons, followed by coffee. As they walked back along the banks of the Seine, Rose noticed how relaxed everyone seemed. Lovers were laid on the grass enjoying their time together. For the first time in five years, Rose felt a romantic feeling go through her, and immediately thought of JP. Then she remembered his eyes, and blocked him out. Back in Hugh's flat, the view of Paris caught her breath. There was a huge moon shining, and she could see the stars. The night lights did make the city so romantic, and not realising it, her hand went to her stomach. Hugh and Ruby had been watching her, and both had tears in their eyes, realising Rose was thinking of a child she could never have. Hugh broke the silence and said, "So would you two like to do the river cruise tomorrow? It does include lunch, and entertainment by a pianist and a violinist. Might even have a singer. We even get a welcoming glass of champagne." Rose and Ruby said they would love to.

In the morning, after a breakfast of croissants and coffee, they made their way down to where the cruises left from, and Hugh went and got the tickets. As they boarded, two of the crew quickly rushed to help Rose and Ruby onto the boat.

Ruby whispered to Rose, "Are all the French men good looking?" Rose slapped her arm playfully. They were shown to their table, given a glass of champagne, and ten minutes later the cruise started. Those who couldn't speak French were given headphones in their own language. Luckily the boat wasn't full, which gave Rose plenty of room to take photos. When she turned and looked at her uncle and Ruby, they were laughing about something, and craftily she took their photo. She studied her uncle, and saw how much younger he was looking. The stress and strain of living with her so called aunt now gone. For once he actually looked relaxed. *I must visit him as often as I can* she thought to herself. The first attraction they passed was the Tour Eiffel, followed by Invalides; Assemble Nationale; Institute of France; Notre Dame Cathedral; Hôtel de Ville; Conciergerie, (which use to be a prison); The Louvre; Place de la Concorde; Grand Palace; Palais de Chaillot, and finally Státue de la Liberté. During all these attractions they were treated to a three-course lunch. Rose took about four rolls of film, and all three of them thoroughly enjoyed themselves.

Ruby asked the question, "Where does the president live?"

295

The captain replied in English, "Our president lives at La Palais de L'Élysée, over there," and pointed in the direction. "Palace is closed to public, except on Bastille Day, when you allowed to visit. Queue's long, up to five hours."

Looking at Rose, Ruby said, "Oh dear, looks like you and I will have to come back next month," and then they both looked at Hugh smiling sweetly.

Hugh laughed and replied, "You can both come back whenever you want."

Ruby then asked, "Does the president have many bodyguards, and we speak fluent French."

The captain replied, "I like to talk English. Many English holidaymakers. Yes he has men who guard him, maybe twenty/thirty. He goes different countries, and takes different men. He away now, gone to Holland, I think, for weekend, but no sure." Rose was pleased at that bit of news.

"You on holiday?" he asked.

Ruby replied, "Rose and I are, but our uncle has just taken over as the new bank manager of Stocks Bank."

"Ah yes I know of this bank. What you do?"

Ruby replied, "I am a journalist and Rose is a photographer/journalist."

"That why young lady take so many photos? Which newspaper?"

Rose replied, "*Gilmac News.*"

The captain replied, "You work here then?" All three of them looked at him and frowned.

"No, *Gilmac News* is in London," replied Rose.

"*Gilmac News* also here, in Paris." Looking up at one of the crew he shouted, "*Stephan, depuis combien de temps Gilmac News est-il á Paris?*"

"*Sept ans, peut-être.*"

The captain said to them, "Seven years maybe."

Ruby thought and then said, "That was about a year before I started. Well, I never knew that! I wonder why Marcus never told us?" Hugh replied that Marcus must have had his reasons. At the end of the trip, they thanked the captain for an excellent cruise. Later on, after looking round the shops, they arrived back at the bank.

"Let me show you the bank," said Hugh. He unlocked the large wooden doors, followed by the opening of glass doors, and they went in.

"Wow," said Rose and Ruby together. The bank was huge.

Four large chandeliers hung from the ceiling. On the ground floor, there was an area where the public could read all about the various banking products. There were sixteen tellers' desk, with the usual glass partitions, and two foreign exchange desks. These were split into nine on one side, and nine on the other. Small gold posts, with red rope threaded through them, marked out where the public would queue. At one side was the reception area, with large settees, armchairs and tables. Rose noticed a terminal and went over to it.

"Uncle what's this for?" Hugh replied it was a terminal that had been installed about property financing, and the client would have an answer within seconds. The floor was covered in a dark blue carpet, and the woodwork was all light oak. The levels could be accessed by either the lift, or the light oak blocked in staircases on each side. The first floor had the offices for Client Investments, Property Management, Investments and Portfolios. The deputy manager's office was also on this level, and had a good view of the bank below. There was also a large room where the telephonists directed the callers, and dealt with general enquiries. Again the woodwork was light oak, but the carpet was a deep red. On the second floor was Hugh's office, along with other offices for clients to discuss their financial matters privately. There was also a large conference room, with a big round table and chairs. The carpet on this level was a light green. The whole of the third floor was the archives, where thousands of files were stored, along with two archive offices, and the carpet was brown.

All the offices had large glass windows, phones, cabinets, and where needed typewriters were on each desk. Rose had noticed a lot of what looked black lights, and asked Hugh what they were. Hugh told her they were security cameras. "It's not that we distrust the staff, but if anything unusual should occur, we have the tapes." Next they went to the basement. The vault was huge but at the moment it was empty. Another large room was split into eight smaller rooms.

There were rows and rows of empty gaps, with a table in the middle. Hugh explained that armoured trucks were transferring all funds from the other banks, and the treasury, over the next two days. The same with the deposit boxes, which were the same size as the row of gaps. So lots of people weren't in the deposit room at the same time, it was decided to make separate rooms. Only two would be filled, but as the bank became more popular, so the others would be used.

The armoured trucks would arrive at the back entrance during the night time, with lots of armed guards. Returning back upstairs, as they went out of the glass doors, they turned left and went down a long corridor. This led to a large kitchen, male and female toilets, male and female cloakrooms and the back entrance. At the back of the bank was a car park for twenty cars. These were for Managers only. Ruby asked Hugh about security. Hugh told her, apart from the security cameras the whole bank was wired up to a specialist alarm system. Once the bank was declared open, if anyone tried to get in or out, without switching the alarms off, the noise of the alarms would wake up half of Paris. The bank would open at 8.30am and close at 4pm, and staff would leave at 5pm. The vault had to have two people to put keys in to open it, which would be Hugh and his deputy manager. All funds would then be put on the shelves, with other important documents locked in a cabinet. The vault would then be closed and locked. Cleaners would then come in and be gone by 6.30pm. Security guards would then check every level to make sure all two hundred staff had left. Hugh, or his deputy manager, would then set the alarms and close the doors. Rose and Ruby realised how much responsibility Hugh now had.

CHAPTER 44

Over the next three days, unfortunately Hugh had to oversee what was going on in the bank, as Friday morning was the grand opening. His weekend would be free though. Rose and Ruby decided they would do as much sightseeing as they could. They visited the Eiffel Tower, Notre Dame and The Louvre. One day they decided to go on a hop on hop off bus ride. Many stops they got off and had a look around. One attraction that caught their eyes was Grévin Wax Museum.

"Do you remember the time we went to Madame Tussauds?" asked Ruby.

Rose replied, "I do, especially the chambers of horrors. Want to go in?" Ruby nodded. They were told the wax museum was the oldest in Europe, and had over two hundred wax figures. Like Madame Tussauds it had state figures, royalty, and cabinet ministers. The music section had various musicians including Edith Piaf, Louis Armstrong, and arriving shortly would be The Rolling Stones. Other waxworks were Charlie Chaplin, Marilyn Monroe, Pablo Picasso, Einstein, Gandhi, and leaders from Charlemagne to Napoleon III. Two rooms contained The French Revolution and the scenes were bloody. There was also a tableau of Charlotte Corday murdering Jean-Paul Marat, and it included the actual knife and bathtub used. They were both surprised to see they had spent over two hours walking round. Naturally they had to go fashion shopping, as the fashions were totally different to London. Another day, they asked Hugh if he could spare Pascal so they could go flat shopping for him. When Pascal wasn't driving, he doubled up as a security guard for the bank. He took them to a huge shopping centre on the outskirts of

Paris. Hugh had given them five thousand francs. They bought curtains and poles, bathroom towels, tea towels, bed linen, and a huge grocery shop including toiletries and other items. Needless to say, there wasn't much change left.

On Wednesday and Thursday, all the staff arrived and sorted out where their positions were, and got acquainted with each other. Vans arrived with cabinets, documents, files and other items to be placed in the correct office. Two of the staff went to the supermarket and bought tea, coffee, sugar, milk, toilet rolls, soap etc. The telephone engineers arrived and by mid afternoon all the phones were working correctly, including the large switchboard. Plaques of the teller's names were placed in front of the tills, and like the London branch, they all had name tags, but they used first names. A stationery list was made, which included pens, papers, pads, typewriter ribbons, etc. That was all delivered on Thursday, and the person responsible walked round and gave the items to the correct person. By Thursday night the bank was ready. On Wednesday and Thursday night, Hugh and his new deputy called Florian Bardet, had to be at the bank for when the armoured vehicles arrived. This had been kept a secret, as Hugh and Florian were worried a robbery could happen, but everything went smoothly. That night the bank alarms were put into use. Back in the flat Hugh noticed everything that Rose and Ruby had done. He thanked both of them, as the flat now looked lived in. Even though the flat was high enough up not to need curtains, they would keep the heat in, especially in the winter months.

Friday morning arrived and Hugh was down in the bank by 8am. Slowly the staff turned up and by 8.30am everyone was ready to go. Hugh wished them all "good luck" and then unlocked the big wooden doors, and was stunned to see a long queue. A banner was at the side, and Hugh pulled it across the open doors.

"Good morning ladies and gentlemen, I am Hugh Brambles the Bank Manager, and I welcome you to the opening of Stocks Bank." A few people clapped and Hugh let the banner fall to the floor. As each client passed him he welcomed him or her. Suddenly the bank was a hive of activity. Rose and Ruby popped in and were happy to see how busy the bank was.

"Miss Brambles, lovely to see you again." Rose turned to see Robert from the London office.

"Hello Robert, so you decided to come with my uncle?"

"Oh yes, Monsieur Brambles is the best." Rose smiled and then introduced Ruby. They shook hands. "Are you here long?" Rose replied they were flying back on Sunday afternoon. "I hope we will see you again soon. Excuse me, but I think a client is looking lost," and with that Robert left them. Hugh had spotted them and walked over.

"Well done uncle," said Rose.

Hugh smiled and said, "Thank you my dear. Where are you two off to today?"

"It's such a lovely day, we are going to do what Parisians do, and walk along the Seine, and sit and relax. Later on, we are taking you out for a celebratory meal."

Hugh replied, "I look forward to that. I'd better mingle. Enjoy yourselves. Rose do you have enough francs?" Rose replied she had fifty francs, which was plenty. "Here take this," and gave her another hundred. Rose kissed his cheek and then they left.

As Rose and Ruby walked out they saw Pascal. "Pascal, can you suggest somewhere nice where we can take uncle for a meal tonight?"

Pascal replied, "Have you been to the Latin Quarter yet?" They both shook their heads. "I pick you up at 8pm, and take you. You will enjoy."

"Thank you Pascal." Rose and Ruby walked along the banks of the Seine, watching people rushing by, the cruise ships, and just enjoying themselves. They found a little cafe and had croissants and coffee. Needless to say, they turned many a Frenchman's head.

"There is one place we haven't been to yet," said Ruby.

"Where's that?" asked Rose.

"A nightclub. We must go before we go home. Let's have a look around and see if we can see one." Without thinking Rose went to cross the road.

"Rose, look out," said Ruby grabbing her arm. A car drove past tooting his horn.

"Sorry," shouted Rose to the driver, who was now halfway down the road. They walked around but saw no nightclubs.

"Might have to wait until after it's dark," said Rose.

"We could go there," Ruby said pointing to a building. "We've never been to a casino before."

"Not sure about that Ruby, as they're gambling places."

"We could ask uncle to take us, just to have a look, nothing else."

Rose replied, "Maybe we could go tonight, after our meal?" Ruby was happy about that. Later on the three of them were in the Latin Quarter.

"Oh this is wonderful," said Rose taking photos. The streets and cafe were buzzing with lovers, tourists and other people, along with street buskers. They walked round for about an hour, looking at the various cafes and restaurants and found one that looked interesting.

Inside, it was like walking back into the seventeenth century. The waitresses wore old, low cut, long dresses. The tables and chairs were solid wood, and the floor was stone. The menu however, was not seventeenth century. They all decided to try something really French, and for starters ordered a small selection of snails, oysters and frogs legs, and shared it out. For the main courses Rose had Poulet de Provençal, Ruby had Steak Diane and Hugh had Filet Mignon with Mushroom-Cabernet gravy. All were served with Gratin Dauphinois and vegetables. After that they finished with an assortment of soufflés and coffee. They also had a bottle of wine with their meal. Luckily they had long breaks in between courses, and didn't leave until midnight. Hugh hailed a taxi and the taxi driver gave them a running commentary on everything they past. One thing he did point out was The Panthéon.

"Best views of Paris you will ever get."

"Perhaps we will come back tomorrow," said Rose. Soon they were back at the bank. Rose said, "Uncle, now the bank is alarmed, how do we get in?"

Hugh replied, "I'll show you." At the right hand side of the big wooden doors was a smaller door, which he unlocked. "This little bit here, and the corridor down to the kitchen etc, is the only bit of the bank not alarmed. Try and open the glass doors and the alarms will go off."

The following day, even though the bank was closed, Hugh had lots of paperwork to do, so Rose and Ruby went back to the Latin Quarter. They walked to The Panthéon, and inside saw the tombs of Voltaire, Rousseau, Victor Hugo and Zola. At the top, as the taxi driver said, the views of Paris were brilliant. As they walked around the streets they noticed underground jazz bars, which stayed open until dawn, and lots and lots of bookshops, and just had to go in. Rose still had a fascination for books and bought four. Walking along cobbled streets they came to the Sorbonne, with a pretty square lined with trees and cafes. They decided to sit at one of the cafes and have a coffee, and just people watch. Later on they went to Jardin du Luxembourg, which was full of rose and lilac filled gardens, with beautiful statues and fountains. There were also lawns and woodlands, and pretty benches to sit on. It would have taken them all day to walk round, so they only saw a small part. Late afternoon they arrived back at the flat. Hugh was busy in the kitchen preparing a meal for later. He was going to miss Rose and Ruby, but they would be back in a month.

Once they had had their meal, Ruby said, "We saw a casino, and wondered if you would take us?"

Hugh raised his eyebrow and replied, "That's not the sort of place I would take you to. It will be full of gamblers and people getting annoyed when they lose. I would much rather stay here and enjoy your company, before you leave tomorrow," so that's what they did and had a great evening. The following day Rose and Ruby did their packing, and later on along with Hugh, Pascal drove them back to the airport. A short while later, after hugs and kisses for Hugh, they boarded the plane.

Just after they'd got settled in their seats, Ruby said, "Rose look. It's that plane with the president on." They watched as it came to a standstill and the door opened. Two black limousines had arrived. Andre, Pierre and Donatien got off first, and looked all around, and stood by the open car door. The president then walked down the few steps, closely followed by Antoine and JP. The president got into the back of the first car, with JP getting into the front passenger seat. The rest got in the second car, and then they drove off.

Ruby said, "They arrive and we're going." Rose didn't reply.

Back in London, it was pouring with rain.

"Some welcome this is," said Ruby.

Rose laughed and said, "Let's go back to Paris."

Ruby replied, "We'll be back next month. I'm dying to know why Marcus didn't mention the Paris office. I was thinking, we need to get time off for next month, so how about we persuade Marcus that we go and can do a report on the La Palais de L'Élysée along with lots of photos." Rose agreed.

At work the following day, everyone said it was nice to have them back.

"Ladies decided to come back to work have you?" asked Marcus.

Ruby replied, "Yes boss we're back and you'll never guess what we found out?" They both saw Marcus's face harden.

"So you know about *Gilmac News* in Paris?" They both nodded. "You met my brother then?"

"Brother?" said Rose and Ruby together stunned.

"You didn't go to the office?"

Rose replied, "No boss we didn't. We had other things to do, but talking about that, we found out that the La Palais de L'Élysée only opens to the public once a year on Bastille Day. We were wondering if you would like us to go, and then we could do a supplement, with photos, for the public to see. Could be quite a coup."

Marcus looked at them both and replied, "I'll think about it," and walked out of their office. Rose and Ruby looked at each other and shrugged their shoulders. About five minutes later Marcus returned.

"Ok, you can do the La Palais de L'Élysée spread, and I'd better explain about my brother, just in case curiosity gets the better of you two, and decide to go and visit.

"Many, many years ago we set up this newspaper. We always got on well, but then fame seemed to go to his head. He started going out partying, getting drunk, gambling and one night ended up in a fistfight. Obviously it affected the business, so I kicked him out. The next thing I knew, he'd gone to Paris. Plenty of gambling places, but he met a woman, who I'm glad to say got him back on the straight and narrow. They married, but she died three years later. He then met another woman and she persuaded him to start the newspaper business up again, and as you know, he did. I last spoke to my brother about twelve years ago. End of story." Rose and Ruby both felt upset for Marcus, and Rose said,

"We didn't mean to pry boss. We only found out because the captain on the cruise boat told us. Thank you for letting us do the spread. What would you like us to do now?"

Marcus smiled and said, "Got just the job for you. A baby competition. Twelve babies are being judged at the town hall at 2pm today. Should be fun, not. Would love to see your photos of Paris. Get Ivan to develop them for both of you."

"Thanks boss," they replied. Rose phoned her uncle and said they would be over in July, whilst Ruby phoned her parents.

Monica said, "Oh I wish we could come to Paris with you, as we've never been." Ruby told Monica to hold whilst she spoke to Rose. She caught Rose's eye, who told her uncle Ruby wanted her. Ruby mentioned what Monica had said.

"Uncle, if Monica and George came with us, can you suggest a nice hotel?"

Hugh replied, "Well they could stay here. I can sleep in the sitting room, and the four of you can have the two bedrooms." Rose said she would let him know. Ruby told Monica to think about it, and let her know, and then they could meet up and make all the arrangements.

Later on they went to the baby competition.

"What a racket," said Ruby as they walked in. All the babies were screaming their heads off, along with some young children.

"Sorry about the noise, but a door slammed so hard, it started them all off," said a lady. "They'll settle in a minute. I assume you're the journalists/photographers from *Gilmac News*?" Rose and Ruby nodded. Slowly the babies and children settled into gurgles and laughs. Rose and Ruby agreed the twelve in the competition were all beautiful, and were glad they didn't have to judge. There were three judges, two women and one man. Rose took the photos from the back of the room, so as not to upset the babies. About an hour later the winner was declared. The parents had won five hundred pounds and a year's supply of nappies. The story was in the following day's newspaper.

CHAPTER 45

A month later, on a very sunny Friday morning, Rose, Ruby, Monica and George boarded a plane bound for Paris. Monica and George had managed to get a long weekend off, but had kindly declined Hugh's offer of them staying in the flat, as it would be too crowded. Hugh had found a nice hotel just down the road, and the four of them were going to stay there, as Hugh got a really good deal. Luckily, that year, Bastille Day fell on a Sunday, so Hugh could go with them.

"Wonder if we'll see Antoine, JP and the others flying out as we arrive?" asked Ruby.

Rose replied, "Now wouldn't that be a coincidence?" and they both laughed. Once they'd landed and collected their bags, Rose spotted Pascal and waved. He loaded all their cases onto a trolley, and then drove them to Paris. Like Rose and Ruby the month before, Monica and George's eyes took in the beauty of Paris. The hotel was huge and went up eight floors. As they checked in, Pascal loaded the cases onto one of the hotel trolleys. They were shown to the lift and the lift boy pressed number eight.

"Oh, we're on the top floor," said Monica.

The bellboy said, "Excuse me Madame, the eighth floor is the Paris Suite. Wonderful views of Paris."

"Thank you," said Monica. When the lift stopped they saw their cases were being put into the room.

"Welcome to the Paris Suite. I hope you have an enjoyable stay." They all thanked the member of staff. When they walked in, all four of them gasped. It was a huge suite, consisting of sitting room, two bedrooms en suite, kitchen and a dining area. Every room had top to floor glass windows.

"This is incredible," said Monica, "look at the views."

George said, "Rose, I must have words with your uncle, this must have cost a fortune."

Rose replied, "Please don't as he would be upset, and he did tell me he got it for a lot less than anyone else would have got it for."

"Very well," said George, "but dinner is on us tonight, and every night."

Hugh met them about 8pm, and said how delighted he was that Monica and George had come. He hugged and kissed Rose and Ruby.

"How are you settling in Hugh?" asked George.

"I'm glad to say very well. The staff are so much more obliging. Anything you need or doing, they're on it straight away. You must see the bank before you go back on Monday." George said he would like that. Hugh took them to a lovely restaurant overlooking the Seine, and they laughed and talked the night away.

On the way back, Monica said, "Oh George look, a casino. Can we go and have a look inside?" George looked at Hugh, who shrugged his shoulders. "That's settled then, come on everyone," said Monica.

Ruby whispered to Rose, "A mum comes in handy sometimes," to which Rose giggled silently. Inside the place was huge. As they walked round, Rose counted twenty eight gambling tables, that were all busy. Fascinated they all watched as the croupier did his/her job, how the people placed their bets, and the disappointment on the faces of the ones who lost, and the smiles of those who won. They went to the bar and order some drinks, and were stunned at how expensive they were. About an hour later they left.

Rose said to Hugh, "Don't worry uncle, I won't be going there again." Hugh patted her arm, which she had linked through his. On the Saturday they did a morning river cruise, and the afternoon and evening they visited the Latin Quarter. Monica and George loved it. Sunday morning, they met Hugh at 7am. It wasn't far to walk to the La Palais de L'Élysée, and when they got there, the queue was already long. The entrance was via the back of the palace, through large cast iron gates, with a rooster on the top, called Grille du Coq. The queue then walked down a twisty path, which skirted a large central lawn, which was cordoned off, and this linked the gate to the palace. Luckily the weather held and four hours later they went into the palace.

Rose had her camera, but only the one with a good built in zoom. Within seconds the camera was out of her bag. Those who wanted a guided tour went with a tour guide, but Rose and the rest of them decided to go it alone. They were given a layout with the names of the rooms. The first room they went into was called the Salle des Fêtes, a huge ballroom with chandeliers hanging from the ceiling. There were six Gobelins tapestries hanging on the walls, and the whole room was in red and gold colours. The floor was covered in a thick piled carpet, which was removed if a ball was taking place. Pillars had rich red and gold drapes attached and tied back, but when pulled together, a smaller area could be made more intimate. The pillars also had small delicate lights attached to them. In one corner was a raised platform where a piano was displayed along with stands for sheet music and other instruments.

"Can you imagine it," said Monica dreamily, "All the ladies in exquisite ball gowns, and the men in dinner suits, and everyone dancing to the music." George took Monica's hand and said, "May I have this dance Madame?"

They both did a quick twirl and then George said, "Now you can tell everyone you danced in the President's Ballroom." All of them smiled. Rose had been listening to a tour guide, and said, "Apparently it's also used as a large conference room."

The next room was The *Jardins d'Hiver* (Winter Garden), which used to be a greenhouse, but was now just an extension of the ballroom, used for official banquets. A Gobelins tapestry was on one of the walls, and three chandeliers hung from the ceiling, which were identical to the ones in the ballroom and the next room, which was Napoleon III's room. It used to be the orangery. It was very lavish, like the Winter Garden, but on each ceiling corner there was an imperial eagle and the monogram RF (*République Française*), surrounded by an olive branch. They crossed a corridor and went into the *Salon des Tapisseries*, which was decorated, as the name suggested, with luxurious tapestries. In a glass cabinet was a copy of the French Constitution. Once they left this room they entered the *Cour d'Honneur* and *Vestibule d'Honneur*. This is where the president would meet heads of states, ministers, and official guests. On the back wall was a very impressive sculpture called "Tribute to the French Revolution" by Arman. On either side of the sculpture was crystal, gilt bronze and Italian marble candelabras, designed by the Chagot Brothers, leading them to winning a prize in 1819. Looking out of the large glass windows, they could see the huge courtyard, which led down to the palace entrance. Next to the vestibule was Escalier Murat, which was the main staircase that linked the ground and first floor. As they walked up the stairs, which again had thick carpet, they noticed the rails were golden with gilded palm leaves. On the landing was a statue called "*La Defense*," which was placed in front of a tapestry called "Europe."

The landing led to two antechambers decorated with portraits of former presidents and decorated in Empire style. The next room they walked into made them gasp. It wasn't called the Salon Doré (Golden Room) for nothing. This was the President's Office. The doors, tables and chairs, and the wall edges were all gold coloured. The room had a Napoleon III crystal chandelier, stunning tapestries, and carpets, and a chest of drawers. However, the most spectacular piece of furniture was the Louis XV style desk that had been created in the eighteenth century. As with other rooms the ceiling was covered in various paintings, in rich colours. "Would have been nice to take a photo of the president sat at his desk," said Ruby. Rose agreed. There were four more rooms on this floor, which were the *Salon Vert* (Green Room), as everything was in green; the *Salon de Fougéres* (Flower Room), because of the floral patterned wallpaper; the *Salon Angle* (Angel Room) which used to be an old dining room; and the *Ancienne Chambre de la Reine* and the *Ancienne Chambre du Rio*, which used to be the bedrooms of former Kings and Queens. When they returned to the top of the stairs, Rose saw a notice that said "Private."

Looking at Hugh she said, "I wonder if that's where the president's private quarters are?" Hugh replied it probably was. Walking down the stairs Rose shivered, but she wasn't cold. She had a strange feeling she was being watched. She looked around, but saw nobody she knew. She did however notice just how many surveillance cameras were around, plus the fact there must have been at least a hundred guards on duty. Every room had four to six.

The next room they entered was *Salon Cléopâtre* that used to be the *Marquise de Pompadour's* dressing room. The name came from the Gobelins tapestry, "Meeting of Antony and Cleopatra." Leaving this room led them into *Salon de Potraits*, which was named after eight potraits on the upper walls. Out of that door and into the next was *Salon Pompadour*, which was her state bedroom. Later it became the bedchamber of Napoleon I. Between the two windows, which overlooked the terrace was a lovely portrait of the Marquise. Tapestries and furnishings from Louis XV and Louis XVI era's also adorned the room. Next came the Salon des Ambassadeurs, which was one of the most prestigious rooms in the palace. A clock sitting on the fireplace, showed the month, moon phases and zodiac signs. There was also a bronze statuette of the Roman Emperor Marcus Aurelius, and the chandelier dated back to the Bourbon Restoration. The rest of the furnishings were exceptional. The *Salon des Aides de Camp* was next, which had a carpet from the *Château des Tuileries*, and a fireplace, which was a replica of Louis XIV's bedchamber at Versailles. The last room of these rooms was Salon Murat. This is where the Council of Ministers met every Wednesday morning, with the President sitting in the centre of a large table, facing his Ministers. There are two paintings by Horace Vernet and a painting of the Trajan Column in Rome. There was also a console table with a porcelain decor dating from 1819.

They were now back where they came in, but carried on down round the corridor until they came to *Salon des Cartes*, a card room. A couple of tables were laid out with cards on top. The next room Rose loved, as it was the *Bibliothéque* (Library). It use to be used as a bedroom for the Duchess of Bourbon, and later it was one of Napoleon III's private apartments. It had a curved wall and is the only original room left from those days. It was then made into a wonderful library with thousands of books. Rose wanted to touch them, but it wasn't allowed. The penultimate room had them shaking their heads. It was the *Salle à Manger Paulin* (Paulin Dining Room). Again this use to be one of Napoleon's rooms, until 1972, when the designer Pierre Paulin was asked to transform the room. It is a complete contrast to all the other rooms. The walls were made from polyester panels, and the chairs had a single leg attached to a round base. Round tables were made of glass. The ceiling consisted of glass panels, with glass balls and rods, making the whole room light and airy. The very last room was the *Salon d'Argent* (Silver Room). This room was the official entrance to the private apartments located in the other wing. The room was decorated in lilac and silver fabrics dated back to the 1800's, but had still kept their soft and delicate shades. The wall features, mantelpieces, sofas and armchairs, along with the tables, all had silver coloured edges. The armchairs had swan sculptures at the sides. On the desk sat Napoleon's signed second abdication, after the defeat of Waterloo. This now concluded the tour of the palace. Rose had taken loads of photos. All five of them had a favourite room and wanted to go back and see it again. It was easily done they just joined the other line of people going the other way.

Hugh said, "Look there's the exit leading into the gardens. Why don't we all meet up at the fountain, say in an hour?" Everyone agreed, and split up.

"Ruby, why don't you have the camera for a bit, as I've got arm ache, but I need to put a new film in? Still need photos of the garden."

"Ok, where are you going?" Rose replied she just wanted to see the library and the president's office again. Quickly she put a new film in. Ruby said she would go with her. They made their way back to the president's office, and both noticed things they hadn't seen before.

"I'm dying for the toilet," said Ruby.

"Ask the guard where they are. I'll make my way to the library." Ruby asked the guard and he pointed her in the right direction. Rose was busy studying the different books in the library, when a voice she knew whispered in her ear,

"Follow me." JP grabbed her hand and led her through a door. They stood and looked at each other for a moment. "I won't keep you Rose, but I need an answer to one question that's bothered me for the last five years. I loved you so much, and I thought you loved me. Why didn't you answer my letters?" There was anger in his voice.

Rose replied, "Because I didn't get them."

JP snapped, "That's a good excuse. All you had to do was tell me it was a mistake and you didn't want me anymore. It might be five years since I last saw you, but now it feels like yesterday. I thought you wanted me. You broke my heart, and I'll never forgive you."

Rose's temper was starting to rise, and snapping back she said, "I loved you as much as you loved me. Things happened and I don't want to talk about it."

JP, who was now furious said, "Oh things happened did they? What got yourself a new boyfriend and left me dangling?"

Rose looked at him with fury in her eyes and shouted back, "No I didn't get a new boyfriend. You really want to know what happened, then I'll bloody well tell you. I never got your letters because someone destroyed them. The night you left, I was kidnapped, raped and beaten senseless, until I was hardly recognisable and left to die." Rose went to the door and opening it, turned and said with venom, "I was brutally raped, not by one man, but four. That a good enough excuse for you?" Rose ran out of the room with tears flowing down her face. The room, alas, opened up into the library, and everyone had gone silent. Ruby ran towards her but Rose told her to leave her alone. She would see them back at the hotel. Rose ran across the garden and out of the palace. She ran across the roads, without looking, and ignored all the drivers tooting at her. She bumped into people and didn't bother apologising. Rose didn't have a clue where she was going, and she didn't care. Suddenly it started pouring with rain, and within seconds she was soaked through to her skin. She was in a park and eventually slumped down against a tree. She brought her knees up and putting her arms round them, put her head down and sobbed and sobbed, until her whole body wracked with pain. Because her breathing was so bad, she actually passed out. When she woke it was night time and she was so cold and shivering uncontrollably, and it was still pouring with rain. She closed her eyes and everything went black.

CHAPTER 46

Rose slowly opened her eyes, and looked around, and wondered where she was. Then she noticed she was linked up to some machines that were bleeping away. The door opened and a young man entered.

"*Bonjour Mademoiselle, comment allez-vous?*"

Rose replied, "*Assoiffé.*" The man poured Rose a glass of water handed it to her, telling her to sip it slowly. "*Où suis-je?*"

The man replied, "*Hôpital Antoinette.*"

"*Où est mon oncle?*" "*Je vais lui téléphoner maintenant,*" replied the young man who then left. Rose closed her eyes, and when she awoke Hugh was sitting at the side of the bed.

"Rose my dear, how are you feeling?"

Rose replied, "I feel totally drained. How long have I been here uncle?" Hugh told her just over a couple of weeks, as she had had pneumonia. "Weeks, pneumonia?" said Rose startled. "I should be back in London. Where's Ruby, and Mum and Dad?"

Hugh replied, "Alas my dear, as much as they didn't want to go, they had to, but they have phoned me every night to ask about you. Rose, if you don't mind me asking, what happened?"

Rose thought for a moment and said, "I know we all went to the La Palais de L'Élysée, which was absolutely beautiful. I remember being soaking wet and sat by a tree. After that I don't know."

Hugh took her hand and said, "Do you remember running out of the library at the La Palais de L'Élysée, very upset, and Ruby calling

313

out to you? You told her you would meet them back at the hotel."
Rose shook her head. There was a knock at the door, and an older
man walked in.

"Morning Miss Brambles, I'm Doctor Meredith, and yes, I'm
English. Nice to see you back in the land of the living. Your statistics
are looking good, but I would like to keep you in a bit longer yet, as I
need to make sure your breathing and lungs have recovered. Just
promise me you won't go out running in dreadful weather again."
Rose apologised for the trouble she'd caused. Doctor Meredith
patted Rose's hand and told her to get as much rest as possible, and
then left.

***

JP sat in his office, still going over the events of two weeks before,
completely unaware of what had happened to Rose. He had sent one
of his men to make very discreet enquiries and was told they had all
returned to London. On that day, he knew Andre, Donatien, Antoine
and Pierre would be in the surveillance room. He needed to check
when Pierre's wife was due to give birth, so Pierre would be with her
and not away. When he got to the surveillance room, he opened the
door and heard Antoine say,

"Look it's Ruby and Rose." Whilst the four of them looked at the
screen, JP edged in quietly, and stood behind a cabinet, so he
wouldn't be seen.

Andre said, "Where's JP?"

Antoine replied, "In his office sorting out the schedules for which
bodyguards are to accompany the president on his trips abroad.
Why?"

Andre raised his voice and said, "You of all people have to ask
that!! Have you forgotten how he reacted when he saw Rose at the
airport? It brought everything back to him, but this time it was anger,
not heartbreak. Whatever happens, he mustn't see her. Where are
they now?"

Antoine replied, "Heading towards the Pompadour rooms. Must
say they are still as beautiful as ever. Looks like they're with company.
Oh, that's Ruby's parents and Rose's uncle."

Donatien asked, "What are we going to do?"

Andre replied, "Somehow, we need to keep JP in his office."

Pierre replied, "I need to see him about not going to Holland, as that's when Emilie is due to give birth again. I just hope it's a boy this time." Donatien gave him a friendly slap on the back.

"You know if one of us can't go, then none of us will. JP likes to keep us four with him, which I like." JP smiled at that remark.

"I'd rather go to London again," said Antoine, "Speaking of London, where are they?"

After a couple of minutes Pierre said, "There they are. Looks like they've split up. Ruby's parents are in the ballroom, Rose's uncle is in the portraits room. Rose is walking towards the library, but I can't find Ruby." Whilst they all scanned the screens for Ruby, JP quietly made his way out. He took the back staircase and made his way to the library. As he opened the door into the library, he saw her stood there. He went and grabbed her and pulled her into the room behind the library. He still didn't understand why he was so nasty to her, but what she shouted at him as she fled from the room, left him reeling with shock. He had vaguely heard someone shouting her name, but the door had closed automatically behind her. Even now, he physically felt sick to think what she had had to endure. One thing he did know, was that Rose hadn't lied to him. He noticed Rose had dropped her bag and picked it up, and could see lots of film rolls inside. Eventually he walked back to his office. His men were waiting for him, and knew something had happened, but assumed it was to do with the president. They had all left the surveillance room before JP grabbed Rose. Nobody had seen it, as when the new team came in, they were all busy talking with their backs towards the monitors.

"What's with the bag?" asked Pierre.

"One of the guards just gave it to me, as he found it in the ballroom." JP put the bag in a cabinet. There was a knock at his door, which brought him back to the present. It was Antoine asking about the rotas. JP gave him the list.

"Antoine, can I ask you something?" Antoine nodded. "Can you remember the name of the bank where Rose worked?"

Antoine gave him a questioning look, but replied, "Something like Slack, Stacks, umm ... Stocks, that's it Stocks Bank. I'm curious, why do you want to know after all these years?"

JP smiled and replied, "I see a branch has opened up here in Paris, and I know they have a good reputation in the UK. My bank's rubbish at the moment. Time for a change. Thanks Antoine." Antoine left thinking no more about it. JP made a phone call.

***

After Hugh had left the hospital, he returned to work. All he had told them was that Rose had been taken ill. Everyone was concerned, and were pleased to hear her recovery was going well. Even though Hugh had only been there a short time, he was surprised at how caring his staff were, especially Robert. That evening he phoned Ruby first, and then Monica and George. All were relieved to know she had woken up. George asked him if Rose remembered what happened. Hugh replied she didn't.

"That means she's suffered a huge shock about something, and has probably pushed it to the back of her mind. All three of us will be over next weekend. I'm sorry we can't get there before, work commitments." Hugh said that would be fine, and he would book them into the same hotel, but then asked, "George, do you think I should tell Rose how she ended up in hospital?"

George replied, "It might help, but you will have to take it slowly. We need Rose to remember herself." Hugh thanked George and said he would phone at the end of the week. Hugh visited Rose every evening, and a week later she was discharged, but was told she still needed to rest and build up slowly, as she was still weak. He was pleased to have her back in the flat. Hugh hadn't told or asked her anything, but one night Rose asked,

"Uncle, how did I end up in hospital?" Hugh was a bit hesitant at first, but decided to tell Rose, as he thought it might help her remember, so he replied, "The first we knew about you leaving the palace was when Ruby told us you had run out crying. She tried to follow you, but lost you in the crowds. You shouted you would see her back at the hotel, so we didn't worry too much. That night I thought you'd gone to the hotel, and Ruby and her parents thought you'd come here. As you know, you were suppose to fly home Monday lunchtime. Ruby phoned me to say you hadn't gone back to pack your bags, and that's when alarm bells sounded. I went to the bank and spoke to Florian, and just told him you'd been taken ill, and then left and went to the hotel. George had already contacted the airline and re-booked the last flight out. They had to leave, as George had to perform an operation the following day.

"We walked back to the La Palais de L'Élysée, and then tried to decide which way you would have gone. When we got to Place de la Concorde, an ambulance went rushing past, and stopped at the Jardin des Tuileries. We all ran there and saw a crowd of people standing around looking concerned. We managed to get to the front, but then a gendarme stopped us. All we could see was ambulance men attending to somebody. When one of them moved, I saw it was you. I explained to the gendarme that I was your uncle and you had been missing since the night before. He let us through. Even though the sun was out, you were still under the shadow of the tree. You were soaking wet, very, very cold and going blue. They wrapped you in blankets and put on a breathing mask to help you. They let the four of us go to the hospital, in the ambulance, especially when George said he was a doctor, and Monica a nurse. You were rushed into the intensive care unit. We had to wait about two hours, and then the doctor came and told us that because you hadn't been breathing properly your lungs had started to collapse and pneumonia had set in. They had you in foil, trying to warm your body up. It was twenty four hours before you started to respond to treatment. Sometimes you were thrashing around in the bed, and out of concern, they pulled the bed bars up, and put pillows at the side, so you wouldn't hurt yourself. Soon, as I've already mentioned, Ruby, Monica and George had to leave. I phoned Pascal and he took them to the airport. Then I just had to wait until you woke up. The rest you know."

Rose replied, "I'm so sorry uncle, to be such a burden," Hugh told her the last thing she was, was a burden.

Rose said, "I have something to tell you, and you're going to think I've gone mad. You know ..."

At that moment the phone rang and it was Ruby. Hugh spoke to her first and then Rose.

"Oh Rose, it's so good to hear your voice. I'm so sorry I had to leave you, but I thought I'd better get back and explain to Marcus what had happened. All he knows is you were taken ill. How are you feeling?"

Rose replied, "It's alright Ruby, don't worry. The last thing we need is to lose our jobs. I feel fine, just my body is weak. Hopefully I will be back very soon. Is Marcus really annoyed?"

"Heavens, no," replied Ruby, "He is concerned, and told me to tell you not to worry. You have to rest and get better." Suddenly Rose thought of something.

"Ruby, do you know where my camera and bag is?"

Ruby replied, "Your uncle has your camera, but we didn't find your bag."

Rose said sadly, "I must have dropped it somewhere, and all my film reels were in it, along with other stuff. All my photos of the palace gone."

Ruby replied, "Rose, we can do it again next year. You are more important than photos." They chatted for another half an hour and then said their goodbyes, but not before Ruby told her all three of them would be over the following weekend. Rose smiled at that.

Hugh had made Rose a hot chocolate, hoping it would help her sleep better. "Your camera is in your bedroom my dear. You were going to say something my dear, before Ruby phoned."

Rose sipped some of her hot chocolate and said, "You know the saying that goes, "when you think you're dying, your life flashes in front of your eyes," well it's true. Under that tree, I don't know why, but I felt desolate, and just wanted to fade away. After I closed my eyes, I was sort of transported back and I floated like a ghost in the background of my life so far. I went right back to when I first met Ruby, and saw myself telling them my story, about my parents and brothers, the orphanage and you and aunt adopting me. I could see the pity in their eyes, but there was also love and concern for me. I saw all of my schooling and looking through aunt's desk; going to the secretarial college and meeting our three musketeers; working at the library; and then leaving and coming to work at the bank, and my lovely flat; meeting JP and his men and then watching them leave; the … the rape. This was really frightening as I saw every detail of what they did to me. I tried to stop them, but I just passed straight through them. I was in the court and saw the trial and heard their sentences, and watched as they were driven away from my life forever. I saw myself in the bank, and noticed most of the clients had pity in their eyes when they saw me, but still smiled. I saw Smetherson and myself arguing, and him asking me if I was playing the poor little rape victim, and then slapping him. I watched as I left Fracton and went to London and started working at *Gilmac News*. Seeing JP and his men in London. I went back to Hayleigh and saw my pa and brothers weren't dead but alive; I watched my pa being buried, and then saw him rise from the grave, and he came over and hugged me, and told me to be strong, and to go back, as it wasn't my time yet. You telling me you were leaving to come to Paris; all three of us flying to Paris; seeing JP and his men at the airport, and the hate in his eyes. Ruby and I returning last week with Mum and Dad. I remembered everything as I floated around the La Palais de L'Élysée, and then I woke up."

Hugh was at a loss for words, but said, "You dreamt all that, including your ordeal. Oh Rose," and he hugged her and kissed her cheek.

"I'm alright uncle, and it actually put a lot of things in perspective. I knew I was a lucky little girl, due to you, but it made me see how lucky I have been in everything else as well, if that makes sense."

Hugh smiled at her and replied, "You are the best thing in my life now and always will be. I love you so dearly Rose."

Rose hugged him and replied, "I love you too uncle, and always will."

Hugh replied, "Well my dear, it's been a long day and I feel my bed calling."

Rose smiled and holding her mug of hot chocolate out said, "I'll drink to that and to new beginnings."

TO BE CONTINUED IN
"THE LIFE OF ROSE BRAMBLES – BOOK 2"